THE
SHADOW
OF THERON

AGE OF SHADOWS BOOK ONE

KATHRYN TROY

THE SHADOW OF THERON
Age of Shadows, Book 1

CITY OWL PRESS
www.cityowlpress.com

Cover Design by MiblArt. All stock photos licensed appropriately.

Edited by Tee Tate.

For information on subsidiary rights, please contact the publisher at info@cityowlpress.com.

Print Edition ISBN: 978-1-64898-296-5

Digital Edition ISBN: 978-1-64898-297-2

Printed in the United States of America

BOOKS BY KATHRYN TROY

"Give him the bow, and let us see whether he can string it or no."
Homer, The Odyssey

1

IT WOULD HAVE BEEN A PLEASANT DAY, IF NOT FOR THE HANGING.

The sun glistened off the newly constructed gallows—it was not often Lighura had a public execution—and people greeted each other in the square, staking out spots with a good view as they consumed their sweet buns and boiled eggs.

Lysandro was not hungry. He couldn't see how good people could be content to stuff themselves before a man was set to die, before the stench of a man expiring in his own piss filled their nostrils. He could smell it already.

Kato brushed against his elbow.

"You'll be able to see better from here, Don de Castel."

"I can see all I care to from here, thank you."

The innkeeper nodded. "As you say, Signor. But if you change your mind—"

Lysandro nodded and planted his feet on the ground, fists clenched at his side.

The crowd snapped to attention as the door to the magistrate's office opened. Lysandro's stomach soured at the sight of Marek. He exuded a sense of utter disinterest in the events of which he himself was the director. But Lysandro saw the glint of malice in Marek's eyes that he was unable to hide. He relished the power over the life and death of the wretch behind him, his broad chest inflated with self-importance. In short, Lysandro loathed him.

His attention turned to the bound man following the magistrate. Two of Marek's officers stood beside him and another behind, forming a diamond around the condemned. It was clear this man would not go easily to his death.

He writhed and twisted his body to get away from the men holding him, one at each elbow, kicking and flailing his legs out in a childlike tantrum. He was so focused on trying to escape their grip that only inchoate groans passed his lips. When they ascended the steps to the platform, the man's struggling became more desperate, more violent. The crowd gasped when the man wrangled one arm free, and it looked like he might escape. But he fell to the ground as two of Marek's men fumbled after him, fighting to keep him in their grip. They forced him to his feet again.

Without saying a word, Marek turned to face his underlings. They redoubled their efforts, squeezing the prisoner tight between them until his feet barely touched the ground. The man's struggling didn't cease, but his range of motion was now severely restricted. The captive's eyes went wide in fear, showing the whites of them like a man held in the throes of a hysterical fit.

Drop back, Lysandro thought. He couldn't stop his mind from racing through all the ways the man might free himself. If he could just loosen their hold on him again, he could run. But he'd never make it. Not without help.

When Marek turned his face to the crowd, his eyes had narrowed to murderous slits, and his jaw was tightly clenched to preserve the façade of a smile that he wore there. He lifted his chin and addressed those who had gathered:

"People of Lighura—Jair Oreyo is guilty of killing Don Aldo Carras, who caught him stealing silver. His crime was discovered by his widow, Doña Sofia Carras, who tripped over her husband's body when responding to his screams."

Lysandro heard the gasps of those around him as Marek recounted the grisly details. Marek was either too stupid or too cruel to show more consideration for Carras's family. They stood huddled together in a tight circle, their faces pointed at the ground, while Marek expounded on the way Don Aldo's brains had been bashed against the stairway of their own home and turned the entryway slippery with blood. The women and children who congregated in the square turned their heads away from the platform as if to shut out Marek's words and shield themselves from the nightmares such lurid descriptions were bound to produce.

Lysandro could feel his face flushing hot. A good man's guts were being strewn about with words. That he couldn't stifle them turned him livid.

Seemingly sated by his talk of violence, Marek shifted to patting himself on the back for a job well done. He turned to his officers and beckoned with a small gesture for the prisoner to be brought forward. His men accomplished it, but with great difficulty.

"Any last words?" he asked in a cool, collected tone.

Jair was foaming at the mouth. Lysandro could see the veins on his neck bulge as his face went purple with rage, and he lunged at Marek.

"Liar!"

Lysandro's ears pricked up. Alarm bells rang in his head like the one in the temple tower—a full-throated clang that deepened his suspicion.

"Murderer!" Jair shouted. "You're just as guilty as me!"

He pled with his captors, who rammed the noose around his neck. "Don't listen to him, he's a liar! *Stop*, or he'll do the same thing to you!"

The knife tucked up Lysandro's sleeve prodded him at the wrist. He calculated the distance and the force it would take to sever the rope swinging from the beam.

He could do it. Avoiding notice, though—that would be another matter entirely. But something else stopped him from sliding the hidden blade into his hand.

You're just as guilty as me.

Jair was a murderer; he just wasn't alone.

The corner of Lysandro's mouth twitched as the officers tightened the noose around Jair's throat, but his fingers remained loose at his side.

THE BLOOD IN LOTHAN MAREK'S VEINS HISSED IN FURY AS HIS BROTHERS dragged Jairo, kicking and screaming, toward the noose. He was being ridiculous. It was one thing to steal from the poor, and another to murder a pillar of the community and think no one would notice. Lothan had no choice but to act. And Jair had the gall to call him out in front of the whole village.

His behavior worked in Lothan's favor. He was acting like a lunatic with his hair on fire, and Lothan expected people to discount his exclamations as the ravings of an almost dead man. Jair's outrage was Lothan's shield, so long as he kept the anger from his face.

Jair had been effective at his job; his taste for brutality had served him well on occasion. He was perhaps the strongest among them, excepting Lothan himself, and it was a bitter shame to kill him. Almost.

All those who shared his blood were a greedy, groveling, worthless waste of a power that should have been his alone. Today brought him one step closer to the magic scattered across their veins being made whole.

Lothan quashed his annoyance as Jair squealed and squirmed to the last minute, wriggling like a worm until the floor gave way beneath him and silence reigned over the square, heralded by a definitive, satisfying crack. Jair's latent power shivered up Lothan's spine. The surge of energy buzzed through him like a current, crackling at his fingertips and the ends of his hair. It was delicious. But not nearly enough.

LYSANDRO WAS GRATEFUL FOR THE SILENCE; IT WAS INFINITELY BETTER THAN a roar of cheers would have been. The Carras family remained clustered together as the knot of onlookers unfurled itself, and people returned to their routines to try to forget what they'd seen. Lysandro made his way toward them. Marek approached at the same time, holding a large wooden box in his hands.

"Doña Carras," he said, presenting her with the recovered silverware.

He looked so pleased with himself.

Don Aldo's widow stared at him, then took the box into her hands with a dumb expression on her face.

Lothan furrowed his brows. "This *is* your stolen silver, is it not? I imagined its return would bring you some comfort." He had to fight to keep the bite out of his voice.

Lysandro could hold his tongue no longer.

"Perhaps she'd be more grateful if you'd preserved her husband's dignity, rather than turn his final moments into a spectacle."

Marek looked up at him, his eyes bright with challenge.

"Or perhaps they'd have been grateful if you had arrested Jair weeks ago, after he'd already been accused of thievery by the blacksmith. Granted, his family's possessions are humbler than this fine collection," Lysandro continued, gesturing at the box of silver, "but had your justice been swifter—"

The widow sobbed, and Lysandro let his accusation hang in the air.

"The blacksmith's account was not reliable. He was not as—"

"Worthy of your attention?" Lysandro offered. His mouth set into a hard line. "I shouldn't need to remind you that the office of magistrate is bound to protect *all* of Lighura, not just its wealthier citizens."

Lothan scowled.

"What did you lie about?" Lysandro asked.

"Excuse me?"

The abrupt turn took Marek by surprise. Lysandro lifted his gaze over Marek's shoulder to the hanged man. "With his last breath, he called you a liar. What did you lie about?"

Marek huffed through his nose and shifted on his feet like a bull in a pen.

"He called me a murderer too. Do you also accuse me of that?"

Marek fixed him with a venomous stare. Doña Sofia's hand flew to her mouth, and her younger children hid their faces in her voluminous black skirts.

Lysandro didn't flinch.

He waited for an answer with feigned curiosity. Marek had walked into the trap himself. Lysandro wasn't about to help him out of it.

Marek's gaze slid to the widow. "I did my duty here today. No one can say I didn't." He turned his back on them both and left.

Doña Sofia let out a sigh of relief. "Thank you."

"Someone had to say something."

She looked down again and brushed her fingers against the grain of the box Marek had given her as her children came out of hiding. Lysandro smiled at them and ruffled the younger boy's hair before turning his gaze back to their mother.

"Is there anything you need?" he asked.

"We'll be all right. Thank you again."

Lysandro nodded and looked to her eldest son. "Take good care of them."

The young don was a strapping teenager, who tried to act older than he was by appearing to be unmoved by the whole affair. He was managing it badly. The boy's eyes darted from one end of the square to the other, not finding an answer to the question forming on his lips.

"There's so much to go through. So many papers. I don't even—"

"There's nothing that can't wait a few days' time," Lysandro interrupted. "I'll come see you soon, help you get everything sorted. Let's see if we can't make any sense of it."

"Thank you."

"It's my pleasure," he replied. "Take care."

Before departing from the square himself, Lysandro spared one last look at the hanged man, cast in silhouette by the sun's rays as Marek's officers worked to cut him down. Lysandro wondered at all he might have inquired of the dead man—all the questions he could never ask.

The cheerful weather was wasted on the somber mood that hung over the dusty little village until nightfall. Lysandro called on his father for a late supper, having finally found his appetite after a full day's abstinence. He greeted the doorman genially.

"Good evening, Diego."

"Good evening, Don Lysandro. You'll find him in the dining hall this evening."

"The dining hall?" Lysandro asked. "Does he have guests?"

"No, Signor. He simply said he longed for some formality."

Lysandro raised an amused eyebrow. He thanked the man and headed through the familiar hallways of the house in which he had grown up and found his way to his father. Don de Castel the elder was already seated at the head of a long wooden table in an elegantly papered room of cream and burgundy. Cheeses, warm bread, and a stiff fortified wine lay fanned out before him.

"Standing on ceremony today, Father?" Lysandro asked, seating himself at his father's right hand and pouring himself a drink.

"Indeed," Elias answered, not looking up from his plate as he tore off a piece of bread from a larger loaf and soaked it in a spiced olive oil.

"In your dressing gown?" Lysandro asked.

Elias grunted in the affirmative. "It's my best one."

Lysandro smiled and took in the image of his father. His robe was one of fine fabric, luxurious and warm against the chill in the air coming off the sea. The wine-colored gown was elevated by an intricately embroidered scroll pattern, with golden threads woven into the cuffs and collar. His father's face was thin, but sharp, and marked by an imposing chin and a well-kept, respectable beard of silver to match the hair smoothed back on his head. Yes, Lysandro thought, his father looked every ounce a don.

"Marek hung Carrass's murderer today," Lysandro said.

"Mm."

"How *he* got to be magistrate I'll never know."

"That's easy. You didn't try for it."

Lysandro sipped at his wine. "Surely there are other able men in this village."

"There's so much influence you could wield, if only you would. There's no one sitting on the Andran Council now for Lighura."

"I doubt the Council would take kindly to my views."

"You still think you should give up all your land, and have it owned by the peasants who live there?" Elias asked.

"I clearly can't manage it on my own. Why *shouldn't* they own the fruit of their labors?"

"Without their rents you would be impoverished."

"I've known many men poorer than I who lead much happier lives."

Elias reclined in his high-backed seat and studied his son's reserved expression. "The social season starts in a few days. Will you attend the opening ball?"

Lysandro's heart constricted at the mention of it. He tried to dodge the question by digging into the slice of pork loin on his plate, but his father's expectant stare was unwavering.

"Why?" Lysandro asked, swallowing. "So I can mix with ladies almost ten years my junior and talk about the latest fashions?" Women saw his wealth and his title, and little else.

"That problem will get worse the older *you* get without choosing a bride. You're almost thirty."

"I seem to have exhausted my prospects."

"You only need to choose one."

If only there was one, Lysandro thought. *Just one.*

"You ask too much," Elias said.

"I just want what you had with Mother. Is *that* too much?"

Elias's eyes softened. "No. Maybe some travel would be in order. You've always longed to see Mirêne for yourself."

"Perhaps." Though Mirêne was more attuned to the Goddess's loving and more artful face, and better reflected Lysandro's own inclinations, he couldn't leave Lighura now—not after what had happened. There was a tension in the air, a sense of trouble brewing into something darker. More sinister.

He returned home and descended into the cavernous rooms carved out from underneath his estate. The space was sparsely furnished, with only a small dresser and a low bed covered in soft, dark furs. Wax puddled at the bases of the wrought-iron candelabras that flanked the corners of the room and lent it their dim light.

Lysandro considered what his father had said. He might find more in common with the people of Mirêne, but his heart belonged to Lighura too. Lysandro couldn't leave the fate of its people in the hands of Marek. Lysandro's belief that he was a thief and a murderer was stronger than ever. But he needed proof to remove him. Proof that might finally be within reach.

The trading ship that had quit the port yesterday had left heading north, rather than back the way they'd come. It would be easy for them to round to the other side of the coast unseen, rather than out to sea.

He stripped down to his skin and donned much simpler attire, dyed black to blend with the coming night. The worn fabric often felt more familiar and reassuring to him than the fine clothes he wore in the daytime. Too fancy an outfit would give him away and would more than likely get in his way. He didn't wear any metal or ornamentation that might glint in the moonlight; he had to be able to weave in and out of the darkness unseen. He completed his ensemble with a broad hat, leather gloves, and a sword honed to a fine point. He wrapped a strip of black cloth tightly around his face, revealing only his eyes, and tucked his long hair, kept in an older, more distinctive style, inside his shirt.

Lysandro abhorred violence. In the full light of day, it went against the example of kindness he worked so hard to set. But the edge of a sword carried a certain sense of rightness. So he sought justice from the shadows.

LIGHURA'S COAST WAS TOO SMALL TO BE A TRUE HARBOR. IT COULD ONLY manage two ships at once, three in an emergency. Tonight, as most nights, the port was empty, leaving the water to creep slowly up the narrow beach without disruption. The only sounds for miles were the breaking of the surf and the call of gulls. But Lighura had pride of place in Andras. Aside from its beautiful coast, it was reputed to be the birthplace of the hero Theron, though exactly *where* he had lived had been lost to the passage of time.

As Lothan made his way down the sloping path to the shore, past the grass-covered dunes and toward the thin strip of sand, he spied the merchant vessel he sought approaching from a distance. They were still too far away for Lothan to tell if they carried any genuine relics aboard. If they truly possessed what they claimed, he would know—just as the work of Argoss sang in his veins, the lingering sense of the goddess sent his skin crawling. The only thing he felt in that moment was the blade pulsing against his abdomen. Under his coat blossomed the scent of fresh blood—a river's worth of it.

The drums of the broken metal shard's magic beat furiously between his ears. It was perhaps the only proof in the whole world that the goddess had failed—Argoss may have lost his life, but his sorcery was beyond her ability to destroy. A hot determination overcame Lothan as he brushed his fingers against the makeshift handle at his belt, drenching them in gore. What the goddess's whores insisted did not exist was his birthright, to bend and shape to his will. It had eluded him until now, with no clean or clever way to adhere the bleeding metal to the handle of his cheap knife, no symmetrical point or edge to pull them neatly together. But Jair's energy had come to roost in him, and he willed the broken fragment to cling to the grip. This time, it had obeyed.

The flow of blood racing along its jagged edge made him sticky, lapping at his skin like a wonton lover. It turned his blood feverish, and made his mouth run dry. He licked his lips as a distraction.

The sense of triumph he had first experienced when the shard had come into his possession had waned. What good did it do him if he couldn't find a way to salvage what remained of the once-mighty Blood Sword? It was so small. And he was not a blacksmith or a sorcerer. At least, not in the true sense of the word. He'd managed to find its location, and had it transported from the farthest edges of Andras without raising suspicion, but that had been accomplished through instinct and sheer luck. The "why" of it eluded him. It was a constant source of frustration. When Lothan jabbed it through the air for the first time to test it, blood didn't fly off the edge in a venomous spray, which was a bit of a disappointment. But this was only one piece—Lothan consoled himself with the prospect of finding more, and one day wielding the full blade without squandering its power as Argoss had.

He had half a mind to slay his brothers right where they stood and take back from them what was his. But he was tied to his post, and much of what he craved lay beyond his grasp. He needed them. Although at this particular moment, the furtive glow of the lanterns on the beach was infuriatingly stationary. Lothan quickened his steps, and almost barreled into Jenner.

"What are you doing just standing there like an idiot? Spread out! Who do you have on the cliff?"

"That was Jair's job, Lord Lothan."

Lothan stared at him, and the man's legs nearly buckled as he spun on his heel and hurried to do the job himself.

They scattered at his command, taking up their positions as the ship made land.

Lothan was incensed by the illicit goods as they received the smugglers. They had only trinkets to offer— illustrated pages and "blessed" bits of junk, useless things that allowed deluded fanatics to feel nearer to the goddess and their hero—but nothing that bore the mark of

Argoss. They had promised him more. They had promised him the Cerulean Key. Lothan did not take kindly to being lied to.

He turned to the man standing at his left and whispered in his ear.

"Get Gorin down here."

His brother retreated up the cliff face to recall the lookout. The more of them Lothan had nearby, the quicker he could dispatch the two-faced captain and his crew.

Lothan was still waiting for the pair of them to come back down when Jenner handed the captain his money. The captain in turn handed it to his second, who scurried up onto the boat. Lothan shot a piercing look to the cliffs, but neither man was anywhere in sight. He'd just about lost his patience when a single head popped into view.

"He's gone!"

"What do you mean, gone?"

"Like he's just vanished into thin air."

Lothan's skin prickled. Then he heard a scream, and a splash. That's when he knew they were not alone.

The sailors aboard the ship drew their swords, but it was useless against an invisible enemy. One man came flying in their direction and landed face-first in the mud. Another two, from Lothan's vantage point, seemed to disappear entirely, as if the floor had opened up from under them. Pandemonium erupted on the small vessel, but no one could discern the cause.

"It's him!"

"It's the Shadow of Theron!"

Marek's men watched but made no move to help, their eyes round in the lantern light. They grew skittish, wavering in place like horses ready to bolt.

He screamed at his men —better they fear him than some impostor who styled himself after a ridiculous excuse for a god. But his raging was drowned out by another voice that echoed across the sea.

"Ho, there! Looking for this?"

The Shadow of Theron appeared out of the darkness. He stood balanced on the thin outcropping of the ship's prow, with the sack of coins Jenner had just given over to the captain dangling from his hand.

The realization that he'd snuck past the lot of them without so much as a ripple out of place seized Lothan with a fit of rage. For too long, the Shadow had plagued him. Whenever he had come close to achieving even the smallest of his aims, Theron's Impostor had been there; he always knew the precise moment to strike, and always came away laughing— leaving Lothan chasing after him like an empty-headed fool. He reached for the bleeding dagger at his belt.

Not this night.

"Get him!" the captain shouted.

Jenner lunged for the chest, but the captain kicked the lid shut with his boot and caught him by the hand.

"No money, no trade!" The captain scooped up the ill-gotten treasure and sped back to the ship. The sailors seemed to have the Shadow cornered, stuck as he was on the thin bowsprit poking out over the water, but he batted their swords away with ease, their seething violence no more than a child's game to him. He pretended to lose his balance and flung the coins far out to sea.

A blood vessel in Lothan's neck threatened to burst; the smugglers howled in indignation. But when they charged him, he cut one of the lines connected to the foremast and used it to sail clear across the water to the stern. He bounded off the ship and landed on the beachhead with the grace of a jungle cat. He turned his back on Lothan, not showing a care in the world, and waved the ship off.

"Safe journey! Be careful of those rocks, they're trickier than they look!" Then he returned his gaze to the men on the beach, and grinned.

All Lothan needed was to get close enough to deliver one small slice. But the Shadow was untouchable. He dodged Marek and his men with nimble steps at every turn, cutting through their number as he stayed always just a hair's breadth out of reach.

In a matter of minutes, Lothan's lieutenants lay sprawled flat in the sand, bloodied and unconscious. Lothan slowly worked to close the circle tighter and tighter as the Shadow danced around him. He was close enough now that the Shadow could see what it was that Lothan held; the broken blade shimmered brilliantly in the moonlight. The Shadow grew more careful, pushing Lothan to the brink of his endurance.

Lothan shot him a grim smile and tried to knock him off his balance.

"Was Theron himself such a coward in the face of great magic, or is that just you?"

But the Shadow was relentless, and deftly avoided his blows.

Lothan was rewarded for his patience. He thrust straight ahead, causing the Shadow to twist away to the side. But instead of righting himself, Lothan stepped into the dodge, leaving himself exposed, and retracted his arm back at rapid speed.

It was a shallow cut on the upper arm, nothing more. But Lothan felt the edge of the blade bite through the Shadow's sleeve, and the soft release as it rent open his flesh. The tang of blood filled the air as the tiny droplets joined the flood along the enchanted metal. The Shadow staggered backward, his chest heaving.

Lothan shivered in triumph. But he didn't stop. He struck again, aiming high for the head. The Shadow of Theron deflected the blow with more force than Lothan thought possible. But the power that pulsed at his fingertips didn't lie. Lothan stood grinning in the moonlight as the Shadow turned and ran for his life, although he was somewhat perturbed by the Shadow's speed. He shouldn't have been able to run at all.

The others were rising from the ground as his enemy shrank back into the shadows.

"Where did he go?"

"Should we go after him?"

"Let him be," Lothan said, a devilish grin on his face. Lothan was giddy, drunk with victory. "I cut him. With this." He held out the vermillion remnant of the Blood Sword of Argoss. His brothers gaped and dropped again to their knees, pressing their heads back into the sand.

"It may not be what it was. But if it has even a fraction of its old force…he won't live through the night."

2

LYSANDRO RACED HOME IN A DEAD PANIC. THE SWEAT ON HIS FOREHEAD soaked into his stallion's neck as he slumped forward and gripped his mane.

"Please," he whispered. "Hurry."

The pace of Hurricane's hooves thumping in the grass matched the beating of Lysandro's heart. His vision swam.

Lysandro was no stranger to wounds. This one was barely a nick, not even deep enough to merit stitching. But he felt his life leeching out of him.

His thoughts descended into delirium, and a shrinking, numbing sensation took hold of his limbs and his fingers. His legs felt as if they were dissolving beneath him, reducing him to only the pounding in his chest. The cold wind on his cheek that sliced through his mask and bit into the tips of his ears was the only thing keeping him conscious.

Lysandro was losing his grip on Hurricane. He pulled on the horse's mane to stop from falling off. Hurricane whinnied in pain and jerked his head violently. Lysandro righted himself, but soon slid down again like a heap of dead flesh atop the raging beast.

He collapsed onto the floor as Hurricane crossed the threshold into the stable. The stallion returned to his stall of his own accord, his flanks heaving and shimmering with the exertion.

"Marta!"

Lysandro called out as loud as he could, even as his tongue turned to lead. He felt the shortness of time, and his heart couldn't keep up the pace; it was a thundering in his ear that he feared would send him hurtling headlong into oblivion.

"Marta!"

His voice was so full of fear, it frightened him just to hear it as he crawled on his hands and elbows, dragging his legs behind him as he tried to reach the bed. The candle flames burned black in his eyes; the contours of the room wavered like a dreamscape.

The sound of Marta's steps flying down the stairs from the main house sounded like salvation.

"Don Lysandro!" she screamed.

He tried to respond, to peel his tongue off the roof of his mouth, but he failed.

She bent down and turned him over onto his back. His breathing was shallow, like a fish plucked from the sea. Lysandro gripped the hem of her apron as she knelt beside him and heaved him up off the floor with trembling hands. Together they lurched over to the bed, where she stripped off his boots, hat, mask, and shirt.

Then she screamed. She must have seen what he felt, the darkness clawing at his vision, death rushing through his veins. Even the whites of his eyes were tainted, streaked with dark lightning. His arm felt like it belonged to a dead man, the insignificant cut now a puffy, angry red surrounded by dying flesh.

"I'm calling Rafael right now!" She turned to race up the stairs and shouted to the groomsman to ready the coach.

Lysandro tried to call her back. When she turned to him, her eyes were wild with fright. That was all he could see of her—the fear in her eyes.

He moved his lips, but Marta had to move closer to her.

"I don't want to die alone."

Tears spilled down her cheeks and disappeared into the black cloud surrounding her face. She put a cool, gentle hand to his forehead.

"I won't be a second."

"No," he said with all the force he could muster.

Marta disappeared. He felt himself slipping away, his heartbeat slowing to a dangerous murmur. He fought to wait for her, so she could hold his hand and whisper kind words in his ear, but he was sinking. He felt a tickle against his cheek as fear turned to sadness. Then he slid into darkness.

* * *

A stinging pain in his arm shocked Lysandro back into consciousness. He opened his eyes to find the world no longer enrobed in shadow. Rafael peeled away a bandage at his side.

"Oh! You're awake!"

Rafael dropped the soiled bandage in his hands as their eyes met and pressed the back of his knuckles to Lysandro's forehead.

"Your fever's broken," he exhaled.

Lysandro heard a sob to his right. He turned his head to see his housemaid wiping away tears with a handkerchief worn down to the barest threads. He tested his fingers. They were stiff, but responsive. Marta rushed to his side and squeezed them. He smiled at her.

He looked around the room and shifted under the blankets. "Did you tell my—"

"No," Rafael replied. "I didn't drag him out of his slumber to witness his son's last minutes. But I should have."

Lysandro pressed his hands to either side of him to sit up, but Rafael stopped him with a litany of questions. "Are you dizzy? Nauseous? Does anything hurt? How's your appetite?"

"I'm ready to eat as soon as you stop peppering me."

Rafael cocked his head in confusion. "You appear to be fine."

"I feel fine. Just sore."

Marta hopped from her seat without being asked. "I'll be back with food. Lots and lots of food."

As soon as Marta's footsteps could no longer be heard in the stairwell, Rafael turned to Lysandro with an intense stare.

"What *happened*?"

"Marek. He cut me." His name was like a foul breath on Lysandro's lips.

"I've never seen such a virulent, fast-acting poison."

It was no poison—it was death itself that had stolen into him, had held his heart tight in its grip. The thing Lothan had attacked him with should have eaten his flesh right down to his bones, and then eaten through that until there was nothing left of him. Whatever medicine Rafael had used to pull Lysandro back from the brink was nothing short of a miracle. But that was a thing not supposed to exist.

Lysandro didn't dare tell Rafael any of this. He would only worry that he was delirious.

"I didn't get what I needed," Lysandro said, shifting the conversation.

Rafael leaned back in his chair and took up a stone mortar and pestle. He placed it next to Lysandro on the bed and ground its contents into a fine paste.

"What does that mean?" Rafael asked. His mouth pressed into a thin line, and the muscles of his jaw worked as he pounded at his concoction.

"I found proof of their activities, or at least some of them, but nothing tied directly to Marek."

Rafael laid the pestle aside and applied the poultice liberally onto the discreet line on Lysandro's bicep that had almost been his undoing.

"This is not a game anymore. It has to stop."

"It was *never* a game to me. People don't feel safe enough to—agh!"

Rafael had wrapped the bandage tight, pulling the ends into a knot against Lysandro's skin.

"I can't keep putting you back together like this. I almost lost you this time. What would I say to your father? What then, Lysandro?"

"He has to be stopped, Rafael, or none of us are safe."

Especially now.

"And how exactly are you going to stop him? What if he poisons you again?"

The thought of that blade touching his skin was enough to send Lysandro's mind spiraling. But he let the fear slide off his back and said simply, "I'll find a way."

Rafael shook his head. "Goddess damn you, Lysandro. You're as stubborn as your father."

Lysandro offered him only a wan smile in response.

Rafael pointed to a powdered substance in a worn pouch. "Try to drink at least two cups of that a day. And mix some with linseed oil and change the bandages just as often."

Lysandro raised an eyebrow. "You want me to dress it *and* drink it?"

"I want you to get as much of that into your body as you can." Rafael packed up his belongings.

"You're a good friend, Rafael."

He grimaced. "A good friend? A good friend would stop coming every time you call, so maybe you'd stop this madness."

"A world without justice *is* madness, my friend."

Rafael sighed and turned to go, and almost crashed into Marta at the door. She held a silver tray loaded with a day's worth of food.

"Oh, Signor, I made a plate for you upstairs. Please take it with you."

"I will Marta, thank you. You be sure to call me if his condition changes." He cast a final glance back at Lysandro, flashing him a wry smile, then left.

Marta laid the tray on Lysandro's lap. "Is there anything else you want, Don Lysandro?"

"I don't think you could possibly fit anything else. Thank you."

"I'm just so glad you're well. You eat now. The Shadow of Theron needs his strength." She beamed at him with an eager, hopeful expression that smoothed the lines of her face and made Lysandro think he was looking into the face of Marta as a young girl, full of hopes and dreams. People needed someone to protect them from humanity's worst instincts, even if that meant risking life and limb. Looking into her face, he knew that as soon as he was able, he'd do it all over again.

"Go get some rest. I'll call you if I need anything."

She scurried back up the stairs and left him alone with his feast. She'd piled the tray high with all his favorites—warm bread with fresh butter, clotted cream, lemon curd and a soft cheese, a bowl of cherries, a lidded pot of shredded lamb—all the fatty foods he deprived himself of when he was training. It was like a final meal after the fact.

When he could eat no more, he pushed the platter off his lap and attempted to rise. He had to lean heavily on the chair propped beside the bed to steady himself. *Now* he was dizzy.

Lysandro drew in deep breaths. His limbs ached, but the discomfort was infinitely better than not feeling his body at all. He splashed his face with cool water poured from a jug into a bronze basin and slipped out of his pants and into a clean dressing gown. He grimaced as he put his bandaged arm through the sleeve, still marveling at the damage wrought by so tiny a wound. On the far side of the room, he spied the garments he donned as the Shadow, already mended. The broken and remade seam was invisible, like it had never been cut at all. From an inner pocket, he withdrew the papers he had pilfered from aboard the ship.

He hadn't had the time to rifle through everything in the captain's quarters. He'd just grabbed anything he could. He sorted through them now, setting aside mundane records and manifests that seemed to be in order. One paper among the stack was curious, providing only place names, numbers, and odd phrases.

Lareina – stones – 4, 6250
– flowers – 100, 250
Selonia – illuminations – 12, 860
Milagra – key – 1, 8000

Lysandro scowled at himself for not looking more carefully before taking the documents. The whole thing made no sense. Whatever it was Marek was after, Lysandro consoled himself with the knowledge that he had prevented him from getting it. *This time*, at least. He wondered how Marek had ever come across something so insidious, borne more of legend than truth. He would have to be so very careful.

Lysandro picked up the untouched fruit from his plate and walked outside to his second stable. Hurricane stood idle, hanging his head out at the smell of food in the air.

"You look better than I do," Lysandro said in a soothing voice. The stallion took the food and left nothing behind. "You deserve it."

The horse nickered in agreement.

Lysandro reached for the brush and started to groom him in long, smooth strokes. He inhaled sharply at the extension of his injured arm, but he needed a simple task like this to work through his pain. He didn't have the luxury of time; he had to get back on his horse as soon as he could. And the day he couldn't brush down his own horse was the day he'd stop breathing. He worked on Hurricane's coat until it shone like silk.

He ran his fingers over Hurricane's sides, feeling a prick of emotion in the corner of his eye.

"You rode like the wind," he whispered. He held the stallion's head in his hand, and pressed his forehead to Hurricane's long, sleek nose.

Lysandro struggled to break free from overwhelming stiffness and lethargy, like tendrils of death curling themselves around him. Uneventful days gave him time to rest, and time for reading. But indulging in his favorite tales sharpened his yearning to experience for himself the great adventure of falling in love. He didn't want to be a bachelor all his life. He didn't want to be a bachelor now, but he had limited choice in the matter. To stop himself from being consumed by the loneliness spurred by tales of knights and their princesses, he trained.

He kept coming back to the strange manifest. Who in his right mind would pay such exorbitant sums for such ordinary items? Eight thousand lyra for a key? It had to be a code for something, but Lysandro didn't have the first clue what. More unbelievable still was that Marek hadn't been affected by the weapon he carried. How was he able to touch it without killing himself? Lysandro needed answers. And he knew just who to ask.

SANCIO BUILT UP A SWEAT DOING THE SIMPLEST THINGS. SWEEPING, KEEPING the candles lit, and making sure the brazier stayed hot caused *him* to overheat in short order. He ducked into the private prayer booth and wiped the sweat off his forehead with the pale blue sleeve of his robes. Reaching under the bench, he recovered the cheese-covered roll he had secreted away there. He'd earned the treat with a morning of hard work, even if it was his third of the day. Or was it the fourth? It was definitely the fourth. But the stress of staring at the flaky, buttery bun only made his hunger grow, and the baking at Arun's temple house was so very good.

He sat quietly in the booth and enjoyed his mid-morning snack. It was shaping up to be a beautifully warm, sunny day, and there were no worshippers about that needed tending to. The only sound in the temple was that of his lips smacking together. But before he could finish, he heard someone enter the temple and make their way into the other half of the booth. He wrapped the rest of his food into its little white cloth and placed it next to him on the bench, licking his fingers and brushing the crumbs off his belly before addressing the person whose face was obscured behind a carved wooden screen.

"Share what troubles you, friend, and together we'll ask for Arun's strength."

"I am guilty of not taking the story of Argoss and his sword seriously, and I have come to deeply regret it."

Sancio immediately recognized the smooth baritone. He jerked upright and straightened his robe.

"Lysandro?" he whispered. "Where have you been?"

"On the edge of death, my friend. Won't you hear my confession?"

Lysandro related his encounter at the harbor.

"He had a dagger with a crooked blade, with blood running along the edge of it, just like in the sacred stories. He cut me with it, and my whole body was wracked by death in an instant. Only Faelia knows why I did not succumb."

Sancio's mouth gaped open, and he sputtered for a response. "Are you sure that it wasn't a hallucination? Or the effect of some poison or fever?"

"You're the acolyte. You tell me."

Sancio grunted. He and Lysandro left their ends of the booth at the same time. Lysandro stood over a foot taller than Sancio and was impeccably groomed for someone who had almost met the Goddess in person. Sancio's heart fluttered.

Lysandro spun round in one graceful, effortless move and followed close on Sancio's heels as he approached the altar.

"If the high priestess catches us, she'll tan my hide." They both knelt on the marble floor, letting their right knees touch the ground before climbing the few shallow steps. Sancio had trouble getting to his feet again. Lysandro grabbed him by the shoulder and hauled him upright.

"Maybe if you stopped eating so many of those cakes, you could do this all by yourself."

Sancio's face turned a bright pink. He fidgeted with his robes.

"I'm sorry Sancio, I didn't mean to—"

"It's nothing," Sancio cut him off. "You're probably right." He gave his friend a weak, self-effacing smile as he put his hand underneath the front flap of his robe to reveal a small brass key on a chain. He unlocked the glass cabinet beneath the pulpit, pulled out the temple's copy of *The Histories*, and laid it out on the altar. Sancio mumbled to himself as he flipped through the pages.

"Why didn't you pledge to serve Morgasse?" Lysandro asked.

Sancio's fingers stilled on the page. "What?"

"You would have excelled at serving the Sorcerer, with your affinity for books. It would have suited you better."

What Lysandro meant was that Sancio was not fast, or tall, or strong enough to be counted among the Aruni.

"I didn't want to leave Lighura," Sancio answered, feeling his cheeks redden. "And may I remind you, that you are also a lover of books?"

"I didn't take holy orders."

"Here it is." Sancio opened the tome to a pair of brightly illuminated pages, bordered by an interlocking pattern that showed the Lover, the Warrior, and the Sorcerer looking inward at the illustrations. On the right-hand page was a portrait of Argoss. He was tall and broad, with dark feral eyes and a malicious smirk. In his right hand was an enchanted sword almost the length of an entire man. Its tinted edges flared a shimmering red.

"Is that what you saw?"

"That's what I saw. What can you tell me about it?"

"Nothing you don't already know. Weren't you listening all those years when you sat quietly in temple?"

"You can't blame me for assuming there was some exaggeration involved."

Sancio looked scandalized.

"I'm listening *now*," Lysandro said.

Sancio pointed to the image on the opposite page, depicting a coil of snakes. Their scales sparkled in gold and black against the underlying red.

"They're eldur vipers," Sancio explained. "There's a small population of them lining the side of Mount Aetnus. They're said to look like flowing lava when they move. They can withstand the volcano's heat, and their venom is derived from something in the ash. It's their poison that taints the blood on this sword."

"It was only about this big." Lysandro held his index finger and thumb apart to show a length more common to a paring knife than a sword. "It was rough and uneven all over. I know the Blood Sword was shattered by an arrow fired from the Hand of Arun. It could have been a piece that broke off. But that's impossible, isn't it? Nothing was left of the final battle with Argoss. I remember *that* much."

Sancio became uneasy on his feet. He nodded in agreement, but the look in his eyes had shifted.

"Sancio?"

"I'm not...I'm not supposed to—"

"*Sancio.*"

His shoulders slumped. "There *were* some things left of Argoss's enchantments. Not much, but... I've been sworn to secrecy. If anyone finds out that I told you..."

"Were there shards from the shattered sword?"

"Yes," Sancio whispered.

Lysandro rocked back on his heels.

"How did Marek get it?"

Again, Sancio hesitated. "Relics have been... disappearing."

"*Disappearing?*"

"Insignificant things, mostly. Bits of soil where Theron may have walked. Flowers touched by Faelia. It's been happening all over Andras."

"Has Lighura been robbed?"

"No."

"That's conspicuous, isn't it?" Lysandro stopped himself and tried to keep his rioting thoughts in order. "How would Marek be able to wield this weapon? Would he have to be a sorcerer?"

"Most likely. Or..."

"*Or?*" Lysandro pressed.

Sancio returned the heavy volume to its place and locked the cabinet. "There's a rumor," he said, "a very old rumor, that Argoss sired several children, with the aim of building an army of sorcerers. Theron killed him before they came of age. Some say the Aruni slaughtered his bastards after the final battle, others believe they turned to dust upon his demise. Either way, it was never proven."

"It seems the temple keeps quite a few secrets, doesn't it?"

"What good would it do for the world to know all this? If no one knows about the dark relics, they can't fall into the hands of treasure seekers or people hungry for power."

Lysandro accepted that reasoning grudgingly.

"So, if that's what he is…"

"We don't know that."

"But if it *is* true, then how do I stop him?

"*You* don't. The Council of Three has appointed Examiners, priestesses from each temple to recover the relics. There's going to be an announcement about it tomorrow."

Lysandro took the manifest out of the folds of his coat and handed it over.

"Will this help? At first, I thought it was a code for something else. Now I'm not so sure."

"Where did you get this?"

"Onboard *The Siren* the night Marek cut me. Give it to the Examiners when they come."

"Whom shall I say I got it from?"

Lysandro shrugged.

"You could write your name, or something. Not your real name, obviously, but you know…the other one?"

Lysandro shook his head. "I just want Lighura to be safe, and for its people to thrive. I'm not Theron, and I'm not his shadow."

"The people you protect think you are."

"I can't control what people think, or what they call me."

Sancio sighed and tucked the parchment into the folds of his robe. "I don't like this."

"Me neither."

3

LYSANDRO ROSE EARLY FOR MORNING SERVICE. HE DONNED A COAT OF DEEP blue that offset his eyes, and a thick banded ring of burnished silver. His boots were buffed to perfection. It was the first time he'd been to the temple since his brush with death, and he was eager to give thanks.

He found his father in front of the temple as people mulled about. It was easy enough to do; Elias de Castel was one of the tallest people in Lighura, set apart by his dignified silver head, his noble bearing, and his fine wardrobe.

"Good morning, Father."

Elias turned. "Morning. You're looking rather dapper today. I missed you on Tyrsday."

"I'm sorry, I've been ill."

"Oh?"

Lysandro shook his head dismissively. "Nothing serious," he lied.

Elias smiled. "Good. Nothing that would stop you from attending tonight's ball, then?"

Lysandro rolled his eyes. "Father, please. Must we talk about this every time we see each other?"

"Tell you what—you settle down and find yourself a lovely bride, and I'll never ask about another social event again."

His father's sly grin was contagious. Lysandro turned his head to look out over the crowd and saw a vision of beauty descending from a coach on the far edge of the circle. She was slender, with hair the color of spiced honey that cascaded to her waist. An ivory dress with bright embellishments accentuated her golden strands. Her skin was so pale, nearly untouched by the Lighuran sun, that it seemed luminescent. He stood awestruck.

But even from a distance, he could see that there was no light shining in her eyes. She stood detached from her parents; her whole appearance gave off the impression that she was a ghost, just a shell of a girl who wasn't really there.

Elias, not realizing his son's enchantment, turned away from a neighbor he'd been speaking with and addressed Lysandro.

"Shall we go in?"

Lysandro's eyes didn't leave the girl as she and her family drew nearer to him. For a moment, he was afraid to say anything, for fear that she might be just a phantom, and that to call attention to her would banish her from his sight forever. He tried to shake off the notion.

"Who is that?" he dared to ask.

Elias followed his son's unwavering gaze. "That would be Signorina Alvaró, I should think."

"Alvaró?"

Lysandro knew the name. They were a good Lighuran family, though they had fallen on hard times. If she'd been in the village before, he would have noticed her. He couldn't tear himself away from her elegant profile now.

"Yes," Elias answered. "They sent her away to be educated. She must have just returned."

Lysandro said nothing. The smirk on his father's face went unnoticed as Elias stepped out in front of him and greeted the girl's father with a broad smile.

"Good morning, Don Alvaró."

The stout man seemed surprised to be so warmly saluted. They exchanged pleasantries until his father's voice became a dull, soft tone in Lysandro's ear. Close up, Lysandro admired the girl's delicate features—a sleek little nose, an enticing mouth, set in an expressionless straight line, and warm, intoxicating brown eyes that were rimmed in red. She looked positively heartbroken. It made Lysandro's own chest ache.

His father's voice became clear again in his ears as it veered toward a new subject.

"And who is this fine young creature?"

She did not meet his gaze but continued to stare forward and down toward some invisible point. Her mouth didn't make the slightest twitch in an intention to reply, but the moment went unremarked by all, except Lysandro, as her mother readily filled the void.

"This is our daughter, Seraphine. She's just returned from Romagna, where she attended one of the finest schools for young ladies."

"Lovely. How was the capital, Signorina?" Elias asked.

With a straight face, not looking at him, or at anyone, she answered in a subdued voice: "I wouldn't know."

Her father shot her a warning look, then laughed awkwardly. "You'll have to forgive her, Don de Castel. She's had a very long journey and hasn't had the chance to rest or get her bearings yet. The ship bringing her back to us just arrived this morning."

That's not it, Lysandro thought. Why would a girl who had spent the majority of her life in Romagna claim to know nothing about it?

She settled back into a distant silence, and the subject was dropped as they made their way inside the temple.

The villagers filed into the six long wooden rows at the front of the temple. Lysandro quickened his steps to seat himself next to Seraphine. He put a hand on his father's shoulder and pushed him aside, nearly vaulting over him.

"Oh for heaven's sake," Elias grumbled, but Lysandro never heard it. He tried to catch the girl's attention as people settled into their seats all around them, but she stared stubbornly at her hands, folded on her lap. It was unbearable to see her so distraught.

Having never conversed with such a beauty before, he was keenly aware of her nearness. It turned his head to mush, made his palms sweaty, and caused his voice to tremble.

"Signorina," he whispered. "Are you alright?"

He feared somehow that he'd made her mysterious condition worse just by asking. Her eyes took on an added gleam. Despite the steady curve of her mouth, her eyes looked as if tears might burst forth at any moment.

Very subtly, she shook her head in the negative.

He suddenly had the urge to soothe the storm clouds brewing in her eyes, and would have done anything to learn the reason for her silent anguish.

A novice in pale blue approached the brazier near the right-hand wall and stoked it back to life, signaling the start of the service. Lysandro turned his gaze away from Seraphine to reflect on the sacred window illuminated by the flames, and remember why he had come. Cut into nine panes, the window of the Temple Arun depicted the moment the arrow from the Hand of Arun was loosed. Inside the larger panes, bits of colored class were cut up at odd angles to make the window appear shattered, representing the chaos surrounding Argoss. He towered over Theron, who crouched and took his aim. The sky was black, reflected in smoked glass. Lysandro thought the heat shimmering against the window made the figures look sweaty and alive, caught in a mortal struggle. The brilliant diamond at the tip of the arrow lent the scene that magical, Goddess-blessed quality.

The high priestess entered the chamber and ascended to her place behind the altar. All eyes turned to her. Throughout the series of songs, Lysandro did not once hear the voice of the girl beside him join in the chorus. As the high priestess led them through a litany of prayers, Seraphine still did not join the swell of supplicants. But her lips did move.

What she said to herself was a prayer not to the Warrior Arun, but to Faelia, the Lover. Faelia was no more the favored face of the Goddess in Romagna than She was in Lighura. *All* Andran cities, large and small, gave homage to Arun. But Faelia *was* the predominant aspect found in the temples of Mirêne. His thoughts lingered on it, but he turned his attention back to the high priestess as her voice increased, and her tone deepened.

"We must never forget the story of the hero preparing to fight Argoss. From the humblest origins, he took upon himself the task of challenging the mighty sorcerer with a black heart, second only to Morgasse in power. He commanded an army of monsters and unspeakable things, pulled up from the Abyss to do his bidding. And yet, even as Argoss grew in skill, Theron prevailed. He saved his own defenseless village with no weapons but his bare hands, his cunning and his wit, and his unfailing courage. Armed with only these, he killed the goblin that threatened to ravage this village and raze it to the ground. In this way he gained the attention of the Honored Warrior, the Mighty Arun, the Defender of Men, who rewarded his bravery by bestowing upon him the weapons that cleaved through the wicked sorcery of Argoss. All that Arun had given Theron, and all the blessings of the sorcerer Morgasse and the lover Faelia, are our windows into the realm of the Three-faced Goddess. Those blessings are kept in sacred trust by our sisters and brothers, protected by her high servants and the Council of Three. That sacred trust has been broken. The temples of Andras have been robbed of their relics."

A murmur rippled through the temple. Lysandro noticed that she did not mention the fact that some of the pilfered items were forged with an evil intent, and could still be used to prey upon the vulnerable.

The high priestess allowed her words to sink in before she continued.

"It is our duty to protect and retrieve these relics and return them to those chosen by the Goddess to safeguard them. The Council of Three has therefore called for Examiners to be sent from the Temples Arun and Morgasse to seek out these sacred gifts, restore them to the temple, and punish those who would challenge the Goddess by seizing her powers for themselves."

There was another round of whispers at this. The notable absence of a Faelian Examiner meant there would be no escape from Morgasse's gaze, no tempering of Arun's rage. The message was clear.

Lysandro scanned the gathering, looking for Marek. He wanted to see his reaction to this news. But he wasn't there. Come to think of it, Lysandro had never seen Lothan present in the temple. He considered the possibility that Lothan *couldn't* enter the temple.

Nothing would give Lysandro greater pleasure than to hand Marek over to the Examiners to await their judgment. Nothing, perhaps, except to see Seraphine Alvaró smile.

The high priestess closed the ceremony with a prayer for the Examiners' success in their solemn mission and a departing song. Again, Lysandro noticed that the girl next to him remained silent. His gaze happened to fall on the prayer book she held limply in her hands. He cocked his head. As he inched closer, he caught the fragrance of citrus coming from her hair. He savored it, but before he could make a fool of himself by leaning forward for no reason, he cleared his throat in a soft, deep way that only she could hear, took the book from her hand, and flipped it around.

She looked down at the pages before her, now sitting upright, and one eyebrow went up. She nodded subtly, as if Lysandro had just solved a most perplexing conundrum. Her lips remained motionless, but the amusement was evident in her eyes. A light flickered on inside. She turned to Lysandro, and met his gaze for the first time.

He swallowed hard, caught in her intense expression. Never had he beheld such perfection. Lysandro was afraid that the pounding in his chest was audible.

The song and the service concluded, the villagers exited their seats and made their way back out again into the square. Lysandro's father resumed his conversation with Don Alvaró as if it had never been interrupted.

"I'd be honored if you and your family would join my son and me for dinner tonight."

Lysandro could have cut out his father's tongue.

Doña Alvaró answered. "We'd love to, but we can't tonight, I'm afraid. Tonight is the first dance of the season, you know."

Elias rocked back on his heels, with his hands folded behind his back.

"Ah, yes. It's been a long time since I've gone to such a thing myself. So easy to forget these things at my age," he said with a foxy smile.

Lysandro snorted. If *they* had professed not to know, Lysandro was sure his father would have remembered for them.

Elias ignored him.

"Oh, yes," Seraphine's father chimed in. "She's missed her own season here, but it was well worth it, to have given over a child in exchange for a well-bred lady."

Lysandro noticed Seraphine's ears prick up at her mother's next pronouncement.

"They always do such a nice job planning these events for the young people. I believe this year they were inspired to do a Mirênese theme, with their connection to the Maghreve Desert."

"Of course," Elias replied. "Another time, perhaps."

"You are very gracious to think of us," Don Alvaró said. "We look forward to the day when we can all dine at the same table."

"Indeed."

With that, Seraphine and her family departed.

ELIAS HAD JUST SAT DOWN TO SUPPER WHEN LYSANDRO ENTERED THE ROOM unannounced. The pains he had taken with his person were obvious—his long, dark hair was prim and glossy, and his clothes were finely cut.

"Good evening son," Elias said evenly.

Lysandro's reply was clipped. "Can I borrow your sapphire studs?"

Elias wiped the beef drippings from his lips. "I thought you had no interest in going out tonight."

"Father, do you want me to go, or don't you?"

Elias swallowed his meat and grinned. He rose from his chair and retreated to his wardrobe, returning in a moment with the requested jewels. He stood in front of Lysandro and helped affix them to the cuffs of his sleeves. He could feel the tension in Lysandro's muscles.

"I did rather like Signorina Alvaró. She's the right age for you, and from a good family."

"Mm."

"Lysandro, you're a handsome young man. You're a don. You've got land, and

wealth—"

"I'd rather a girl didn't choose me for my wealth."

"Yes, yes, but...it never hurt. You can have any girl you want. You're a fine man, with a good heart."

"Father..."

Elias clapped him on the back of the neck. "Alright. Good luck tonight, and have fun."

"Thank you."

Elias sat down again to his meal as Lysandro left, and found himself humming a love ballad through his next mouthful.

THE LARGEST BALLROOM IN LIGHURA HAD BEEN TRANSFORMED INTO AN oasis. Sensuous purple, indigo, and gold silks were draped across the austere marble pillars lining the circular dance hall. Soft cushions replaced the chairs, and low platforms had been brought in to serve as makeshift tables. The orchestra included additional players on the sitar and drums to inject a more authentic sound into their repertoire.

Lysandro scanned the crowds for Seraphine. He didn't see her amber tresses among the cacophony of satin, ribbons, and lace.

As he made his way through the ballroom, another young woman stepped into his path.

"Good evening, Don de Castel."

"Good evening, Signorina."

"It's a lovely night, isn't it? Perfect for dancing."

"Yes."

An awkward silence ensued. This was meant to be the moment when he asked her to dance.

"Excuse me," he said, and rounded past her shoulder.

He moved along the edges of the room, circumnavigating the central space occupied by countless dancing couples. Then he saw her. At the far end of the hall, the normal view out over the coast had been replaced by a painted backdrop of the Maghreve Desert, at the very farthest border of Mirène. She was leaning against a pillar marking the boundary between the hall and its balcony. With her arms wrapped around herself, she looked out over the artificial horizon. She wore a sleek ivory dress covered in gold and copper crystals that left her shoulders daringly bare. It was a tasteful and simple silhouette, not overwrought in bright bows or flounces. That now familiar ache that hadn't left him since this morning grew more pronounced.

As he observed the faraway, wistful look in her eyes, he realized he recognized it—homesickness. He took a deep breath and called on well-used skills to smooth his nerves and keep them tightly tucked away under a charming façade.

He inhaled the hypnotic scent of her hair again as he stood close to her, and almost lost his nerve. He agonized over what to say, knowing he might have only one shot to get her attention.

"Is the city of stars as beautiful as they say?"

She turned to face him, and he saw the truth in her eyes.

She opened her mouth to speak, then closed it again, her attention drawn away from him. He followed her gaze. At the edge of his vision, a gaggle of young women were mulling about near the banister. More than one pair of eyes darted quickly away as Lysandro took notice of them.

He turned back to Seraphine and extended his hand. "Would you care to dance?"

He closed his fingers over her smooth skin and pulled her into the privacy provided by the swell of dancers. He pressed his luck again.

"You've come from Mirène, haven't you?"

"Yes."

"I don't understand. Your parents said they'd sent you to school in Romagna."

"They did. I had to leave for my own safety."

Lysandro gaped at her. "Why didn't you ask your parents to bring you home?"

"They'd already sent me away, even though I didn't want to go."

Lysandro saw sadness return to her face at her confession of feeling unwanted.

"Don't tell them," she pleaded. "Don't tell my parents."

It had not yet been five minutes, and already she was asking him to keep her secrets.

"You can trust me, Signorina."

"Sera."

"Hmm?"

"My friends call me Sera."

He feared staring too long into her eyes and being ensnared by her gaze. But he couldn't bear to look away.

They fell more fully into the dance. Lysandro's senses came alive everywhere their bodies touched. Every brush of their hips as they spun round the other dancers, and the press of her fingertips against his shoulder sent shockwaves of desire straight through him. The dance ended all too quickly.

"I'm sorry, Don de Castel."

"Lysandro, please. What are you sorry for?"

"I haven't been a very good dance partner, I'm afraid."

She started to break their frame and step away from him, but he didn't relinquish his hand on her waist. Instead he pulled her closer, closer than she was before. Her cheeks flushed a glorious shade of pink.

"Can I have another?"

They floated across the floor. At the end of each song, they were interrupted by other gentlemen seeking a turn with her. Every time, Lysandro steeled himself to acquiesce to her wishes, even if it killed him. But she refused them all.

More than her blinding beauty and flawless grace, it was her words that had his blood racing as they danced the night away.

"So, if you can't tell me about Romagna—"

"I can't."

"Tell me about Mirêne."

Her eyes took on a dreamy quality. "It's the most beautiful place in all the world."

"Do you read?"

She pierced him with a scrutinizing look. "I may not be a graduate of some overpriced finishing school, but I did manage to learn to read. In *two* languages."

Lysandro's face turned scarlet.

"That's not what I meant. I mean, do you read for pleasure?"

"Very much," she answered, not seeming offended in the least. Lysandro stopped holding his breath.

"I prefer mysteries."

"Oh no. Not those sordid tales of spurned mistresses, bastard children, and nefarious plots to gain a fat inheritance?"

"Those *sordid* tales are the only thing worth reading. If someone isn't missing or murdered, I'm not interested."

He flashed a curious smile. "What a morbid sense of taste."

"It's not the violence that intrigues me, it's the grand puzzle. Following the clues, discovering the culprit…"

Lysandro spun her around; when she came back into his embrace, her hand slid up the length of his arm and came to rest on the back of his neck.

"What sort of reading material would be more to your liking, Don de

Castel?" she asked with an upturned nose. A shiver ran through him as he met her fiery gaze.

"I'm partial to the classics. Particularly Romantic legends."

"You mean fairy tales?"

"No."

She pursed her lips, skeptical.

"Not every tale contains fairies."

"Uh-huh. Stories written for children are more appropriate reading material?"

"It's a sad world, don't you think, where stories of valor and heroism are only for the young?"

Her expression changed from one of amusement to admiration. "You know, you're right."

He smiled at the compliment.

"But mine are still more interesting."

He raised an eyebrow in challenge. "Is there ever a moral to those stories?"

"Of course. Don't get murdered."

He laughed.

"Don't covet what isn't yours. Don't marry for money. Never keep candlesticks in your home, and *never* go out on the moors at night. It teaches you to be observant."

Lysandro thought this a useful skill. If he'd been more observant, he might have noticed Marek's constant absence from the temple and caught on to him earlier.

While he might take umbrage at her taste in books, she *had* taste, and it didn't include manuals claiming to be the authority on the proper decorum for a wife. She was articulate, witty, and possessed in spades what scores of high-bred girls lacked—the art of good conversation.

Lysandro led her to one of the dining tents erected in the corners of the room as the orchestra rested between sets. Mirênese and Maghrevan fare was piled high atop silver platters. They both reached for the hand-held pastries stuffed with a savory filling, a desert delicacy.

"Does it taste like the real thing?"

"Nope."

She was so quick to answer, laughter bubbled up in his throat and he had to cover his mouth to keep the food in.

"They've left out the pistachios."

"I don't think I've ever had those."

"No, I imagine they're too expensive to import. They're delicate, and they spoil quickly. But it gives it a warm, earthy flavor. I wish I would have thought to bring some with me, but my mind was elsewhere. I wasn't actually expecting to leave."

She averted her gaze; she'd said something she hadn't meant to. Lysandro couldn't help himself.

"You don't have to answer, but, how did you come to be here?"

"Someone was supposed to meet me before I was set to leave, but…"

Lysandro began to understand what she was trying to say, and it sliced him to the core.

She shrugged. "I trusted the wrong man."

Jealousy and outrage warred within him, rendering him mute.

"I should have known. Everyone else did."

"You should have expected a man you cared for to betray your trust?"

It was unthinkable. Unforgiveable. Lysandro would kill the man who had abandoned her, and left her on a ship bound across the ocean, away from her life, her friends…

She only sighed. "He did what he had to. I just…I never should have expected anything else from him."

Lysandro was incredulous. "That's awfully cavalier of you. How can you be so forgiving?"

"Oh, I'm not. But two months at sea has faded my anger. I'm mostly mad at myself. I had a way to keep myself where I most long to be, and I didn't take it."

Though Lysandro didn't relish the idea of competing with a phantom, he admired the fact that she had dared to love. He wondered if her heart would have the courage to take another chance.

"If you had stayed, I wouldn't have the pleasure of your company now."

Her eyes softened. "That's sweet of you to say. You needn't feel obligated to stay by my side all night. Surely there are others here that might be more cheerful company."

"I've always felt out of place at these things," he said. "And the more seasons that pass, the truer that becomes."

"Why are you here then?"

"I came to see you."

The words came out too quickly for him to stop them. She blushed again, and his shoulders relaxed.

The conversation of another couple sitting in the tent with them grew heated, and became difficult to ignore.

"How am I supposed to feel safe on the way home? What if we cross paths with the Shadow?" the girl asked.

The hair on Lysandro's arms stood on end.

"What shadow?" Sera asked.

"The Shadow of Theron," the gentleman next to her answered.

"He's a criminal," the girl said.

"He's a *hero*. What has he ever done that was criminal?"

"If he's not a criminal, why does he wear a mask?"

The young man sighed.

"See?" the lady asked, turning to Sera.

"Hmm. Well you can't both be right."

"How do you suggest we break the stalemate?" the gentleman asked.

"With a third opinion." She turned to Lysandro.

He flushed hot under his collar. He wasn't sure what he should say.

"The *magistrate* hates him," the lady cut in, saving him from answering.

Lysandro scowled. Sera saw; he wasn't quick enough to hide it.

"Ah. You have one of *those* magistrates," Sera said.

"Sadly."

"And he hates this shadow person, you say?" Sera asked.

"The Shadow of Theron," the man corrected. "With a passion."

"There's your answer."

All three of them looked at her, confused.

"Where's my answer?" the other gentleman asked.

"An impartial magistrate shouldn't hate anyone. For the Shadow to provoke a reaction like that, he mostly likely speaks an inconvenient truth."

Lysandro smiled. She *was* clever.

"Ha!" The gentleman banged his fist down on the table and glared at his dance partner. "What do you say to that?"

The lady in question folded her arms and pouted.

"I can't help you with your next problem," Sera said as her gaze traveled between the put-out young man and the discontented object of his attention. She left them to their predicament and turned to Lysandro. "Ready for another set?"

"Have you spent any time in the desert?" he asked as they returned to the dance floor.

"Why are you so interested?"

"I've always wanted to see Mirêne and its outer environs. I always felt that I'd have been more at home there."

"You're not inclined to Arun?"

"I don't believe war solves anything. To follow Faelia seems like a higher calling—love and art bring out the best in people."

"It is a paradise for that."

"So?"

"Most people, when they first encounter the Bedou, are taken completely by surprise by the richness of their culture. They do so much with so little. Artisans are highly valued in their society—they honor creativity, and pay great attention to even the tiniest details. Market days are absolutely delightful. The museums in Mirêne have large collections of objects with historical significance. Their entire society's memory is captured in song."

"We have so very little access here to that kind of knowledge. Our museum holds mostly objects of Andran culture, and the temples are almost all dedicated to Arun, of course. Our people are great warriors, not great artists, I'm afraid."

"Seeing some Andran culture would be a change for me. And I should probably get better at pretending I've been living in Romagna for years."

Lysandro wasn't sure if she was just favoring him for the night. But he didn't hesitate. "I'd love to take you."

"I'd like that."

Marek entered the ballroom just then, casting an eclipse over Lysandro's elation at her reply. His grip around Sera's waist tightened as his would-be murderer strode directly toward them.

Marek tried to cut in. They both resisted, but he persisted in standing in their path, and they were forced to stop mid-step to face him. Lysandro put himself between Lothan and Sera. The magistrate settled greedy eyes on her.

"Excuse me, I don't think we've met. I'm Lothan Marek, the magistrate of Lighura. And you are?"

"We *were* in the middle of a dance," Lysandro growled.

Marek looked at him with a mix of loathing and satisfaction at seeing him so perturbed. His gaze turned back to Sera as he waited for her to respond. By now, people were paying attention to their exchange from the corners of their eyes and behind their crystal glasses.

There was a prolonged, awkward silence. She held his impatient stare and said, "Seraphine Alvaró. Now if you'll excuse us."

Marek was not accustomed to being dismissed, and was quick to anger.

"I must question your choice of partner. For a dance as robust as this one, you'll want someone who can keep up. *His* blood does not run as hot as a man's should."

Lysandro's blood was just about boiling now.

He felt Sera's grip on his hand tighten, and she said, "Actually, conventional wisdom suggests that a cooler head is a sign of higher intelligence. And I prefer a keen mind to someone too dim to take a hint."

Lysandro's jaw dropped. The murmurs that had taken over the ballroom turned into laughter as Marek's face flashed a bright crimson.

"Goodnight, Magistrate Marek." She turned back to Lysandro, who promptly led her across the dance floor.

Lysandro wanted so badly to look, but Sera stopped him.

"Eyes on me," she murmured as they moved deeper into the ballroom and away from Marek.

"That was incredible. I've never seen him put in his place quite so effectively."

"I'm a member of the Mirênese court," she said, putting more flourish into her movements. "I've learned from the best."

Was it the doge of Mirêne who broke your heart?

Sera was a remarkable beauty, and her charms could not possibly have failed to gain his notice. A doge *would* be the sort of person to offer a woman false promises. But if that were true, it didn't account for the pride in her voice. It was baffling.

Her expression changed as she caught Marek staring after them. One or two gentlemen tried to strike up a conversation with him, but he turned abruptly on his heels and left.

Lysandro could see the gears of her mind turning.

"What are your powers of observation telling you now?"

"I've known men like him, but…"

Her steps slowed as she searched for the right words. He didn't imagine it when her body drew closer to his, and her skin turned cool under his touch.

"He scares me."

"You're right to be afraid." He saw worry cloud her eyes, and he rushed to comfort her, clasping her hand more firmly. "It's alright," he said. "He's gone."

His words appeared to reassure her, but the smile didn't quite reach her eyes.

4

EUGENIE ENTERED THE CROWDED TAVERN CLUTCHING THE OVERSIZED BAG slung over her shoulder. She offered a litany of excuses and apologies as she worked her way over to the communal table that stretched from one end of the establishment to the other. With a slight build and a slight voice, she struggled not to be invisible, and had to jockey her way to a seat. She aimed for a spot facing the door, so she could watch people coming and going. After being crammed shoulder to shoulder with a gaggle of strangers for over half an hour, she saw her chance. As one person got up from the table, she moved to take his place. But a bulk of a man stepped right in front of her. He knocked her off balance and nearly sent her crashing to the ground.

"Hey! I was just about to—"

He waved his hand over his shoulder without looking up, as if he were swatting away a fly.

"About to sit there, you big oaf," she finished under her breath. She would have liked to tell him who she was—that would have been enough to clear the whole table—but the high priestess had told her not to reveal herself until she met the Aruni who would be her partner. So there she was, at the appointed place and time.

She narrowed her eyes at the oaf's back and decided that if he could use his size to simply take what he wanted, so could she. She tightened her grip on her unwieldy satchel. With a swing forward, the bag knocked the man square in the back. His hooked nose dunked into his bowl. He snorted and choked on his food as Eugenie slid herself in between him and the person next to him.

Beef broth dripped from the man's lips, and bits of stewed carrot got caught in his wiry beard. His dull eyes turned fierce.

"Don't crowd me, woman!"

"You're five times the size of me!" she snapped. "I'm crowding *you*?"

He turned back to his food with a scowl, and she tucked her bag between her legs.

She fiddled with her hair, so pale it was almost white, and twisted together in a messy braid that hung over her shoulder, all the while keeping an eye on the door. She was anxious to get started.

Not long after she sat down, she saw a dark-haired woman come through the door. She was much taller than Eugenie, by nearly a head and a half, with broad shoulders. The tavern's weak candlelight glistened off her coppery skin and the blue crystalline beads coiled around her wrists.

Eugenie had never seen this woman before, had never visited any temple other than the one to which she belonged. But she knew a priestess of Arun when she saw one.

The tall woman quietly scanned the room from the doorway. When her eyes met Eugenie's, she walked toward her without a flicker of hesitation.

She stopped at the table and stared down the man sitting directly opposite Eugenie. Her eyes were a piercing, feral green. Their intensity was enough to drive the man from his seat, clutching his bowl to his chest. She sat down and stretched her arms lazily on the table in front of her. In a voice that was less booming than Eugenie expected, the woman greeted her.

"Good evening, Sister."

"Hello." Eugenie was about to introduce herself, but the woman interrupted her.

"You eat yet?"

"No, I—"

The warrior's gaze left Eugenie's face as she got the attention of the barmaid. She made contact over the crowd in a matter of seconds. The warrior held two fingers in the air and then turned back to her.

"I'm Eugenie," she managed, shouting over the raucous din of the other patrons.

"Asha," the warrior replied.

"It's nice to meet you."

Asha responded with a half-smile. She scrutinized Eugenie's face so intently that she blushed, and began fidgeting with her clothes again.

"Where are you traveling from?" Eugenie asked.

"Camarque."

"I've never been that far north," Eugenie laughed awkwardly. "I've never been anywhere."

That made Asha smirk. "You volunteer?"

"Me? No. My high priestess asked me. It's a huge honor, to be tasked with something so important."

Asha nodded. "I volunteered."

Of course you did, Eugenie thought to herself.

The barmaid brought them two frothy amber drinks, and Asha touched the girl's arm gently before she'd scurried away.

"Do you have a room for the two of us?" she asked.

"We've got a single left—one bed only."

Asha nodded. "We'll manage. And two bowls of the stew please."

When the barmaid nodded and left, Asha turned back to Eugenie.

"Have you—"

She stopped herself, shifted her eyes in one direction then another, and searched for the right words. "Have you caught on to anything yet?"

"Not yet," Eugenie said. Only the priestesses of Morgasse had been granted the power to sense the nearness of the objects touched by the Goddess.

Asha pulled a small leather pouch out of her clothes and untied the strings. It blossomed into a circular map depicting Andras in miniature. She laid it out on the table between them.

"I was given a list," Asha said. "I was thinking we could go to the people who lost the most first, then so on."

The pattern that emerged before Eugenie's eyes made her nervous. She dragged an imaginary zigzag through the map with her eyes as she considered Asha's plan.

"I see your point," Eugenie started, unsure. "But that will cost time. Regardless of *what* we're after, it's imperative to recover them all as quickly as possible."

She traced her finger across the map in a gentle arc, following the path with the fastest roads.

"All right, we'll do it your way. If we start early tomorrow and ride hard, we should make it to Lareina before sundown," Asha said.

"Great," Eugenie grimaced. Her backside still smarted from the journey there.

Asha ate two bowls of the stew, then finished Eugenie's portion after she'd had her fill. She paid the barmaid handsomely and quit her seat, heading for the stairway. Only then did Eugenie notice the gigantic broadsword strapped to Asha's back.

"Thanks," Eugenie stammered, scrambling to catch up as she lugged her bag behind her. "I could have paid my way."

"You can get the next one Gin."

"Oh. Um, actually, it's Eugenie."

"Here," Asha said, grabbing Eugenie's bag and throwing it over her shoulder like it was nothing.

"I carried it all the way here," Eugenie said under her breath.

Asha stopped and turned in the middle of the stairway. She held the parcel out to Eugenie.

She took it again as heat flooded her face. "Sorry. I didn't mean to—"

"It's fine Gin. Come on, I'm ready for bed." Asha trotted up the rest of the stairs. The sword on her back may as well have been a feather.

Eugenie sighed and followed after, her bag smacking her in the ankles as she dragged it behind her.

The landlord led them to a narrow room at the top of the landing and dropped the key into Asha's hand.

"When they said single room, they meant it," Eugenie said as she reached the door and peered in. It looked more like a closet that the owners had cleaned out for the purpose of earning Asha's coin.

Asha unstrapped the scabbard from around her chest, laid it on the ground next to her, and sprawled out on the solid pine floor. Eugenie rushed to her side.

"That's not necessary. I wasn't suggesting—"

"I was planning to sleep on the floor anyway. Good for my back after today's ride. Hand me a pillow, would you?"

Eugenie sat on the bed, and was pricked in the rump by the rough hay that comprised the mattress. She took one of the small lumpy pillows and passed it down to Asha.

"You're sure?"

"I'm sure." Asha tucked the pillow at the base of her skull and laid herself out flat. She folded her hands behind her head and closed her eyes.

Eugenie couldn't get comfortable. No matter which way she turned, she was stabbed by the sharp needles of the straw poking through the tired bed linens. Every muscle ached, every inch of her spinal column felt painfully crooked. She leaned over with a grunt, and took another stab to her hip to look at Asha. She was a picture of serenity.

"Oof!"

Eugenie tumbled out of the bed, and pulled another needle of hay from her elbow.

Asha opened one eye as she watched Eugenie fumble onto the floor and flip over onto her back.

"Oh—oh yeah," Eugenie groaned. "That's better." She felt the beginning of divine re-alignment.

Asha pushed the bed all the way against the wall with her foot, giving Eugenie a little extra room.

"Thanks," she exhaled.

"Mmhmm."

Eugenie still couldn't sleep.

"What do you think we'll find?"

Asha opened her eyes again.

"I mean, why do you think anyone would steal the relics?"

"I've been thinking about that," Asha said. "It's not a coincidence that they've been disappearing all at once."

"You think the thefts are coordinated?"

"I do. But by whom, or why…that's what we have to figure out."

"When we do…will you kill them?

"Maybe."

It was hard for Eugenie to think of herself as sending people to their deaths, but ultimately, what Asha did to channel Arun's wrath was not for her to decide. At least, she thought, she would be able to tell with certainty who deserved it. No amount of hiding or lying would stop her from knowing if someone had a relic in their possession. The thought comforted her little as she drifted off to sleep.

Eugenie and Asha dressed before the dawn, both donning black robes with silver clasps instead of their traditional colors—blue for Asha, purple for Eugenie—and took their breakfast with them as they set off at a brisk pace.

They stopped only once for lunch and to water the horses. As they swallowed their last bites of bread and cured meat, Eugenie reached inside her satchel and pulled out a soft leather pouch with the sigil of Morgasse burned into the side, a perfectly rounded eye with a smaller circle in the center. She knelt down and scored the dirt with the symbols for the sun, the moon, and the positive and negative elements into a diamond pattern, with the sigil of the Goddess in the center.

Asha crouched down beside her. "You any good at this?" she asked.

"Best in my temple."

"Better than your high priestess?"

Asha raised her eyebrow when Eugenie didn't answer.

"I've never had a false positive before. But I've also never divined something on quite this scale."

She began to murmur to herself; Asha refrained from straining to hear.

Eugenie cast the stones in her hand in a wide arc. She gasped as she opened her eyes to see the pattern the runes had formed.

"Something wrong?" Asha asked. She observed Eugenie's pinched features and nervous gait as she paced back and forth before the casting, stopping often to crane her neck to read the positions of the runes like a map.

"Deception and trickery are ascendant."

"Does that mean we shouldn't expect people to be cooperative?" Asha asked.

"Maybe not, but divination is meant to give insight about what lies beneath the surface."

"So…"

"Deceit is a reminder that things may not be as they seem. It's a warning to be watchful, vigilant."

"Any idea why this is happening?"

"It's showing—" Eugenie grunted, confounded by the configuration laid out before her. "The placement of the stones are too perfect. Like they've been there before." Something like this was not as easy to read as whom to marry or where to stud your horse. But she didn't like the implication.

What truly made her shudder was where the stones had landed. Though she had aimed for the middle where the Goddess was positioned, none of the stones had come close to Her. They were spread out in a fan all around the rune, as if they had been repelled by it, like a sunburst radiating outward. She had the sense that it was familiar, like time repeating. But it was spinning the wrong way, as if time were working backwards, but also forward at the same time.

Asha didn't need to be a seer to observe that the positive aspects of bravery and hope were diminished in stature, clustered together as if in hiding.

* * *

Their horses neared a full gallop as they raced to avoid the angry storm clouds brewing overhead. The townsfolk, attuned to the impending weather, were shut up in their homes. The streets of Lareina were deserted by the time Eugenie and Asha passed through the gates of the walled city. They headed for the town square, where a temple to Faelia, their first destination, lay at the center.

"Your horse needs new shoes before we leave," Asha said as they led the beasts into the stable. "They should have never let you take her in that condition."

"I didn't think to inquire about that."

"I grew up around horses. My family breeds them. She's a good horse. She just needs better shoes."

The horse whinnied, pleased at the compliment.

The Examiners pulled their cloaks tight around them to keep out the rising wind that was kicking up dust from the road into a swirling vortex. The heavens opened up behind them just as they passed the threshold to the temple house's main hall.

"Come, come Sisters!" a stout, bespectacled woman called out as she approached them. "We're honored to have you here, and only wish it were under better circumstances."

"Thank you for welcoming us,—"

"Mirabel. I'm the high priestess here. We're pleased to serve the Goddess in whatever way She needs. You've arrived at a fortuitous time. We were just about to sit down for supper."

Eugenie could see the awe, the fear even, in the Faelians' eyes as she and Asha were escorted to the dining hall. True to her Goddess's aspect, the high priestess was the most welcoming of all. The Examiners were given a place of honor at her table.

Asha looked down at the bowl of steamed rice and mushrooms in front of her. Her hands curled and uncurled.

"Is there—um—some meat I can have with this? A side of beef maybe? Or pork?"

Eugenie cleared her throat quietly. The high priestess offered only a smile in reply.

"Oh. Right. I forgot about that. I hope I didn't offend—"

"Of course you didn't," Mirabel insisted.

"It's just that I'm so damn hungry," Asha said under her breath.

"Thank you, High Priestess, for your hospitality," Eugenie said, casting a sideways look at Asha. She'd buried her face in her bowl, determined to eat as much food as she had to to fill her stomach. Eugenie passed her bowl over to her when she was finished.

"You will begin your search soon, I imagine?" Mirabel asked.

"First thing in the morning," Eugenie answered. "We'll need to speak to the entire village. We've no time to waste."

"I'll ring the bells in the morning. They will come."

"Thank you."

"Can you tell me," Asha managed between mouthfuls, "how many new acolytes you've taken on?"

Eugenie gave her a puzzled look.

"Five, this season."

"Is that a lot?"

"A bit, but we're happy to have them." Mirabel smiled at the uninitiated.

Eugenie was beginning to understand. "Are you all from the village?" she asked, directing her query to the novices.

"We are," one girl said, indicating the girls to either side of her. "But Marcus and Hairo have come to us from Milagra."

"We are dedicated to the principles of Faelia, and this was the closest temple to us," one of them said with a broad smile. "We are so happy to be here."

"You traveled together then?"

The dark-haired boy, Hairo, opened his mouth to answer, but the freckled one beat him to it.

"No, actually we met on the road."

As Hairo's gaze shifted from Marcus to Asha, his eyes narrowed. He tried to mask his annoyance. But Eugenie hadn't imagined it. Asha marched ever forward.

"Is there more than one road out of Milagra?"

The boy's lips pursed tighter as he contemplated his reply. Eugenie squeezed Asha's knee under the table, and she felt Asha lean back in her seat; her interrogation ceased, for the time being.

Eugenie's gaze kept returning to Hairo. At times, his smile contorted into a wicked grin. Sometimes it turned into something grotesque, like another face swimming just beneath the skin that occasionally surfaced. It was gone again in the blink of an eye, and she tried to convince herself that it was an illusion, just a trick of the dappled shadows from the storm outside, punctured by sudden flashes of lightning. She forced herself to look away, to avoid the young man's constant gaze without betraying what she may or may not have seen. But her gaze kept sliding back in his direction, and every time it fell unbidden upon him, her stomach muscles clenched.

Eugenie was not alone in her unease. She saw that Asha had unconsciously dropped her hand from the table and rested it on the handle of the dagger poking out of her belt.

"Thank you," Eugenie said as a handful of novices cleared the table at the conclusion of the meal.

"You've had a long journey," Mirabel said. "I assume you'll want to turn in early."

Asha shook her head. "Show us where the relics were taken from."

"That might be difficult," Mirabel answered, turning her head meaningfully toward the window.

Asha grunted.

"What can you tell us?" Eugenie asked.

"Sisters, come with me."

Asha ducked to avoid a bough of drying flowers hung above the lintel of the high priestess's private chamber. Vines crawled up the whitewashed bricks, weaving themselves into the wooden beams of the ceiling and stalking up the stone columns, making the interior of room appear as a secluded alcove, an extension of the greater garden beyond. Blossoms of violet, magenta, and sunshine yellow stood atop the columns and stretched their verdant tendrils down toward the floor like a company of graceful dancers. Open shelves hewn from dark wooden beams held countless glass jars filled with leaves, roots, mosses and berries, fresh and dried.

The insistent rain poured in through the open balcony. Mirabel rushed forward and pulled closed the glass doors, crisscrossed by a metal frame that formed a diamond pattern across the panes.

"Here, sit," she offered, gesturing to a pair of wicker chairs that she collected from opposite corners of the room. "The storm will provide our conversation some protection."

While Asha and Eugenie took their seats, Mirabel poured them each a cup of rosehip tea with lemon from an ornate silver service.

"This will warm you right up," she said with a smile.

"Thank you," Eugenie said. She allowed the sweet, gentle fragrance to reach her nose before bringing the drink to her lips.

Mirabel nodded in satisfaction at seeing Eugenie savor the brew and began without prompting.

"I woke up just before dawn, as I usually do, to pray and to do some early gardening. When I arrived at that part of the labyrinth—"

"You have a labyrinth?" Asha interrupted.

"Yes. You can't see it just now on account of the weather, but it is quite extensive. It's where our treasure rested in secrecy. But when I came upon that spot, the soil was overturned, and the Sorrow Stones were missing."

"Was that the only spot that was disturbed?" Eugenie asked.

The high priestess furrowed her brow. Then her face lit up.

"Why no! There were several rows where the soil had been upturned. At first, I'd thought we were dealing with a rabbit, or a mole even. When I saw that the relic had been taken, any thought of rabbits completely left my head."

"Do you have a map of the labyrinth?" Asha asked.

Mirabel stretched over the arm of her chair and picked up a small, unfurled scroll from the cluttered work desk.

"Show us," Asha said, "where it was disturbed."

"I replanted the soil that very day," Mirabel said as she marked several pathways leading to into the labyrinth. "Faelia be praised one of my predecessors had the foresight not to keep the stones all in one place."

"You're sure?" Asha asked.

Mirabel gave a deep nod. "I checked all the other locations myself, and buried them again just as quickly. The rest of the stones are still here."

"That's something, at least," Eugenie sighed.

But Asha wasn't satisfied. "Did anyone else see you do this?"

"No," Mirabel said with conviction. "I completed my task before waking the others."

"How did the other priestesses respond when you told them?" Eugenie asked.

"As you might expect. But I didn't immediately make it known."

"Why not?" Eugenie asked.

"I wrote to the Council of Three straightaway, of course, but I didn't wish to create a panic in my own temple. When I received word that other temples were experiencing similar problems, I no longer believed in the need for secrecy."

"Have you questioned them?" Asha asked.

"They have all assured me—they saw nothing, heard nothing, know nothing."

Eugenie exchanged glances with Asha. She caught an inquisitive light in Asha's eye, and had that sense that Asha wanted her to be the one to ask the next question. She wondered if Asha didn't trust herself to be anything but blunt.

"Tell us about your new inductees," Eugenie said.

"They're a fine bunch. Carla is showing quite an aptitude for healing and midwifery. I allow her to assist me. Rielle and Marcus share an equal interest in it as well but have slightly less talent. Jinnifer is especially helpful during public services. She's a local girl, and everyone flocks to her for their prayers and confessions. Hairo…"

Asha shifted in her chair, stilled only by a sidelong glance from Eugenie.

"Hairo will find his place here soon enough. He's taking a bit longer to adjust, but that is not uncommon for those who come to us from so far away."

And that is precisely why they hadn't appointed an Examiner from among the Faelians, Eugenie thought to herself. The highest-ranking members of the temple were blessed by Faelia with seeing the good in people. Mirabel couldn't sense what Eugenie did when she looked upon Hairo's face; she didn't become ill in his presence. That a Faelian temple had been one of the first to be stripped of their relic made perfect sense to her. They made an easy target.

"How many people have access to the labyrinth?" Asha asked, bringing Eugenie's attention back to the map Asha held in her hands.

"It's open to the public during sunlight hours. We invite people in to pray, to reflect on their lives…"

"What time did the last person leave on the day before?"

Mirabel raised her eyes to the ceiling in contemplation. "It had been overcast that day. Our last visitor stopped by a little after lunch."

"You know this person well?"

"Yes, she comes here often. I always thought she'd make an excellent Faelian, but she took a husband instead. Her children are absolute cherubs."

"When did *you* last go into the labyrinth on that day?" Asha asked.

Her tone made Eugenie uncomfortable, but the high priestess answered the question with her smile intact.

"After sunset. The labyrinth was as it always is when we lit the lanterns for evening prayer."

"This was done inside the labyrinth?" Eugenie asked.

Mirabel nodded. "It was fine when I left."

"Who douses the lanterns?" Asha asked.

"Anna Maria. She's been here longer than I have."

Asha rose from her chair. "Thank you for being so forthright."

"Of course," Mirabel said, rising as well. "I'll have the bells rung at seven o'clock."

Eugenie didn't speak again until she and Asha were shown to their room, a well-appointed little alcove at the back of the temple. Two narrow beds lined the walls, with a thin space between them, and two matching windows looking out over the extensive gardens. They could barely glimpse the sacred space in the darkness. The high priestess bade them goodnight and closed the door.

Eugenie set her things in the corner and went about lighting the fresh taper on the shared night table nestled between the windows.

Asha stretched out on her bed, but Eugenie thought she didn't look as comfortable as she had the night before, not as much at ease.

"Hairo didn't come from Milagra," Asha said. It wasn't a question.

"Plenty of priestesses and priests have traveled to be closer to the Goddess's face that they most see in themselves," Eugenie observed.

"It was the *way* he said it. There was something in his eyes, something that seemed...not right."

Eugenie nodded in confirmation. "His eyes were disorienting. When he spoke, I felt positively ill."

"What does that mean?"

"I'm not sure." She reached into the lumpy, overstretched satchel.

"What is all that you've been carrying around?" Asha asked.

"Books," she answered. "A prayer service book, volumes one and two of *The Histories*...I thought it might be useful if I could easily reference the items we recover. Maybe they will help us understand why they were taken in the first place." She held the book closed with her hands, shut her eyes, and began to move her lips without making a sound. It went on for so long that Asha felt compelled to break the silence.

"Gin?"

"We're taught to seek signs not just in the runes, but everywhere. Even the smallest thing can speak the language of Morgasse."

She released the corners of the book, and let it fall open onto her lap. "Impossible…"

Asha peered over her shoulder and read the passage that had been made familiar to her just before she'd left her temple. To see the scant lines about what happened in the aftermath of Theron's triumph again so soon made her hair stand on end.

Eugenie stared wide-eyed at the pages that told of how the descendants of Argoss had been discovered in a cave in the desert, with not a scrap of food or clothing between them. The nauseous feeling from dinner returned in full force.

They were slaughtered, Eugenie reminded herself. *They were slaughtered*.

Her face taut, Eugenie flipped through the pages, hoping there would be something to explain the dread she'd felt as the young man's gaze had fallen upon her, something other than what she suspected. There wasn't.

"They're alive."

Eugenie craned her neck up to stare at Asha.

The warrior cleared her throat. "The Faelians advocated mercy. We vowed that we would keep track of them and their offspring, but…we lost that knowledge. It's our temple's greatest shame."

Eugenie blinked.

"My high priestess told me," Asha continued. "She shared all of Temple Arun's secrets with me in case I might need them. I'm telling you now."

Eugenie's high priestess had done the same.

"You alright?' Asha asked after a long silence.

"Yes," Eugenie said.

Asha exhaled through her nose. She wasn't sold on it either. "You look pale."

"I'm always pale."

Asha unfolded the map again and held it out to Eugenie. "This is the pattern of someone who doesn't know what they're doing."

"Or it might have been made to appear that way," Eugenie countered.

Asha grimaced. "Why not do it all, then? The disruptions don't go any deeper. Once he found the first set of Sorrow Stones, he stopped."

If there was a flaw in Asha's logic, Eugenie didn't see it.

"The only reason to dig up the labyrinth and draw attention to himself," Asha reasoned, "is if he'd already looked everywhere else."

When Eugenie said nothing, Asha drew her sword from its sheath and headed for the door.

"Wait a minute!" Eugenie cried, leaping from her bed and reaching for Asha's wrist as she was halfway out of the room.

"Wait for what? We know what he is. We know he's responsible. I say we strike hard and fast, and don't give him a chance to run."

"*You* said you thought these thefts were coordinated. I believe you."

Asha huffed like a raging bull. But she didn't move.

"If Hairo had disappeared for long enough to reach the other towns, Mirabel would have told us," Eugenie pressed. "There are others. There must be. And if we're too hasty here, we may never recover the relics."

Asha's face twisted in confusion.

"If these acts are coordinated, then the relics are not just being stolen. They're being moved. We need to find out to where. Especially…"

Asha rocked back on her heels, absorbing Eugenie's line of thought. With the disappearance of the relics, the balance of the world had already begun to shift. If the dark relics found their way into the hands of Argoss's bastards, it would plunge the world into chaos.

"He's our only link," Eugenie said. "He must lead us to the others, or we might already be too late."

Asha shifted, unsteady on her feet. "So what do we do?" she murmured.

"He must have had help getting the stones out of the temple," Eugenie answered. "His accomplices may point us in the right direction."

Asha sheathed her sword with heavy reluctance. But before settling back down, her head snapped up, and she turned her bright, intense stare back at Eugenie.

"You can tell that the missing stones are not in the temple?"

Eugenie nodded.

"What about the rest of the town?"

Eugenie donned her cloak again and followed Asha out the door and down the main hallway back into the temple nave. In wordless tandem, they stopped and knelt before the image of Faelia giving succor to Theron in the Cave of Sorrows. Faelia knelt before a collapsed and bleeding Theron, his face obscured. Sharp angles depicted his broken body, and a spray of rubies glittered in a halo of blood. Faelia's face was hidden, covered by her hands to stop the tears that flowed.

As Eugenie prayed to be steadfast in the face of what the night might bring, the image grew darker in the wake of the storm. The water pouring from the sky flowed down the colored glass, threatening to wash away all they had known, all that had come before.

5

"Too dim...that slut."

Lothan walked through the dark streets and away from the ball wearing a scowl. He'd made sure his boots were buffed, his face was clean-shaven, and his hands clean. None of it had mattered. He would have liked nothing better than to soil that girl's dress by slicing open Lysandro's stomach and watching horror and pain play in his eyes. It made his skin itch to be away from his dagger for so long. He cursed himself for leaving it at home. But he couldn't keep his shirts clean; the blood just would not come out. And Lysandro was still too powerful to kill outright. Worst of all, the thing that made him more wrathful than the rest, was that things remained unsettled—the damned Shadow was still among the living.

His men had scoured the village until dawn on the night the Shadow had fled. But there had been no masked corpses anywhere. He briefly considered that the Blood Sword might not be as powerful as he believed, but he had seen the terror written plain on the Shadow's face. He knew with a certainty deep within his bones that when he'd cut the Shadow, he'd been moments away from his doom.

Lothan had gone to the ball to see who looked like he had one foot in the grave. Nothing he'd seen there put him on the scent. He half wished it was Lysandro, to have both of his rivals out of the way in one blow. He immediately dismissed the thought for being ridiculous.

He took the long way down to the southern shore, avoiding the lane occupied by the temple. Passing its gleaming whitewashed columns made his flesh crawl.

The night was not a total loss. Lothan had never seen the girl before, and though he had no interest in the fairer sex beyond his natural cravings, he *was* interested in the way Lysandro had been looking at her.

Lothan felt his brothers gravitate toward him as he entered the cave, like pinpoints of darkness. They were moths, and he was the flame. The closer they got to him, the brighter he burned.

The pitted ceiling poured moonlight on them, casting everything in a pale blue glow. Lothan took his customary place, only half listening as Gorin worked them into a frenzy.

"Argoss invoked the goddess's wrath when his sorcery overshadowed hers, mastering the great fathoms of the Abyss. She used deceit and trickery to work her will through a mere farm boy to humiliate him. But Argoss is not destroyed. He lives! Our day is coming, and the world *will* be made over!"

The horde of bastards descended upon the pair of eldur vipers coiled together in a central pit. They provoked the creatures with sticks and rocks, drawing their ire and causing their gargantuan fangs to swell with venom.

Lothan looked on as the others feasted on the reptiles to strengthen the magic in their blood and make them invincible against a poison for which there was no cure. They collapsed upon each other, convulsing and rolling their eyes to the backs of their heads. One of them fell perfectly still, too weak to withstand the vipers' vicious attack. Lothan felt his energy increase by barely a trickle.

He hated listening to them fawn over Argoss. Argoss was a fool. He'd had all the power in the world, and he'd squandered it. Yet Lothan's brothers could think no bigger than working to bring about his return. That was the last thing Lothan wanted.

But even achieving his preliminary aims felt further and further out of reach. He needed what had been promised. He directed Gorin to refill their coffers.

"From where?" he asked. "The Shadow tossed what we had into the sea."

"I don't care. Just don't *kill* anyone this time, or it'll be your neck I snap!"

"Yes, Lord Lothan."

Nothing ever seemed enough. Lothan let the disquieting thought simmer as Jenner approached him.

"We got this prayer book, and I was cutting out the illuminations to sell piecemeal, like you said—"

"Can you get to your point?"

"Yes, Lord Lothan. Sorry. I noticed that there are things in here that I've never heard them say in the temple before. Things they've been leaving out."

Lothan sat upright.

"What *exactly* are they leaving out?" he asked.

"Mostly little things, like a change in the wording. But other times, it's whole pages. There are stories here that I've never heard."

"Like what?"

"Like this one here, about the goddess traveling *with* Theron. Not just appearing and disappearing all fairy-like. So, did I do good?"

Jenner was so eager to please him, Lothan could hear the thumping of a dog's tail in the mud behind him. But he plastered on a smile.

"Indeed, you did." He was convinced that somewhere there was a book of spells, or a cache of objects, or *something* that would allow him to crack the barrier of Argoss's knowledge. Jenner could enter the temple unaffected—at times, his weakness was useful.

Eager anticipation cut Lothan's anger. He shifted his attention to the shrouded figure bent over in the corner, cloaked in dark rags. The hunched shape emanated a black purplish flame that roiled over his form, but did not burn. Lothan crossed the distance between them.

"How did the Shadow survive?" Lothan asked. "The dagger should have killed him."

Lothan waited patiently for the figure to respond. Then his eyelids grew heavy with understanding.

"Of course...of course he had help."

The aura surrounding the shrouded figure flared.

It all made sense. And he knew just how to deal with his betrayer.

Lothan reached for the figure's hand, obscured by the long sleeves of its robe. Only three bony fingers remained. With a firm yank, he detached the index finger at the knuckle and ground it up into a fine powder. The aura of its owner remained, and furled around the stone edges of the bowl Lothan used to pulverize the digit.

Lothan had no idea what effect his dabbling would have. But he knew it would be anything but pleasant.

6

Sancio was preparing a guest room for the Examiners' arrival when Lysandro surprised him, appearing at the open window from out of nowhere.

"Sancio!"

Sancio screamed and stumbled backward, tripping on his robes and landing on the wooden floor with a hard thunk.

"Don't ever do that to me again!"

"Sancio, I'm in love!"

Sancio's back stiffened as he scrambled to his feet. "You're in love?" he repeated, smoothing out the front of his robe.

"With Signorina Seraphine Alvaró. Oh, Sancio," Lysandro swooned, dropping onto the bed against the left wall and rumpling the newly washed linens that Sancio had just spread out with great care. "She's absolutely perfect."

"*No one* is perfect," Sancio replied. He turned his back to Lysandro as he folded the linens on the other bed into prim corners.

"She's perfect to me. She's smart, and witty, and worldly, and her beauty—" Lysandro stopped and swallowed hard. "Her beauty is like staring into the sun. It's overwhelming."

He hadn't slept a wink; the small hours of the night had been devoted to reliving every step of their unending dances, the way she'd felt in his arms, and the conversation that had struck a chord deep within his soul.

"You barely know her," Sancio murmured without turning around.

"I'm *getting* to know her," Lysandro countered. "I want to know everything. She's agreed to come to the gallery with me."

"Of course she did."

Lysandro blinked. "What does that mean?"

Sancio turned, his face tight. "How do you know she's being honest with you?"

"What?"

"How do you know she's not just putting on a face, telling you what you want to hear, so she can trap you into a marriage?"

Lysandro laughed. "Marrying her would be a wish come true."

Sancio shook his head in dismay.

"You're just jealous!"

Sancio's head snapped to attention. "No I'm not. What? No! Why would you think

that—"

"You're jealous that I'm free to marry and you're not."

The heat prickling on Sancio's cheeks faded slowly with each breath he took.

"We danced and talked all night," Lysandro said, his voice deep and dreamy. "She wouldn't dance with anyone else. And she had plenty of requests. She even refused Marek!"

Lysandro sat up on the bed, his eyes glittering. "He tried to cut in while insulting me at the same time."

"That must have been pleasant."

"She called him an idiot, and we just floated away. It was brilliant! Sancio you should have *been* there."

"That was a mistake," Sancio observed.

Lysandro's face turned grave. He opened his mouth to speak, but Sancio answered his question before it could even form on his lips.

"When has Marek *ever* let someone make him the butt of their joke and let it slide?"

Lysandro bounded off the bed and was already halfway out the window again.

"Wait! What are you going to do?"

Lysandro was deaf to his friend's pleas as he raced across the temple garden back the way he had come. He leapt onto his chestnut bay mare and headed for the Alvaró family home. He was already dressed for it, he thought. He had planned on calling on Sera that morning, but as his friend's warning echoed in his ears, his purpose for visiting changed dramatically. It would not be easy or convenient for Sera's father to turn Marek away if he came calling. But if he could just talk to Don Alvaró and get him to agree, Lysandro would be able to keep Sera safe. He pushed his mare as fast as she would go, wishing for the speed of Hurricane underneath him.

As the Alvaró estate came into view, Lysandro began to sweat. He wiped his slick palms on the supple coat of his horse's neck. He struggled to compose his thoughts. A great many odes to love danced and flitted away from him, taunting him, so near but just out of reach. The ballads and tales he held sacred abandoned him now; he had no idea what he was going to say.

The main house was constructed of pale yellow bricks. Deep green vines crept up the impressive front, giving it an inviting appearance. There was no sign of Seraphine at any of the iron-framed windows. His heart lodged itself in his throat at the prospect of seeing her.

He left his mare outside the wrought-iron gate marking the edge of the property and entered a small but well-kept garden. The first person he encountered was the groundskeeper, who stood as Lysandro approached.

"Good morning, Don de Castel," he called out with a smile.

"Good morning. Is Don Alvaró at home?"

"Yes, Signor. Please come in."

Lysandro followed him into Don Alvaró's study. He did not spy Seraphine in any of the rooms they passed. He tried to smooth away his fear. He folded it up and tucked it underneath a cool, detached bearing as Don Alvaró entered the room.

"Don de Castel, what a surprise to see you again so soon," he said, coming to shake Lysandro's hand.

"A good surprise, I hope."

"Yes, of course. Please, sit." Alvaró gestured toward a pair of leather-backed chairs. "Can I get you anything?"

"No, thank you." Lysandro's tongue was so dry he could barely speak.

"So, to what do I owe the pleasure?"

"I'm here to inquire after your daughter."

"Ah, yes. She's a beautiful young girl, no?"

Lysandro's mouth only twitched in response, showing a mere hint of a smile. He turned the conversation in another direction. "Our families are well-matched. Better matched than an appointed official, such as a magistrate."

Alvaró's face widened in a knowing grin. "Yes, but perhaps she would be happier with a man with more vigor. You're a fine gentleman, Don Lysandro. But perhaps too gentle. She may choose a bold, assertive man who can protect her."

Lysandro's hackles went up. But he just wanted this conversation to be over so he could have a conversation with Sera of an entirely different sort.

"Marek has no lands and no money," Lysandro answered in a blunt tone. "He's not a don. He will never be able to provide her with the security and stature she deserves."

"What you say is true. Under any circumstances, you would undoubtedly be the highest bidder."

Lysandro didn't appreciate Alvaró's language at all. He understood perfectly well that Marek was not a viable suitor. But Lysandro was meant to believe he was, to drive up the bride price. Seraphine was Goddess-sent, a vision of charm and beauty. She was not the base means by which Alvaró could enrich himself. He grimaced, but said nothing.

Alvaró continued. "What would you have me do?" he asked.

"I have no desire to compete for a bride."

"You would have me turn Marek away?" Alvaró asked, incredulous.

"And anyone else. At least until I have an answer."

"Wooing her holds no interest for you either, I presume. It's a long journey between our houses—all that riding and song-singing would be too much exertion. I'll make your case to her, if you wish."

What Lysandro wished was to punch him square in the jaw. He was about to protest when he heard a sound that froze his blood. The voice of an angel.

"Lysandro?"

He stood and turned, his eyes wild with not knowing how much she had overheard.

"Sera..."

She stared unbelieving at him, then at her father. The storm that gathered in her eyes sunk Lysandro's heart like a stone into a bottomless pit. His hopes of earning her affection crumbled to dust.

"Daughter," Don Alvaró said, rising to his feet, "Don Lysandro de Castel has asked me to give you to him in marriage. He may be the best offer we'll get for you, but in the meantime—"

Don Alvaró's voice was a death knell in Lysandro's ears. He kept his eyes on Seraphine; her stare was withering. His instinct was to cower in some faraway corner.

But her stony façade soon cracked. Pain bubbled to the surface of her rage. She stepped backward, turned, and fled from them without saying another word.

Don Alvaró put his hands up before him as if to say, *court her if you can,* then slipped out of the room through a secondary door. Lysandro raced after Seraphine.

She was fast, but Lysandro caught up with her in moments, taking hold of her elbow and spinning her round to face him.

"Sera, wait!"

"*Don't touch me!*" she screamed.

Lysandro flinched and pulled his hand away immediately. "I'm sorry."

Sera's entire frame trembled with her fury.

"How could you? After everything I—" she bit her tongue and turned her head to the side to stop the tears that were flooding her eyes from falling. "And you were so charming."

Lysandro wanted to die. The lump in his throat grew so large he had difficulty forming words.

"Seraphine," he managed, "I—"

Her words cut him so deep he could barely stand upright. In all his beloved tales and poems, never had the prince ever won the object of his love by making her cry.

In this one thing that he wished for most in the world, he had failed. Horribly. She'd already been let down, already had her heart broken, and he had trampled on it anew as if she meant nothing to him.

"Let me explain, please. *Please* Seraphine."

"No," she answered. Her voice was firm, with a finality that Lysandro knew was not limited to allowing him an explanation. "No." She turned and left him standing alone in the corridor.

* * *

He couldn't leave. He absolutely could not leave things like that. But she wouldn't talk to him. Lysandro shuffled his feet on the way back to his mare. As he reached for the saddle, he paused. Hanging in front of him was his large leather satchel, where he kept an extra set of his night clothes and a mask for emergencies. If he could fasten the cloak over his clothes and tuck his hair into his collar, he could just get away with it. He led his horse out the way he had come, but then rounded the building, and set the mare as a lookout in a secluded spot not likely to be discovered.

After donning the garb of the Shadow of Theron, he crept among the high grasses and flowers, slinking along the edge of the wall. He was hiding in the shadows offered by the overhang of the third-floor balcony when he heard Sera's voice.

She was crying. Crying so hard and so deep she sounded beyond consolation. Lysandro felt a tight pain in his chest; he was drowning in her tears.

He adjusted his mask, screwed up his courage, and scaled the wall. Pulling on the vines for support, he bounded over the edge of her balcony, and landed gracefully at her feet.

"Please Signorina, don't cry."

Seraphine screamed and jumped from the balcony's edge where she sat with her knees hugged to her chest. Lysandro lifted his hands in front of him to plead with her.

"No, I beg you, peerless beauty, don't be afraid."

"Are you a thief? A murderer?!" she cried.

"I am neither."

"What do you want with *me?*" She stepped back, pressing herself against the stone column that separated her balcony from the inner recesses of her room.

Lysandro got down on his knees. "Signorina, I mean you no harm. I do not think myself fit to kiss the hem of your garment. But please, don't cry. I cannot bear it."

She inhaled a sharp breath and ventured away from the wall, inching toward the balustrade, nearer to Lysandro.

"You're...the Shadow of Theron?" she asked.

He rose from the floor and crouched next to her at the edge of the balcony.

"That is what I am called, when I wear this," he said, touching the brim of his hat. But I do not think so highly of myself as that."

"Why do you wear a mask?"

"I seek to do justice, Signorina, but that is a dangerous prospect these days, and must be done from the shadows."

"Why are you here?"

"Because the sound of your sorrow is tearing apart my soul."

Her taut frame relaxed, disarmed by his affectionate entreaties. She wiped her face, almost ashamed of her sadness.

"Tell me what pains you so, that you make the skies quake with your sorrow."

She hesitated.

Lysandro inched closer to her, so that their hands on the ledge were almost touching.

"Don Lysandro..."

"Don Lysandro is a fool. I'll kill him with my own hands if that will stop your tears."

"No, don't do that," she sniffed.

"He most certainly deserves it. You would have me show mercy?"

"I just—"

She shuddered as she exhaled, stifling a sob.

"My goddess, my sweet, brilliant angel, I will guard your secrets with my life."

"You are a dealer in secrets, it seems."

"Never in secrets of the heart, dear one. Never have I seen such wonder in a woman's eyes, never have I wanted to kiss such a graceful hand, that I would cut off my own for the chance of it."

Seraphine blushed.

"Why does he cause you such suffering?"

"It's the second time I've been asked to marry a man who didn't love me."

"Oh...oh my angel..."

Lysandro felt like he'd been stabbed clean through. He was worse than a fool. He was a villain, that he could have been so careless with what was most precious to him.

"The first was bad enough, but this—"

A fresh tear fell into the stream staining her cheek.

Lysandro's voice broke as he reached for her. "Oh, no..."

He came closer still, his hand trembling when his fingertips touched her cheek. He held her face in the palm of his gloved hand.

She flinched, afraid of his touch. But she calmed as their eyes met, and she studied the streaks of cobalt in his gray eyes.

"You are the most perfect creature I have ever seen. It would be utterly impossible for me not to love you."

Lysandro felt his own tears burning at the back of his eyes. Sera's heartbreak felt like his own.

His words had a soothing effect, and she allowed him to stroke her cheek with his thumb. But after a moment, she pulled away.

"You don't know me," she protested.

"I will spend a lifetime correcting my sin."

"I don't know you."

"I will tell you all."

She reached tentatively for his face. Her fingertips rested on the edge of his mask.

Lysandro clasped her hands before she was able to lift it off him. He feared that if she recognized him now, it would all be for naught.

"There are men who make it dangerous for you to know my face."

She dropped her hand, and Lysandro saw the light flee from her eyes. He panicked.

"I *will* reveal myself to you, dear one, and you will know what is in my heart, that there is room for nothing but you. From this day, I pledge myself to your protection and your happiness."

"Seraphine?"

They both turned at the sound of Doña Alvaró ascending the stairs.

"You cannot be found here. Go," Sera said.

"I cannot bear to part with you."

"You must."

"Only if you promise not to shed another tear over that wretch Don Lysandro, who should taste the steel of my blade for his crimes against your sweet heart."

"Go, before you are found!" she hissed.

"I would have your promise, Signorina," he said, desperate.

"I won't cry," she insisted, "but she's coming!"

"It means nothing to me if I die, if I cannot see you again."

"Please!"

"Your promise!"

"I promise you can see me again. Now for your own safety go!"

His eyes met hers as he descended the balcony. "You won't forget, will you?"

"I won't. I promise I won't."

"Then I am the luckiest man in the world."

He let go his grip on the balcony and was gone as suddenly as he had come.

Lysandro's hands shook as he held the reigns of his mare on the slow ride home, his disguise once again buried deep in his saddlebag.

"That went alright. For the Shadow, not for me. You think she'll forgive me? You're a female—would *you* forgive me?"

The horse whinnied.

"Maybe she will. At least I can see her again. So long as she's not really looking at me. Stop your nickering. I'm quite aware that I'm losing my mind. But I can't help it. I get all twisted up when she's near. I acted a right idiot. I wouldn't blame her if she *never* forgave me for it."

Lysandro couldn't concentrate on anything but Seraphine. He couldn't leave it like this forever, her shunning him by day and only welcoming him at night. It wouldn't be nearly enough. He had to make this right between them.

After barely touching his dinner, he made the long journey back to the Alvaró household as twilight fell. When he came upon the place, he saw Sera sitting by herself in the front garden, her dress tucked under her feet and staring up at the stars. A gentle breeze played about the tips of her hair. She seemed calm, her ire cooled and her sadness abated. He wondered if he was responsible for that.

He cleared his throat, and braced himself for shattering her serenity. "Seraphine?"

She looked at him, her blank stare seeing right through him. She turned her head away and back to the heavens.

"I won't be a bride of convenience. I won't."

He dismounted, and clasped the handle of the gate, not daring to pass it.

"You can't know how sorry I am. I would never want that. And I never wanted to hurt you."

She didn't respond. He persisted.

"I don't agree with what your father said. Not at all."

"What about what *you* said?"

"My behavior was inexcusable. But if you'll let me take you to the gallery like we planned, I can explain everything."

She tucked her light, airy dress like moonlight even tighter around her.

"I've had enough of men who don't mean what they say."

Lysandro took the hit to his chest, and hung his head to absorb the blow. "I *never* wanted to be counted among their number. I'm so sorry Sera. Please, listen what I have to say. If after that you never want to hear from me again, I'll leave you alone."

She bit her lip, considering.

Lysandro couldn't breathe. He gripped the gate for dear life, knowing this could be the end of everything. Her voice came like the soft peal of a bell into the quiet night.

"Goodnight, Lysandro."

He'd lost her. She'd dismissed him, in the same way she had dismissed Marek. He cursed himself for being so unthinking with his words and turned to go, feeling lower than a dog with its tail between its legs.

"I'll see you in the morning," she called over his shoulder.

He spun to face her.

"I'll be here." He smiled, but she didn't smile back. He realized that he'd never seen her smile. He knew then. If she never smiled, if he was never able to *make* her smile, then he would never himself be happy again.

7

"So, she hates your guts, but she's interested in the Shadow? That's rich."

"She doesn't *hate* me. Hate is a strong word."

Lysandro took another draft of his ale, but it did little to assuage his wounded heart. He set the frothy amber back down on the small table in their corner of the tavern, turned boisterous after nightfall.

"There goes your happily ever after," Sancio said.

"I'm not giving up. I'm seeing her tomorrow. I can try to smooth things over."

"If you manage not to insult her, or make a fool of yourself again."

Lysandro grunted. "Haven't you ever gotten tongue-tied talking to someone you were attracted to?"

Sancio only blinked, and responded with a sympathetic smile.

"Well, multiply that by a million. Her father said she might be happier with someone bold, and assertive. I *am* bold and assertive!"

Sancio raised a mischievous eyebrow. "Are you?"

Lysandro drew back. "How can you say that?"

"When Marek throws barbs at you in public, do you answer him?"

Lysandro floundered.

"No. You hold yourself aloof. Sometimes you don't help yourself."

"Should I show him my right hook every time he speaks to me?" He lowered his voice and added, "sacrilegious activities excepting. I don't need to answer Marek on his terms. I want to set an example, to show men there's a better way to deal with their differences."

"But you can't do that if you don't have their respect."

Lysandro rocked back in his chair, causing the aged wooden legs to creak. His face fell.

"Am I not respectable?"

"You *are*," Sancio reassured him. "You're kind, and generous, and not just to the dons, but to everyone. Especially those who need your kindness the most. You're the only respectable man I know, the only one worth looking up to."

"Thank you, Sancio."

"But the Shadow of Theron is called that *precisely* because he takes necessary action to uphold the right and punish the wicked. People respect men of action, not just words. And I know..." he lowered his voice, and leaned his elbows on the table. "I know you are both. But never at the same time. And that's the problem. Maybe it's time to..." He gestured with his hands, not really sure what he was suggesting.

"Maybe. But Marek is at a disadvantage because he doesn't know his enemy. And I need every advantage I can get. If he knew, then everyone the Shadow loves would be at risk."

Sancio pushed his lips to the corner of his mouth, conceding the point.

"It sets me on such edge, knowing what he's walking around with. What he's capable of."

"Leave it to the Examiners, I told you."

"And when are *they* getting here?"

"I don't know. None of this has ever happened before, so no one knows what to expect—how long it'll take them to get to each town, or even how many Examiners there are."

"Marek won't wait to strike again."

"What are you going to do?"

"I can't do nothing. You still have that manifest?"

"It's safe," Sancio answered, shifting uneasily in his chair.

"Maybe I can use it to anticipate his next move, somehow."

"You can't get close to him. Not now," Sancio protested.

"I don't have to get close to him. I just have to frustrate his plans."

* * *

Lysandro's ears pricked at the sound of Marek turning the key in the lock and the crunch of the gravel as he departed the magistrate's office. Lysandro rolled off his back and slid down the roof, where he'd lain hidden for longer than he'd expected to, and landed noiselessly on his feet. He fell into step behind Marek.

Lysandro kept his distance, mimicking Marek's gait and hiding his own presence in Lothan's footsteps. They continued like this down the main path, past Marek's humble dwelling on the edge of an older part of town, and began the long sloping curve down to the sea. In front of one of the last houses in a weather-beaten line, a little boy crouched in front of his door, playing with a pair of wooden figures in the soft light from his kitchen window. The boy looked up as Marek approached, then to the Shadow following behind. Lysandro watched the boy's gaze shift to Marek and back to himself again. The child covered his mouth to suppress a giggle, delighting in the game but not understanding the rules. Marek turned a sharp look in the child's direction.

His mirth died on his lips.

Lysandro's grip on his sword tightened as the boy by increments pressed his back against his mother's door. When Marek turned his head to the left, Lysandro circled to the right, outside of Marek's line of vision as he turned to glance behind him.

Lysandro was invisible. Marek bristled, but turned back again and resumed walking toward the coast without further suspicion. As Lysandro passed the boy, he touched his fingers to the brim of his hat before the child scurried inside, never to tell what he had seen.

When Marek made the final dip down to the slender beach, Lysandro stayed above him, ducking down into the high whistling grasses and tracking Marek's movements from the cliff's edge. The sound of his approach was engulfed by the crashing of the waves upon the rocky shore. After following Marek from above for half an hour, Lysandro's eyes grew round with disbelief when Marek suddenly disappeared.

It happened without warning; Lysandro's heart beat furiously in his chest as he crept closer to investigate, imagining that at any moment Marek would rematerialize behind him and try to lodge his nightmarish blade deep in his back. When he came to the spot directly above where he had seen Marek vanish, he saw immediately—there was a secondary wall, a hidden formation of stalagmites that guarded the mouth of the cavern behind it and, from a distance, made it appear as if Marek had moved through the solid granite when he'd slipped behind the outer wall and into the cave.

A faint echo met Lysandro's ears. There were voices—at least a dozen. It was all garbled together with the thrashing surf, but its heavy cadence and rhythm sounded wrong somehow in Lysandro's ears in a way he couldn't define.

He lay sprawled on his belly above the mouth of the cave for hours. The position of the moon told him it was past two in the morning. He'd considered trying to burrow a hole into the cavern's roof to get a better look, but was afraid that any noticeable amount of falling sediment would spell the end of his being there undetected.

He needed to keep his nose and mouth covered with his handkerchief to keep out the charnel stench wafting up from beneath him. His skin crawled at the memory of the slick edge of the weapon that had nearly robbed him of his life.

He sensed movement at the mouth of the cave, and the swell of voices echoed as a handful of men exited the cavern and made their way back up the beach to the village. Keeping his head low, Lysandro spied their faces over the edge of the bluff. His stomach lurched. They were all Marek's officers, the only law enforcement Lighura had. There were none in which Lysandro could confide, none whom he could hope would aid him in bringing Marek to justice. The people of Lighura were entirely at Marek's mercy.

Lysandro rolled over onto his back, and laid his sword beside him, retrieving the pistol from his belt. The howling winds would mask the sound of anyone approaching; slowly, silently, he loaded the weapon and cocked it. He kept his hand on the trigger as he laid it across his chest, and prayed to all three of the goddess's aspects to give him the strength and the wisdom to live through the night, so he might not miss his date with Sera in the morning. The possibility that he could go to his grave without confessing his true feelings broke his spirit. He found himself hoping that if his body were found and his identity discovered, that she might understand. The thought choked him, but he shook free of it to watch Marek, the last of the pack, climb up the road to the village without so much as a glance in his direction.

Lysandro slunk down to the beach when Lothan was completely out of sight, his pistol still in his hand and his sword in its sheath. He dropped down into the shelter between the outer and inner walls of the cave, listening to see if he'd miscounted, if there was still someone inside. There was no sound, no movement as Lysandro rounded the stalagmite that had shielded him, until he could see plainly that the cave was empty. He traversed the space with slow, unbelieving steps. The hair on his arms and the back of his neck stood at attention as he peered down into the shallow, muddy pit carved out of the cave floor. In the center of the depression lay the carcasses of at least three eldur vipers, their blood steaming as it dyed the mud of the pit a hellish red. To his right he spied a smoothed bit of the cave's formation, a long gleaming shelf, stained by the glistening trail of blood. Lysandro realized what he was looking at, and it curdled the blood in his veins. It was where Marek sat, presiding over whatever dark doings had transpired, with that infernal weapon dripping its gore down into a widening puddle. Averting his eyes, Lysandro caught sight of a strongbox beside the seat. First with the tip of his sword, then with his gloved hand, Lysandro prodded the box, satisfied that its surface was safe for him to open. He pulled a hairpin from the back of his head and bent it out of shape to make quick work of the lock protecting the box's contents. Inside was a pile of illuminated pages, torn loose from their bindings, and a strange, dark-colored stone that glowed like an ember from within. He avoided the stone and rifled through the pages. He recognized the prayers and service instructions from the temple, but didn't understand their value to Lothan. Why would he steal what he could simply listen to if he ever set foot inside a temple? Then he found a handwritten log tucked in between the other pages, buried so deep in the pile that he'd almost missed it.

Lysandro grinned. He'd always known Marek lacked intelligence, but he never expected him to be so stupid as to record his own crimes. Near the bottom of the page, the date listed had not yet passed; another exchange was still expected. He laid the page atop the rest and closed the lid when he heard a subtle whispering behind him. He whirled around, pistol raised, and cried out in horror—in the corner, a skeleton cloaked in rags sat upright, staring into nothing. Curling around its edges was a dark purplish haze, like a shimmering mirage.

Lysandro heard the whispering again, a wet, pregnant echo of a noise not yet borne on the wind, and drew slowly closer. He could almost understand it, but he didn't want to. It spoke of terrible things—insane things—and Lysandro knew that if he came close enough to truly hear it, he would go mad. The sound poured out in a slow steady stream like a poison river that threatened to overtake him. He backed away, gripping the lockbox under his arm and scrambling to escape the maw of the cavern. After a few fortifying breaths of fresh sea air, he laid the box down in the grass and pulled at the leather pouch of gunpowder hanging from his belt. Cleaving through the dirt-covered rock with his sword, Lysandro poured a line of powder across the overhang of the cliff. When he'd spilled all he had with him except what was loaded in the pistol, he picked up the box, retreated ten paces, and took his aim.

The shot lit up the night like a flash of lightning, followed rapidly by the roar of thunder as the ground beneath Lysandro's feet trembled and gave way. He fled across the bluff as the hanging edge of the rock collapsed upon itself, filling the mouth of the cave.

* * *

"Sancio," Lysandro whispered. "Sancio wake up, *now.*"

Sancio groaned and rolled over in his sleep. He only opened his eyes when Lysandro gave him a firm slap on the top of his head.

"What? What?!"

"Get the high priestess. I have something she needs to see."

"Now?"

"Yes, now."

Lysandro's masked face disappeared from the window, and Sancio scrambled out of his bed. He woke Beatríz, who was even less pleased to be summoned by a bumbling acolyte to the front entry of the temple, where the Shadow of Theron stood with an unremarkable metal box in his hands.

"You dare to come here wearing that mask," she scowled, "presuming to be the sacred hero, the worker of the Goddess's will?" Her chastisement echoed off the stone columns framing the nave.

Lysandro answered in a calm, quiet voice. "I don't claim that name myself. It was given to me by the people of Lighura."

She rebuffed him. "You don't correct them."

"If I thought serving the Goddess could be done in the daylight, this would not be necessary."

The high priestess opened her mouth again, the rage of being woken from her sleep blazing in her eyes, but Sancio interceded.

"High Priestess, please, if he has come here at this hour, he must have a reason. Let's at least hear it." At the turn of her head, Sancio hunched his shoulders, trying to hide himself from her murderous stare, but there was nowhere to go. She turned again to face Lysandro, her expression unyielding.

He stepped forward and opened the box as he handed it to her. He told all that he had seen. When he spoke of the broken shard from the Sword of Argoss, her voice stiffened.

"You're mistaken. The Blood Sword was destroyed."

Lysandro knew she wasn't telling the truth. Even *she* didn't sound like she believed it. "Lothan Marek is at the center of this. I saw him with my own eyes."

The Aruni shot him a skeptical glance before eyeing the papers inside the box. "I won't deny these are Temple property. But not our temple; thankfully, we have not been thieved."

"Yet," Lysandro added. "Marek smuggled those into the village. For what reason I don't know. But to strike the temple in his own district would cause too much suspicion."

"*Someone* transported these here," she conceded. "You can't say for sure it was Marek."

"Surely ships do not come and go without his notice?"

The high priestess flinched, but she stood her ground. "You have proof of something but not *someone*. You'll forgive me if I don't just take your word for it."

Lysandro realized that she was right; Marek had been stupid enough to create an account of his activity, but *not* so stupid as to sign his name on the ledger.

"Take me to this cave, then," the warrior said.

Lysandro started. "I can't."

She raised an impatient eyebrow.

"I destroyed it. I thought...I thought it would be safer, for everyone."

The priestess's eyes narrowed. "How do I know it's not you? You've already established a flair for flirting with sacrilege."

"Why would he come to us, then?" Sancio objected.

One look said what the priestess thought of Sancio's opinion.

"Marek has never entered your temple," Lysandro pressed.

"Sure he has," the priestess hedged.

"Name one occasion."

"I could say the same of you, hiding behind a name that isn't yours."

There was an awkward pause, but Lysandro continued. "Will you call the Examiners down, at least, tell them there's no time to waste?"

"I'm quite sure their time *isn't* being wasted. And besides, I couldn't contact them even if I wanted to. There's no way to tell who or where they are."

"If you sent a rider, asking for people who have seen the Examiners, you *might* find them..." Sancio suggested.

"And who will go, *you*? You're not fast enough to catch a slug."

Sancio bowed his head. "I would if I could, High Priestess."

Beatríz sighed. "I will keep these safe, until the Examiners see fit to come."

"*Will* they come? Why would they if we've had nothing stolen?"

Beatríz's face darkened two shades. But she gave no answer.

Lysandro raged inside his head. But he knew it would be worse for him if he argued further. He stepped back, leaving Lothan's lockbox in the high priestess's hands.

She handed it to Sancio, who disappeared behind her. He caught up with Lysandro as he passed through the temple's outer columns and clasped Lysandro's hands in his own.

"Thank you for bringing this to us. You are a true servant of the Goddess."

Lysandro kept his eyes on his friend as he felt a folded slip of paper pass into his hands. Lysandro squeezed Sancio tighter, and left. Alone in the street, he unfolded the paper to find the last page of Marek's ledger, the one saying where he would be expecting more stolen relics to arrive, and when. He secreted it away in his garments, then disappeared into the night.

8

LYSANDRO ROSE WHEN HE COULD WAIT NO MORE. HE GAVE HIMSELF A CLEAN shave and agonized over his attire, dressing himself in multiple garments and then tossing them onto the bed if he didn't deem them flattering enough. He settled on a white silk shirt with a high collar and a slight billow to the sleeves, paired with charcoal pants and a coat with notches cut out at the hips. It was lined with bright silver buttons and a pewter embroidered pattern along the hem. He brushed his dark hair until he achieved a glossy shine. A simple ring of burnished silver with a topaz stud was his only jeweled ornamentation.

The coach ride to Sera's home seemed to take forever. When he finally arrived and knocked on the door, he hoped he would not have to see Don Alvaró.

Sera answered the door in a flowing dress the color of pale sunshine. Her hair tumbled in loose waves of shimmering gold and copper in the morning light. She looked more ethereal than ever. Once again, Lysandro was dumbstruck.

"Good morning," she greeted him.

"Good morning." He led her up into the coach and seated himself on the opposite bench. With a gentle knock on the ceiling, they left the Alvaró estate and headed west.

They turned on to the main road toward Lighura's sole repository of Andran art and culture in an awkward silence. Sera looked at Lysandro expectantly, and he realized he should have practiced what he was going to say. His brain raced through the possibilities of what to tell her, petrified by indecision, until Sera's anxious expression turned to one of impatience.

"I was trying to protect you from Marek!" he blurted out.

"What?"

Lysandro took a deep breath to calm his rattled nerves. "He will not let your insult stand. As much as I loved watching you humiliate him, he might make trouble for you."

"Trouble…"

"He's a dangerous man, Sera. He doesn't respect the law, and holds himself above it."

Sera's brow furrowed. "So you want me to marry you?"

"I thought that if your father agreed to let me court you exclusively, then Marek wouldn't be able to harass you."

She leaned back in her seat, absorbing his confession.

Lysandro balled his fists in his lap as he waited for her reaction. Whether she would continue talking to him or tell him to turn the coach around hinged on this moment.

"Yesterday was a disaster," he added, a final plea.

"That's putting it mildly."

Lysandro's face reddened, and he was grateful for the shadows enveloping the corners of the coach. He leaned into them.

"It's a clever ruse," she said finally.

"Oh—"

"But you should have told me."

"I *was* going to tell you. But I barely had time to speak to your father, and I didn't get the chance."

"You should have told me *first*."

He bowed his head. "I should have told you first."

He clenched his jaw. She'd called it a ruse. She believed his entire proposal to be false, his intention to marry her a lie.

He didn't know what to say, or how to fix it without angering her further. So he stayed silent. And cursed himself for a coward.

"I didn't want to believe it," she said, turning her head toward the window to hide her expression. "I didn't want to believe that you could be so cruel, to barter for me like a...a..."

"Sera. I would never think of you, or of any woman that way. What your father said...it stunned me speechless."

"I've always known what I meant to him. And what I didn't."

Sancio's voice echoed in Lysandro's head, chiding him about silence more often than not acting as his enemy.

"I should have said something," he muttered.

Sera turned her gaze away from the window to look at him.

"No one should be allowed to speak to you like that, not even him. I should have defended you."

She clasped the silver pendant of an angel's wing hanging from her neck. "That might have been nice..."

Lysandro closed his eyes to shut out the pain her words inflicted. Sancio was right. His reticence to show his true feelings had robbed him of the chance to be her champion.

She sighed. "You're forgiven."

He shouldn't have been. The men in her life—her father, her mysterious first suitor who'd proposed, but not out of love, and the cur who abandoned her at the docks of Mirêne—had made the fair maiden sitting opposite him feel unworthy of love. It seemed to him the world's greatest injustice. But he couldn't turn his thoughts into words; they tumbled and dissolved on the journey from his heart to his lips. Constant was the fear that no matter what he said, no matter what soulful confessions he made, they would never be enough to upturn the corners of her mouth.

The carriage pulled to a stop in front of a tall stone edifice of gleaming alabaster. Narrow steps led up to a column-lined portico that gave way to the marble floors inside. At this hour, the influx of patrons was modest. Lysandro reached for Sera's hand. He allowed himself to hope when she didn't pull away.

"Thank you for listening to me. If you would prefer for me to take you home now, I'll understand."

"I'd prefer to go inside, if you don't mind."

Lysandro smiled. "It would be my pleasure." He opened the carriage door with a crisp turn of the handle and let Sera out into the early sunshine. They were met in the first room of the gallery by a collection of primitive Andran statuettes and fetishes dating back to before the Age of Theron.

"How did it start?" Sera asked, peering at the carvings on a ritual dagger made of obsidian, displayed on a stone pedestal.

"Hmm?"

"This feud between you and Marek."

Lysandro cocked his head.

"He didn't try to cut in on anyone else but you and me, didn't insult anyone but you, and went out of his way to do it."

"It seems since the moment he arrived, we've been at odds," Lysandro said.

"What does he have against you?"

"I'm not charmed by him."

"Is that all?"

It was more difficult by the day for Lysandro to separate what he knew of Marek from what he could safely say—what he could admit to knowing without revealing himself. He chose his words with deliberation, careful not to lie.

"He has no care for his position, or the people he's meant to protect. The only thing that matters to him is the power that his post allows him."

Sera pointed out what Lysandro wasn't saying. "And I suspect you've made your feelings known?"

"I've not made a secret of it."

After kneeling to admire the craftsmanship of a stone altar inscribed with interlocking characters and symbols that made little sense to her, she straightened.

"Is it safe, for us to talk about this?"

Lysandro scoffed. "He would never be found at a place like this. He resents that too; it undermines his influence in the village."

"What does?"

"My title, my family name, my ability to afford finer things."

"And appreciate them," she countered. "Money doesn't buy intellect, or taste. And this place *is* open to the public."

"That way of thinking would be lost on him."

They moved to the next room, which showcased several depictions of the Age of Theron in paint.

"So, when you say dangerous…" she asked, "how dangerous?"

A shadow passed over Lysandro's eyes. He heard the dark echo of a skeleton whispering in his ear. In his mind's eye, he imagined the skull turning on its defunct moorings to face him, and he gave an involuntary shudder. He moved to stand behind her, and looked up at a painting of the hero battling a horde of goblins astride his horse. He craned his neck and whispered in her ear.

"He has blood on his hands."

She swallowed a gasp. "Why hasn't he been removed?" she whispered back.

"Knowing and proving to the satisfaction of his superiors are two different things."

"Thank you," she said. "For concerning yourself with my safety."

Lysandro's voice was deep when it came, and sterner than he intended.

"Don't ever thank me for what I did yesterday." He squeezed her arms just below the shoulders, and stole a breath infused with the spiced orange scent of her hair. "You deserve better than that."

Sera didn't answer him; she continued to gaze at the painting, studying the brush strokes that lent Morgasse her all-knowing aura as she conjured the storm clouds gathering in the corner of the image. Lysandro was unsure if Sera's interest in the painting was genuine, or if she stared at it to avoid meeting his eyes.

He wouldn't push the matter of the kind of proposal she deserved if she was unwilling. "I think you'll like the next room. We have some panels from a sacred window, though I can't recall what temple they're from."

Sera spun and stared at him. "You have panels?"

"Yes…" he said, not understanding the dire urgency that had flooded her countenance.

"Where?!"

"Just in here—"

She darted away from him. "What is She holding?" she cried over her shoulder.

"What?" he called out, taking long hasty strides to catch up as he crossed into the next space.

"What's She holding?"

Sera stopped her frantic dash when she found what she was looking for. The circular room was enclosed on every side by adjoining spaces, cloaking the room in complete darkness, except for the large brazier illuminating the colored glass panes suspended in an iron framework from the ceiling. Empty rectangles of iron adjoined to where the missing sections of the window ought to have been.

Sera stared wide-eyed at the panel hanging in the center. "A key! Of course! A key to what?"

Lysandro fell into step behind her.

"I think it's meant to be the Cerulean Key. Why all the excitement?"

"The unlocker of every door..." she said in awe. "I have to tell Fabien."

"The Doge of Mirêne?" Lysandro asked, his ears pricked.

She nodded. "He has the sixth and eighth panels. You can see Morgasse's face, and the position of the fingers in her right hand, grabbing something, but not what. Well, wait a minute," she said, peering closer. "What's this hand doing?"

Behind the right hand in the foreground, the index finger of the left hand was outstretched. Sera copied the movement, following its trajectory to the northwestern corner, where an iron rectangle lay empty.

"The first panel," she mumbled to herself. "He's got to find the first panel." She turned to Lysandro to explain. "It's said that this window belonged to the Temple Theron."

"There's a temple just to Theron?"

"There was one once. But it was destroyed by fire, and the panels of its window were scattered, believed to be lost forever. Fabien tracked down every scrap of history and lore he could find. He discovered that clues to where Theron was buried were hidden *inside* the image. If you can decipher the clues, you can find Theron's tomb. And with him, the Hand of Arun." She reached out to the fragmented window and pressed her fingertips to the bottom-most corner of the glass. "The key...what does it mean?"

"I have to admit, I'm intrigued," Lysandro said. "I've never heard that bit of legend before."

"The doge has been obsessed for years. It's become his life-long quest. He's going to be positively giddy when I tell him about these."

Lysandro started. "So he's not—" he bit his tongue, and let the air out of his lungs without forming the rest of his words.

"Not the one who abandoned me?" Sera finished. "No. Fabien is my dearest friend in all the world. He's the one who warned me about his—"

Sera caught herself, but it was too late. She scrunched up her face.

"His brother," Lysandro finished.

"I realize how ridiculous that sounds. But Fane has a way of drawing people into his orbit."

"You were seduced…by the king of Mirêne," Lysandro said. The words were sour on his tongue. "I hear he's quite good at that."

"*Not* seduced," Seraphine answered stiffly. "'Seduced' implies he got what he wanted. I may have been a fool to pay him any attention, but I have more care for myself, and for whoever my future husband might be, than to do something as downright stupid as that. I have no desire to share, or to *be* shared."

Her plain talk made the tips of Lysandro's ears blush.

"You deserve a husband who's earned your loyalty. One who keeps his promises."

"You kept yours," she said in a soft voice.

"I did? When?"

"You said you had a reason for visiting my father, and you did. Even if it came out all wrong," she finished before he could interrupt her. "I'm glad you came back last night."

His heart thudded hard in response. "So am I."

She tucked an errant strand of her hair behind her ear. "I'm sorry, I've been leading you around since we got here. What did you want to see?"

"We're quite close, actually." He led her through the next three rooms with a cursory glance and stopped in a long, wide hallway on whose walls hung an enormous painting of a pair of lovers embracing in a field, their lips close to touching.

"What a beautiful picture." She admired the classic image of Elard and Galaine, immortalized by the epic poem of the same name.

"It's my favorite."

"That's not the least bit surprising. This is a lovely rendering though."

"Of all the iterations of this tryst, this one has the most transcendent sky. The sunrise is sublime." Lysandro allowed himself to soak in the painting's joy.

"The color *is* exquisite. It casts everything in a soft, golden glow. A timeless moment."

Lysandro's smile ached on his face, his heart swelled to bursting. "That's precisely how I've always thought of it." He stood beside Sera, gazing at the portrait of the immortal young lovers—at the man he always wished himself to be. Something stirred in him.

"I wish you *would* consider marrying me."

She looked up at him, but said nothing.

"When I told your father I wanted to court you, I meant it. I delight in your company. It's important to me that I share a deep bond with my wife, that I would rather spend the whole day with her than do anything else. I want my life to be something I share."

"You value friendship in a marriage?"

"Very much."

"And what about that?" she asked, turning her gaze again to the painting. Lysandro saw her eyes glisten.

"I've seen that look, when Fabien is with the one *he* truly loves but can't marry. I know that *that* kind of love...is real. And I am envious." She swallowed, trying to conquer her emotions.

Lysandro stepped closer to her so that their shoulders were almost touching.

"You don't need to give me an answer now. We've only been acquainted for a night and a morning. But in time, we might be everything to each other."

There was a pause. Lysandro prayed to Faelia that his heart would not be broken in the next moment.

After what seemed like an age, Seraphine spoke. Her voice was soft, no more than a murmur.

"Okay."

Thank you, Sweet Goddess.

Lysandro's fingers brushed against Sera's in silent query as they hung by her side. She answered him, opening her hand and folding her fingers together with his. Lysandro felt like he could fly.

"I promised Don Carras I would have lunch with him and help him sort out his father's affairs," Lysandro said as they exited the gallery and climbed back into his coach. "Will you come to my house for dinner tonight?"

"You really *do* enjoy my company, don't you?" she said in a coy tone.

"Will you come?"

"Mmhmm."

"Wonderful. I'll send the coach for you."

"Thank you for a lovely morning," she said as she climbed out of the coach. Steadying herself on his arm, she stretched up on her toes and laid a kiss on his cheek. "I'll see you tonight." She waved to the driver and got a smile in return.

Lysandro had stopped breathing and stood grinning like an idiot as he watched her disappear through the front doors. Once he closed the doors, Lysandro collapsed on the floor of his coach.

"Salla," he called through the ceiling, "Am I dreaming, or did that gorgeous girl just kiss me?"

"Indeed she did, Signor. Saw it with my own eyes. Well done." He clicked his tongue and led the horses back down toward the main road. "I think I'd like having her as the lady of the house, if I may say so."

"So would I, Salla. So would I."

* * *

"Are you sure you won't stay for dinner?" the young don asked as he locked his father's desk with a small brass key.

"Thanks, but another time. I already have plans for this evening." Lysandro gathered his coat. "We've gone through a good amount today, and we've sorted what to do with the most pressing matters."

Carras nodded. "I wouldn't have understood the half of it on my own. But I think I've got a feel for it now. I'm in your debt, Don Lysandro."

"Not at all. You're doing a fine job. Your mother and sisters are enormously proud of you."

"I know," he said, bowing his head.

Lysandro placed a reassuring hand on the adolescent's shoulder. "Don't be afraid to ask them if you need a hand. I'm sure they'd jump at the chance. And I'll come back in a few weeks, to see if I'm needed."

"Uh—can I ask you something?"

"Of course."

"Your dinner plans…are they with a girl?"

Lysandro smiled. "Yes, as a matter of fact."

"Who?"

"Signorina Seraphine Alvaró, if you must know." Lysandro puffed his chest out at the sound of her name on his lips.

"I've seen her! She's real pretty."

"Yes. Yes, she is."

The boy pouted. "You have all the fun."

Lysandro laughed. "You'll get your chance. Now I've got to be going. You should never keep a girl waiting."

Lysandro walked home on a cloud, counting the seconds until he saw Sera again. Before going to the Carras estate, he'd sent word to Marta that he wanted the house immaculate from top to bottom, and brightened up with fresh flowers. He wanted the house that might one day be Sera's home to be at its best to welcome her.

So he was not at all pleased to walk into his dining room to find his father seated at the table, sipping at a glass of wine with a plate of perfectly cubed cheeses laid out before him.

"What are you doing here?" he asked in a curt tone.

"Nice to see you too," Elias replied. "It's Tyrsday, isn't it?"

Lysandro groaned and covered his eyes with his hands. "It is. I'm sorry Father, but you've got to leave. I'm expecting company."

"Mm. She's in the kitchen."

Lysandro's brain temporarily ceased to function. "What did you say?"

"She's in. The. Kitchen," Elias repeated. He nibbled on another block of cheese.

It was suddenly unbearably hot in his dining room.

"Where's Marta?"

"I gave her the night off. A potential bride *should* be able to cook her husband a decent meal."

Lysandro couldn't form words. The meteoric rise in his blood pressure made his hands shake.

"Get out!"

"I beg your pardon?"

"I love you, but you need to leave now or I swear I'm going to strangle you."

Elias huffed as he threw down his napkin. "You're going to make me miss whatever is responsible for that fine smell?"

Lysandro heaved his father out of his chair, shoved him through the front door, and slammed it in his face. Then he raced to the kitchen as fast as his legs could carry him.

"Stop, stop, stop!" he shouted, barging in through the set of double doors. "Put that down this instant!"

Seraphine stood at the counter chopping carrots, calm as anything, with a pan of mushrooms sizzling away on the stove behind her.

"I did *not* invite you here for this! I can't even believe that my father sent you in here. And Marta! That traitor! She should have never allowed this. You're to be my guest, not my cook. How can I make this up to you Sera? I can't, can I? And who could blame you? I've been nothing but a complete ass. Merciful Faelia, why am I cursed with such terrible fortune?!"

Lysandro only stopped to take a breath and bury his head in his hands.

Sera looked at him, emitted a curious sound, then turned her head back to her work.

Lysandro's head popped up. "What was that? Did you just—" He got off the stool he'd collapsed onto and came daringly close to her. "Your face—it just did the strangest thing."

Her expression widened. A bright flush infused her cheeks, and she turned her face away.

"There it is again! The corners of your mouth, they—they curled upward! Can you do it again?"

"Stop," she giggled.

He stepped back, his eyes wide and his hand playfully clasping at his chest. "Incredible!"

"Have you never seen a smile before?"

"Not on you. I would have remembered."

Her flush deepened. It was contagious.

"Please stop. I beg you." Lysandro placed his hand gently atop hers to cease her chopping. "You must know I had nothing to do with this. I'll call Marta back."

"Don't you dare, or I'll never smile again. And you'll miss out on the best meal of your life."

"I'll what?"

"Sit down. Can't you see I'm cooking something here? I'm perfectly fine. Better than fine." She smiled again.

"You're serious?"

"I'm dead serious."

"But—"

"Lysandro. I'm happy to do it."

He was utterly flummoxed. But she was smiling—finally smiling—and it was glorious.

"Well...can I help, at least?" he asked, taking off his coat in favor of just his shirt.

She raised an eyebrow. "Can you?"

He narrowed his eyes at her. "I *am* capable of cutting vegetables, yes."

"We'll see," she said, and pushed the board of carrots in front of her toward him. She turned around to toss the mushrooms and remove them to a plate holding crisped bacon.

"I need those," she said, pulling another board in front of her, this one stacked with peeled potatoes.

"I'm almost done."

Sera's eyes kept darting to the carrots in Lysandro's hands as she turned her three potatoes into a pile of perfectly uniform cubes in a matter of seconds. She gathered them up and tossed them into the pan with a resounding sizzle, turning to wait for Lysandro. She pressed her hands to her hips until she couldn't take it anymore.

"Give me those, will you? You're driving me crazy." She took the carrots back from him and finished mincing them in the blink of an eye, the knife in her hand doing the work in rapid, confident movements.

"Sorry." Lysandro frowned.

"It's all right. If you want to help me, you could tie my hair back."

Lysandro jumped up at the invitation to runs his fingers through her silken tresses. He came to stand behind her as she tossed the contents of the frying pan with no more than a few quick flicks of her wrist. He took his time, gathering her hair delicately in both his hands, then wrapped the lot around his index finger. It was as smooth as he imagined, and equally soft. He tied a loosely twisted bun at the nape of her neck, then placed his arms on her shoulders.

"Is this okay?"

"Perfect. Thanks. You know, Marta really *wasn't* having it. But I insisted. Don't scold her for it, please."

"I won't."

"Can you imagine? My parents won't let me near our kitchen at home, telling me it's beneath my station."

His cheeks burned. "I didn't want you to have the wrong idea about why I invited you here tonight."

"And yet, your father seems to think I *should* be cooking dinner. You Andrans are so peculiar…"

"Are you not Andran?"

"Not in any of the ways that count."

"So—help me understand. Your parents sent you to a finishing school in Romagna…"

"Yes."

"And yet you've returned from Mirêne."

Her breath rose and fell as she contemplated her answer. After some consideration, and splashing the vegetables with the wine from the table, she said, "the boarding school my parents sent me to was expensive, which of course in their mind meant it was the best. But they had a certain reputation."

He raised an eyebrow in query.

"For beating their girls."

Lysandro felt the blood drain from his face.

She gave a sad, self-deprecating smile. "I was an unruly child."

He swallowed hard, his stomach dropping somewhere in the vicinity of his knees as he watched the smile fade from her face.

"I crossed the border into Mirêne in less than a year."

"How did you support yourself?"

Her expression turned rueful. "I found a job working in a kitchen. A very fine one."

Lysandro furrowed his brows. "I thought only boys were allowed to work in restaurants."

"*They* didn't know I was a girl," she said with a bat of her hand.

He blinked. "How could they miss that?"

"I'd cut my hair long before then. I learned very quickly that it was safer for me to travel as a boy."

He sighed in weary relief at that. At least the loss of her sun-kissed hair had afforded her some protection.

"You were not harassed, then?"

"Of course I was harassed. I was a foreigner who got the better jobs because I'm faster with a knife. But getting beaten was better than the alternative."

That settled it. He would go to Mirène and slaughter the lot of them.

"How did you bear it?"

"I already told you."

He cocked his head. "Did you?"

She flashed a wide smile, and the corner of her eyes crinkled. "I'm faster with a knife."

He laughed then, and reveled in the brightness of her eyes.

She removed the pan from the flame and allowed its contents to cool. "After a few years I was hired to work in the palace kitchen, where the young doge had a habit of spending his days." Her eyes glimmered, lost in a memory. "He knew the minute he looked at me that I was no boy. We've been thick as thieves ever since."

"How did he figure it out?"

"I don't know. I suppose I was getting older by then. Couldn't have kept it up forever."

Lysandro licked his lips at the obtuse reference to her curves. It was impossible that any man could miss them. But then again, the idea of any other man paying her his attentions soaked his thoughts in murder.

"And your parents know nothing."

She caught him in an intense stare. "Of *any* of this."

He rested his hand atop hers. "You can trust me."

"Thank you."

"I just hope you don't think I would expect you to cook, if you agree to marry me."

"For someone who has remained a bachelor for so long, you mention marriage a lot."

"I'll never do it again."

"I guess I'm just curious as to why you're not already married," she said, fanning all the vegetables she'd fried and preparing a long, thin cut of a young calf. "I've been listening all day to my mother alternatively complain that she and I have not been invited anyplace by the other mothers and preen herself on the thought that we haven't been invited because all the other girls have failed to gain your attention."

Lysandro shrugged. "I can't talk to any of them about art, tawdry mysteries—"

"They are *not* tawdry!"

"Or the hidden tombs of ancient heroes."

"Still. They seemed pretty enough."

He chuckled under his breath and shook his head. "None of them is even half as beautiful as you."

Lysandro's breath caught in his throat, not realizing what he'd said until after he'd said it.

"What?" Sera asked, batting her eyelashes. "Did you say something wrong?"

His voice dropped an octave. "Did I?"

"No." She returned his smile as she placed a layer of vegetables atop the meat, then a layer of bacon.

"Oh my," Lysandro said, turning the conversation. "That looks decadent."

"Here's the best part." With slow, deft fingers, she rolled the meat, tucking the filling into a tightly swirled bundle.

Lysandro handed her the spool of string set to the side without being prompted, and Sera tied it off and slid the roast into the oven.

"Okay. On to dessert." She wiped her hands and retrieved a bowl of eggs, a canister of sugar, and a jug of fresh cream from the corner.

"Dessert too?" he asked.

"What is dinner without dessert?"

She combined the eggs and sugar with ease, snapping her wrist with incredibly fast, almost invisible movements that produced a pale yellow foam. Without stopping, she nodded toward the jug of cream. "Pour that in here in a slow, steady stream."

Lysandro did as he was asked, watching in wonder as the mixture combined to form a smooth custard.

"Do you have shallow bowls, like for pudding?"

He rummaged through the cupboards above her head and pulled down a set of small porcelain vessels.

After filling them with the custard, she swiped at her cheek with her wrist, leaving a trail of sugar on her face.

Lysandro was mesmerized by the way her skin glistened. Little golden tendrils had escaped her coiffure, framing her slender chin and that provocative curl of her mouth. It drove Lysandro to distraction.

"Done with *that*," Sera said, leaving the tray next to the oven to wait their turn. When she opened the oven door, a scent of perfection came wafting toward them.

"Sweet heavens above that smells good," Lysandro said.

"Oh. I thought you didn't want me to slave away over a hot oven."

"Never mind what I said. Shall I carry that to the dining room?"

"Whatever for? We've got a perfectly good table right here."

She laid down the roast and slid the custards into the oven, straining the gravy that had been simmering away all the while. He sliced the meat to reveal a perfect spiral. When she lifted the plates to place on the worktable, he leapt to take them from her, setting them down on the adjoining corners.

"Allow me."

"Thank you."

Lysandro quickly became obsessed with her glittering skin; he couldn't think anymore. All his thoughts circled back to that sweet, shimmering spot high on her right cheek.

Sera caught him staring as if in a trance. "Is everything alright?"

"You—"

Her eyes questioned him as he stepped closer to her, and he put his hands to her cheek, pressing his thumb to that part of her skin that was sparkling.

"Oh—"

Lysandro gathered the sugar onto the top of his thumb and put the digit in his mouth. He watched her eyes for any sign that his touch was unwelcome. There wasn't one.

He returned his hand to her face, losing his fingers in her hair, and brushing that now clean spot on her cheek with his thumb. Sera gazed into his eyes as he closed the gap between them, and let out a sudden gasp.

He stepped back, crestfallen.

"I'm sorry. I—"

"No," Sera protested, brushing her cheeks to chase away the heat that had blossomed there. "Don't apologize."

Lysandro steadied himself and helped Sera to her seat before taking his own. He hid his embarrassment in his first bite of their meal, where his mind was redirected.

"Oh, that is sinfully good."

She beamed at his compliment. After a few quiet mouthfuls, she said, "I keep hearing about this Shadow of Theron."

Lysandro's food caught in his throat. "The Shadow of Theron?" he repeated.

"His name is on everyone's lips. Is he a villain, or a hero, do you think?"

"Why does it matter what I think?"

"I've heard so many things. One more opinion wouldn't hurt."

He considered his answer carefully.

"I wish I could say he wasn't necessary. But he makes the villagers feel safe, I think. Someone is looking out for them, even if Marek is not."

"He's not a criminal then, flouting the law by night?"

"I've only ever heard of him hurting anyone in defense of others."

"So he *is* like Theron."

Lysandro shook his head, burying his expression in his plate. "I don't know. There are no monsters here for him to slay. Only corrupt officials. Not really the same, is it?"

"Depends on the official, I guess."

She had unwittingly hit the nail on the head. Marek *was* a monster. What was Lysandro doing, if not fighting him?

"I imagine Marek would like nothing better than to clap him in irons," Sera said.

"With extreme enthusiasm."

"He's earned his title then, if he's willing to protect an entire village from Marek."

Lysandro willed the heat prickling his cheeks to fade.

"Perhaps."

Sera stood up to take the custards out of the oven. "I'll just clean up while these are cooling."

"Oh no, please, that really would be too much."

"Lysandro, I am *not* going to leave Marta's kitchen filthy after she so graciously let me use it."

"*Her* kitchen?"

"Don't kid yourself."

She hastily tidied the room, with Lysandro helping her at the pace of a mere mortal. He spied some blackening bananas on the edge of the counter and made to toss them in the rubbish bin before she leapt at him.

"What in six hells are you doing?"

"What? These are no good anymore."

"I'm going to teach you a lesson about *never* throwing away fruit."

In a matter of minutes, a batter of the imperiled bananas, sugar, butter, flour, and chocolate was rising in the oven. By then, dessert was ready.

Lysandro dug into the caramel crust with a satisfying crack, and moaned as he swallowed.

"You are always welcome here."

"Thanks, but I thought I was already."

He looked up and found she was already looking at him, giving him a sweet, perfect smile.

"You are. Next time, though, I'd like to treat *you*. There's an establishment a few towns over that I think will be up to your exacting standards. Will you come with me?"

She nodded. "What should I wear?"

"Hmm. Something you might wear to the theater."

"Understood."

Lysandro inhaled the newest fragrance in the kitchen, a heady blend of banana and chocolate. "I'm going to get very fat if you stay here much longer."

Sera pulled two golden brown loaves from the oven. "This one is for you—" she swatted his hand away— "not now, have it for breakfast, and this one's for Marta. Will you give it to her in the morning, with my thanks?"

"You're putting an awful lot of trust in me right here."

She cast him a look that set his blood on fire; it took everything he had not to gather her up in a passionate embrace.

They talked deep into the night. They laid in the grass of Lysandro's garden, gazing at the night sky as Lysandro reintroduced her to Lighura's constellations. It was quite late when he escorted Sera back to her house and bade her goodnight.

Sera rushed up to her bedroom. She stared smiling at the ceiling in her nightgown, thinking of how Lysandro had looked at her tonight, when their lips had almost met. His eyes were heather gray with streaks of cobalt—the same gray-blue eyes that had gazed into her soul and dried her tears from behind the Shadow of Theron's mask. Sleep evaded her as she recalled every exquisite word of his lovestruck entreaties.

9

LIGHURA'S BEST AND ONLY SURGEON OPENED HIS DOOR PROMPTLY ON THE second knock.

"Yes? Oh—Magistrate Marek. Is anything the matter?"

Lothan pushed through the door Rafael held closed in his hand without much effort and seated himself in the nearest chair. Its legs scraped against the black-and-white tiled floor of the parlor.

"Won't you have a seat?" Rafael asked in a curt tone. But Lothan's officious manner was unshakeable. He inspected the examining room with an air of distaste.

"No patients at this hour?"

"It's a slow morning."

Lothan nodded and gestured for Rafael to approach, as if it were his own home and Rafael had been the one who'd entered uninvited.

"What can I do for you, Magistrate?"

Lothan's face settled into a smug smile. He was eager to see how quickly the surgeon's expression would change once he understood the matter at hand, and how long it would take him to give Lothan what he wanted.

"You've benefitted from our friendship, haven't you?" he asked.

"Of course," Rafael answered, suddenly uneasy.

Lothan beckoned him closer. Rafael complied, sitting opposite Lothan and bringing their eyes level.

"So," Marek continued, "why would you sour that friendship by aiding my enemy?"

Lothan saw the corner of Rafael's mouth twitch in response. He pulled a mirror compact from his pocket and opened it to reveal a fine gray powder. A dark purple haze smoke furled from its surface like gunpowder on the verge of ignition.

Rafael's eyes widened in shock.

It was then that Lothan blew hard across the mirror, sending a wicked cloud into Rafael's eyes. He screamed and reeled back, toppling his chair. Blood streamed down his face from underneath the seams of his eyelids. Lothan wondered whether Rafael would resort to clawing his own eyes out to dull the pain, although of course it wouldn't.

Rafael lunged for the small table against the wall by the door, knocking over his surgical bag and sending his tools clattering to the floor. He groped the slick tiles and the remaining contents of the bag blindly, running his fingers over the labels of his many glass bottles and tinctures in vain.

Lothan clicked his tongue in mock sympathy. "I suppose you need your eyes to be a surgeon, don't you?"

Rafael's search grew more frantic as his pain intensified.

Lothan became irate at being ignored. He leapt to his feet and kicked the surgical bag out of reach.

"Why don't you heal yourself, you treacherous fool? The same way you healed the Shadow of Theron!" He stepped on Rafael's hand, crushing his fingers beneath his boot. "With the benefit of *my* generosity!"

"I...can't!" Rafael screamed. "Haven't...got it...anymore!" His whole body quaked. The pain shooting through his skull caused him to retch.

Lothan pushed his boot harder into the surgeon's hand. "Careful doctor, or pretty soon they'll be nothing left of your livelihood," he said through grinding teeth.

"Gone! Gone!"

"On the Shadow?!" Lothan demanded.

Rafael trembled.

"Used...everything! Please! I...need more!"

Lothan removed his foot and crouched down, bringing himself nose to nose with Rafael's mangled face.

"Tell me who the Shadow is, and maybe I'll give you something for your eyes."

Rafael screamed, and Lothan saw a fresh stream flow down the channels staining his cheeks.

"The Shadow!"

"I...don't...don't know!"

"You dare lie to me?!"

"Swear...ngh...Goddess..."

Rafael's oaths darkened Lothan's temper; he didn't want to believe them. He wanted to dash the surgeon's brains across the table.

"How could you not know?!"

Rafael moaned, his words turned incoherent.

Lothan grabbed him by his collar and pulled him to his feet. He shook him hard.

"The Shadow! The Shadow for your eyes! And *don't* fucking mumble at me like an idiot!"

Rafael inhaled sharp rapid breaths that scorched his lungs.

"I...I heard a noise, at my window! He took my bag—when he gave it back, the stones were gone! I never saw him! Please, Marek! My eyes! My eyes..."

Lothan peeled the lid of Rafael's left eye open.

Rafael's pitch jumped two octaves when air hit his pupil. Lothan stared curiously as he watched the ground bits of bone rove over the surgeon's eye like starved carrion beetles, searching out his blood vessels and tearing them to shreds. Lothan seethed, but he believed that the surgeon was telling the truth. The man would never withstand such ruination if he could help it. He growled and released the surgeon's collar.

Rafael crumpled to the ground. He was still screaming Lothan's name when he left the surgeon sprawled out in a pool of his own blood.

HE SHOULD HAVE USED THE SURGEON TO SET A TRAP. IT MIGHT NOT HAVE been as satisfying as slicing the Shadow open, but having someone he trusted poison him would have sufficed. Lothan had been too eager, too quick to confront the surgeon without a plan. Nothing concerning Theron's impostor was easy, and he should have known this would be no different. Marek had missed an opportunity, and it put him in a foul mood.

He preoccupied himself with the preparations for the coming night to stop his squandered revenge from gnawing at him. His deputies huddled around his desk, peering into a nondescript crate.

"We were able to pinch two silver candlesticks, a silver service and a porcelain tea set," Jenner said, rifling through their loot.

"Any jewels?" Lothan asked.

"Nothing to speak of, really. A small pearl brooch, a gold wedding band. A timepiece. Nothing exotic. You told us not to hit another don's house, so we went middle of the road."

"Hmm. This might be enough for the upcoming trade, but it doesn't recoup what we lost from Carras. Have we heard back from the *Siren* yet?"

The deputy swallowed. "We have."

"Well?"

"They said they'll only come back if you can double their price."

"Double?!" Lothan repeated.

Jenner nodded. "Said it's not worth their while otherwise. Rumors of the Examiners are heating up, and they don't want to tangle with the Aruni."

Lothan grimaced.

Then he felt the gentle lapping of the broken blade at his hip like a seductive whisper. His expression hardened.

"Tell them it's a deal."

His brother's brows lifted in confusion, but his countenance slowly shifted as understanding came over him. Jenner bared his teeth, mirroring Lothan's wicked grin. He nodded, then headed off to set it up.

Lothan and his men put on their best faces when the newly burgled head of the Montes family came storming in before lunch.

"Right here, Signor, go straight in to see the magistrate himself," one of the lieutenants said, and led the fuming man through the doors to Lothan's office.

"Good afternoon, Signor Montes," Lothan started. "I'm so sorry to hear of your losses. Won't you sit down and—"

"Look here, Marek. It's your duty to keep this village safe. Now I've lived here all my life, and never have I felt compelled to lock my door at night. But since you've taken up this post, I can't name a single soul who feels safe, even in their own homes. Arun's sake man, I have young children!"

Lothan breathed steadily through his nose, and chose his words with care.

"We take such crimes very seriously. I assure you, we'll do everything we can to—"

"Like you did for the blacksmith? Or Don Carras? Quite frankly, Marek, I don't think you could catch a mouse. But when you hung that man, you promised us this nasty business was over!"

Considering the man hadn't lost much of value, Lothan thought his response was a bit extreme. But this was exactly the kind of sentiment he couldn't allow to grow. Being ousted prematurely would see all his fine plans ground to dust. He clenched his jaw to restrain himself, which only lent to his air of indifference. He didn't like the man's condescending tone. He responded by infuriating the man with protocol.

"If you'd like to fill out a report and describe what's missing, I'll send two deputies to your house to investigate, and—"

"To six hells with your report! What are you going to *do* about it, Marek! What?!"

"I can do nothing without a formal complaint from you, Signor."

"You can't do anything *with* it either, it seems. Don't you worry about a formal complaint. I know *exactly* where to lodge it!"

Montes slammed the door on his way out.

Lothan dug his fingernails into the wood grain of his desk. "Gorin!" he barked.

The deputy manning the front desk came scrambling in. "Yes, Lord Lothan?"

"Signor Montes is displeased, and plans on filing a formal complaint against this office."

Gorin just stared, unsure of the response Lothan expected.

"Intercept his mail, imbecile."

The man nodded with vigor. "Sure, right. Of course. Leave it to me."

Lothan let out an exasperated sigh. If he'd still had Jair, he wouldn't have had to spell it out. And the result might have been infinitely more to his liking.

"Out!" he shouted, and he was quickly left alone again to wallow in his setbacks. The only consolation was the slick metal that beckoned on his skin. He yielded to it, feeling his temperature rise as the scent of blood filled his nostrils.

When the need to act on his hunger rose to a pitch he could no longer ignore, the Alvaró girl came to mind. He left his post in the middle of the afternoon to pay her a visit, but again he was stymied.

"I'm sorry, Magistrate Marek, but we have to make the best choice for our daughter," Don Alvaró said when he opened the door.

"And you think de Castel is the best thing for her?" he snorted.

Alvaró laughed. "He said almost the exact same thing about you."

"Did he..."

"Look, I understand how you feel, but you can't deny that he has good qualities."

"Such as?"

Alvaró gave him a patronizing smile. "Come on, Marek. I shouldn't have to explain this to you."

Lothan said nothing, betrayed no hint of understanding.

"I'm telling you this not just as Seraphine's father but as your friend. De Castel has titles. He has wealth. He comes from the finest family in Lighura. He can offer my daughter greater security, and a position in the village that's more worthy of her birth."

Lothan's eyes narrowed. "I'm not looking to marry her, Carlo, I just want to have a chat. Maybe take a walk around the village."

"Ah, see, but de Castel *is* looking to marry her. And she's agreed to entertain his suit, for the time being."

Lothan took a step back. He hadn't expected Lysandro to move so quickly. Or for his so-called friend to put up so much resistance.

"I have given Don de Castel my word that I will not hear any other suitors until Seraphine has rejected his offer. Good day, Marek."

Alvaró shut the door. Just like that, Lothan was relegated to whatever scraps de Castel left behind. He hadn't even made it into the house.

Marek didn't go back to the office. He chose instead to release his fury on the middle-aged widow who lived two houses down from him. He replayed his conversations with Alvaró and Montes in his head as he bore down on her.

No matter where he turned, even among his allies, he was a public servant. He fumed at their fixation on the condition of his birth, how his inability to claim a prestigious lineage prevented him from getting the respect he deserved. If they only knew. If only…

"Not so rough, Lothan," the widow bellowed from beneath him.

"Shut up."

He gripped her hips harder, clawing at her skin as he ignored her protests.

"You bastard!" she cried as he released her. "Don't come back here."

"I'll do as I please," he retorted, and tossed a few coins to the floor on his way out.

He came later than usual to the coast, approaching his dark sanctuary carved into the cliffside close to midnight. He was surprised to find his brothers milling about on the beach near the entrance.

"What the fuck are you all doing out here? Are you asking to be seen?!"

Lothan scanned their blank faces with rising impatience. And then he saw it. The mouth of the cave was collapsed, sealed shut.

"What in six hells…"

There was no other way in. Lothan put his hand to the wall of granite to test it, but it was no use. Even if they worked all night and managed to shake the rubble loose, more would just come crashing down upon them.

Lothan howled with rage, and bloodied his fingernails against the unyielding barrier. Then a slow, subtle sound slipped into his ear. He closed his eyes and cocked his head to listen. The steady lapping of blood at his hip became a rushing tide as he strained to hear the infernal voice beyond the wall.

After a long silence, his eyes snapped open. He spun around to look upon his brothers. They were hungry for his words, for a command that would dispel their confusion. Their fear.

"Theron's Impostor has done this," he snarled.

The faces staring back at him hardened.

"He has taken from us what was ours. Now we are going to take something from him."

Sancio was just about to sit down to a late supper of juicy beef and boiled potatoes when High Priestess Beatríz hooked him by the elbow and pulled him away from the table.

"You've had enough food," she said as she led him into the hallway.

He craned his neck to spy his untouched plate, then turned back to her stern face.

"I haven't eaten anything yet."

"You ate enough food this morning to last you a lifetime."

The high priestess's harsh words stung. He didn't know how to respond.

"There's a Morgassen temple in San Treya. Do you want me to recommend you?"

"What?" His appetite evaporated.

"You're not cut out to be an Aruni. You're better suited to the life of a scholar. We both know it."

"But I don't want to leave," Sancio protested.

Beatríz sighed in exasperation. "When you first came to us, I thought your aim was to break out of that bulbous shell you call a body. If anything, you've gained more weight."

Sancio's face flushed. He'd noticed, of course, but he hadn't thought anyone else had. "It's not exactly easy to shrink my waist when there's salted meat and butter everywhere I turn," he said in retort.

"That food is meant to help energize those who *use* their bodies. Almighty Arun, Sancio, you don't even try, and you reward yourself by eating three times more than the rest."

Sancio felt tears stinging the corner of his eyes, but he refused to let them fall.

"The intention was never to shrink you," Beatríz continued, "but to turn your size into a weapon. You could be a giant, if only you fed strength and endurance, rather than being a slave to your belly."

Sancio said nothing.

Beatríz gestured with her chin, and led him through the training grounds, past the novice hall into the arena for advanced acolytes. It was a space he had only ever entered to clean.

Sturdy ropes swung tauntingly from the ceiling, and weapons big and small lined the walls. Heavy beams were erected at varying heights and odd angles, scattered throughout the space to create a simulated mountain range. From here, trainees were expected to battle each other. Sancio had seen the grievous injuries incurred from falling, or from an opponent's blade when someone was preoccupied with trying desperately *not* to fall. The scent of blood and sweat hung permanently in the air. He sensed that whatever the high priestess said next was going to be painful.

"Go on, then," she said.

Sancio's eyes scanned her face, then the arena, looking for some clue.

"Go on then...what?"

"Cross the ridge, if you wish to stay."

He laughed, but the sound died in his throat at the sight of the scowl forming at the corners of Beatríz's mouth.

"How can you expect me to—"

"The same way we expect it of *every* Aruni," she cut him off. She turned to the wall, grabbed the heaviest broadsword perched there, and strapped it to Sancio's back. His knees buckled under the sudden weight, and Beatríz pulled him upright by the scruff of his neck.

"Don't forget your weapon," she said, her voice frosty.

Sancio could already feel his legs screaming at the injustice. His eyes bulged when the high priestess turned to leave.

"How long must I do this?" he called after her.

She whipped her head around to stare at him, and Sancio stumbled backward.

"If you haven't had a heart attack by morning, maybe I'll let you have breakfast."

Sancio had no breath to complain. And after ten minutes of trying and failing to mount the first crest, he was positive that there wasn't enough air in the entire arena to fill his heaving lungs. Each time he attempted to climb, he fell, dragged down by the ungainly sword and his own clumsiness. Each fall was more damaging than the last; whenever he landed on his back, the thick handle of the blade dug into him. Angry red welts swelled with every twitch of his shoulders as he clambered for a foothold. After a particularly nasty crash that had left him dizzy, he slumped over the first bar, and waited for the world to come to a standstill.

Stopping for breath was almost worse. His face felt like it was on fire, and sweat stung his eyes. He wanted to throw up, but couldn't because his lungs were working so hard just to keep him from passing out. His heart hammered in his chest and he was afraid to move, afraid he would collapse if he loosened his grip. He'd be found dead in the morning, he was sure of it, just a useless puddle of bruises and sweat.

For more than half an hour he hung immobilized, clinging to the first bar like an infant to his mother's skirts. If he was to survive this night, Sancio decided, he was going to need something to eat.

He peeled himself off the edge of the mountain made of wood and shuffled his feet toward the door. He tried to unfasten the sword the high priestess had strapped to him, but his fingers were like jelly, and he couldn't manage the buckle. He had no choice but to take it with him in search of food.

It was a little past midnight. The temple was robed in blackness save for the small heat of the glowing embers in the brazier and the soft moonlight that gleamed off the pristine white columns. No one else was around to ask why he was holing himself up in the confessional with a broadsword. He sat down with a heavy thunk, and nearly went head over heels when he bent to retrieve the half-eaten chicken bun from lunch that he'd stored there. He stopped short of shoving it into his mouth in one bite.

If he didn't do as the high priestess ordered, she'd cast him out. He'd never heard of anyone casting off temple robes against their will, but it was reasonable to assume that the shame of it would be unbearable.

Lysandro made such physical tests as Beatríz demanded look easy. Sancio imagined him hopping from one crest to the other with ease, brandishing his sword in the air as if it weighed no more than a wooden stick. That wasn't him. It would *never* be him.

But Lysandro would be married soon. There wasn't any scenario in which Sancio could see the Alvaró girl not agreeing to marry him. Lysandro was wealthy. He was kind. And he was drop-dead gorgeous.

There was no girl on the planet that could resist him. And once Lysandro took a bride, he'd have precious little time to spend with his childhood playmate. Sancio loved his friend and wanted him to be happy. He just wasn't prepared to be there to see it.

His mind made up, Sancio opened his mouth to enjoy his hard-earned dinner. But a commotion at the front of the temple made him drop his bun.

He had his hand pressed to the door to open it and investigate when he heard the magistrate's booming voice.

"Be quick."

Sancio had just enough time to duck his head before Marek and a dozen or so of his lackeys passed the confessional door. How he wished he could shrink now, wished he could make himself as small and as insignificant as an insect as he wriggled silently into the gap underneath the bench. His head and his shoulders poked out, but he was flat against the floor and could not be seen. The echo of heavy boots masked the sound of the scabbard sliding around his chest and landing on the floor.

"Lift this thing up," Sancio heard Marek say. From the distance of their voices, he guessed they were trying to upend the altar. The idiots. It was solid marble, carved from a single block from the top to the base, and built into the floor in a perfect interlocking design. There were no easy seams or corners, no way to lift it by so much as an inch. He heard a tremendous amount of grunting and swearing, but the marble was silent, immovable.

Marek hissed at his men again. "They're hiding something powerful here, something worth more than this whole stinking village. Find it!"

Sancio's thumb grazed the handle of the sword. He gripped it, for a sense of security, if nothing else. It was no use pretending he could use the weapon, or that Marek wouldn't slice him open the second he was found. But if he could manage to get the sword out of its scabbard without detection, it was just possible that he could unwittingly skewer someone if they barged in on his hiding place. Even a few seconds more might make the difference between life and death if Beatríz heard the clamor. Which was increasingly likely, as Marek and his officers tore the temple apart.

Their search seemed haphazard to Sancio's ears, first in one corner, then another; they had no clue where to look for whatever it was that they hoped to find. Sancio was a young, untested acolyte, and not privy to the secret of what sacred treasure the Aruni protected in his own temple. The open layout of the temple was unforgiving. There were no easy nooks or crannies, nowhere obvious for something to hide. Except the prayer booth.

Sancio heard the splintering of wood, and the echo of books and undefinable objects being tossed to the floor.

"Here it is!" This is what I was telling you about," another man said.

Sancio's breath caught in his throat. What were they after that they had now found? He prayed that they would take whatever it was and leave, but his pleas to the Goddess went unanswered.

"Tear up the prayer books. All of them," Marek said. "I will find what I seek in the ashes."

The brazier crashed to the floor, followed by the crisp snapping of paper. Then he heard the worst noise of all—the shattering of glass. The temple window, the sacred image honoring Theron's triumph over Argoss and the pride of Lighura, was gone. Sancio pressed his hand to his mouth, feeling its loss deep in his chest. But he didn't make a sound.

Footsteps approached and stopped in front of the door to the booth on the other side, away from Sancio. The door fell inward, torn from its hinges and heaped onto the flames. Sancio couldn't pry the sword loose from its scabbard. The hilt was lodged against the door at a bad angle, and was insanely heavy.

The door he hid behind was kicked in, and came swinging fast at his head. His body was already in such twisted agony that he barely registered the pain. He ground his teeth and bore it in silence. His vision failed; he blinked, but the world stayed stubbornly black. The planks comprising the booth had fallen in on him, keeping him from view as the center structure and the wooden divider were ripped apart. At any moment, he expected the plank to be lifted off his head and given to the flames. He readied himself to be discovered in the same moment. But that moment never came. There was another noise, one from the far end of the temple behind the altar. The Aruni were coming.

Sancio heard the snapping of fingers, and Marek's men retreated, gone before the high priestess could lay eyes on any of them.

Sancio was up like a shot, exploding from his hiding place to help smother the flames as warriors and novices poured into the temple.

The prayer books were burnt beyond repair, but not much else. The stone pillars had resisted the flames, and the brazier was quickly righted again. But the temple window was reduced to a gaping hole with its center hollowed out. The servants of Arun cleared away the debris, treating the shards of colored glass with the utmost reverence. The diamond that had been the focal point of Theron's arrow was found intact among the rubble, but it was a small consolation.

The Aruni went about the work of restoring the temple to order, as much as it could be, with empty expressions. No one spoke for more than a few seconds, and even then, their words came out in disbelieving murmurs.

When there was no more that he could do, Sancio approached the high priestess. She was standing behind the altar, staring into a locked cabinet that had been forced open.

"Beatríz?"

She turned, her face ashen. "It's gone," she said, looking in his direction but not really seeing him.

"What did they take?" he asked.

"The Histories."

Sancio shook his head; he didn't understand. "But why would they—"

"There are things in those books that could prove dangerous, if discovered by the wrong people."

Of course. Having never come to a service himself, Marek would know very little about the faces of the Goddess and the Age of Theron. Marek had been guessing up to this point, but it had only gotten him so far. If Marek truly wanted to possess the power of Argoss, he had to know where to look.

"I was here, High Priestess," Sancio said in a soft voice.

She looked up at him, suddenly seeing him.

"I was here when it happened."

"Did you see them?"

"No. But I heard...I heard Magistrate Marek."

She snorted. "How can you be sure, if you didn't see them?"

"I'm *sure*," he insisted. "It is as the Shadow of Theron told us."

"The Shadow of Theron," Beatríz moaned, squeezing the bridge of her nose between her forefinger and thumb.

"We should trust him," Sancio urged.

Beatríz ignored his comment and looked more closely at him. She furrowed her brow.

"You're still wearing the sword."

His gaze turned quickly over his shoulder, then back at her. "Oh. Yes. Couldn't undo the strap."

She raised an inquiring eyebrow.

"I was...I was looking for food. And, thinking on your offer," he said.

"Where did you hide?"

"What?"

"They didn't notice you. Where did you hide?" she asked, louder.

"I was in the prayer booth."

"The prayer booth's destroyed."

"They kicked it in when there were setting fire to the place."

Beatríz folded her arms across her chest. "They didn't discover you then?"

"No."

"Didn't you cry out?"

"No, High Priestess."

She took his hands in hers without warning and flipped them over to inspect his palms. She cocked her head, confused.

"You held the sword."

"Yes. Well, sort of. I was thinking one of them might run themselves through with it if they weren't expecting it. But I didn't have enough room to unsheathe it."

"You didn't run."

"I hid," Sancio corrected.

"You hid yourself in the place where we have the most to hide."

"I—what?"

Beatríz ignored the question. "You stayed."

"I didn't really think I could outrun them," Sancio said shortly.

"So. You managed not to get yourself killed. And you've been here all night, and all morning. With that sword strapped to your back."

Sancio paused. "Yes." He felt awkward under her scrutiny for so long, and wished to evade it. "I'll stay as long as you need me to, but I have thought about what you said. Your suggestion may be for the best. I'll go to San Treya, if they'll have me."

Beatríz tongued the inside of her cheek as she considered him.

"For now," she said, "I have something I need you to do."

"Of course."

"Something you can't tell a soul about."

"Anything."

She stepped closer to him. "It must be done now, and no one must see you."

Sancio nodded. Her grave tone made the hair on his arms stand on end.

Beatríz's gaze drifted to the floor above which the confessional used to stand.

"Get the hammer from the swordsmith's."

10

Eugenie was alone and freezing. The wind above her head howled. Hidden in the snow beside her was a body.

She scrambled to uncover the grave, clawing at the snow with her hands, but it was futile. Then suddenly the air stilled, and the swirling wind died all around her. She heard the footsteps of someone approaching. But it wasn't Asha. It was a man—the most beautiful man she had ever seen, with fair hair kissed by sunlight and eyes a fathomless gray, streaked with the blue of storm clouds. He towered over her. In his hand, he held a gleaming white sword of carved bone. She tried to read the runes carved into the groove of the blade, but they wouldn't come together. Strapped across his back was the golden bow.

He was so brilliant she needed to shield her eyes, but she couldn't. She dared to look up at him, this sun made man, and then he was gone, as if he had never been there. She saw him in the far distance, pacing back and forth on a ledge high atop the mountains. The wind whipped his fair hair across his face, but still he trapped her with his eyes.

He whispered to her, low and urgent. But the wind filled her ears and she couldn't make out the words. The sound was too faint and far away. It was only enough to know it was there.

"I can't understand you," she pleaded. The current beneath the air became sharper, more insistent. But his words were battered by the winds, their edges worn away by time. The contours of his mouth as he gave shape to soundless words carved themselves into her memory. Her gaze lingered there, on the curve of his lips, as a cheerful knock at the door startled her awake. Her eyes snapped open. Behind her eyelids, he was still there—his urgent, pleading eyes and the voice she could not fathom. The knock came again, and snapped the tether that bound her to her dreams. Her chest fell as the image of him faded. But not completely.

Her limbs were chilled and wooden, her tongue felt glued to the roof of her mouth.

Asha spoke first; it was more of a grunt than a word.

"Good morning, Sisters," Mirabel called out from the other side of the door. "I thought you might join me for an early walk, as we discussed."

Asha groaned. "Give us a minute."

Asha's face was at the same time haggard and murderous. Eugenie imagined that she didn't look any better herself. They'd spent the better part of the night riding through Lareina, crossing the entire town headfirst through the brunt of the storm only to realize that their mad search was in vain. The relics of the temple were not hidden in some unknown cabinet, but had been removed beyond Lareina's borders. Though their task had just begun, the prospect of having already fallen behind dampened their spirits.

Asha threw the blankets off herself. They landed on Eugenie's face.

"Hey!" she cried as she flailed her arms to free herself.

Asha groaned again in apology. She lumbered over to the fireplace where the flames she had stoked only scant hours before were reduced to embers.

"These aren't dry yet," Asha said, feeling the sodden fabric of their Examiner's robes. She poked and prodded the fire back to life, then pulled the garment she'd worn to bed over her head and rummaged through her belongings for clean clothes.

Eugenie didn't mean to stare, but the way the muscles of Asha's shoulders rippled as she dressed was hypnotic. Her body was hardened and powerful. Her own soft, fair flesh felt insignificant by comparison.

The scoring between Asha's shoulder blades didn't mar Eugenie's perception of Asha's perfect body; it was proof that it was capable of anything, that it could carry Asha through the six hells and come out the other side.

Eugenie got to her feet and threw her usual robe on over her thin nightgown.

"That'll scare 'em," Asha said. She pointed to the frilly border of her sleeping dress poking out from beneath her robe.

"I didn't bring a lot of extra clothes," Eugenie snapped back.

"Couldn't fit them in that giant bag of yours?"

"Hey listen!—"

"Yeah?" Asha stopped Eugenie's advance with a raised index finger. "*That's* the face you need to put on in front of the villagers today." Asha gave her a wry smile. It caught on Eugenie's mouth too.

Together, she and Asha followed the high priestess into the garden at the rear of the temple. It was the most extensive cultivated plot Eugenie had ever seen. Neat rows of vegetables and berries gave way to a riot of color blossoming in every shape and size. Mushrooms flourished on the shaded footpaths. They clustered near tree roots or, in some instances, grew out of the trunks themselves, like a stepladder for fairies or winged imps. Lush plants and spotted foliage forged a winding path throughout, connecting the different areas with a maze-like logic. The vegetation grew thicker as they progressed along the circuitous route. Eugenie turned around, expecting to see the windows lining the eastern temple wall. But the pink glow of the impending sunrise saturated what *should* have been the northern sky. She'd been turned around somehow, reoriented when she wasn't expecting it. The labyrinth was not some collection of neatly trimmed hedges just around the next bend, Eugenie realized. Her eyes glimmered.

"It's not quite what I expected," she said, not caring to mask the wonder in her voice.

"That's true for most," Mirabel replied. A proud smile crept up the corners of her mouth. "But losing oneself in here often leads to finding that which you most seek. If you'll look down, you'll see—"

"Don't stop." Asha interrupted her in a low, brusque voice. "Just take us to the center."

"Y-yes, of course," Mirabel answered. Her footsteps faltered only a moment before she carried on, squeezing her thick frame through two intertwined olive trees seemingly caught in a lover's embrace. She beckoned the Examiners to follow. Eugenie slipped through the gap with ease. Asha struggled, and pulled at her sword in its sheath. It appeared to have wedged itself into the small crack where the two trunks were woven together.

"Just a minute." Asha grunted, putting her foot flat on the trunk to give herself more leverage to pull.

"I'm afraid not," Mirabel said. "You won't pass through no matter what you do."

Asha stopped and looked up. "Is that right?" she asked with heaving breaths. Mirabel's gaze didn't waver. "There is no violence permitted past this gate. You may leave your weapons on the ground. They will remain untouched."

Eugenie watched with interest as Asha pulled her weapon free from between the two trees, back in the direction from which she'd come, without any fuss. She turned the blade over curiously in her hand, and tried to push it through the gap, pointed edge first. It met hard resistance, like stabbing an impossibly clear window.

"Huh," was Asha's only reply. She laid down her blade in the grass, and added a set of throwing knives, a dagger, two drams of a viscous black fluid, and a vial of a fine colorless powder alongside it.

Eugenie crossed the threshold and rejoined Asha. She pored over the bark and peered under the leaves at the tree's base.

Asha raised an eyebrow. "Lost something?"

"No," Eugenie said, her smile going wide. "Found it." She pulled back a thick patch of brambles and exposed one of the leftmost tree's thick roots. Etched on the edge of the bark before it dipped into the soil was a pair of strangely curved symbols.

"A dear friend inscribed that many years ago," Mirabel explained. "No one's ever found those wards before," Mirabel replied, nodding in approval at Eugenie.

"It wasn't *that* well-hidden," Asha said.

"It's not just the brambles that cloak the wards," Eugenie said. She let the leaves covering the markings fall into place and gestured to Asha. "Try it."

Asha knelt and sifted through the growth in the same spot. "Wait—"

With two hands, she ruffled the leaves in a wide arc, looked under every crevice and shadow. She still couldn't find them again. She stood, put her hands to her hips, and grunted.

"We're almost to the center," Mirabel said. "Come." She led the Examiners around the edges of a small orchard of trees that reached no higher than Asha's shoulder, then through a dense, thorny thicket before emerging into a clearing with a reflective pool in the center, surrounded by polished stones that glittered like crystals. Eugenie heard the faint twinkling of glass as lanterns swayed in the gentle breeze. She sat on the edge of the pool, but she could not spy the bottom of the clear water. It was more of a well than a pool, but without the expected darkness.

"I apologize if I offended you earlier," Asha said to Mirabel. "I only wished not to draw any attention to our true destination."

"Of course. I understand."

"This labyrinth is quite overgrown in places."

The high priestess bristled. "Everything in the labyrinth is as we intend it to be."

"What I'm trying to say is, given the abundance of nature here, how sure are you that the ground was undisturbed? Is it possible that the digging took place not over the course of one night, but several?"

Eugenie didn't hear Mirabel's answer. Her mind was bent on something else. She pulled out a thick leather roll from inside her robe, bearing the same Morgassen symbol burnt into the leather as her bag of runes. She unfurled it along the crystalline edge of the well and extracted a vial of a fine white substance, a brown speckled feather of a greater horned owl, and a small stone drill with sigils carved into the side. She was about to retrieve the other necessary items from their places when she heard the high priestess and Asha coming closer. She quickly folded everything up before either of them could see.

"You ready Gin?" Asha asked. "Mirabel's going to ring the bell."

"Just a minute. I'll find my own way."

Asha's eyes narrowed as she tried to decipher the intent behind her words. She leaned down to press her hand to Eugenie's shoulder.

"Keep them out," Eugenie murmured.

Asha nodded and headed back out of the labyrinth after Mirabel.

Eugenie was quick, but thorough. She tried to work in an orderly fashion, but the logic of the labyrinth thwarted her. More than once, she found herself following her own tracks, and at least twice she came upon entirely new areas that Mirabel hadn't shown them. As much as she could, she raced against the tolling of the bell as it summoned all of Lareina to the temple. No one disturbed her; if anyone had tried to enter the garden, she was too far away to hear it. It was far more likely that Asha had scared them off with that look that was more like a snarl.

Drawing down the power of Morgasse drained her. By the time Eugenie finally emerged from the labyrinth, her knees threatened to give way beneath her. It was a relief to see Asha's solid back come into view from behind one of the trees marking the entrance to the garden.

Just one more, she told herself, and knelt at the roots for one final surge of sorcery.

Hairo approached from the temple just as Eugenie braced herself against the heavy trunk and stood up.

"All the village is assembled," he said.

"Great," Eugenie sighed.

Startled, Asha turned around. Eugenie waved off the concern in Asha's wide eyes.

"Hairo, I think I left something at the center, but I'll never find my way back again in time. Fetch it for me, will you?"

"With pleasure."

He moved past Asha, but he stopped almost dead in his tracks as he neared the trees that marked the beginning of the labyrinth. He started backward, then forward again like a spooked horse. His brows furrowed and he lifted his face, seeming to sniff the air. His wild eyes settled back on Eugenie.

"You know, uh, maybe it'll be better if I get it after. So you're not late."

Eugenie managed a smirk. "Fine."

Hairo spun around and scurried back to the temple.

"What did you do?" Asha asked, turning an incredulous face to Eugenie.

"The kissing tree gave me the idea."

"You set wards on the *entire* labyrinth?"

"What I could find of it. I'm not sure if I caught all the loose ends. He can't pass through here again, at any rate."

"That's good work. Eugenie, listen…"

Eugenie looked up, suddenly attentive.

"We didn't come here to make friends. They should be afraid. Afraid that you can see right into their souls."

"I *can*," Eugenie retorted. "With a little effort."

Asha nodded. "But they must believe it. When you look at someone, really *look* at them. Make them think their lies have nowhere to hide."

"They don't."

"Alright." Asha pulled her hood up. Eugenie did the same, grateful for the excuse to hide the exhaustion in her eyes.

The curious murmur of the townsfolk ceased when the Examiners entered the temple. Asha pulled the heavy doors closed behind them with a resounding echo. Eugenie saw more than one set of shoulders jump at the thunderous noise. The gaping faces turned as Mirabel addressed the crowd from behind the altar.

"Brothers and sisters, today I bear grave news. A few weeks ago, a relic from the Age of Theron, and other sacred objects, were stolen from our temple."

The news revived the people's humming. Eugenie found it curious that Mirabel had waited until now to reveal even this much. What she said next surprised the congregation even more.

"Such dark days have come not only to us, but to villages across Andras. As you well know, it is the sacred duty of the priestesses of Faelia, Morgasse, and Arun to hold and protect these proofs of the Goddess's powers. The theft of them is a severe infraction against the temple, against Andras, and against the Goddess herself. To answer these crimes, the Council of Three has sent us Examiners from the Orders of Morgasse and Arun. Their duty is to examine your conscience, to recover what has been stolen, and to punish those who have offended the Goddess with their selfishness and greed."

As Mirabel spoke, Eugenie slowly paced around the temple. She set out a path for herself in her mind to give her steps the air of determination. As she passed, children clutched their mothers, as they in turn clung to their husbands. Most only peered at her out of the corners of their eyes. Some turned their heads sharply away—in fear, Eugenie supposed, not outrage. Some stared straight ahead, pretending that Eugenie simply wasn't there. At one point, she stopped at the end of an aisle, purely for dramatic emphasis. The reaction was dramatic indeed as the air in the temple stood still. Only when she began walking again did the worshippers release their collective breath. A frail-looking woman in her middle years dropped to her seat in a dead faint and had to be carried out.

"It has been decided," the high priestess continued, "that the priestesses of Faelia, myself included, will play no part in the role these esteemed Examiners must now play, except to open our arms to them and offer whatever aid they may require. I ask you to do the same. Open your homes to them. Welcome them to your table. Provide them with all the comfort, generosity, and kindness that mark us as the children of Faelia. And above all—you will share with them what you know, to help them in a speedy recovery of the treasures of the Three Temples, and to expunge the sinners from our midst."

Mirabel lifted her gaze from her congregation to Asha, who was as still as a statue against the temple doors. Her hood obscured her face in shadow. The hilt of her sword was the only thing about her that was plainly visible. Her voice boomed in the solemn space.

"Those who present themselves to us will receive mercy. Those who fail to submit to the Goddess will suffer Arun's swift justice."

Silence reigned in the temple. Asha stepped aside and opened the doors to let in the morning sunshine.

At first, not a soul moved. They dared not even breathe. Then a wealthy-looking family from the front returned to their senses and exited their row, shuffling their feet through the doors and back into the daylight. The day did not seem so bright as it had a moment before.

Asha ground her teeth as she met Hairo's gaze and moved along the current of people pouring out of the temple to catch up to him.

"You made quite the impression, Madame Examiner," he said. "May the Goddess bless your efforts."

He couldn't even manage to make it *sound* sincere. Any effort to do so was undermined by the smirk that he failed to suppress. He and his brethren had disturbed a centuries-long peace, and had done it with pride.

"Actually, there's something you can do to aid us in our task," Asha said.

"Yes?"

"I asked the High Priestess if I could enlist the service of someone she trusted highly. She directed me to you."

Hairo's shoulders broadened, and his smile gleamed white. "Whatever I can do to help the Goddess in these dark times."

The way he invoked the Goddess was like a jeer on his lips. Asha wanted to knock his jaw out of alignment just to stop him from saying it. But there was more at stake than the need to satisfy her rage. So she stayed her fists and instead stepped closer to him, lowering her voice to a conspiratorial tone.

"This letter *must* reach the Council of Three without delay. It is of vital importance," she said. She held out a small scroll in her hand.

"Have you discovered something?" he asked.

"Yes. But the contents of this letter are for their eyes alone."

"Oh of course."

"I am entrusting you with this, Hairo. The fate of the world could very well rest in your hands."

He clutched the scroll tight.

"You haven't got a moment to lose."

"Should I take your horse, then?"

Her eyes flared. The bastard had real balls. But she kept her composure.

Go ahead, you stupid shit, she thought. *Let's see how far you get.*

"Of course," she answered. "Make haste."

Hairo turned on his heels and rushed to the stable. He had taken the bait. Now she had to see how deep into their nefarious network he would lead her.

She found Eugenie up to her eyeballs in books when she returned to their room.

"I've got to borrow your horse."

Eugenie looked up. Asha wasn't sure if the confusion on her face was from her question, or from whatever Eugenie had just read on the page in her lap.

"I thought—"

"I gave the bastard something he's sure to pass along. I have to follow him, so we can figure out how they are communicating, and where they're moving the relics to."

"But...shouldn't I come with you?"

"No. Stay here. We shook people up this morning. See what you can get out of them."

Eugenie considered, then finally nodded.

"Alright," Asha said, standing reluctantly in the doorway. She knew she had to leave quickly if she was going to pick up the bastard's trail, but still. "I'll come back soon," she promised.

"I know. Good luck."

Hairo hadn't bothered hiding *her* horse's tracks. Asha followed them with ease, pushing Eugenie's mare as hard as she would go. Asha could tell from the length of his stride that her own horse wasn't traveling at his fastest. It was less than an hour before Asha spied him far down on the road. She guided Eugenie's mare up onto the hill abutting the dirt road, suspended out of sight. Not that Asha ever saw him look over his shoulder.

When he stopped a little ways ahead of her, Asha dismounted, leaving the horse to graze while she followed the rest of the way on foot. She watched as he stopped in front of a nondescript pile of rocks by the road. He removed the topmost stone, placed her false message (with a broken seal) inside, and replaced the top of the hollow cairn. She ducked her head deep into the grass as he remounted her horse to leave, but she did not hear the pounding of hooves.

Asha realized what the problem was. He couldn't return to the temple. The Council of Three lay more than a mere hour's ride away, and he had to at least maintain the appearance of having performed his task faithfully. Her horse whickered impatiently as Hairo wavered with indecision. This was the extent of his involvement, as far as any line of inquiry with him would go.

Asha gave a low whistle; her horse reared up. She heard a scream, followed by a crash. Asha rose to her full height at the crest of the hill and surveyed the damage. The way Hairo lay in a twisted heap told her that his back was broken. His eyes grew round when he saw her, and his screams crescendoed. She whistled again—two short, high notes that brought the stallion's powerful front legs down upon his chest and cut his wailing short. The sound of his ribs cracking drifted up to Asha on the wind. When she descended the hill, she saw that one of the kicks had landed near his eye socket. His skull was split open like a ripened melon.

"Alright boy," she said, stroking her horse's nose. "You don't have to let him ride you ever again." She pulled a thin length of cord out of her satchel, and tied one end around Hairo's left foot, and the other end around her wrist, taking it up into the saddle with her. They were off with a click of her tongue, down the sloping side of the road and out of sight.

When she returned to the cairn, she was on foot. She camouflaged the trail of blood she had made down the hill, leaving a sole crimson puddle that would only be seen by someone as they stood before the cairn. She walked back down the hill directly opposite the cairn, laid down in the grass on her belly, and waited.

* * *

The sun had set and risen twice. Still, Asha waited. When night fell for the third time, she began to worry that she'd made a mistake. She'd left Eugenie alone for longer than she'd meant to, and she worried that if Hairo's contact didn't show himself soon, they'd be in a worse position than they were before.

The hard, yeasty biscuits she'd brought with her were turning. Tomorrow, they'd be inedible. She was chewing through the last of her cured meat when she felt the ground vibrate beneath her; a rider was approaching. She dropped the meat and reached for her dagger. She waited until she heard the rider dismount before poking her head over the crest of the hill.

His foot stepped into the bloodied smear on the ground, kicking up a cloud of dust dyed red as he reached for the top stone of the cairn. Asha smiled, and silently thanked Arun for rewarding her patience. She was on him before he could turn around.

"Where you headed, stranger?" she asked in a cool tone. The man struggled, but he was shorter than her by a head, and nowhere near as strong. All he managed to do was slice through the skin of his own neck as he wriggled against her dagger.

"Take it easy now. Answer my question and you'll walk away with your head. Where are you going?"

The stranger grunted, then spat out an answer. "Lareina."

Asha clucked her tongue. "Lying to me won't help you, or your kinsman."

"If you hurt him—"

"Clearly he's hurt. That's his blood you're splashing in."

His struggle increased, but still it was no use.

"I know your little secret," Asha taunted. "Descended from Argoss, are you?"

She felt the stranger's muscles tighten under her iron grip.

"You can't be worthy of his name, if your grand plans will crumble with just a single word from you."

"Argoss is rising," he crowed. "He will wash over the land in a great unending wave."

"He will, will he? You want to live to see it? Tell me where the relics are," she growled. Her dagger bit into his neck. Fresh blood seeped onto her knuckles and between her fingers.

The stranger's stifled rage gave way to pain, then transformed into a mad laugh that echoed in the night.

"He is rising," the stranger cackled. The shrill glee in his voice set Asha's teeth on edge. It assailed her ears and pierced the calm of the world.

Asha shook off a sudden chill.

"Where?!" she demanded.

The infernal bastard's laughter continued unabated.

"*Where?!*"

"From the Boundless Sea, he rises!" he screeched, howling wildly into the air. "Hail the Divine Lord Argoss! Hail Lord Lothan, standing at his right hand! Hail Ar—"

The maniac dropped at her feet. Asha was grateful for the return of silence, drawing it into her lungs in deep gulps as she wiped her blade clean.

From the Boundless Sea...

The village closest to the sea, surrounded by it on all sides, had not been marked on Asha's map. But if that was the heart from which darkness stretched across the land, then to Lighura they would go.

11

SERA ALREADY REGRETTED TELLING HER MOTHER THAT LYSANDRO HAD invited her to a formal dinner. They'd only been at the dressmaker's for five minutes.

"What about this one? Or this? Oh, this is nice."

Marietta Alvaró held up bolts of silk and satin in midnight, indigo, cerulean, and periwinkle.

"They're all blue," Sera replied, not moving from her perch as the gentleman who owned the establishment measured her for her form.

"Of course. Don Lysandro loves blue."

"Says who?"

"*Everyone.*"

"You mean, all the girls he *didn't* marry?"

Sera turned her head quickly to the sound of the dressmaker coughing near her waist. The graying man wasn't ill; he was trying to contain his laughter.

"You're a sharp one," he said. He and Sera exchanged a friendly smile.

Doña Alvaró tossed the fabrics down on the table and smoothed her own dress.

"I look better in whites and ivories," Sera said in a soft voice to the dressmaker.

He nodded in agreement. "Lighter shades don't compete with your hair. Would you consider a soft yellow?"

"Mmhmm," Sera mumbled absent-mindedly. She had been happy with the simpler dresses she'd brought with her up to now, but just then she was missing her most extravagant gowns. Whenever Fabien had insisted on something new—a new color, a new cut, a new fabric—she'd rolled her eyes at his excess. Now she was sorry for it, and would have given anything for just one of his stunning creations.

She wanted to look her best the next time she saw Lysandro. Her head was still spinning with the revelation that he was the Shadow of Theron. The man who had suggested they marry for friendship was the same man who had climbed her balcony and proclaimed to harbor such intense passion toward her.

You're the most perfect creature I've ever seen. It would be impossible for me not to love you.

She licked her lips as his voice echoed in her memory. Sera couldn't get him out of her head. But so many questions danced together in a tangle at the tip of her tongue. Why did he conceal his identity when he did nothing criminal? Why proclaim to adore her from behind the mask, but not while courting face-to-face? Why did he hide his feelings from her, if she was to take the Shadow's expression of love as truth?

She understood, or thought she did, that it might all amount to nerves. The thought was endearing, and his clandestine visit to her balcony *was* very romantic. It was exactly the kind of thing she imagined a man of his tastes would do. When he had shown her the portrait of the lovers, Elard and Galaine, she'd had the feeling that it was the first time he'd been genuine.

We might be everything to each other.

Remembering his raw sincerity brought a pang to her chest. But ever since she'd discovered his secret, she couldn't stop wondering why it was a secret at all—his good deeds, his attraction to her—any of it. For all her love of mysteries, Lysandro was the greatest enigma she had ever encountered.

And the most handsome. *By Faelia,* he was handsome. His piercing eyes and finely sculpted features put the king of Mirêne to shame. And those glossy black tresses—she'd had no idea how much she liked long hair on a man until Lysandro had run his fingers through it, completely unaware of his own charms.

"Seraphine, please pay attention!"

Her mother's voice cut her daydreaming short. "Sorry. What?"

"What do you want?" Marietta asked, gesticulating at the dressmaker's inventory. "You can't wear white every time he sees you."

"Umm…"

Sera scanned the possibilities without leaving her pedestal. But nothing jumped out at her, nothing felt quite…special.

"If you'll excuse me just a moment Signoras, something new came in this morning, and I think it might be just what you're looking for."

The dressmaker was gone and back in an instant. When he returned, what he held in his hands brought tears to Sera's eyes.

"Oh," Marietta swooned. She fawned over a bolt of exquisitely cut spun gold, and a collection of delicate, gauzy fabrics that glittered at the slightest movement.

"A cutting-edge fashion, straight from Mirêne."

A hard lump formed in Sera's throat. "It's perfect."

"Excellent. Now, do you want it in the true Mirênese cut? I warn you, it's quite daring, very close to the skin."

"I'd have it no other way."

The dressmaker smiled, reveling in his work as he draped the fabric over Seraphine. He pulled the sheer white, like newly fallen snow, from the table behind him.

"The gold's too open on its own, so I'll line it with—"

"No," Sera said. "Use the pale pink."

The dressmaker shook his head, flustered. "If I may, Signorina, a cleaner color will better showcase the gold."

"The man's an expert, Seraphine," her mother chided.

She looked the dressmaker straight in the eye. "Trust me."

He blinked, then did as she asked, and slipped a measure of the shimmering blush underneath the golden overlay. His eyes went wide.

"Well, aren't you clever."

Her mother's intake of breath was so sharp, she was close to fainting. The dressmaker moved to rearrange the pillows around her to prepare for the eventuality.

Sera beamed, admiring the rosy golden hue as it sparkled in the mirror.

"That color is absolute perfection on you. Look how it goes with your hair," the dressmaker said. "It's like it was made just for you."

And of course it was. *Shen je, Fabien. Shen je.*

"Could I have a bit more sleeve than this?" Sera asked, pulling at the string of beads that had been sent as accompaniments. "Maybe with the sheer?"

The dressmaker draped the twinkling pink over her shoulder, then cocked his head to look at her reflection.

"That will add a bit of drama," he said. "I think I'll give you some flair on the train too. Oh, I'm going to enjoy making this very much."

"If this doesn't send Don Lysandro to his knees, nothing will," her mother said. Her eyes shined with pride as she selected a jewel-encrusted comb with golden flowers to pin up a section of her daughter's hair, highlighting its effortless wave.

"If she doesn't have that effect on every man in Lighura, I'll eat my hat," the dressmaker chimed in. He hummed as he took additional measurements for the cutting of the gown.

Doña Alvaró snorted. "To think that your idiot father would even *entertain* Magistrate Marek as a suitor for you. That man could work himself into his grave and still never afford to give you a dress like this."

"Hold still, please. You all right, dear?"

"Yes, fine."

The mention of Marek sent a chill down Sera's spine. It frightened her how right Lysandro had been, that the magistrate would pursue her to spite them both. She wondered how much of Marek's crimes Lysandro had seen with his own eyes. Being in the dark about his activities as the Shadow made her nervous. She knew just enough to be grateful that she hadn't been home when Marek had come calling.

Her innermost thoughts were interrupted again, this time by the tolling of the temple bell. The three of them turned their heads in the direction of the sound in tandem.

"That's odd, isn't it?" the dressmaker said.

"Are we expected to go?" Sera asked.

"I suppose so," Marietta answered.

Sera shifted her feet to descend the pedestal, but the dressmaker stopped her before she could.

"Don't move."

Once the dressmaker released them, Sera and her mother crossed the short distance to the temple. The minute they stepped inside, the reason for the bells was painfully obvious. Arun's acolytes had swept the shattered glass away before summoning the village, but there was no softening the blow of seeing a gaping, ragged hole where the image of Theron had once been.

The murmurs of the gathering crowd quieted as they passed the threshold, and became sobs that echoed off the marble columns. Their unmoving sturdiness was the only solace to be had that morning.

When the temple could hold no more, the high priestess spoke. Her voice was muted at first, but then her rage boiled over.

"Who did this?"

There was no answer.

"*Who did this?*"

Sera scanned the congregation. The faces staring back at the high priestess were blank, some of them tear-streaked. But still no one answered.

"The guilty will be shown no quarter. Magistrate Marek," she called, lifting her gaze to the back of the temple, "this is to be your singular priority."

Everyone turned to Marek, who stood just inside the two columns holding up the entrance to the temple. At this distance, Sera couldn't be sure, but she had the unsettling impression that, although his lips were pressed into a thin line, on the inside, he was smiling.

The silence hanging in the air grew taut as all of Lighura waited for him to respond.

The magistrate sucked in a deep breath and said, "It is not the habit of my office to involve itself in Temple affairs. This is a matter best left to you."

"You will do nothing, then?!"

Lysandro's voice was explosive. Like a clap of thunder, his reproof heralded a torrent of outraged voices. Marek stood in the eye of the storm, unmoved by the cries of injustice that bore down on him. His stark refusal to do his duty was the last straw, and Sera heard more than one voice demand his removal, declaring him disloyal to Arun and to Lighura. Just as many, if not more, rebuked the magistrate with threats of a different sort.

"The Shadow of Theron will not stand for this!"

"*He* will not sit idly by while our temple is destroyed!"

Marek bristled at the naked criticism, and lifted his hands in front of himself as if they could stem the flood.

"For all you know, this is the work of the masked impostor that you hold so dear."

Sera looked to Lysandro. He held his tongue as the village's temper boiled over. But his eyes were vicious.

"Horseshit!" another man called. "The Shadow of Theron is a champion of the people, and of Arun!"

"He is nothing more than a common criminal, and you are wrong to put your faith in him," Lothan said.

"So we should trust *you*?" Signor Montes spoke up. "You've never lifted a finger to help anyone unless it suited you!"

"If the three Temples have seen fit to send Examiners for the crimes against themselves, then there is no need for me to interfere," Lothan retorted.

"This is ridiculous," Sera's mother fumed beside her. "What good is a magistrate who throws his hands in the air and says, 'it's not my job?' It most certainly *is* his job. But not for much longer, by the sound of it."

Marietta was right. The unrest in the temple was reaching riotous proportions. When Marek turned his back on the village and strode across the square to his office, the villagers followed after him.

Seraphine's mother took hold of her arm. "Let them pass. Better for us to go home, and not mix ourselves up in this ruckus."

Sera had to agree to that. Angry or no, she had no intention of banging down Marek's door. She had already garnered more of his attention than she cared to. As the temple cleared, she saw that Lysandro also lingered. His gaze was lost in the center of the ruined glass.

He approached the high priestess, who was speaking to the blacksmith. Sera followed. The bear of a man was shaking his head as she drew near.

"The last window was made before even my great-great-grandfather's time. I don't know where to start, and I couldn't begin to do the work on my own."

"Surely there must be someone, somewhere with the skill to restore this," Beatríz pressed.

"Maybe, but that someone isn't me."

"Then find someone who is," Lysandro cut in. "Metalworkers, glassmakers, artists—the best in their trades."

The blacksmith wiped his forehead with a grease-smeared cloth. "That'll take some doing."

"Lighura deserves to have their temple restored to them. I will bear the cost."

All mouths dropped open at Lysandro's pronouncement.

"That's very kind, and *very* generous, Don de Castel, but—"

"Spare no expense," he said to the blacksmith.

The man's demeanor shifted, and he nodded. "I'll make this day look like a bad memory if it's the last job I ever do."

Lysandro turned again to Beatríz. "High Priestess, where is Sancio?"

"On an errand for me."

He turned to leave, and noticed Seraphine for the first time. "Sera."

"I wish I could say good morning," she greeted him, not really knowing what to say. Now that she had his full attention, she saw that Lysandro looked sick to his stomach.

"The village will be grateful for what you're doing," she said by way of comfort.

"They would be more grateful if it had never happened."

"You can't help that," she replied.

Shame and dejection warred across his features. His hands were balled into fists at his side. He was trying hard to contain himself, she could tell, but he was losing the battle.

"Did *you* break the window?" she asked as they both stepped away from the altar and moved toward the exit.

His gaze slid sideways to the floor.

Sera wondered then if he believed that something he had done under the cover of night had provoked the attack. But if his prime adversary was Marek, did that mean *he* was the one responsible? It was unbelievable, that he would show his face there after such an assault. And it also made perfect sense. But why? What—

A million questions bubbled to the surface of her mind, but she pushed them all away and focused on Lysandro, who had not yet answered her question.

"*Did* you break the window? No? Then it's not your fault."

He sighed, wretched with grief, but a bit calmer. "I suppose not."

"What will you do? About Marek."

He flashed her a grim, self-effacing look. "What can I do?"

"More than you think."

It had been his voice that had woken the village from its stupor and directed its anger at Marek. Whenever he gave them an opportunity, they followed him. But Sera suspected that wasn't very often.

"The village needs you," she said. "They want you to stand with them and be their voice, and not just help them from the shadows."

Seraphine bit her tongue. She hadn't meant that as a reference to his actions as *the* Shadow, but she could see that he had caught the double meaning of her words and was turning them over in his mind. It was to her great relief that suspicion did not blossom across his face.

Lysandro was still formulating a reply when a small scrap of a boy raced up to him and tugged on his coat.

"Don de Castel! Don de Castel!"

"What's the matter?" he asked.

The boy pulled Lysandro down to his knees and whispered in his ear. Sera watched his expression shift from one of desolation to alarm. The urchin scampered away as Lysandro got to his feet.

"Sera, I'm so sorry—but I have to go." He headed off at a quick pace, taking a different road than the one down which she had seen the boy disappear.

"Lysandro, wait—"

"Yes?" he said, turning back to her.

He had enough to deal with already, only some of which she understood, but she needed him to know.

"Marek did come to my house, just as you said."

His face drained of its color.

"My father turned him away."

He looked like he was barely breathing. Sera worried that she had made a mistake.

After a moment, he said, "I have no right to ask this, but please—don't leave your house without your parents or me."

"I—"

"I'll come by later. I promise. Please be safe."

He turned and rushed away before she had a chance to say goodbye.

"You too," she whispered under her breath as her mother rejoined her side. The rapidity with which she'd found her told Sera that her mother had never been that far away.

"Where is he off to in such a hurry? What did you say to him?"

"Nothing," Sera replied.

Marietta huffed. "Nothing. *Nothing* sent him running in the opposite direction. I swear Seraphine, sometimes it's easier talking to the goats."

"Yes. If only they didn't smell so terrible."

Doña Alvaró scowled, but this time she couldn't hide the laugh lines quivering at the corners of her mouth.

THE HOUSE WAS DARK WHEN LYSANDRO ARRIVED. HE CRACKED OPEN THE door, but there was nobody there. Or so it seemed. He called out in a hoarse whisper.

"Rafael?"

His voice echoed weakly off the marble floor, but there was no reply. Lysandro's hand moved instinctively over his shoulder to grip a weapon that wasn't there.

He stepped into the space and closed the door behind him. It cast the room in total darkness, save for a candle a few feet away that was flickering out. Lysandro fumbled over the small narrow stairs that led into the parlor, and reached for a wooden table against the stairwell going up to the second floor. He replaced the sputtering light with a fresh taper and surveyed the room.

The house looked abandoned. Stretching the candle's halo of light wide in front of him, Lysandro caught sight of an overturned chair, lying in streaks of blood.

A jolt ran through him at the sight. There was no sign of the boy who had urged him to come, nor his friend. He considered checking the upper floor first, but then he heard a faint moan that sent him running.

"Lysandro…"

He found Rafael crouched against the wall of the room beyond the parlor. The contents of the shelves where he stored all his medicines were in shambles. Glass bottles lay spilled on their side, some shattered altogether. Lysandro knelt down and passed the light over his friend's face.

"Merciful Goddess…"

Rivers of dried blood stained Rafael's face. And his eyes—the seams of his eyes were ragged with black lines, like the face of a man who'd been attacked with burning coals.

"Who did this to you?"

"Who else? Get me another drink, will you? I seem to be out." He lifted an empty decanter in his hand. "Underneath the cupboard, to my right."

Lysandro set the candleholder down on the floor. He found the fortified wine, and handed it to Rafael, but not before pouring a glass for himself.

"I brought what you asked." Lysandro withdrew a muslin pouch from his coat, the last of the powder that Rafael had brewed into tea for him.

Rafael nodded. "There should be a bottle of linseed oil above my head, if I haven't already broken it."

"I've got it." Lysandro added a small measure of it to the bag until it formed a thick paste. He dipped his fingers inside, then pressed them tentatively to his friend's eyelids.

Rafael cried out.

Lysandro caught his flailing arms. "Hold onto me," he insisted as he continued to apply the poultice across Rafael's eyes until there was nothing left. He grimaced.

"Can you open your eyes? Just a little bit, to get some under your lids."

Rafael's grip tightened on his friend's arm, digging his fingernails into that still-tender spot on Lysandro's bicep. A shiver ran through him at the unexpected pressure, but he ignored it.

"Okay," Rafael relented. "Just—just a little."

The second Lysandro saw his eyelids flutter, he shoved the paste through the gap.

Rafael screamed and writhed.

"It's done! It's done already. Here—"

Lysandro knocked over a pile of clean bandages, found what he was looking for, and wrapped a long strip of cloth around the surgeon's face.

Rafael settled down, and brought his drink to his lips again as Lysandro soaked another bandage in a bowl of water and began to wipe his face clean.

"He knew," Rafael said. "He knew I'd helped you."

"How?"

Rafael turned his head to the side, and Lysandro saw him clench and unclench his jaw in the dim light. He looked down at the bandages in his hand.

"Rafael...what's in this poultice?"

The surgeon let out a heavy sigh. "When Theron first confronted Argoss, he was mortally wounded by the Blood Sword. Theron fled, and took shelter in a nearby cave. There, Faelia appeared to him. She stayed with him as his life drained away, and washed his wounds with her tears."

All this Lysandro already knew. He had heard the story many times.

"When Theron awoke, his wounds were healed, and he walked out of the cave as strong as he'd ever been." Rafael gestured toward his eyes with his hand. "This is made from the stones of the wall of that cave."

The words shocked Lysandro to silence.

"I'd seen the Cave of Sorrows in my travels, when I was still an apprentice. I think my teacher meant it as a lesson about our mortal limitations...how *we* could never perform miracles, and all that. But I'm a scientist. I've only ever believed in what I could feel...and see."

Rafael swallowed hard. Lysandro filled his glass again with the dark amber liquid. He downed half of it in one gulp.

"Even if I believed the story, I didn't believe that Theron's recovery was Faelia's work. I thought it must be some special composition of the soil, the rocks. That if I could just study it, I could unlock its secrets, and end so many people's suffering. But the cave is guarded by Faelians. There were some individuals who were willing to overlook that obstacle, for the right price."

Lysandro didn't like this story at all. But he was hardly in a position to judge.

"I thought it was for the best. And that, if there truly was such a thing as a goddess, she would want the world to benefit from the gifts she had bestowed upon it. But in order for it to reach me here, it first had to board a ship."

Lysandro's gut wrenched at this turn in the story. For he knew what had happened next.

"Marek found out, I have no idea how, and threatened to arrest me for stealing Temple property. When I tried to explain its potential benefit to humanity, he released me, and let me keep the stones. I suppose I should have known then that something was wrong. All that has been stolen from the temples since, I think…I think I might have given him the idea."

Rafael finished off the liquor in his glass. "Yesterday, he came and blew something into my eyes. Some kind of dust. But it *burned*. With a black, purplish flame."

Lysandro remembered that precise shade, furling itself around the hooded skeleton inside Marek's hidden cave. The memory of its obscured face and its infernal song rippled just beneath the surface of his mind. He gave an involuntary shudder.

"He offered to restore my eyes if I told him."

Lysandro took the blow hard. "My secret was not worth your eyes. You're the best friend any man could ever ask for, but—"

"Don't be daft. I knew better than to take him at his word."

They sat for a while in awkward silence.

"Do you feel any change?" Lysandro inquired at last.

"I don't know. I'm afraid to find out. But the pain is gone, at least. Lysandro…"

"I'm here. I'm here, my friend."

"I know what I said before, about staying out of trouble, but…you have to kill him, or soon all of us will be plunged into darkness. You may not like the title Lighura has thrust upon you, but it's who you are."

Lysandro's expression hardened in the shadows.

"I was at your deathbed, Lysandro. Your *deathbed*. You are alive only through divine will. That I do believe."

Lysandro didn't like what Rafael was implying. He preoccupied himself by moving the candleholder to the side and attempting to clear away some of the debris on the floor.

"Merciful Goddess!"

"What?" Lysandro cried.

"That light! I could see that light!"

Rafael untied the bandage from his head so furiously Lysandro could barely help him. He used the grimy scrap to wipe away the poultice from his eyes and dared to open them. Rafael gasped, then started to cry.

"Praise be to Faelia! My friend, never have you looked so good!"

The pair embraced, and Lysandro helped the surgeon to his feet. Rafael reached out a shaky hand to lift the candle from the floor. Lysandro could see that his blood vessels had burst open, and his irises looked much darker than normal.

"You're a bit blurry," Rafael admitted, "but I'll take it."

Lysandro didn't leave his friend's side until he was fast asleep in his bed. He didn't know how long Rafael would be able to stay there. Marek would be furious if he discovered that Rafael's eyes were healing. The only safe place for him was Lysandro's own house.

He felt a dark pall drape itself around his shoulders like a cloak as he stepped out into the street. He couldn't meet Sera with death reflected in his eyes. Rather than go to her straight away, he visited his father to help regain his composure. He bumped into an unexpected visitor on his way through the door.

"Sancio!"

"Oh! Sorry Lysandro, I didn't see you there."

"What are you doing here?"

Elias came to the door just as Sancio answered.

"Looking for you. Obviously, you weren't here."

Odd, Lysandro thought. Sancio hadn't come knocking at this door since before Lysandro had moved into his own residence.

"I asked after you at the temple. Beatríz said you were running an errand for her."

"Oh. Yes," Sancio waved his hand in the air in dismissal. "That's done already." He continued down the steps past Lysandro.

"Wait a minute," Lysandro called out.

"Yes?"

"Where are you going?"

"Back to the temple."

Lysandro's brows furrowed. "Didn't you come to see *me*?"

Sancio hesitated.

Throughout this exchange, Elias remained motionless by the door.

"I did," Sancio admitted, "but I've stayed longer than I should have. Beatríz will be expecting me. I'll catch up with you later." Above Lysandro's head, Sancio nodded to Elias. He returned the gesture.

Lysandro cocked his head as Sancio again turned to leave. He couldn't put his finger on it, but Sancio looked somewhat different as he walked away. Taller.

"Hello, son. Come in."

Elias opened the door wide, and talked to Lysandro over his shoulder as he led the way into the drawing room. "Have you eaten yet?"

"No," Lysandro answered. Any thought of food had flown away at the sight of his friend's face, butchered by that demon Marek.

Elias had a cold side of beef brought, sliced thin along with a crusty loaf of bread and boiled potatoes. Lysandro washed it down with a fine glass of port.

The grandfather clock standing in the corner struck the hour. Lysandro turned his head in its direction. He studied it for a moment.

"Did you do something to it?"

"To what?" Elias asked.

"The clock."

Elias shifted in his chair. "No."

"It sounds…different."

It wasn't the sound that was off. It was something else, something Lysandro couldn't quite identify. He'd never paid it much mind before. But the chiming of the bells seemed to demand his attention now. Their echo rang in his ears long after they had finished their song. He couldn't figure out why it bothered him. He shrugged it off.

"I've offered to pay for the restoration of the temple," he told his father.

Elias's fork hung suspended in midair. "That will promise to be quite a sum."

Lysandro nodded absently. What else could he do? It was Marek's revenge for the cave-in. He couldn't let the village pay the price of his own recklessness.

"Do you need help?" Elias asked.

"No," Lysandro answered, thinking it over. "Thank you. I'll be fine."

Elias chewed over his next words carefully.

"Such an expense could prove unwise, on the eve of a marriage."

Lysandro said nothing, but took another drink of his wine.

Elias drummed his fingers on the arms of his chair. "At the risk of being throttled, how fares Signorina Alvaró?"

Lysandro didn't have enough fight in him to resist this line of inquiry.

"She's fine," he replied in a listless tone, "as good as can be expected."

"What does that mean?"

"We're courting...*I'm* courting *her*, I guess."

And?

It was at the edge of his teeth, but from the look on his son's face, Elias guessed that he wouldn't like the answer any better than Lysandro himself did. He didn't want to push a sore point.

"She'll come around, eventually."

"Yes. That's exactly how I'd like to have my proposal accepted, to say that she 'came around' to the idea."

The side of Elias's mouth quirked upward. "I'm saying that she will make her decision once she has been satisfied."

Lysandro's eyebrows shot up. "Excuse me?"

"Do you see her?"

"What? I just told you, we're—"

Elias shook his head. "All women wish to be appreciated. Not just as potential wives and mothers, or for whatever money they will bring to the marriage, but for themselves—their passions, their fears, their talents, their moods—the things that make you love them above all others. The girl wants to be seen. Do you see her?"

He did. At least, he was beginning to. But did she know that? How could she, when he kept so much of himself locked deep inside his skin?

"Father?"

"Mm?"

"What did *you* see? In Mother?"

Elias put down his fork and swallowed the morsel of beef he'd been working on.

Lysandro clasped his knees under the table. "I'm sorry. I—"

"Fire," Elias answered. "Your mother had such a bright, determined spirit. No one could ever tell her what to do. Not her parents, when they told her she could do better than a don in an out-of-the-way little village, not when the Andran Council said she couldn't hold the seat for Lighura, not—"

Elias pressed his eyes closed. A tear fell onto his plate with a silver tinkling. Lysandro's breath caught in his throat.

"Not when the midwife told her she would never hold a child of her own."

Lysandro's mind swirled in confusion.

"She had five miscarriages, before you. Five. And every one of them cut her worse than the last."

Lysandro could barely breathe—the lump in his chest had become too great to bear.

"But she wouldn't quit. Even when I told her that she was enough, that I'd sooner raise a foundling child than see her go through that again. But here you are." His father smiled through his tears. "She lived her life just as she wanted to. I was beyond blessed to have shared in it." Elias sniffed and wiped at his eyes. "Never hesitate to bring her up, understand? Or worry how I might take it. I think about her every day, whether you ask about her or not. I'd just as soon you did."

"Alright," Lysandro nodded meekly.

Elias reached for his son's hand across the table, kissed his knuckles, then resumed his meal.

"Oh—I can't keep our standing dinner date this week."

"Why not?" Lysandro asked.

"I'm going to pay Aleksander a visit. This business with Marek and the temple is untenable."

"Untenable" didn't even begin to describe it. Marek was out of control. But with that cursed dagger, there was little Lysandro could do to get close to him. He doubted anyone could, unless Marek was overcome by sheer numbers. Even then, the resultant loss of life before he was subdued could be severe.

Lysandro was reluctant to admit that Sancio had been right all along, that Marek's crimes were too big for him to deal with alone. But still—

"Are you sure that's wise? I wouldn't want Marek finding out that you were the one lodging a complaint with his superiors."

"I'm not the only one. Montes just came back from there. He didn't have much luck, it seems, but I've known Aleksander much longer. He'll talk to me. We can't let everything fall on the Shadow of Theron's shoulders, can we, much as he does to keep this village standing."

"I suppose not."

"Some things must be settled in the full light of day. Though I'm sure the Shadow will make Marek's life miserable."

Summoning the chief magistrate might be enough to start moving things in the right direction, but Marek's actions suggested that the constraints his position imposed on him were slackening. Lysandro could still prevent him from acquiring any other dark relics and stop his power growing. It didn't come close to satisfying the call for his utter destruction screaming through Lysandro's veins, but it might make all the difference when the Examiners finally arrived. For the first time, Lysandro found himself hoping that the Aruni and Morgassen would be strong enough to combat him.

A sense of dread took hold of him at the thought. Marek had done his damnedest to kill the Shadow. He'd blinded Rafael. He'd defiled the temple. And he'd set his sights on Sera over the smallest slight.

"I think you might be underestimating the danger that Marek poses."

Elias said nothing to this as he stood from the table and moved toward the door. He didn't know the half of what Marek was responsible for, what he was capable of. There was only one way to warn him.

Lysandro cleared his throat. "Father...?"

"Lysandro?"

I'm the Shadow of Theron. I don't have time to explain, but trust me when I say—it isn't safe.

It was on the tip of his tongue. Then Rafael's face raced across his mind.

"Have a safe journey. And be careful. I know Aleksander is an old friend, but he did appoint Marek. He must have done so for a reason."

"I know. And I intend to discover what that reason is."

"Will you bring your pistol?"

This gave Elias pause. "I will, if it sets your mind at ease."

"It would."

"Fine. I'll see you in a few days."

They shared a warm embrace before Elias let his son out into the fading sunlight and closed the door.

Lysandro hoped he had made the right choice. He had the sinking suspicion that the people who he told his secret to would be the ones most at risk. That included Sera.

"Oh damn!"

He'd lost all track of the day. He craned his neck toward the darkening sky and cursed again. Sera would be having her own meal now with her parents; it would be too late to call on her afterward.

He resolved to see her first thing in the morning. If she forgave him, that is. If he lived through the night. Tonight was the night Marek had marked in the ledger Lysandro had pinched from the cave. The magistrate was expecting a delivery. Lysandro wasn't about to let him have it.

12

LOTHAN'S SKULL WAS ABOUT TO SPLIT OPEN. BLOOD AND BRAINS WOULD splatter everywhere, getting in his lieutenant's eye and adding to the grime on the ceiling. That's how it felt, with the constant banging on the door and the windowpanes. It seemed to only have increased in the last hour. He'd closed the shutters; at least he didn't have to look at the rioters. But he couldn't block out his brothers, who made just as much of a racket within the magistrate's office as the people without.

Lothan pinched the bridge of his nose, then spread his middle finger and thumb outward to his eyebrows to relieve the pressure building underneath.

"How many are still out there?" he asked.

The one closest to the window peeped through the wooden slats obscuring the mob outside, then turned his head back to Marek and shrugged.

"Just as many as what followed us, I'd say. Doesn't look like anybody's gotten tired yet."

Lothan emitted a low sound from deep in his throat. He needed them to go away. His head had been throbbing since he'd entered the temple the night before. Whatever the bitches of Arun were hiding in that temple, it was powerful. Just by being near to something so strongly tied to the goddess had nearly overwhelmed him, *aside* from the skull-splitting torment. He'd broken into a cold sweat, and the urge to vomit hadn't left him until he had passed through the stone columns marking the exit. He'd had to endure it all night without showing the slightest hint of provocation. He couldn't very well have collapsed into convulsions on the temple floor, though that was the only thing he'd had enough energy to do.

But this morning had been different. This morning's brief entry into the temple had not sent his brains and his guts reeling anew. There was only one explanation. Whatever had lain hidden in the temple, whatever had made Lothan cringe every time he passed it on the street, had been moved. To where, he couldn't tell. Nor was he keen to find out.

He couldn't comprehend why something so obviously valuable would be kept in so insignificant a place as Lighura. He wouldn't have believed it if he hadn't felt it down to the marrow in his bones. Maybe it would make more sense to him once his mind cleared.

That, however, seemed further and further away as the banging continued at a sustained pace.

"What do they expect to get out of this?" Lothan asked, exhausted. He needed food, drink, rest…but with that obnoxious cluster outside, he would have none.

"Your resignation, Lord Lothan."

He snorted. "That's what de Castel wants."

"He's got them well and truly riled up now. If you ask me—"

"I didn't."

The younger officer was crestfallen. "Sorry, My Lord, I was just saying, it's all his fault, isn't it? I mean, he's the one who spoke out against you, in front of the whole village."

"He's not out there now, is he?"

"No, My Lord. He and his father are about the only dons *not* standing outside."

"Of course not." The coward. He had the gall to start something, but not the balls to finish it. And this time, his whining was echoed fifty-fold. The sound of it curdled Lothan's brain. He barked at the man closest to him, making him jump.

"Find out if we can arrest de Castel for inciting a riot he isn't present for. A night of our hospitality is what *he* needs."

The officer bounded out of Lothan's office into the front room without another word. He appreciated that, at least—until the door slammed shut behind him with a resounding crack.

"One of these days," he murmured to himself as he pressed his hands to his eyelids, "I'm going to kill every single one of you."

Through the cacophony, an idea occurred to him. It had been a while —years—since he'd done anything like it, and never on this scale. It might turn whatever was left of his mind to mush. But it was worth a try.

He hauled himself out of the chair, gripping the armrests to mask his dizziness, and lurched through the front door. The minute he opened it, the outcry of the crowd pierced his ears all the more sharply. He nearly crumpled then. But he buried his snarl behind a smile, mustered all the concentration he had left, and addressed the crowd in dulcet tones.

"Don't you think it's time you left? Go home and have a nice dinner with your family. This business with the temple will all be sorted when the Examiners arrive."

Lothan caught some subtle movement toward the back of the crowd. They had followed others to his door; they would be the easiest to sway. He continued.

"Go home. Your families are waiting for you. The Examiners are the best suited to deal with this."

Marek breathed a sigh of relief when a handful of protesters broke away from the pack. "Lock your doors—the Shadow of Theron could be out and about tonight. You never know what new dangers that menace will bring," he added.

There was some pushback on this, but Lothan persisted.

"He's an impostor, and a criminal. He's the one who needs to be stopped."

It seemed to be working. Lothan continued to soothe the villagers away from his door. He whittled them down with his words, repeated them over and over again, until it became a chant. Those who had led the charge were the hardest to crack. It was for the best that Don Lysandro wasn't there, or it might have been a total failure, but the thinning of the crowd and the fanning of their tempers did the work for him. It was enough discouragement for even his staunchest critics to find themselves standing alone. Eventually, they too headed for home.

Lothan was drained. The only thing left of him was the pain in his skull. It dulled some as the riot fizzled out, and he hoped he was through the worst of it.

Chaos returned as he entered his office. His lieutenants erupted in cheers and fawning compliments.

"Shut *up*."

His brothers fell quiet, and at last, Lothan felt like he could breathe. But it was no time to rest.

"Any word on tonight's delivery?" Lothan asked.

"They should be here at eleven, as agreed."

"And the Examiners?"

"It's hard to say. None of ours have spotted them, or we would have heard."

He turned to Gorin, leaning idly on the wall to his left.

"I want the whole village ready to throw the Shadow at their feet by the time they get here. We need to cut him off from the people that protect him."

"Didn't you just finish convincing them all that he's the enemy?"

"It will wear off," Lothan said, "unless we remind them. Have some new broadsheets printed, urging people who know anything of him to come forward. Offer them money."

"What should I say he is guilty of?"

Lothan's eyes narrowed at the man's impudence. "Theft. Vandalism. Fomenting civil unrest. The destruction of Temple property."

"Right. Of course."

Lothan didn't expect the Shadow to surrender. Not after what they'd done to the temple. A grin crept back to his face when he thought of how it must have been for him to be called to the temple that morning, only to find it destroyed. No, a few dark marks on his reputation wouldn't stop him, but it would preoccupy him long enough for Lothan to take the measure of the Examiners before deciding his next step. If he could deter them from their course, or eliminate them along with the Shadow, then his post will have served its purpose, and he would at last be able to move about at will. And if he could take another relic out of the goddess's hands tonight, he'd be that much closer.

Who destroyed the temple window? Marek?
Why was the temple window destroyed?
What did the Shadow of Theron ~Lysandro~ do to make him angry?

SERAPHINE SHUFFLED THE QUESTIONS SHE HAD COMMITTED TO PAPER around on her walnut writing desk the way a magician might rearrange the cards of a divination deck, hoping that a solution might appear, willed into existence by an invisible, omniscient hand.

No such luck.

She pushed up from her chair in a huff, carrying the slips bearing the three queries at the foremost of her thoughts, and pinned them to the papered wall with the others. Her pincushion was nearly empty. She'd used almost half of a ball of ivory thread connecting all she had learned about the feud between Lysandro and Marek, the Shadow of Theron's reputation, the disappearance of the relics from the temples, and the destruction of the Aruni window. At Fabien's side, Sera had decorated countless palace walls this way in the doge's mad quest to find Theron's tomb. It had led to incredible and unlikely discoveries; the ultimate solution was just out of reach.

But this was different. There was no center, no shocking revelation to be had along the ropey logic from one slip of paper to the next. There were only questions. Questions upon questions with no end in sight. Whenever Sera applied herself to the problem, she only realized there was one more thing that she *didn't* know.

She wondered what Fabien would make of all of this. But he was a man possessed by a different mystery, and she owed him a letter. Taking her seat again, she created a rough image of the panels from the Temple Theron, adding in the panels she had seen in the museum. Sketching the window and writing down her theories provided a safer, more distant problem, and one in which she had at least made progress. Several additional sheets chronicled her days with the kinds of details she knew Fabien craved. Multiple pages were dedicated to Lysandro's beauty, and another two were filled with their evening together at the so-called Mirênese ball. She recited every word that had passed between her and Lysandro—even the ones he had spoken as the Shadow of Theron. Fabien had been her lifelong confidante in all things. He was the very picture of discretion. Plus her missive was entirely in Mirênese, and spelled out in a way that Fabien would understand without being explicitly told.

Signing her name to a letter that was more like a novel, Sera stuffed it all into an envelope and sealed it, then turned again to the puzzle laid out in cotton on her wall. The raw material had been heaped upon her in bulk, along with measures of lace, colored ribbons, and other finishings by her mother, who had been shocked to learn that Seraphine had returned home without having made her trousseau.

"How is it possible that such a fine school sent you home without enough dresses to get you through your season, or the necessities of becoming a bride?! I have a mind to write them a strongly worded letter and demand they tell me exactly what my money was spent on," she had said.

Sera laughed at the thought. She lacked a great many things her parents had paid for, but in Fabien's court, she had wanted for nothing.

As far as a trousseau was concerned, she had been expected *not* to know how to make her own bedclothes—she had learned fashion, not production, at the doge's hand, as well as witticism, playacting, stage fighting, how to win at cards, how to sing like an angel and drink like a devil.

Sera did love to sing; she wanted so very much to sing. She also wanted to drink. She wanted to sing while drunk, but she was fairly certain her parents would not approve and anyway that was an activity best enjoyed among similarly soused individuals.

No: knitting, sewing, or anything truly practical did not become a member of the doge's court. So now she used the string to collate all she knew and hoped for an epiphany to jump off the pages affixed to her wall by intersecting lines of ivory gossamer thread.

So many uncertainties danced in circles round her head. The only answer glaring back at her was that she needed a walk to clear her mind. The northern coast lay just beyond the edge of her parents' property, and Sera remembered it fondly as a quiet spot where she could sit and read for hours, though now she was fresh out of reading material. The gardener had confessed, the heroine's good name was restored, and all the family ghosts had been laid to rest within the leather-bound confines of her latest book. It was one more thing she wished she had packed more of, if only she'd known she was going away for real.

The sun's heat cooled as Sera approached the shore and the burning orb began its descent into the horizon. It dyed the clouds in fiery yellows and intense purples that reflected off the long blades of grass. Sera found a familiar spot at the edge of the cliff and fanned her skirt out in front of her in a wide arc. The air was cool, and the wind sprayed her cheeks with a fine mist as it carried seawater up from the shore on its back. Seraphine breathed deep of the fresh air, and let her worries drift away.

The weather turned brisk as the sun dipped beneath the waves. But what made Sera stir was the sound of male voices drifting up to her from below.

"Spread out. I don't want any mistakes like the last time."

She opened her eyes and inched toward the edge of the cliff. Her feet dangled out in front of her and she clutched at the high sturdy grass as she slid, very slowly, down the slope of the hill. The muddy surf came up to her ankles as she dropped the final distance from the cliff's overhang to the beach, and she instantly retreated, pushing her back up against the stone underbelly of the bluff. The growing shadows that overtook the day as the moon ascended in the sky acted as her refuge.

"If the Shadow dares to meddle with me again, he will not escape his death a second time."

The voice was clearer now, closer. And it was unmistakably Marek's.

Before Sera could kick herself for not adhering to Lysandro's plea that she not venture out alone, the ground trembled above her and sent a sprinkling of gravel into her hair. One of Marek's men crossed the spot where she had sat only minutes before. Even if she had turned and run at the sound of Marek's men, rather than descending the slope, they would have noticed her. And now the path back to the safety of her house was cut off. To her right was a small incision in the rock wall. It was just big enough. She wormed herself into the tight space and tucked her skirts under her feet as she willed the niche to swallow up the bright fabric of her dress and make her invisible. Seraphine wrapped her arms around her knees and prayed that Marek was right—that the Shadow would come.

* * *

Tracking the path of the moon as it made its way across the sky did little to inform Sera of how much time she had passed huddled in a small hole in the cliffside wall. All she knew for certain was that it was a lot.

The tide was higher now, and it rushed at the base of the cliff and into her hiding space in brisk, foamy waves. Her bottom lip was bitten raw; she swallowed her cries every time the icy surf broke upon her, climbing the hem of her skirts up to her collarbone, and leaving her soaked and shivering by degrees.

The gaggle of voices that kept her trapped there crescendoed. She gathered from their exultations that they were expecting a ship and had just caught sight of it. Sera's heart hammered louder in her chest. She didn't know how much longer her hiding place would protect her if more men poured onto the beach. Or if the tide continued to climb and turned her refuge into a tomb. Drowning was one of the most painful ways to die —or so she had heard—and she wondered half-heartedly if the frigid temperature of the water would numb her to the worst of it.

Without warning, the soil of the overhang shook and released a cloud of dirt down on top of her head. It was too much of a disturbance to be caused by only one pair of feet; some sort of scuffle was happening above her.

It was over quickly. Sera curled herself into an even tighter ball as the victor descended silently down the slope, much as she had. Her heart gave a little leap as she recognized Lysandro's lithe figure. But it occurred to her that she had no clue how to get his attention without gaining the notice of anyone else, and possibly dooming them both.

Lysandro kept his eyes focused on the cluster of villains before him as he trod softly on the beach. True to his name, he sidled along the edge of the cliff's base, keeping to the shadows as he made his advance. If he would just step a little closer to her...

He snuck right by without noticing her. When he completely obscured her from view of the others, Sera saw her chance. She darted out at him before he stepped out of reach. Her fingers just caught the edge of his pants near his calves. She gripped the coarse fabric for dear life and pulled him backward with all the force she could muster.

The Shadow of Theron wheeled around and took in the miserable sight of her at his heels. His eyes looked ready to pop out of his skull. He tossed a quick glance over his shoulder to see if anyone had noticed him, then ducked down before her.

Sera pulled on his sleeves, drawing him closer. He felt so warm, and she was so terribly cold. She wanted to curl up inside his embrace and not emerge until the shivering ceased—and even then. But the Shadow pulled away from her, mouthing furiously without making a sound.

"Signorina! What are you doing here? Go home right now!"

She stared at him, incredulous. Her voice came out as a raspy whisper against the crashing waves.

"How? I was already here before they came—I've been here for hours!"

From behind his linen mask, Lysandro's eyelids peeled all the way back in horror as his gaze raked over the ruined condition of her dress. Her skin had taken on an unearthly blue tint.

"I'll distract them, and you run. My horse is at the top of the hill," he whispered.

"They'll kill you!"

"I can protect myself, Signorina, but not if my mind is on you. I need to know that you are safe and far away from here."

"There's too many of them," she protested.

"The magistrate's goons are no match for me."

"There's more coming—look!"

She pointed behind them at the unassuming merchant ship making its way ashore.

"Then you must go—now!"

"No!"

Seraphine clapped her hand over her mouth. Her protest hadn't been a shout, but it wasn't a whisper, and enough of her voice carried to make the sentinel nearest them turn his head.

In a shorter time than it took Sera to blink, Lysandro twisted around, putting his back up against her and pressing her deeper into the rocky recess, blocking her body from view with his.

Panic rose in Sera's throat. She tried to swallow it and pressed her fingertips to the back of his shoulders to brace herself. She felt Lysandro's muscles tense under his shirt as his form coiled, ready to pounce if the lookout should stray too close. Lysandro cloaked the gleam from his dagger, now drawn, in the crook of his forearm. As the wary stranger approached, Lysandro dipped his head, shielding his face with the dark, wide brim of his hat. Sera pressed her forehead against him and closed her eyes as the man's footsteps drew nearer, nearer, and then finally turned and faded away again as the man returned to his post further up the beach.

Sera finally allowed herself to breathe. A rush of water at their feet sent another shock through her, but she gnawed her lip again and kept her silence.

Lysandro tucked in his chin and turned his head just enough that she could see the edge of his sleek profile. His face was sublime in the moonlight, but now was not the time to moon over him. The steely look he shot her made her wince.

The Shadow remained with her, using himself as Sera's shield when the incoming vessel shoved its prow into the surf. She could no longer hear Marek's voice, now that he wasn't barking orders, so Sera tried to catch a glimpse of the men disembarking. There was a tiny opening between the curve of Lysandro's shoulder and the brim of his hat. Through that little window she spied two stout, well-muscled men descending from the ship, carrying a heavy wooden chest between them. Marek stood at a distance with his arms folded as their leader made a big show of presenting their wares. They were too far away for her to make out what passed between them, but both parties went about their business without suspecting they were being spied on.

Sera was relieved that the transaction was going smoothly. She hoped that meant they would leave soon, and Theron's Shadow could escort her home. It took her completely by surprise when Marek grabbed the man he'd been speaking with by the scruff of his neck and plunged a glowing red knife into his throat. She muffled her gasps in the dip between Lysandro's shoulder blades. He flinched, caught just as much by surprise as she. The merchant's skin grew black, sucking in the darkness of the night until it swallowed him whole. The rest of the ship's crew cried out; there was nothing left of their captain as his clothes fell to the ground.

The air became soaked with the tang of blood, and Sera had to hold her breath to calm her stomach as chaos erupted mere feet from them.

LOTHAN KNEW THE KEY WAS A FAKE BEFORE THE MERCHANT CAPTAIN EVEN opened his trunk. The true Cerulean Key was near—near enough to produce an acute buzzing between his ears like a swarm of locusts. But it was not in the chest the captain laid at his feet. It had to be aboard the ship still. But here the captain was, boasting in great detail about the pains he had taken to steal the relic, gesticulating at the trunk as he turned the opening of the chest into a dramatic performance. The more he went on, the more enraged Lothan became.

"Stealing into the temple of Morgasse takes meticulous planning, an insider's knowledge, and, most of all—someone clever enough to do it. We have faced great peril to bring you such a prize, which is worth twice as much as my humble crew and I have agreed to take. Ten times more, even."

He finished with a flourish and placed a key in Lothan's hand. It was cheap tin, painted to effect a mysterious glow where the moonlight struck it. The design was intricate, impertinent, overwrought. The key that opened nothing was light in his palm, as dead and devoid of sorcery as the pebbles littering the beach.

The flow of blood across the jagged blade at Lothan's hip quickened, mirroring his rising ire. Lothan shivered with its impatience.

"Ten times as much?" he asked. "When you've already doubled your price?"

"Easily, Magistrate. No one can deny the dangers of procuring such a treasure. Don't forget, this is the second time I've come to this shore to do business. Last time was anything but orderly. And, forever after, I'll be unable to tell a soul about my exploits. You must admit, that is a great cost to bear for a reputation such as mine. A little indulgence is all I ask for."

"Is it worth your life?"

The hard lines of Lothan's face glowed in the lantern light.

The captain's smile vanished. Before his expression could shift entirely, Lothan plunged the dagger into his neck and severed his vocal cords.

"That's what your lies have cost you."

Lothan withdrew his blade, causing the wound to spray blood on his face. He didn't mind. This time, he was not robbed of the satisfaction of dealing death. He reveled in watching one who would cheat him turn to ash. If only his true enemy was here now. There would be no escape.

His lieutenants took this as their cue. Outnumbering the merchant's crew by at least half, and positioned so well they hadn't even noticed, the rest of the crew didn't have time to run. In a matter of moments, the beach was littered with corpses. Lothan was pleased.

"It's here," he said as his bloodied brothers gathered around him. "Search the ship, and get this place cleaned up."

A LOW GROWL ESCAPED LYSANDRO'S LIPS, BUT HE STAYED WHERE HE WAS. Sera knew that if it hadn't been for her, he would have tried to stop it. Guilt roiled the meager contents of her stomach. If not for her, and her flippant ignorance of Lysandro's warning, some of those men might have lived.

Or Lysandro would be dead.

She didn't think he'd see it that way. Men had died because he had chosen not to act, all to save her—and it was her fault.

Marek and his crew kept their heads to their work as they raided the boat and loaded the bodies of the slain back onto its deck. Lysandro turned his face to Sera and whispered low in her ear.

"You're going to climb, nice and slow, back up the ridge. Now, while their attention is elsewhere."

"I'm not leaving—"

"I'll be right behind you. Now come on."

He shifted his weight so she could pass by him, and yanked her out of the crevice with a firm grip on her wrist. The wind was merciless; her soaked clothes presented no obstacle. But she crept, steady and silent, back the way she had come.

Lysandro drew his sword and stayed so close he was almost on top of her.

There was a shuffle of movement beneath them, accompanied by angry whispers. A shaft of light came soaring up from below, sweeping the cliffside.

Lysandro lunged, caging Sera under his body and pressing her down into the dirt. Though they had not been spotted, the lighted remained focused on the top of the hill, unsatisfied.

The top of Sera's head butted against Lysandro's chest, and her hands were crushed underneath her. Lysandro lay still as a stone, save for his labored breathing, but her thumb grazed the handle of the dagger at his belt. Not exactly a small or light knife, but she would only get one shot, so it would have to do.

The beam of light made another sweep across the grass. From its arc, Sera estimated the man holding the lantern was almost directly beneath them. In the split second when the beam went as far out to the east as it could before coming back again, Sera slipped the dagger free from Lysandro's belt, ignoring his frantic protests as she flipped the blade in her hand and threw it.

The sound of shattered glass went up, and shouts were followed by angry footsteps—heading in the wrong direction.

"Go, go!" she hissed.

They scrambled to their feet and broke into a wild run across the field under the returned cover of darkness. Lysandro kept his fierce grip on her hand until a black stallion came into view. He hoisted her up by the waist into the saddle without stopping and jumped on behind.

He kicked the beast hard, and it flew across the open ground at a dizzying pace. Sera struggled to keep her balance, and groped for something to hold on to before she was jolted violently out of her seat. Lysandro's thigh muscles tightened around her, and his arm wrapped around her waist. He bent forward, pushing her low until her nose was almost pressed up to the saddle. The position stopped her from flailing at this breakneck speed. She clung to the saddle, and didn't dare to look as the ground whizzed past beneath her in a blur.

They had crossed onto the Alvaró estate when Lysandro finally slowed his horse's pace to a canter and Sera felt steady enough to sit up. When her house came into sight, she let out a sigh of relief. The sensation of calm was replaced in an instant by a flood of questions aimed at the man sitting behind her, in between whose thighs she was nestled.

"What was that knife Marek was holding? Did *he* destroy the temple? Why would he—"

Lysandro pulled up on the reigns, hopped down from his stallion, and brought her down gently from the saddle before clapping her by the arms and shaking her silly.

"What were you thinking?! Did you see what Marek did to those men? What he could have done to *you*?!"

She blinked back tears.

"I'm sorry! I didn't know..."

A high wind whipped at her, slicing her right to the bone. This time, she cried out as the cold damp of her dress battered her skin.

Lysandro released her and ripped the blanket out from underneath his horse's saddle. He grimaced at the sight of it and tried to brush it clean of horsehair and dirt. It was useless. He wrapped it around Sera's shoulders with an expression akin to shame.

"Forgive me, angel, I have nothing better to offer you at the moment."

It was heavy and coarse, and absolutely perfect against her chilled body.

She mumbled a thank you, not daring to look up at him. If not for the ice running through her veins, Sera's cheeks would have been burning. She felt so very stupid.

As if reading her mind and wishing to soothe her thoughts, Lysandro drew her close, pulling on the edges of the blanket until their cheeks grazed each other under the shadow of his hat. Sera was sure he could hear her heart pounding.

"Are you alright?" he asked in a voice as soft as velvet.

"I thought it was safe," she lamented.

"Nowhere is safe anymore."

"I feel safe now," she whispered, and buried her face in his chest.

Lysandro swallowed hard and brushed his gloved fingers against her cheek. He lifted her chin and brought her gaze up to meet his. The brilliance of his blue-gray eyes was so intense, Sera was liable to lose herself in them.

"You frightened me something terrible. If something had happened to you…" Worry gave way to agony across his face. He clutched her closer. "I would lay down my life to keep you safe."

She squeezed him around the waist. He was the only thing that felt familiar in this strange, dangerous place, and she craved his comfort and his warmth as much as his affection.

The Shadow of Theron clasped Sera's hand as he led her through the gardens of her father's estate to the front door.

"No, not that way," she said. "They don't know I'm missing."

"Signorina! Who would have come for you then, with no one to realize the danger?"

"You came."

A smile tugged at the corner of his lips. "And I always will."

"I can find my way inside from here," she whispered, stopping in front of a crack in the stone wall that stretched into the larder.

"Goodnight, Signorina, and please, I beg you—no more walks by yourself."

"I am like a prisoner then."

"I will do what I can to rid Lighura of its villainy. But that will be very little if I must constantly worry for your safety." He released her hand and stepped back.

Sera turned to go in, but just as quickly she found herself trapped again in the Shadow's arms. She savored his touch, breathing in his clean grassy scent, mixed with warm spices and the salt of the sea.

Lysandro nuzzled her nose, her cheek. His lips came dangerously close to hers, brushing against the corners of her mouth. The air was charged with anticipation, but he did not stir. His voice came like a gentle ripple across her skin, making her shudder in his arms.

"How I long to kiss you, Signorina. But I dare not. Not now, with my face hidden from you."

"Even if that's what I want?"

He groaned in exquisite agony. His grip on her tightened, his mouth was so close she could feel his warm breath on her face.

"I fear you would not say that, if you knew who I am."

"I know you well enough."

The weight of his refusal formed a sharp ache in her chest. He could remove the obstacle he had placed between them if he wanted to. Her feet backed away as if on their own, withdrawing her from his false embrace.

But Lysandro held her fast. "No," he pleaded. "Don't leave me like this, with a storm brewing against me in your heart."

"Why should I stay?" she whispered.

He searched her eyes, and found his own want mirrored there. He dipped his head and took her bottom lip between his own, tugging at it ever so gently, so that the feel of their mouths together was as soft as a dream. They parted again all too quickly, with only a whisper between them. Desire crackled through his embrace like a lightning bolt, and he pressed his mouth to hers again.

Sera had never been kissed like this before, fiercely, and yet gently, from a deep well of longing. He was living for this kiss; it turned her knees soft. He squeezed her tighter as she buckled in his embrace. Lysandro kissed her like he might never again.

She met his eager affection with her own. Her skin thrilled at the feverish grip of his gloved hands on her waist, in her hair. She fell deeper and deeper into his caress until the whole world faded away. When her heart was near to bursting, he broke from her, leaving the smallest lingering touch. The light, feathery passes of his tongue over her bottom lip made her desperate for more. She couldn't think or even breathe—she just wanted to live inside his kisses.

His name almost escaped her, but she feared shattering this perfect moment.

Lysandro pressed his forehead to hers, resting his sleek nose against her cheek. "Now I am doomed, you beautiful, bewitching thing. Promise me. Promise me you'll always be mine."

Sera brushed her thumb against his mask, slipping her finger underneath to feel the smooth skin of his cheek.

"Whose?"

He flinched. "I can't. You may never forgive me if I do."

She could be patient. And she could play his game. "You must, or you will lose me to Don Lysandro."

His pulse jumped beneath her fingertips as she spoke his name.

"Will you marry him?" His eyes were bright with hope, though he tried to force the pretense of jealousy into his voice.

Never had Sera felt so wanted. He was undone, and it made her heart glow.

"I may."

"Then I must hurry. I *will* find the courage to reveal myself to you."

"Promise?" she pleaded, nuzzling her face against the curve of his chin.

"I promise," he answered fervently.

He brushed her cheek with his knuckles, then released her with a reluctant sigh.

The Shadow was still in the courtyard, staring up at her as she came to the balcony of her room to bid him a final farewell. He pressed his fingers to the brim of his hat and blended back into the shadows.

13

ELIAS CLOSED THE DOOR AFTER HIS SON AND RETURNED TO HIS CHAIR. HE leaned back, taking his glass of wine with him.

If Sancio said it was Marek who had ordered the destruction of the temple, then it was. Elias didn't understand why the high priestess would doubt him. Especially after what had happened. Marek's own inaction, coupled with Sancio's testimony, was damning. Anyone with brains in his head instead of rocks would conclude the same.

As to why Marek would commit such an act, Sancio had been more reluctant to talk. He had never been a good liar. Even as a boy, he could never sit still while protesting his innocence over whatever new trouble he and Lysandro had gotten into. He had told Elias the truth about the temple raid, but not the *whole* truth. He had his reasons, Elias supposed, and it didn't much affect his decision to visit the chief magistrate. Elias had always trusted his friend's judgment, but the glaring aberration of Marek's appointment seemed a grave oversight.

But the preparations for his journey could wait until morning. First he had to deal with the relic. Elias rose from his chair and retrieved it from behind the grandfather clock. Sancio had tucked it behind at the sound of Lysandro ascending the stairs to the front door; it was up to Elias to put it back where it belonged.

The weapon was surprisingly light for its size. Had it been crafted anywhere else but Morgasse's forge, it would have easily weighed ten times as much, and been impossible for Elias to lift. He'd grown thinner as he'd aged, and had worried whether he could do what was required as he watched Sancio struggle with it.

He *had* struggled with it, Elias recalled. Sweat had poured from Sancio's forehead as he crossed the threshold, and many minutes had passed before his breath had become steady enough for him to explain himself. But the object Elias now held in his hand felt no heavier than a bread knife.

Elias had known his family's legacy since he was a boy. The secret pride of the de Castels had been passed down through the ages, always kept on their ancestral land until the Aruni had insisted on locking it away for themselves. He had long dreamed of the day when he would see the relic with his own eyes, and use it to save the world as his ancestor had once done. But the vigor of his youth had come and gone, and no monsters had risen up from the Abyss for him to fight. The specter of the past had not reared its frightful head. Until now. And now the sacred weapon that had always belonged to his family was returned to him.

But it was not meant for him. Its destiny lay with a young man who had not heard the stories Elias had been told at his own father's knee; Lysandro's mother had abhorred violence, and begged him not to fill their child's head with visions of slaughter. Lysandro had matured into a gentle soul. Elias worried that he had left off telling him for too long.

He pushed back against the feeling of having failed his son and those who had preceded him as he left the wine cellar built underneath the kitchen and stepped into a tunnel hidden behind a pair of stacked barrels. The path carved into the hard-packed dirt spanned the distance between the de Castel estate and the parcel of land Elias had bestowed upon Lysandro to build his own home. The ground sloped steadily downward as he walked, and the thinning air aggravated his breathing. He followed the meandering path for a little over an hour before he came to his destination, a cavernous space dug out beneath a small thatch-roofed house where a humble goatherd used to live. Craning his neck upward, Elias could see that Lysandro had not discovered the rooms above. The ladder leading up into the house, half-buried into the wall itself, was brittle with disuse, and a city of cobwebs sprawled across the entryway. The weak light of the lantern Elias held stung his eyes. He would have struggled in the increasing darkness if he had not known where to look. Against the wall on the far left, two wrought-iron vessels were embedded into the dirt a little above his head. Dipping his finger in, he found them both full of oil. Elias decided against igniting them, for fear the oil had turned, and instead bent down to place his own light on the ground, illuminating the long chest before which he knelt. Touching his fingertips to the dark grain of the wood sent an echo of his father's voice rushing back to him.

It may be empty now, but what belongs in this chest has been ours since Morgasse forged it, and put it into Theron's hands. It belongs to you now. If the Goddess calls, it will come to you. You must be ready to use it.

Tears pricked at the corner of his eyes. His vision adjusted, and he saw how much the space had changed. The place where he had spent so much time with his father training, preparing for a day that had never come, had fallen into disrepair. That day *was* coming. It was coming for his own son, and he wasn't ready for the task that seemed to be falling to him. Elias knew he should have risked his wife's wrath. He had robbed himself of those precious hours with Lysandro. Now they were lost forever, and the whole world might be made to pay the price.

Elias opened the chest. The red satin lining was as brilliant and pristine as he remembered it. He lifted the relic and wiped it with the hem of his robe until it shone before placing it back where it had come from.

Almighty Arun, have mercy on your poor servant, who neglected his sacred duty, and lend your power to my son. Test the strength of his heart, and you will find him worthy.

He closed the chest and leaned his hand against it, his body as heavy as his soul as he struggled to his feet. His knees groaned under the strain.

"Get up, you old fool," he grumbled to himself. "You've got a long journey ahead of you."

Elias went to bed late and rose early, as was his habit. He left before sunrise and headed west toward the city the chief magistrate called home.

The jostling of the carriage did little to soothe his aching body. Any time Elias attempted to doze off, his neck snapped back from the shock of a rut or a rock caught under the wheels. There was no perfect position that eased the crick in his spine, and Elias grumbled at how much the condition of the dirt path had deteriorated since he'd last used it. But he knew that was not an honest assessment; the road had not changed so much as *he* had—his body was no longer as tolerant of the journey. Today he felt his age. It was little wonder Lysandro requested that he carry his pistol with him, given the current state of things. That his son, who loathed violence where intelligence and sharp wit would suffice, had insisted on it, was sign enough that the situation had turned dire. His fingers stroked the handle of the firearm tucked into the inner lining of his coat for reassurance, then flailed forward again to grip the seat in front of him as the carriage flung itself into another crater.

In keeping with the urgency of his purpose, his driver only stopped long enough for lunch, then continued on until late before stopping for the night at a small inn. Elias slept more soundly than usual, grateful for the reprieve on his rattled bones.

Traveling another day and night like this brought him to the edge of Tolours on the third day just in time for a midday meal. Elias strode down the main thoroughfare with a gait borne of familiarity, and found the chief magistrate in the same tavern, sitting at the same table, and in the same chair that he had occupied for more than twenty years. His eyes lit upon de Castel the minute he passed through the doors.

"Elias! What a surprise to see you here!" The chief magistrate rose from his chair and opened his arms wide to embrace his friend.

Where Elias had thinned with age, Aleksander had increased. Limbs that had once been all wiry sinew now bulged with muscle. His friend had become a sturdy, solid fellow with a warm smile, perfectly suited to his job. He was affable and trustworthy, but still highly capable of intimidating would-be criminals.

Elias wondered how much of a surprise his appearance was; Montes had only just returned from making the same trip, and a slight twinge in Aleksander's brow, a questioning in his gaze, flickered across his expression before it had opened up in a wide grin. His hesitation had only shown on his face for a fraction of a second. But it had been there.

Elias took up his habitual place to Aleksander's right as the man ordered him a glass of grog.

"You've never met Carrick before, have you?" Aleksander asked.

"No, I don't believe I have." Elias extended his hand to the younger man seated to the magistrate's left. "Don Elias de Castel. It's my pleasure."

"Yes, he's mentioned you a few times."

"Carrick has been with me for, what, three years now?"

"Five."

"Five? No wonder you've been bugging me for a raise."

"Mmhmm. So how about it?"

"I guess so."

"Great. The wife'll be pleased." The deputy took a swig of his drink, then left an empty mug and a few coins on the table. "I'm heading back to the office. Feel free to stay here for a while."

"Thanks Chief," Aleksander quipped.

"No problem." He touched the tip of his hat, then left.

Aleksander turned back to Elias. "Can't remember one year to the next anymore."

"I know that feeling." Elias gulped heartily at his drink. It tasted just as he remembered, tart with a lingering sweetness at the end that made you want to suck on your teeth. An effective trick; customers were compelled to buy more food just to soak up the sugar.

"Where are you staying?" the chief magistrate asked.

That was quicker than Elias expected.

"I haven't decided yet." That was a lie, technically. Elias *had* decided that he would be staying with Aleksander, but he couldn't very well tell his friend that before he'd been asked.

"*I* have decided," Aleksander said predictably. "You will stay with me and Caterina."

"That's very kind."

Aleksander nodded. "How have you been, my friend? What brings you to town?"

How he responded to even his initial inquiries within earshot of the townsfolk would tell. Elias gave a noncommittal sigh.

"Things have been rocky lately. You've heard of the temple robberies here as well, I'm sure."

Aleksander's smile faded into a thin line. "Of course. But we've yet to see any temple officials."

Elias leaned back in his chair. "I would have thought the bigger cities like this one would be first in line for the Examiners' assistance."

Aleksander shrugged. "Who knows why the temple does anything the way it does. I would have thought your little corner of the world wouldn't have such problems."

"Quite the opposite. We've seen an uptick in violent crime. And less than a week ago, our temple was vandalized."

Aleksander's brows furrowed, pressing deep wrinkles into his sun-bronzed skin.

"Vandalized?"

Elias nodded. "Our window was shattered."

The magistrate let his breath out with a puff of his cheeks and rubbed his stubbled jaw with his hand.

"Wow. I didn't know."

"How could you?"

Elias watched his friend closely. Aleksander's face slid away from his, drifting down to the golden fathoms of his drink. Elias hadn't mentioned Marek's name; he didn't plan on doing that until later, when they were alone. But he knew the look on his friend's face. The chief magistrate looked guilty, for something that had happened many miles away. His reticence to talk only confirmed for Elias that he had much to say.

"I'd better get back to work," Aleksander said, digging his hand into his pocket as he stood up.

"Of course." Elias stayed the chief magistrate's money with a hand. "It's the least I can do if I'm to be your house guest."

"Wouldn't have it any other way. Come by around seven, I'll be home by then. The girls will be happy to see you too."

"Looking forward to it."

Elias was left with his thoughts and his grog; he purchased a boiled capon and buttered potatoes to sop it up along with a hearty bread. When he was finished, he browsed the shops on the main road and picked up a pair of silver bracelets inlaid with turquoise for Aleksander's daughters, whom he loved like nieces. He whiled away the rest of the afternoon on a bench in the square, taking in the sunshine and the people passing by. Despite the fact that a relic had been stolen from their temple, life seemed to be carrying on as normal here. They did not live with the same sense of gloom clinging to them like shadows, the feeling that their lives were contracting around them. Aleksander was responsible for that. He made them feel safe, allaying their fears rather than provoking them. The knowledge that Lighura alone suffered so acutely set Elias's jaw in determination.

He arrived at the home of the chief magistrate at the appointed hour, and was greeted at the door by Aleksander's daughters. Elias presented them both with their gifts, wrapped in brightly colored paper.

"Oh how wonderful! Thank you!" the younger of the two squeaked.

"You're quite welcome my dear. My, but you have grown since I saw you last. Another spring or two and you'll be fending suitors off with a stick."

The girl's eyes sparkled at the compliment. Carmen, her older sister, stretched onto the balls of her toes to peer over Elias's shoulder, all the while trying to keep her tone cool and disinterested.

"Is Don Lysandro with you?"

"I'm afraid not. Just me this time."

"Oh." The girl's face fell, but she recovered quickly. "Don't be silly, Signor, we're very happy to see you."

Elias smiled and allowed himself to be led into the dining room. Carmen was quite pretty, with dark eyes and raven hair. He would have been pleased to join his family to his friend's, but he laughed to himself as he recalled Lysandro's reaction to the girl's not-so-subtle flirtations. The sheer horror that crossed his face when Carmen had mistaken one of the characters in his beloved books for a style of tying up one's hair was something Elias would never forget. Even now, he had to drown his mirth in his wine as Aleksander passed him a glass. He didn't look quite as pleased to see Elias as he had this afternoon, but invitations had been offered and accepted, with no chance of retraction. Elias took pity on his old friend, doing his damnedest to retain his welcoming demeanor.

His wife came in at that moment and laid a feast on the table. The braised pork with stewed apples and crackling melted in his mouth.

"This is absolutely delicious. I can't remember having a finer meal, or finer company," Elias said.

Caterina ducked her head. "Thank you, Don de Castel. It's not every day we have such a gentleman as yourself honor us with a visit."

"I apologize for my son's absence. Matters at home have him preoccupied."

The girls inclined their heads, but Aleksander deftly turned the subject away from less pleasant topics.

More talk best saved for later, Elias mused.

"How is Don Lysandro? Is he married yet?" Aleks asked.

Elias waved a warning finger in the air, then pressed it to his lips. "Don't jinx it."

"Ah," Aleksander chuckled. "I won't say another word about it then."

At the end of the table, somewhere in Carmen's vicinity, Elias thought he heard a sob.

The meal passed quietly enough, with the conversation never straying toward the darker turn the world had taken. After bidding the ladies of the house a good night, Aleksander offered Elias something stiffer in the drawing room, a space steeped in shadows with a handful of candelabras standing watch from the corners of the room. He seemed resigned to it now; there was no way to avoid the conversation hanging in the air. Elias let his host settle into his chair and take his first draught of whiskey before he began.

"All is not well in Lighura, my friend."

"So you said."

"When a village is plagued by tragedy, as we have been, people need to feel the appropriate measures are being taken. To know that foul misdeeds carry with them dire consequences."

Aleksander pursed his lips.

"I have never questioned your judgment. You know that. But Marek has not eased our minds," Elias said, pushing past the magistrate's reticence. "He's dropped all semblance of performing the duties of his office."

"I'm sure it may seem that way, sometimes. But the job of a magistrate is more complicated than it appears. He must balance the benefit to the few against that of the many."

Elias offered his friend a sad smile. "Signor Montes said you'd say that."

Aleksander shifted in his chair, and tightened his grip on his glass.

"He lets his lieutenants run amok. There is no order in the village. And…he defaced the temple, Aleks."

The chief magistrate took a hard swallow of his whiskey. His cheeks and neck glistened in the candlelight.

"That's a very serious accusation."

"I wouldn't have come if it wasn't. But it's true."

Aleksander lashed out. "True," he huffed. "Can you prove it? That's what counts."

A reply to Aleksander's outburst wasn't necessary. Elias saw through his friend's blustering façade to the uncertainty beneath. But he was implacable.

"It will look bad for you, if you don't remove him."

"I knew this would come back to bite me. *Again.*"

Aleksander poured himself another whiskey and sank deeper into his chair. Elias waited. After a long silence, Aleks spoke, staring out into the darkness beyond the windows.

"Do you remember that abandoned farmhouse in San Treya, the one full of grain?"

It was hard to forget. Without that food, their whole regiment would have starved to death that winter.

"Everyone congratulated me on being clever enough to find it after that terrible storm," Aleksander continued, "but I…" His voice faltered. "I'd meant to be long gone by the time you passed that way. But we'd been marching for so long, and I was so cold…I slept like the dead. When the regiment came upon me, you all just assumed I'd gone on ahead to scout for food. No one suspected."

Elias couldn't think what to say. He didn't understand what one of his closest friends, one he'd bled beside and had risked his life for, was telling him. His mind went quiet.

"I've never told anyone that. Never. But he knew. One day, out of the clear blue sky, he appeared in my office, and informed me that he would be assuming the post of magistrate in Lighura. I laughed at him. And that's when he told me."

Elias shook his head to dispel the confusion, and forced himself to focus on the present.

"Why didn't you come to me?" he asked.

"How could I, with something like that? You were always so brave, so ready for the fight. I used to think you craved it. I never could stand the sight of blood." Aleksander paused. "I only thought of myself that day, and I've regretted it ever since. I didn't want to burden you with my problems."

"But now it has become my problem," Elias said. "My village is no longer safe."

Aleksander leaned his elbows on his knees and cupped his chin in his hands. "What can I say, Elias? There's no excuse for what I did. Or what I have done since to keep my secret. I'm as much of a coward now as I was then."

"You have no idea where he came from?" he asked.

"None. He may as well have descended from the sky, for all I know."

"Why us, I wonder? Why request an out-of-the-way post when you could blackmail your way into any city?"

Aleksander reddened at Elias's cavalier tone about the guilt he'd harbored for years, and how Marek had tortured him with it by demanding a betrayal of the office he'd never truly felt he'd earned.

"But that's precisely why," Aleksander answered. "He'd have less oversight, be under less scrutiny. Can you forgive me? I've made a mess of things."

Elias leaned forward and gripped the magistrate reassuringly on the shoulder. "We all make mistakes. But we aren't all in a position to do something about it."

Aleksander swallowed hard, seemingly frightened at the thought of confronting Marek after all the time that had passed. He must have made some impression, Elias thought, to still intimidate him.

"He won't go quietly."

"No. Which is why I'm asking you to come back with me."

Aleksander's shoulders shot up in alarm, then slumped just as quickly again. He cast Elias an uneasy look.

"You're not giving me much of a choice, are you?"

"No."

14

THE ASCENSION OF ARGOSS

On the eve of a new age, Argoss coveted the robe of the Head High Priestess of the Temple Morgasse. He was one of two sorcerer priests who had ascended through the ranks and was being considered by Priestess Imelda to succeed her.

Argoss was of middling birth, but had shown an aptitude for reading and casting runes early in his training. It was rumored that he exceeded the skills of the Head High Priestess when she had been his age. Fortune seemed to favor him. But in her own writing, Imelda expressed her reservation of bestowing her position upon him, for Argoss could not hide his ambition. She admitted in her journals that of the two candidates, Argoss was the superior diviner. But she devised a series of tests by which to examine their souls. What she found there, she described as a black, blinding fury.

Imelda discovered in his possession a trove of ancient runes, spells written in stone before the worship of the Three-Faced Goddess overtook the Allied Lands. They belonged to the cult of Anruven, whose magics called to darker elements, summoning them with blood and death and pain.

Imelda resisted calls to condemn him, hoping his interest in such dangerous sorcery was purely academic. But she contrived a way to observe him unseen. This revealed the true source of Argoss's power. Threading the archaic runes into Morgassen incantations, Argoss had gained the power not just to read the divining stones, but to move them, to bend fate to his will and forge his own destiny.

Argoss was declared guilty of corrupting the Goddess's gifts. As a sorcerer cannot be stripped of his power, he was sentenced to death. It took a great many Morgassen to bind him strongly enough for the Executioner to do her work. He was pierced through the heart with her sword, a blade whose tested strength as a family heirloom was enhanced by spells inscribed on the blade. This was the first time Argoss was killed.

THE FIRST TIME?

Lothan paused in his reading. The tight quarters that served as his bedroom had grown considerably darker without his notice. He replaced the nub of a candle left burning with another taper. Not a new one—he didn't have any of those—but one that stood tall enough to cast a decent light. He took another hearty gulp of cheaply barreled ale. When the amber liquid dribbled down the side of his cup, he swiped his hand across the heavy tome in his lap.

His mind had finally settled enough to decipher the florid script on the illuminated pages without making his vision swim, but there was still much that confused him. He had expected the temple's recorded histories to reveal how his sorcery had surpassed that of the order of Morgasse; he was dismayed to learn that it had been *built upon* their secrets, rather than made up of something else altogether.

The mention of Anruven held some promise, but Lothan had never heard the name before. He didn't know the first thing about the cults that had preceded the three temples. And he would never have access to Morgassen spells. He'd discovered fairly early in his endeavors that their sorcery was passed down orally. He couldn't steal what they didn't write down.

Such obstacles would have normally boiled his blood, but killing the captain had filled Lothan with a sense of supreme calm. He could think more clearly than he had in what felt like ages. For deep in the bowels of the ship, he had found what he sought. It lay now underneath a rotted floorboard in the corner of the room. Its pulsing magic made his skin feel tight, but he ignored it, confident that, with enough time, he would be able to tolerate handling it. By then, he would know exactly where to use it.

For now, he was content to read the stories that the Temple Arun hid even from its own members. But the text was rife with mysteries. Most puzzling of all was the last line. Had the rise of Argoss been in spirit, but not in the flesh? How many times *had* he been killed, and in how many ways? If he was to avoid Argoss's fate, he needed to understand the dangers. He read on.

A sword through the heart was not enough to destroy Argoss. He had already grown too powerful. He crumpled to the floor of the temple, but before his body could be removed, he opened his eyes. A purple flame enveloped him, and he rose to his feet, pulling the sword out of himself and hurtling it at the Executioner. She was killed instantly. A whole temple of sorcerers was not enough to bind him, and he slaughtered his enemies. Only a handful of priestesses survived. It is through their eyes that we are told of what happened next.

He sunk the Executioner's sword deep into its owner. When he lifted it out again, the blade dripped with her blood from tip to hilt, and seemed like it would bleed forever. He corrupted the runes etched into the steel, and turned its enchantment to a curse. This is how the Blood Sword of Argoss was made. The edge of the blade flowed with the lifeforce of its victims, its menace enlarged with every life taken. When later he added the blood of eldur vipers, the cursed sword was further tainted, and spewed a venom that gnawed at the flesh and bone of any close enough to be splattered by its spray, reducing them to dust.

He had risen from the dead, returned from the blackness beyond. He did not come alone. In an ancient tongue no longer remembered, Argoss ordered the ground to cleave itself in two. Creatures of the Abyss wriggled and crawled their way forth, taking to the sky and blotting out the sun, sinking into the oceans, and burying themselves deep in the forests. He commanded them with a whisper, and his legions tore the world asunder, devouring all hope.

This is all very fine, Lothan thought, *but how?*

He began to flip through pages without reading them. The passages about Argoss devolved into a bestiary of all the monsters under his dominion. Each was illuminated in excruciating detail, with a record charting the average size of each monster, its habits regarding hunting, nesting, and breeding, its behavioral tendencies and vulnerabilities, and the largest of its kind that Theron had killed.

The illustrations piqued Lothan's interest, but ultimately, such records were useless. Then came an even longer list of Theron's many triumphs, as well as a record of the injuries he sustained with a weird symbol marked alongside, a downward curve with two short strikes underneath. He skimmed a little less quickly here, looking for information he could turn to his advantage.

Lothan couldn't comprehend what Theron had done to deserve the goddess's many blessings. He was no one in particular, and had done nothing of note that merited such divine favor. All the Aruni managed to say about their precious warrior was that he was exceedingly strong, wielded with ease the sword, axe, and bow alike, and conquered his enemies with an unlikely courage and unrelenting ferocity.

There was mention of Theron's weapons being enchanted, along with many other boons from the sorcerer goddess. But where there was great depth and breadth dedicated to battles and monsters, the *magic* with which he was able to do it received only the barest summaries.

And then it hit him.

"Of course," he muttered aloud. That's why it was called *The Histories*. There was more than one. Authored by the Aruni, the book in his hands focused on the concerns of the warrior, and would reveal little of the sorcery that lent Theron his supernatural strength. He had stolen the wrong book.

Even Theron's most formidable weapon, the so-called Hand of Arun, was described in simple terms. It was a golden bow, bestowed upon the goat herder after having proven himself in a battle against a horde of goblins with his bare hands. The arrows it loosed never missed their target. There was a lengthy passage about the tussle with the goblins, the appearance of Arun to bestow this gift, and that of Faelia to give him healing and protective potions, but none of that was *explained*. How the bow had been forged, how it managed to never miss, and how it could destroy something that had already been dead remained steeped in the shadows of the past. Even if such answers were recorded in the pages of the Morgassen *Histories*, temples everywhere were on their guard. And while the Aruni would protect their boundaries with brute force, the Morgassen would undoubtedly employ more sophisticated methods, ones that Lothan was unsure he could breach.

He slammed the book closed, and was about to toss it into the fire, but something stopped him. He laid the book on his lap again and pulled his hands away from the binding, letting the book open of its own accord. His eyes drank in the sight of the engraving staring back at him with a luminous hunger.

THE EYE

The origins of Argoss's pendant remain unknown. There is a school of thought that says Argoss crafted it himself, and that it allowed him to concentrate his indominable will and to impose that will on others. But there are certain parallels between the necklace that Argoss was seen wearing after the slaughter at the temple and the Eye of Anruven.

Tales of the Eye go back for many generations in some pockets of the world, with the majority of the village keepers claiming that the stories regarding the Eye were considered ancient even in the time of their great ancestors. As is always the case with folklore, the tales are often nonsensical and frequently contradictory. Still, there is general agreement upon some basic points. One, that the bearer of the pendant possesses the power to influence the minds of those he comes into direct contact with. Two, that the Eye imposes its will upon the wearer in equal if not greater measure than its wearer does upon others. And third, that to covet the Eye is to court your own doom.

Among the variations in the lore, the pendant is commonly believed to have greater powers still, to unleash the wearer's will onto the world and turn his deepest desires into reality. Those who hold to this say it was the Eye that created Argoss's desert fortress. But such a power is warned to come at the cost of one's own soul, reportedly consumed by degrees until the will of the Eye has swallowed that of its owner. Then it moves on, like a parasite, calling out to its next host. To become the owner of such a prize, a great sacrifice is allegedly required to satisfy Anruven's notorious lust for blood.

Such tales enjoy supremacy in the mountainous regions where the cult of Anruven once thrived. Given Argoss's own connections to the obscure cult, the view that he sought out the Eye and was successful bears the ring of truth. In return for unspeakable acts of cruelty, Argoss is believed to have been granted the boon of his Lost Fortress, the impenetrable citadel obscured by the shifting sands.

There is some debate among scholars of the temples as to the fate of the Eye following Theron's victory over Argoss. Some argue vehemently that it spirited itself away, returned to its primal source, and that it lies in wait for a new owner. Others insist that it was not destroyed, nor did it disappear, but that it was sealed away, with such nearly insurmountable difficulty that a number of Morgassen assigned to the task surrendered their lives in order that the seal might succeed.

Lothan tore his gaze away from the graven image, its center a deep inky black, a reflection of the Abyss itself. The next page bore an illustration of a twilit desert with a forbidding citadel towering over a walled city of stone. The shadows of the dunes in the foreground took on shapes of their own. The image was framed from a great distance, its imposing scale and mazelike structure shrouded in darkness. Lothan tilted the page in his hand, trying to get the dim light to reflect off the golden ink etched across it. All he could make out was the simple description written at the base of the page.

THE LOST FORTRESS—*Argoss's hidden stronghold. Obscured and impenetrable until Morgasse produced from her forges the Cerulean Key, which pointed the way and allowed Theron to hunt down Argoss in his own domain. The site of the final confrontation.*

Lothan squinted. In the weak light, the ink from the reverse page was seeping through. He flipped the page to find what appeared to be a map, except that it had no names.

There were no words, no markings of any kind except for the crudely drawn sand dunes, what might have been a canyon or mountain ridge, and a diminutive source of water. Lothan assumed it represented what the Aruni knew of the location of the fortress—in other words, nothing.

He leaned back in his chair. His heart was now set on the Eye. A deep craving for its power had already taken root. It was not unreasonable for him to assume that, whether sealed or hidden, it would be found where Argoss had breathed his last. But far more important—Lothan no longer lamented his limited ability to acquire more shards of the Blood Sword in the hopes of reforging a complete weapon. It would grow on its own; he needed only to use it.

15

SERA DIDN'T KNOW HOW SHE WAS SUPPOSED TO LOOK AT LYSANDRO AND
pretend that last night hadn't happened. She'd barely gotten any sleep.
When she had, she had dreamed of Lysandro, and losing herself in his
never-ending kisses.

He was thinking about it too. She could see it in his eyes as he stood
opposite her in the doorway.

The morning light played on the strong lines of his face, and the gentle
curve of hair that fell past his shoulder. Lysandro's gaze shone with an
eager hopefulness, kept in check by the barest hint of a smile. There was a
quiet, seductive quality to his eyes that she hadn't seen before. His
attention drifted downward to her lips, sharpening her own hunger and
causing the butterflies occupying her chest to flutter violently against her
ribcage.

Lysandro swallowed hard, and greeted her in a subdued voice.

"Good morning."

"Good morning," Sera replied.

Lysandro bit his lip. It made Sera dig her nails into the doorway to
keep from swaying on her feet.

"I wasn't sure if you would see me."

Sera blinked, confused. "Why wouldn't I?'

"Yesterday. I promised I'd come to see you, and then—"

"Oh." Right. Of course. She wasn't supposed to know that Lysandro and the Shadow were the same, and that she *had* seen him. She should be cross. But it just didn't feel right.

"I…assumed it was for a good reason." Sera hadn't forgotten the horrors she'd witnessed on the beach, or the cold misery of the hours preceding them.

Lysandro's cheeks colored, and he shook his head.

"You're being too easy on me. I'm not in the habit of breaking my promises, and it pains me deeply that I broke one to you. I'd like to try to make up for it, if I can."

"What did you have in mind?"

Lysandro extended his hand. She was not the only one to feel a thrill rush through her as their hands touched; she was sure of it. But neither acknowledged it as they climbed up into his carriage and sat opposite each other.

"Did you sleep well?" he asked. His unease was palpable. For all he supposedly knew, she hadn't been drenched to the bone for hours only to witness a bloodbath. But that didn't stop him from worrying about her. Her sleep *had* been disturbed, but the Shadow's warm embrace had given her mind the excuse it needed to chase her nightmares to the very back of her thoughts.

"I'm okay," she said. And she was, given the circumstances.

He nodded, and didn't press her further.

Long minutes passed wordlessly by as they made their way to the main road. Sera didn't know what to expect this morning. She half-hoped that he would tell her who he was, then and there in the privacy of his carriage, and end this need to feign a detachment that contradicted every impulse of her body. Then she might be able to make sense of what she had seen from behind his shoulder.

But he didn't, and that left Sera feeling unsure of what to do. After giving it some thought, she tried to feel around the edges of what they weren't saying.

"Is everything alright?"

"Hmm?"

"With—" she hesitated. "I don't know what, I guess. With whatever it was that called you away."

"No," he answered after some deliberation.

It wasn't what she wanted to hear, but she was grateful for his honesty.

"Still," he continued, "it's not an excuse for my absence. I wouldn't want you to think that—"

He avoided her gaze, turning his face out toward the window.

"I hadn't forgotten about you. I know I haven't made the best impression, but I want you to know that any confidence you put in me won't be misplaced."

She could see why he would be upset. Without knowing what she knew, Lysandro's behavior would appear erratic. But she understood the root cause of his distraction all too well, and couldn't help but be sympathetic. The fact that she was a consideration at all, given the state of things, showed how much he cared.

She thought about their upcoming dinner date, and how it would stop the Shadow from being where he might be needed.

"We don't have to go anywhere tonight, if you don't want," she said.

His face snapped to hers, creased with worry.

"I mean, we can go another time, if that would be easier for you, once things are more...settled."

Lysandro's frown increased. "No. No I don't want to do that."

"Lysandro, the world is turning upside down."

He winced.

"The streets are not safe to walk alone, according to you, Marek has thrown care to the wind, the temple is in ruins..."

"All the things you've said are true, but not every hour of every day needs to be consumed by them. Come with me tonight. Please."

If he could spare a few hours with her, then maybe things were not as terrible as they seemed. Sera wanted to believe that.

"If you insist."

The light returned to Lysandro's face. "I do. And now, I owe you a proper apology."

The carriage stopped, and he let her out into the middle of a road lined with shops, right in front of the—

"I thought jewelry at first, but that didn't seem quite right. Too predictable, not sincere enough. Then I thought perhaps something edible," Lysandro continued, his smile reflecting the pure delight on Sera's face. "But given your impeccable talents, I didn't think any of the confectioner's shops were up to the task of impressing you. So I asked myself, what would Sera most enjoy…"

She was deep into the labyrinthine pathways of the bookshop before Lysandro could finish. By the time she felt his stalwart presence behind her, she already had a book in each hand.

"I'd nearly forgotten about this one. It was set to be released just as I was leaving Mirêne." She weighed the tome in her other hand. "This one though, is much harder to find." She balanced the books in her hands like scales, and settled on the rarer book before moving on.

Time fell away as Sera rifled through books she had never heard of nestled next to more renowned tales.

"What do you think? Stolen portrait or hidden staircase?"

"Hidden staircase, of course," Lysandro replied. "Sounds much more dastardly than a musty old painting gone missing."

She would have been overcome by the urge to smack him, had he been serious. But his snooty air was accompanied by a wry smirk. He was teasing her, and she relished it.

"You never know. The painting could be haunted."

He laughed and threw his hands in the air. "Sure. Why not?"

"Fine. Neither of those then." She replaced the competing titles and drew another from the far-right side. "Maybe this one. His stories are a little on the weird side, but always satisfying. So what's left then? A cursed jewel, always in style, something hidden in the attic, no doubt a lunatic—"

"Naturally."

"A murder at sea, and…" she pulled again at the latest adventure of her favorite detective, discarded earlier in favor of the rarer find. "Still thinking about this one."

She laid them all out next to each other on a narrow table in the middle of the aisle, designed for customers to examine precious texts. "Now: to choose."

Sera assumed a posture of deep thought, but Lysandro just laughed under his breath, shook his head, and began stacking the books one on top of the other.

"Oh no—" She tried to stop him, but his strides were long, and he reached the counter before her.

"We'll take these."

The storekeeper's eyes lit up. "Certainly, Don de Castel."

Sera scrambled up from behind him, pressing her back to the counter and putting herself between him and the shopkeeper.

"Lysandro wait. I didn't mean—"

"Sera. If you agree to marry me—"

"We're on *this* again?"

"Mmhmm. It'll be up to me to provide for your every need. And your every wish."

As he said this, he touched the tip of her nose with his index finger. The affectionate touch and his warm smile sent a shiver across her skin.

"Thank you," she said. "You didn't have to."

"It's my pleasure. I really *am* sorry about yesterday."

"I know. I'm not angry." She never had been.

"I wish I could take you to lunch, but I do have some other things that need taking care of before tonight," Lysandro said as they resumed their seats in the carriage. "Now at least you'll have something to keep you occupied."

Sera wondered if that wasn't his intention all along, to keep her nose-deep in a book so she wouldn't go wandering about again and get herself into more trouble. Either way, it worked.

"Why didn't you get anything for yourself?" she asked.

Lysandro shrugged. "I'm not in need of new books just yet. There's still some life in my well-worn favorites."

"But can any of them rival the likes of these?"

Lysandro's head lilted to one side and arched his eyebrow.

Sera rose to the challenge. She unwrapped the neat bow tying her purchases together, opened the book at the top of the stack, and read aloud.

"True! Nervous—very, very dreadfully nervous I had been and am, but why will you say that I am mad?"

Sera closed the front cover, aloof to it, and returned the book to the pile. Lysandro stared at her with an expression that was unreadable.

Neither of them said a word. Sera very calmly began to retie the string atop the books.

"You can't just stop there." Lysandro left the opposite bench to sit beside her and took the book from her hand before she could fasten it to the others. Sera smiled in triumph as he put his arm around her, opened the book again on her lap, and began to read over her shoulder.

"Not too sordid for you?" she asked, looking up at him through veiled eyelids. "I'd hate to ruffle your delicate sensibilities."

He was ruffled, all right. The fire in his eyes nearly melted her, and turned all her witty remarks to pudding inside her head. She quit needling him and settled into a comfortable position. The scent of open fields and spiced soap from Lysandro's skin, so close to hers, warmed her cheeks. His fingers curled around her shoulder, then began absently twirling her hair around themselves.

Sera couldn't read like this. The words on the page swam in front of her eyes, her head spun in feverish circles. All her concentration was directed to the places where he was touching her. Any words or movement threatened to shatter the intimacy of the moment, so she stayed still, only daring to lean deeper into his embrace. Her heart raced at a furious gallop, and she wished that Lysandro would toss the book aside and kiss her, wildly and without restraint. She couldn't be sure, maybe she only imagined it or wished it to be so, but she felt his body curling tighter around hers. His face was so very close, enough so that if she only dared to turn her head…

"You can turn the page now."

Sera inhaled sharply as if waking from a dream, and did as he asked.

I have no idea what that said.

Lysandro's fingers didn't leave her hair until they left the carriage. He carried the books for her up to the house, but she held the one they'd been reading (*he'd* been reading) out to him.

"You first," she said.

"But it's yours."

"Husbands and wives do share books sometimes, don't they?"

Lysandro went very still.

"It makes for good conversation, I imagine." She extended her arm out to him further, pressing him to take it. She saw the notch at the base of his throat bob as he did so.

"I'll be back at six o'clock."

She smiled. "I'll see you then."

"I don't like her."

"You've never even met her," Lysandro protested. It had taken him a while to catch up with Sancio, but now that he had, he wished he'd put it off for longer.

"Even so," Sancio said. He uncrossed his arms to take a swallow of his ale, then tucked them back again.

"*What* don't you like about her?"

"She's lying to you, for starters."

Lysandro balked in disbelief. "When? She hasn't lied to me once."

"She's supposed to be engaged to you—or almost—and she's spending her nights in the arms of someone else."

"But it *is* me!" he hissed, dipping his voice below the din of the tavern's midday crowd.

"She doesn't know that," Sancio pointed out. "Doesn't say much for how faithful she'd be as a wife."

Lysandro tried to rationalize it, to unfurl the knot his friend's words were tying in the pit of his stomach.

"We're not married. Not yet."

"That doesn't give her the right to throw herself at other men behind your back."

"You don't understand..."

Lysandro's mind was a whir. He couldn't bring himself to doubt Sera's sincerity. Although she hadn't said yes to him yet, she *hadn't* said no. The more time they spent together, the less he believed she would. This morning with her had been perfect. Or nearly; he'd stopped himself from sweeping her up into his arms in the coach. Now, of course, he was kicking himself for not seizing the moment. The feel of her body nestled beside his, the closeness of her soft curves, were enough to drive him mad. He could have told her everything. He should have.

Things got more complicated when he considered how things might have been, had she rejected the Shadow's advances. He wouldn't be as close to her as he felt now; they might not have been on speaking terms at all. And that kiss—he'd never wanted that kiss to end. He *would* tell her the truth. But for now, he trusted that dizzying feeling he had whenever she was near, and the sparks that flew between them whether they met in the open or under cover of night.

"She's playing with your heart and you're letting her."

The words came out louder than Sancio meant them to, but Lysandro was just being so thick-headed. "At the end of the day, *you're* courting her, and *she's* giving her affection to another."

Lysandro's expression soured. "Why do you always have to spoil everything?"

"You want to blame me? Fine. But you know I'm right."

Something ugly boiled up inside Lysandro. He tried to bury it by changing the subject.

"Why did you come to see me at my father's house?"

"I don't remember anymore. Nothing for you to worry about now."

Lysandro sat back in his chair. "Which is it?"

Sancio dodged the question. "I've got to go, or I'll be late for my training."

"I thought that was Lundays and Tyrsdays."

"The Aruni train every day. And I am an Aruni." Sancio stood abruptly and left.

Whatever change had come over his friend, Lysandro didn't like it. He finished his meal in solitude, and tried to remind himself that his friend was going through a lot. He had to face the ruination of the temple every day, and Lysandro was sure tempers were running high there, with no clear person to direct their anger at. But it was no excuse for talking about Sera like that. He didn't know her, didn't know the first thing about her. And whatever Sancio said, Lysandro *was* the Shadow and Sera *hadn't* given her affection to another. If she was falling in love with the Shadow, she was falling in love with *him*, or, at least, a part of him. He just hoped she would fall in love with all of him.

Lysandro paid his tab and walked the short distance to Rafael's house. The door was locked, the windows reflected only darkness from inside, and no one answered when he knocked. Everything was exactly as he expected. Casting a glance over his shoulder to make sure he was unobserved, he slipped through an unlocked window on the east-facing side of the house. He fastened the sill shut again the minute he was inside. The candle was where he'd left it. It was almost down to the nub, and Lysandro had a hard time making out the surgeon's handwriting on the slip of paper he'd given him.

"Feverfew...Goldenseal...Valerian..."

Lysandro plucked the vials and jars Rafael requested off the splintered shelves and gathered them up on the floor. It was still streaked with blood. The air was fetid. It crept into Lysandro's nostrils and wrought havoc on his full stomach, urging him to finish his work quickly. Seeing the blackened pools of gore staining the tiles made Lysandro want to march straight into Marek's office and remove his head from his neck. But he knew it would be a mistake. He couldn't afford to goad the magistrate any further. He needed to give his father time, and maybe by then even the Examiners would be there to help. There had been no visible response from the Shadow for the destruction of the temple window. As much as it stuck in his craw, it suited Lysandro's purposes to let Marek think he'd had the last word. Lysandro hoped that if he kept his own anger in check, the dangers that Lothan posed would not continue to multiply.

Some of the things Rafael had asked for were destroyed, covered in a sheen of shattered glass. But most of it had been untouched in the wake of Lothan's attack. He grabbed a handful of Rafael's tools, shoved them into his medical bag, and then promptly spilled them back out again.

"Stupid, stupid."

If Marek and his men came back, the missing bag would raise suspicion. Forced to improvise, Lysandro wandered into the kitchen and upended a sack of rotting potatoes onto the floor. He stuffed the sack full again with his findings and slipped back out the window, walking along the empty streets behind the line of houses until he met up with his coachman.

"Bring this in with you," he told Salla as they approached his own front door.

The driver hefted the sack off the bench and brought it in through the kitchen, meeting his master there. Lysandro thanked him and headed to the tucked away spare bedroom where Rafael had taken up residence.

The curtains were drawn, letting in only a sliver of light. Rafael turned to greet him at the door.

"Did you find everything okay?" he asked.

"I think so. Some of them I couldn't salvage."

Rafael inspected the labels, bringing them very close to his face before setting them down on the maple bureau. "These would have been harder to replace. Thank you."

Lysandro sat in a nearby armchair. "How are your eyes?"

"Better, I think?"

"Are you settling in?"

"Yes, yes."

"It's only until—"

"Yes, I know. Still, you *will* tell me if someone needs my help, won't you?"

"I don't think that's a good idea. Sort of defeats the purpose of hiding, doesn't it?"

"What's the point of saving my life if I can't help people?"

Lysandro groaned.

"Thank you. So, what's for dinner tonight?"

"Whatever you like. I'm going out, remember?"

"Oh right, sorry. Who is she again?"

"Seraphine Alvaró."

Rafael took the seat next to Lysandro and crossed his legs. "I think I saw her, at temple a few weeks ago. She's a redhead, right?"

"More like golden amber."

Rafael's grin widened in the darkness. "My mistake. Did you tell her who you are?"

Lysandro licked his lips. "I'm…working on it."

"Uh-huh."

"Oh, not you, too."

"Me too what?"

"I may have…told her how I feel…disguised as someone else."

After a beat, Rafael let out a low chuckle.

Lysandro sighed, and slumped deeper into his chair. "I didn't mean to. It just sort of happened."

"I'm sure it'll be fine," Rafael assured him.

"You think so? Sancio said that—"

"Never mind what Sancio said. Have you ever seen him get within a hundred feet of a girl?"

Lysandro hadn't.

"Trust me. If she's still seeing *you*, after she's already had her head spun by the Shadow, it means she hasn't ruled you out. She'll probably be relieved not to have to choose between you."

"I hope you're right."

"Of course I am. I know a lot more about women than you do."

"That so? You're not married any more than I am."

"I'm a bachelor, not a virgin. There's a difference."

Lysandro raised an eyebrow. "Excuse me?"

"Sorry friend, I don't kiss and tell. But I will say: all those girls whose hearts you broke by never deigning to notice them…they had to dry their tears somewhere."

Lysandro huffed. "You're terrible."

"The fairer sex would tell you otherwise." Rafael's grin assumed a wolfish glint.

Lysandro just shook his head. He was glad the darkness obscured the rising heat in his face.

"Will you tell her tonight?"

"Maybe. I don't know."

"What are you waiting for?"

Lysandro wasn't sure how to answer that. Things were going really well between them. And he *did* want her to know. He just didn't want to ruin it.

* * *

Lysandro never ceased to be dazzled by Sera's beauty, but this…this was something else altogether.

Her delicate, rose-golden gown glistened as she approached. As if by reflex, Lysandro reached for his heart to check that it was still working.

He hadn't yet regained the power of speech by the time they were both in the carriage and on their way to dinner.

Compliment her, he chided himself. *Say something, you damned fool, and stop staring*. But he couldn't. He just could not take his eyes from her.

The angel sitting opposite him noticed his struggle, and was the first to speak.

"Is something wrong?"

"No! No, it's just that…you look…that dress…" Lysandro closed his mouth to gather his jumbled thoughts. Then he spoke in a clear, soft voice. "You take my breath away, Sera. That's all."

Her face glowed at his words. He yearned to reach out and stoke the flames rising in her cheek with his palm.

Sera changed the subject as they left Lighura behind.

"It's been a while, remind me—what does Faelsday look like around here?"

"Oh, that's right, that's a big deal in Mirêne."

Sera's eyes glimmered. "There are no words to describe the excess I've been a party to."

Lysandro tilted his head, curious now. "Try."

She sighed. "Where to start? Probably with the alcohol."

That made Lysandro laugh. He couldn't picture the vision before him as a drunken merrymaker.

"Lots and lots and *lots* of alcohol. There's flowers and music everywhere, singing and dancing in the streets, fancy little pastries, a dizzying theater schedule…and between Fabien and Fane, enough jewels to swim in."

"Swimming in jewels? That sounds like fun."

"It is."

Lysandro had been joking; he raised his eyebrows when he realized Sera wasn't. "We don't get up to anything that grand, I'm afraid. We do have a bazaar though, with some specialty foods on offer, and stalls selling items of very fine craftsmanship. I'd be happy to take you to that."

"Any theater?" Sera asked.

"Do you like theater?"

"If there's *anything* I love more than reading…"

Lysandro tried to suppress a smile, but Sera caught it.

"Lysandro?"

"Hmm?"

"What are you hiding?"

He didn't know how to answer that. It wiped the smile from his face. He said nothing as he offered her his arm as they walked up the steps to a palatial structure made of glass. Light reflected everywhere in the cool evening. The jewels in Sera's hair and the glittering fabric of her gown shone the brightest of all.

Lysandro's heart beat faster as her grip on his arm tightened, and she stretched up toward him to speak softly in his ear.

"Whatever it is, I will find out."

"Is that a threat?"

His collar suddenly felt too close, too tight. He hoped they were still talking about the theater.

"No. But you have been warned." When she smiled at him, all the knots in his chest that made it difficult for him to breathe unfurled.

"I don't know what's planned for the festival, but I believe *The Lady in the Lake* is playing now," he said.

Lysandro felt a jolt run through her. If they hadn't been linked at the arm, she might have sprinted to the playhouse.

"Oh! Can we—?"

"I'm afraid not, Signorina," the man at the next table interjected as she and Lysandro were seated. "They've been sold out for weeks."

Sera took the news hard. Her face fell, becoming the very picture of hopelessness.

"I'm cursed. I must be," Sera lamented.

"It's a shame, but—"

"You don't understand. *Every* time there's a production of *The Lady in the Lake*, something prevents me from seeing it. I'm going to go to my grave without ever having seen my favorite play on the stage. I know I am."

Lysandro bit his tongue. He would *not* smile this time.

The waiter brought them a loaf of warm, freshly baked bread. Lysandro let her dig in first.

"Well?" he asked. "Is it any good?"

Sera let out a little moan of satisfaction that made his hair stand on end.

"I'm glad this meets with your approval. I was worried that you would think Andras was devoid of high culture."

"Excellent bread is a good omen. But I wouldn't exactly call Mirêne's penchant for drunkenness a paragon of 'high culture.'"

"Do you miss it?"

"Being drunk?"

"Mirêne," Lysandro laughed.

Sera's face turned serious, and suddenly Lysandro was afraid of what she might say.

"I miss it less than I did."

Those few words filled him with unspeakable hope.

"I still wouldn't say no to a drink though."

"Is there a particular wine you prefer?"

"It depends on the food. What would you recommend here?"

"Um…"

Lysandro's eyes dropped to the table. When he found the courage to look up again, his smile had been replaced with a sheepish expression.

"I've…never eaten here before."

"But it seems like just the kind of place you'd love."

"I've always thought so too. But…it's primarily for…for couples…"

Sera inhaled, but didn't say anything.

"I was never comfortable eating alone in public. And bringing my father would have been…" he shrugged.

"You've never courted anyone?"

"Just you."

He felt silly saying it, but it was the truth. He'd never had more than a passing interest in any girl. There was just never any spark. Not like the one Sera's warm smile sent thrilling down his spine as she reached across the table and interlaced her fingers with his.

"You can pick the wine."

Her playful tone melted his embarrassment. Lysandro chose a full-bodied, fruity red that made the waiter's eyes bulge at the very mention of it.

It was worth every lyra.

"How is the reconstruction of the temple coming?" Sera asked.

"Slowly. The blacksmith is having a hard time finding anyone who knows how to remake the window."

"And I suppose we're not any closer to naming a culprit."

Lysandro's mouth settled into a grim line. "It would be impossible for Marek to find and punish the one responsible."

Sera nodded, as if she understood his double meaning. He was about to ask but then thought better of it, in this dining hall where their voices might carry who knew how far.

"What do you think the Shadow will do?"

"I don't know." That much was true.

"The villagers are expecting him to do *something*."

Lysandro fiddled with his fork, turning it one way and then the other to reflect the light from the ornate chandelier hanging above them. "I know."

What she said next froze the blood in his veins.

"It should be you."

His gaze snapped to her, and she seemed to falter under his wild stare.

"I mean...Lighura already looks up to you. I've only been here a few weeks, but it's obvious even to me. You're generous. Not just with your money, but with your time. You care. You wouldn't need a mask to gain their support. You already have it."

Lysandro sucked in a deep breath. The ice beneath his feet was very, very thin.

"They want a warrior to wreak vengeance upon their foes. But I've always been drawn to ideals that transcend Aruni principles of justice. I've tried to live by subtle, silent example. But that is becoming harder and harder to do."

Sera pursed her lips to one side. "I understand. And you're right, too. Right to seek something other than violence."

"You only say that because you grew up with a Faelian mindset. Here, if you're not ready to draw blood for even the smallest slight, you're a coward. Goddess knows I've been called that enough times."

"We favor bravery of the heart and mind. It takes a lot more guts to move against the flow than to go with it. It's like I told Marek—brains win over brawn every time."

Lysandro smirked. "I don't think I'll ever forget the look on his face when you essentially called him an idiot."

"He *is* an idiot, for trying to cut in when I was obviously happy with my partner. And he's an idiot if he thinks this isn't going to all come toppling down on his head. It's only a matter of when."

"And how many more people will get hurt before that happens. My father went to see the chief magistrate about it. I just hope he's able to impress upon him how serious this is."

"It can't be easy for the chief magistrate, admitting that he made a mistake."

"No. But my father still holds a lot of influence."

"We've never really met properly, he and I. Except when you shoved him out the door. You *did* offer him one of the deserts I made, didn't you?"

"Mmm..."

"Don de Castel!"

"Yes, yes, of course I did. Not willingly though."

Sera smiled. "I can make you more."

"Don't tempt me. He's a good man, he really is. I'm sorry your first impression of him suggested otherwise. He's just a little *too* excited to see his grandchildren."

Sera shrugged. "That's normal at his age. He probably wants something to occupy his time with."

Lysandro had never thought of it quite that way before.

Dinner arrived in a series of small, carefully composed plates that produced a symphony on Lysandro's tongue. Buttery meats harmonized with floral notes. Fruits picked in the prime of their sweetness paired with decadent, bitter chocolate, rich honeys, and deep caramel. Lysandro watched, transfixed, as Sera licked a bit of chocolate from her lips. His pulse quickened as he imagined putting his mouth to hers to consume that heady sweetness. Goddess, how he wanted to devour her. If he couldn't make love to her then and there, he could at least hold her in his arms.

After the final course the music swelled, inviting couples to dance. Lysandro drew her to the middle of the floor in a smooth, liquid movement, bringing her deeper into his embrace by degrees as the songs grew slower and sweeter.

"Now that you're here," Sera asked, "was it worth the wait?"

Lysandro gazed down at her and returned her warm smile. "Yes."

Her understanding was reflected in the blush that blossomed on her cheeks. Sera drew closer to him, shrinking the light between them as they danced. It sent his heart spinning. Just when Lysandro thought he wanted nothing more out of life, the orchestra began to play an old love song, of a woman staring out to sea, forever waiting for her beloved to return. Above the violin's sad notes, he heard the voice of an angel.

He became enrapt by Sera's lush mouth as it gave voice to the lovesick maiden, praying for mercy from the treacherous waves.

Lysandro had read many tales of women who swooned when serenaded by men. But he'd never understood just how powerful it could be. Gazing at Sera, her eyes full of starlight as she sang, *just* for him, turned his knees to jelly. The room spun around them, but so long as he gave himself over to her song, he was anchored by it, and could keep up with her boundless grace. The melody echoed in his mind, her sweet soprano the perfect lullaby for a small child nestled in her arms. He blinked to stop his emotions from overtaking him.

The song ended in a whisper. Sera closed her lips in a smile, and as they stood facing each other on the dance floor, Lysandro dared to cradle her face in his hands. He lost his heart to her completely.

"I've always loved that song," she said.

"That was the most enchanting thing I've ever heard."

She didn't pull away from him as his thumbs grazed her cheeks.

"Shall we stay for the second set?" she asked.

Lysandro couldn't have stopped smiling if he wanted to. "I would love nothing more. But we have a show to catch."

Sera lit up, and leapt at him.

"Oh, you sneaky—!"

"I *did* say to dress for the theater, didn't I?" he said, tightening his arms around her slender waist.

They left the crystalline palace and walked across the central plaza to the playhouse.

"How did you manage to get tickets?" Sera asked.

"I didn't. I have a box." He led her through a separate entrance where they climbed a set of carpeted stairs. Lysandro's private balcony had a spectacular view of the stage.

"Nothing extravagant, was it? No. Just the best meal I've ever had and a private box to a play I've only ever dreamed of."

"Happy Faelsday."

She smiled, and leaned over the railing to glimpse the rest of the theater house. A luxurious red curtain trimmed in gold obscured the stage, and masterful frescoes inlaid with gold covered the ceiling.

"Oh," she said as she glanced below. "We seem to be causing a bit of a stir."

"What do you mean?" He peered over the edge, casually glancing at the stage while directing his actual focus on the theatergoers below from the corner of his eye. Several couples, more than Lysandro could count, had their heads pivoted in his direction. They looked away to confer amongst themselves, and then back up again to confirm their gossip.

"I think there's a direct correlation between the level of animosity and the speed at which the ladies are fanning themselves," Sera said. "That one in the violet looks ready to kick up a tornado. The only one wearing a more sour face is the man next to her."

"Oh, *her.*"

"She's sort of pretty."

"Not when you look closely. She only cares for herself."

"And how did *you* come by this information?"

"A conversation or two."

"Was it one or two?"

Lysandro raised an eyebrow. Could it be possible she was jealous?

"Two. I tried to give her the benefit of the doubt. It was one of the biggest mistakes I ever made. Close up, that woman is ugly as sin."

That seemed to satisfy her curiosity.

The curtain rose. From that moment on, Sera was captivated by the prince falling in love with a girl's reflection, and who had to fight to free her from the curse that only allowed her to appear on the surface of an enchanted lake. Lysandro's attention was divided. He heard the music, but spent the time admiring Sera's profile, and the quiet contentment with which she watched the tale unfolding below. She only spoke again after the prince had drowned trying to save her, and found his salvation and his bride waiting for him in a kingdom under the lake. Her eyes gleamed.

"Thank you. Truly."

Lysandro tucked an errant strand of her hair behind her ear. "Was it better than one of your mystery novels?"

"They can't be compared. Those stories often don't translate well on a stage."

"Oh," he replied, arching an eyebrow. He wasn't sure, but he thought he felt Sera shudder in response. The prospect of having that kind of an effect on her made him feel bold. He lent a steely glint to his gaze.

"They don't provide the same sort of spectacle."

"You don't say."

"Wipe that smirk off your face. I never said I didn't like classics."

But her admission only served to make him smile all the more.

"You didn't say you did, either."

"I do. Especially when they're performed. The mirror effect they used to make her look ghostly was really special. And her voice was incredible."

"I've heard better."

Sera blushed. "I don't know about that."

"*I* do. I rather liked the prince though, and the fight scenes were impeccable. It's that sort of thing that makes a tale like this one timeless— just that little bit of magic and daring."

He dipped his head closer to hers, and let his voice drop to a conspiratorial tone as they climbed into his carriage, instinctually occupying the same side of the bench as if by habit.

"I *am* enjoying your book," he conceded.

"*Are* you?"

She stuck her pert little nose in the air.

"It's as you said. I have no idea what to expect. I don't even know if I should be trusting what I'm reading. But I'm being drawn in with every page. It's different from what I'm used to. And…"

"And?"

He debated whether or not to tell her. The light in her eyes convinced him.

"And…it's a bit addictive," he admitted, secretly relishing the smile that spread across her face, reaching all the way up to her deliciously warm eyes.

"What was that? I couldn't quite hear you."

Lysandro narrowed his eyes at her. He leaned closer. "I said it's addictive." He wasn't thinking about the book anymore; the book was the farthest thing from his mind. All his thoughts were consumed by her closeness and the intoxicating fragrance of her hair. The look of sheer satisfaction on her face sent chills across his skin. He would spend the rest of his life trying to bring that sly, sweet, contented expression to her lips.

"Don't spoil anything. We'll talk later," she said.

He made a gesture of a key turning in its lock at the corner of his mouth. His heart started racing again when she rested her head on his shoulder and let out a deep sigh. Lysandro's fingers found hers. He'd always hoped for a wife he could talk to, *really* talk to, but he'd only now begun to grasp how fulfilling it would be. He dreamed of endless nights like this one. Except, in his dreams, they returned home together, and the night would be only just begun.

She was asleep when they arrived at the gate to her house.

"Sera," Lysandro whispered. "Come on."

She leaned on his arm as he walked her to the door.

"Thank you again, for everything." She stretched onto her toes and pressed her lips to the corner of his mouth. He parted his mouth in a gentle sigh and drew in a sharp breath. His blood pounded in his ears. She lingered there—hoping for more? Sweet Faelia, he wanted to give her more. He wanted to kiss her and never stop. Paralyzed with desire, he only managed to run his fingers through her hair as she pulled away.

"Goodnight," she whispered. Then she was gone.

* * *

Lysandro called to her from the edge of the balcony.

"Signorina," he whispered.

Sera roused from her sleep, and came to greet him in the moonlight, melting into his arms until their noses met.

"I've missed you," she said.

He raised her chin with his finger and brought her lips to meet his. He reveled in the sweetness of her mouth. When her fingers skimmed across his skin, divesting him of his gloves, his hat, his mask, he shuddered and kissed her deeper. The diaphanous silk of her nightdress dissolved under his fingertips.

Lysandro shook himself out of his reverie as he lay atop his bed. He couldn't give reality to his dream, couldn't visit her in her bedchamber disguised at the Shadow. Who would believe he sought only kisses under such circumstances? *He* didn't believe it, if he was being honest with himself. But more to the point: anticipating her reaction to the truth filled him with an increasing sense of dread. The longer he left it, the more troublesome revealing himself to her became, until it seemed an impossible prospect. Nothing he could say now would explain why he spoke to her for so long in two voices. She had asked to see his face—*twice*—and both times he had refused her. Nothing could justify seeking physical affection under the cover of night while he continued to disguise himself.

No—as much as his body ached for her, he couldn't go to her. Not when there was so much in his heart he couldn't bring himself to say. He had to confess his love without the mask.

But one question nagged at him, circling over and over in his head and barring him from sleep: when he finally did muster the courage to tell her everything, would it be too late?

THE SHADOW WOULDN'T BE PAYING HER A VISIT TONIGHT. AFTER MORE THAN an hour had ticked by, Sera was sure of it. She tried to keep her disappointment in check as she discarded her dress and readied herself for bed. It wasn't so much that the Shadow had failed to come after hours. She was upset that Lysandro hadn't kissed her at the end of the night. He kept all the passion she had felt with the Shadow locked up tight. The evening had seemed perfect, at the time. But now that it had come and gone, and there was still no revelation about Lysandro's other self to be had, it set her mind on edge. As charming as Lysandro was, he kept his distance in the daytime. He was playful, affectionate even, but...aloof, somehow, in some vital way. Did the man who kissed her with such tenderness and passion only truly exist behind the mask? Or was the love he professed to have for her genuine? Which of his faces was she to believe?

16

STEFANO LOOKED DOWN AT THE BROADSHEET ORDER IN HIS HANDS. IT MADE a certain kind of sense, he supposed; the magistrate was in hot water, boiling even, and he needed to do something to restore the people's confidence in his office. His reputation was beyond repair, in the printer's view, but that wouldn't stop a man like Marek from trying to maintain some semblance of authority by feigning control of the situation. Still, no matter which way he turned it, the notice that Marek's deputy had thrust into his hands was absolute rubbish.

The printer put on his spectacles and read it again. The letters were clearer, but they made no more sense than they had an hour ago when Marek's man had burst into his shop, just as he was about to lock up for the evening, and told him—not asked—to print enough notices to plaster the walls of Lighura by morning. And to top it all off, he'd underpaid.

A small voice from the top of the stairs broke in on his thoughts.

"Papa?"

"Yes Antony?"

"Are you coming up? Mama says supper is almost ready."

"I'll be up in a minute. Tell your mama she needn't wait."

Stefano watched his only son's bare toes as he retreated up the stairs like a thunderstorm to relay the message. He sighed, then got up from his chair and went about his work.

What would his son think of him in the morning, he wondered as he began setting the type of his press, if he were to print this latest indictment of his hero?

Theft—Vandalism—Terrorizing the Village—Destruction of the Temple Window—all of it was utter bunk. His own eyes didn't shine *as* brightly as his son's at the mere mention of the Shadow, but still, his presence in Lighura was their only protection against the rising dangers of their little community, their only hope. And he owed the Shadow a debt.

It was last spring when the Shadow of Theron had saved Antony's life, around the same time that there was a growing consensus among the artisans and craftsmen that leaving your door open at night was no longer wise. Any complaints about the increase in break-ins and burglaries were summarily ignored, and it had become clear then that Magistrate Marek believed his responsibilities only extended to Lighura's wealthiest citizens.

But the Shadow of Theron concerned himself with every Lighuran, and exposed Marek's indifference and incompetence for what they were. He made himself the magistrate's worst nightmare. Marek couldn't bear the insult to his pride. While the Shadow remained untouchable, Marek hurled at his feet all the villainy he himself had failed to bring under control.

Something must have happened on that spring day, to have them chasing each other around on horseback in broad daylight like madmen, but all Stefano knew was that, lost in his wild cheering and eagerness to see who would catch who, Antony had gotten too close to the road.

Marek's men were catching up, and showed no signs of slowing as Antony stumbled before them, shaken off his feet by the tremor of the horses' hooves racing toward him.

There had been no time to act, or even think, when he saw what was about to happen. In just seconds, the foaming pack of horses would be on top of them. His wife screamed in his ears and dug her nails into his arms, pinning him in place.

The Shadow shot out ahead of the pack. His obsidian stallion was like a crack of dark lightning, streaking toward Antony at an impossible pace. The Shadow leaned all the way out of his saddle. The printer had been sure he was going to fall, and he and his child would be killed together. But the Shadow held his grip on the beast, and scooped Antony up into his arms. Together they disappeared onto the ridge behind the road faster than Marek or any of his men could follow. Without a clear trail, the horses gave up the chase. Two collapsed and had to be put down on the spot. Antony was delivered to his doorstep in time for supper, with the biggest grin that his father had ever seen.

Not a single week went by when Antony did not tell his story at least twice to anyone who would listen.

Stefano finished setting the last of the type. Sometimes he didn't relish his job. He was paid to print the words of others. In the case of an official notice like this one, the printer had very little choice in the matter. But did he not also have an obligation, a sacred duty to the truth?

He wondered what Marek would think of this lofty argument. Specifically, he wondered which of his bones Marek would consider breaking, or if he would conclude that destroying his press would be a more effective lesson in obedience.

Stefano remembered Marek's cold expression as he'd looked upon him in horror, unable to comprehend how the magistrate would have trampled his son into the dirt without a thought.

Accidents happen, he'd said.

"Yes," the printer said to himself. "They certainly do."

The corner of his mouth curled upward as he removed a few characters and returned them to the set. Nothing blatantly obvious, just enough to make the printer whistle as he laid the ink and made the first copy. He peeled the sheet up off the press and inspected it. The result filled him with glee. He copied it again and again, in honor of the adoring young boy eating his dinner in the apartment above. And the one he carried in his heart.

17

EUGENIE WAS NOT QUICK TO ANGER—NEVER HAD BEEN—BUT DOÑA Sobrino had her at the end of her tether. The scowl that Asha wore among strangers made much more sense now.

"You don't seem to understand. The other families of Lareina have entrusted me with this because they have confidence in my discretion," the gentlewoman said.

"This is *not* your choice, or theirs," Eugenie said yet again. She lifted the neatly tied bundle of pages torn from prayer books that Doña Sobrino had delivered off the table.

"The return of these pages is not enough. I need to know who was in possession of them and how they were acquired."

"Just tell me the penalty, and I will pay it."

Eugenie could barely breathe. She felt her hands beginning to tremble with rage. She hid it by laying them flat on the table.

"Your wealth is not a shield for your sin."

Eugenie stood at her place. She didn't tower over the woman as Asha would have, but Asha wasn't there. It had been three days since she'd taken off after Hairo with her horse. Eugenie had no idea what she might have found, or what might have found her. For all intents and purposes, she was stranded.

She pushed that aside and channeled her frustration into the volume of her voice. It bounded off the temple walls. Asha would have been proud.

"You will tell me where each of these pages came from. And you will tell me *now*."

"I cannot tell you what I don't know."

Casting the stones wasn't necessary to see that she was lying. The same way that she had lied when she'd first approached the Examiner, saying it was mostly *other* people who had secretly purchased stolen pages, but that she herself had only one or two. It told in the skin that drew taut around her neck as she spoke. Eugenie was all out of patience.

Doña Sobrino gave a deep sigh and unwrapped the bundle. She sorted the pages into separate files and inscribed the names of their buyers on small scraps of paper that she laid atop.

"Where did you get them?" Eugenie asked.

"I purchased mine from another lady."

"Which lady?"

The woman scowled. "Doña de Marle."

"And she?"

"She didn't provide me with the details."

Eugenie raised an eyebrow.

"She wouldn't reveal her source. I swear it." After a moment, she added, "she fashioned herself a hub of forbidden texts; didn't want anybody cutting into her business."

Only the resentment in her voice signaled that she was telling the truth.

"She'll tell me."

Doña Sobrino grew irate again, concerned more with the punishment her peers would mete out for failing to keep their names out of it than whatever Asha might do. Several times, Doña Sobrino's pen almost pierced the paper on which she reluctantly betrayed their little circle of thieves.

"None of this would have happened if we were permitted to keep our own copies of the sacred texts," the woman said. "Why does the Temple insist on keeping the faithful in the dark? Who is the High Priestess, or the

Council of Three for that matter, to say who may and may not read and interpret the Goddess's words?"

"This from the mouth of a thief and a liar," Eugenie shot back, "one who disrespected the Temple by putting her own desires above the Goddess and her daughters, and thought she could buy her way out of it."

Doña Sobrino's face tightened. It was obvious she wasn't used to being spoken to in such a tone, or being confronted with her own faults. But Eugenie wasn't finished.

"Do you know the Goddess's true name?" she asked.

Doña Sobrino blinked.

"Tell me," Eugenie pressed. "Someone who thinks herself worthy of the Goddess's secrets must surely know the name of the deity she worships."

Again, Doña Sobrino was silent.

"How do you lift a curse? Or ward your door to keep out intruders? How do you purge someone of the wasting sickness?"

There was still no reply.

"Have you been schooled in runes, or taught to read the stars?"

Doña Sobrino's eyes fell to the floor.

"Do not presume a right to know what you cannot possibly comprehend. The Goddess does not reveal herself to everyone, and certainly never to someone who says that if only the rules were to her liking, she would follow them. Such false pride is a sign of deficient character."

She exaggerated the point. In the age before Theron, many of the more basic wards had been common knowledge. Some things were kept secret by necessity. Other things, however, perhaps less so. But now was hardly the time to express that.

Eugenie reveled in the quiet that followed, and thanked Morgasse for sending a cloud across the sky at that very moment. Shadow poured through the open windows high in the temple ceiling, mirroring the gravity that finally overcame Doña Sobrino's countenance. When next she spoke, it was in a subdued tone.

"You said that those who came forward would be granted mercy."

Eugenie straightened her back. "For those who humble themselves, perhaps. Examiner Asha of the Temple Arun will decide your fate." She collected the papers off the table and turned to go.

"Wait—"

Eugenie kept walking.

"Will the punishment be corporal? Will we be expected to give up our lands? Our titles?"

"Won't you intercede for us? Explain that…that…"

For the first time in days, Eugenie smiled.

Eugenie passed Mirabel in the courtyard. They exchanged polite smiles.

"Doña Sobrino proved helpful, I hope?"

From her lack of comment upon the matter, it was clear that the high priestess had not heard from Asha.

"Yes," Eugenie answered with some reluctance. She would have to inform the high priestess about the nefarious doings of her congregants, and she didn't relish that. Mirabel was a kind soul, and a fine Faelian. It would sting to hear how little the town had taken her example to heart.

"I'm glad of it." The naïve smile that brightened her face before she departed made Eugenie wince.

She grabbed a cheese scone before locking herself in her quarters and spreading out the pages Doña Sobrino had returned to her over the hardwood floor.

Eugenie brushed crumbs from her lap as she made a log of the pages, noting who had been holding them, then rearranging them based on the temples to which they belonged. It was easy to tell by the symbols woven into the decorative border of the pages, but you had to know where to look.

Reaching for the scone from her *other* pocket, she retrieved from her satchel the list of missing relics she'd been given and began to cross-reference her findings against the map. She'd hoped such an exercise would allow her to understand the path by which these objects moved, but the list was incomplete. The true relics continued to elude them. She wondered into whose hands those had landed, and whether the theft of the prayer books had been a distraction.

Eugenie sat back in her chair and rubbed at her temples. She did not look forward to confronting those who had paid for the pages. Not alone, at any rate. But she could not afford to be idle in Asha's prolonged

THE SHADOW OF THERON   207

absence. But before going into the lion's den, Eugenie thought it best to spend some time with her books.

She read for hours. She just couldn't shake the feeling there was something she needed to know. But she had no idea what. So Eugenie pored over every page of *The Histories*, expecting recognition to jolt through her when she hit upon the right spell, the right ward. But she just sank deeper into confusion.

Her last casting had left her unsettled. She had always been able to decipher the stones, usually with very little effort. It was intuitive, the way she used to read the clouds and the flight pattern of birds for weather as a child, a sort of preternatural instinct that had only grown over time. But there was something about their arrangement that she couldn't get out of her mind, something about their positions in relation to each other that muddied her concept of time, and rendered the message highly vulnerable to misinterpretation.

The longer she pondered it, the more akin it was to pulling on a knot that would not unravel. The harder she tugged on the strings, the more intractable the problem became. The possibilities seemed endless, and yet not one that she imagined carried with it that intangible, undeniable feeling of being *right*.

But she was running out of time. That was clear to her, if nothing else. There was only one thing she could do. But she would need some things first.

She knocked louder than she meant to, but it was effective all the same.

"Yes?" Mirabel asked, wrapping her robe tighter around herself as she opened the door. "Is something the matter?"

"No. Not exactly. I'm sorry to wake you, but I'm in need of a few items, and thought you might be able to help me."

"What is it you require?"

"It might be better if I looked myself," Eugenie replied. "It'll be quicker that way." The excuse was not a good one; it made Eugenie's insides coil.

Mirabel appeared to think much the same. Nevertheless, she nodded.

"Of course."

She opened the door to let Eugenie pass, then left her to her own devices. Eugenie hastily pulled jars from the high priestess's shelves, taking only the amounts she needed and replacing them in the precise positions in which she'd found them. She took two more powders that she didn't need just in case Mirabel grew curious in the night and inspected her wares. She had to settle for being as discreet as possible about what she was after.

Elder root, black fungus, sphagnum moss, toad venom...

Eugenie should have gathered everything herself, but there was no time. "Thank you," she said as she exited the room and made her way back to her own.

Though she could fit the sum of the ingredients in the palm of her hand, when put together, her mind could only bear a fraction of their effects at a time. Eugenie pulled infinitely small parts from each element—a few fibers from the moss, no more than a sliver of the tree bark—and placed them into a stone mortar along with sulfur and other herbs from her pouch, and lit the mixture ablaze. A dark gray smoke furled and spiraled before her and settled deep into her lungs. The room started spinning; already the boundaries between the furniture and the floor blurred and wavered. She doused the flames with cornflower nectar and let the concoction steep.

The brew was bitter, with a taste like licking the forest floor after a fire, but she knew she had to allow it to take hold of her. She knew she had succeeded when the shadowy corners of the room began to glow with magic. She took another deep breath, inhaling the rotten stench, and swallowed the liquid in one gulp.

She consumed nothing but her potion the rest of the night and into the next day. It put her in precisely the foul mood she required when Doña de Marle appeared at the temple at her request.

"You have stolen sacred writings and relics that belong to the Temple. You will tell me how you got them."

The smile that had been on Doña de Marle's face as she'd entered the chamber was gone now.

The woman opened her mouth to speak, but Eugenie wasn't having it.

"Don't waste your breath telling me that I'm mistaken. Doña Sobrino has already informed me of your treacheries. In my view, you are guiltier than the rest."

Doña de Marle seemed cowed.

"There's a merchant who comes by every new moon. He's the one I bought them from."

"When did this begin?"

"About three seasons ago."

"Did he possess other sacred objects which you did not purchase?"

"Umm..."

"Speak up woman. I have very little patience today."

"Of course. My apologies, Madam Examiner. It's just that, well, I'm not quite sure if he had more stock or not. I was primarily interested in the texts."

"Why is that?"

"I believe Doña Sobrino already explained that to you."

"Did the merchant tell you where he had acquired his wares?'

"No, Madam Examiner."

Eugenie cocked her head. "Then how could you be assured of their legitimacy?"

Doña de Marle's face reddened. "He said that there were many people in Andras of a like mind as we, regarding the Temple's rules of secrecy. And that there were those in a position to help us."

"Help you how?"

"By ensuring their safe passage."

The only people who could do that were the customs officials—based in the office of the local magistrate.

"Where are these impious officers stationed?"

Doña de Marle hesitated. "Everywhere, Madam Examiner."

A frisson of fear pulled at Eugenie's skin. She stood and gestured toward the temple exit. "Lead the way," she said.

Doña de Marle turned her head toward the outer columns of the temple, and then back toward Eugenie. "Where are we going, Madam Examiner?"

"To your home. I mean to retrieve whatever else you are keeping from me."

"Th-there's nothing else. We regret our actions and have told all."

"You sent another to confess to a crime you are guilty of. You'll forgive me if I don't take you at your word."

Doña de Marle's face turned a deep scarlet. There was no way out.

Walking through the streets of town, Eugenie struggled to maintain her balance. The world seemed off-kilter to her, steeped as she was in sorcery. She walked slowly to steady her feet. It had the additional benefit of throwing Doña de Marle into a state of pitched nervousness. That suited Eugenie fine, and she leaned into it.

Where before Eugenie could sense the closeness of the relics, now the doors and walls of the houses they passed seemed just a visual distortion, as opaque as a gossamer veil. She scanned the entirety of Doña de Marle's estate steps from the main entrance.

"Won't you come in?"

"Bring me what you are holding in the small blue box in the rightmost corner, underneath the floorboard of the master bedroom."

Doña de Marle's jaw dropped open. If she was uneasy before, she was terrified of Eugenie now. It was about time. Then she turned her gaze at her grown sons, who had exited the estate and were now approaching their mother with concerned expressions.

"Don't come any closer!" she cried. "Go get it."

The brothers looked at each other, then back toward her. "Get what, Mother?"

That was the last straw for Doña de Marle's overwrought nerves.

"Don't act the fool! Do as I say!"

They scrambled back into the house and returned in moments with the box that Eugenie had described.

"What's going to happen to us?" Doña de Marle asked.

"That is for her to decide."

"Who, Madam Examiner?"

Eugenie jutted her chin toward the eastern gate. The road appeared to be empty. Doña de Marle furrowed her brow.

But Eugenie saw. After several minutes, the sound of horses approaching was loud enough to reach any ear. A cloud of dust preceded Asha, astride her own horse and carrying the reigns of Eugenie's mount in her hand.

When Eugenie saw that her mare was without a rider, she knew Hairo was dead. At the sight of Asha's face, red and glistening from the exertion, Eugenie's stony façade became cracked and brittle. She felt grounded again, on more solid footing than she had been for days.

"Gin!" Asha cried, pulling up hard on the horses and leaping down onto the road.

Eugenie held the contents of the box up for her to see.

Doña de Marle's attention turned to the warrior. She fell to her knees in the middle of the road and pressed her forehead into the dirt.

"Mercy! I beg you, please!"

Asha ignored her. "Gin—we've got to go. Now."

"There are people here awaiting your judgment."

"They can wait some more."

Eugenie observed Asha's hardened stare, and nodded.

* * *

"What's wrong with your face?"

They were alone now on the road. Doña de Marle and her sons had scurried inside to the safety of their estate as the Examiners had ridden away in haste. Asha's eyes narrowed as she investigated Eugenie's widened pupils. A terrible thought occurred to her, and Asha drew back in alarm.

"Did you put Morgasse's Eyes onto yourself?!"

Eugenie supposed she shouldn't have been surprised that Asha had figured it out. After all, it was the formula that was the secret, not the existence of the spell itself.

"We were stuck. We needed to be unstuck."

"That stuff can make you mad!" Asha protested. "At least, that's what I've heard."

"Only if you ingest too much of the potion."

"And did you?"

Eugenie shook her head. "Just enough."

"You should have waited for me."

"It's done now. Where are we going?"

"To Lighura."

Eugenie blinked. "That's not on our map."

Asha replied in a dark, ominous tone. "Argoss is rising…"

The utterance made the hair on the back of Eugenie's neck bristle. "What did you say?"

"That's what the bastard that Hairo led me to said. 'From the Boundless Sea, Argoss rises.'"

Lighura was the perfect place for it, Eugenie admitted. It was far from the scrutiny of a larger city, but connected enough to the main roads crisscrossing Andras to be the true destination of the relics.

Eugenie shuddered at the thought of so many of them in one place.

The world must feel upside down there.

They rode hard, stopping only for a few hours to sleep. But Eugenie couldn't sleep. With Asha snoring next to her, she laid on her back in the grass, staring up at the starry sky. Her breathing calmed, and she slipped into a fugue state that left her feeling heavy and light at the same time. When she saw the stars begin to tremble and shift in the night sky, she simply blinked, and let the stars do what they may. They drew together in a pattern that Eugenie was very familiar with—one that she couldn't put out of her mind. Then they all shifted in tandem, like a spiral turning inward, and the sky darkened. A star that lay at the outer edges of the pattern winked out.

Eugenie felt cold inside. She didn't want to watch anymore, but she knew she must. The firmament continued in their dance, swallowing light into itself until the sky was nothing but an inky expanse, a black void.

The stillness of the night crept into her ears, a deafening silence. Eugenie pressed her eyes closed against the sky that had eaten itself, and prayed for sleep to take her. She was afraid that if she continued to watch, the whole world would be swallowed up in it.

* * *

An invisible hand yanked hard on Eugenie's middle, drawing her back as they crested a hill the following day.

"Stop," Eugenie called out.

"It hasn't been that long since breakfast," Asha said. "If we push through, we could be in Lighura by supper. Not that that matters, when all you eat is sludge."

"We need something. Something that's down there." Eugenie turned her horse around and pointed its nose down the hill to their right.

"What is it?" Asha asked.

"I don't know."

ASHA JUST SHOOK HER HEAD, AND GUIDED HER STALLION DOWN THE GRASSY slope after Eugenie.

It was deceptively steep; more than once Asha had to steady her horse to prevent him from slipping down the side of the hill. Eugenie's mare fared much the same. But when Asha reached over to help steady her, Eugenie just kept her gaze trained forward. Forward and down—down, down, down, to what seemed more like a treacherous pit than a nondescript hill in the middle of nowhere. Asha suspected there was sorcery at work, but she didn't want to ask. All her focus was on the ground beneath that grew more perilous with every step they took.

Asha's back jolted when her horse stepped onto level ground without warning. She craned her neck to see how far down they'd gone. The sky seemed so far away, and they were hemmed in on all sides by menacing inclines. She doubted this place could be seen from the surface. She knew *she* hadn't seen it. But down here, the hills were no longer covered in bright grass. The base of the mountains rising all around them was dark, bare-faced rock. Grass had grown here at one point, it seemed, but the bottom of the incline was charred. The ground was nothing but dirt and soot.

"Where are we?" she asked.

Eugenie turned her head back to face Asha. The severe look on her face caught Asha off-guard.

"Don't you see?"

Asha's gaze traveled over Eugenie's head toward the very center of the hidden valley, where the edges of the ridge seemed to press together and form a sharp corner in the earth. There, tucked between the two hills, was a stone structure in ruin. The only elements visibly standing were the columns marking the entryway, halfway embedded in the rockface itself. Asha inched closer. Then she recognized the sharp, beautiful features and aggressive stance of the figure carved into the columns. All the hair on her body stood on end.

"This is the Temple Theron." If she'd been anyone else, she might have screamed.

Eugenie waited for Asha to match pace with her before crossing the barrier into the temple. Almost immediately, Asha had to duck. A stone lintel hung precariously just inside the entrance. It was locked in a dangerous downward angle by an equally slanted column from the opposite side. The inner room was expansive, but despite the brilliance of the mid-morning sun, the whole of the temple was shrouded in darkness, with only a sliver of light passing through from the entryway.

"There's a light here," Eugenie said, bending down and righting a stone pillar. Atop it she placed a wide, shallow bowl that had toppled over on its side. She reached up and brushed her fingers against the surface of the bowl's interior. They came back greasy.

Asha took her fire-making stones out of the pouch at her hip and sparked a flame that flickered and danced in the bowl. The oil trapped deep in the stone's pores produced a low flame, just enough to see another upended bowl and pillar a few steps away. The Examiners worked together in silence until the nave of the temple was ringed in the faint blue light.

There had been a fire. At the back of her mind, Asha had already known that, but she furrowed her brow nonetheless. A fire explained the charring and ash; it didn't explain the chaos.

EUGENIE STEPPED INTO THE CENTER OF THE SPACE. HER EYES TOOK IN THE heaps of rubble piled in every corner. Some held collapsed columns, others the pulverized remains of the stone tiles that had comprised the floor. Pandemonium threatened to leap out at her, the cause for the disarray buzzing back to life. The screams of those who'd borne witness to the destruction echoed low in her ear, a layer below the silence. She caught movement out of the corner of her eye. It was gone by the time she turned to look, only seeing chaos erupt in its wake. She heard something roar, felt the heavy swing of its spiked tail just outside the bounds of her vision. The sound of crashing stones and the crunch of bone followed close behind.

"A wyvern," she said, catching at last a glimpse of the shimmering crimson scales like a reflection in water. She couldn't tell if that had been the beast's true color, or if it had bathed itself in the gore of its victims. "Trapped. Stuck in the overworld without a way back down."

All the abominations Argoss had summoned up had been cast back down with him in Theron's moment of triumph. But in this place, Asha could believe that one such monster could have been left behind. The lack of bones as proof of its demise unsettled her.

Eugenie closed her eyes, attuned to the demon's murderous thrashing. There was a high-pitched crash to her right; the sacred window set before the brazier had come loose from its mooring. Then the brazier itself had come toppling down.

"The fire started here," she said. She knelt before a pile of darkened embers that crumbled to ash in her hands, just as a phantom priestess ran screaming through her as the hem of her garment caught.

Asha lowered herself to her knees and pressed her head to the floor in a sign of respect for those who had breathed their last. After a time, she wondered aloud if Theron himself had ever stood where they both now knelt.

But Eugenie was compelled by something else. She turned her head and stretched her chin toward the upended brazier. "Help me with this, will you?"

Asha complied. But when she saw what lay underneath, protected by the large brass bowl, she nearly dropped the brazier out of her hands.

"I got it," Asha grunted, tightening her grip.

Eugenie slid underneath and retrieved a colored pane of glass. As soon as she was sitting back on her heels and out of harm's way, Asha let the brazier fall from her hands with a deafening gong.

"Is that what I think it is?" Asha asked breathlessly.

Eugenie smiled. The first panel of the window to the Temple Theron. The only one in the world. It depicted a snowcapped mountain peak in cloudy, pearlescent white against a pale blue sky. Eugenie heard the harsh wind at the top of the mountain whistling in her ears, and wrapped her robe more tightly around herself. She'd heard that wind's high call before, creeping in on her dreams. The gale swept across the panel, covering the mountain in a fresh coat of powder. She lifted it gingerly, braving the frost that blew across the surface of the glass and onto her fingertips, and handed it to Asha, who wrapped it carefully in an extra shirt.

"How will this help us?"

Eugenie wasn't quite sure. She only knew that they were meant to take it with them. She reached for her casting stones, made her preparations, and threw. When she saw how the runes scattered across the floor, she screamed.

Asha did her best to comfort her, but her nerves were shattered by the telling that lay before her.

"It's the same, isn't it?" Asha asked. "The same as last time?"

"Exactly the same. Only..."

The pattern had turned. That's what horrified Eugenie more than anything. "I've seen this," she admitted. "Last night. In...in my dream." She'd been about to say, "in the sky," in the stark reality of consciousness, but something stopped her. It was like a terrible dream that demanded you keep its secret, lest its insanity seep into your waking hours. "It's the same pattern as before, only it's shifted now, like..."

"Like a clock."

The suggestion raced down Eugenie's spine. "Yes. That's exactly what we're looking at."

"Argoss is rising," Asha muttered, repeating again what the bastard had warned of. A bitter wind attacked them, slipping in through the cracked stones and ruined columns. They both felt its truth. The balance of the world was shifting, the boundaries of the ages coming undone at the seams. Without thinking, they put their noses to the wind. It smelled acrid.

"Does that mean something has happened?" Asha asked.

Nothing had winked out yet. None of the stone's surfaces had been expunged, their deeply carved runes wiped clean. They were on the cusp, teetering toward the edge. But that would not hold.

"Something *is* happening," she said. "It *will* happen, unless we stop it."

Asha jumped up and made for the exit.

Eugenie pulled at Asha's wrist. "Wait. The Goddess's true name is Morgasse."

Asha looked down at her. "What?"

"She is the supreme deity of old, the one that was worshipped before the Three."

"*No,*" Asha protested. "The Goddess has three *equal* faces. United, the one true Goddess has no name."

"Morgasse *means* 'no name.' Her first temple is underneath us. Out of abundant love for Theron, she rededicated it to him. She had bestowed so much upon him, made him so full of strength and power, magic and sorcery, that by the time he defeated Argoss, he *was* a god. Faelia and Arun were borne out of her infatuation with him, and her interference in mortal affairs. They are never mentioned before their interactions with Theron."

Asha opened her mouth in retort, but only a hollow sound came out.

"They're *never* mentioned. They didn't exist before then. The priestesses who wrote *The Histories* just assumed they did."

Eugenie was smart, full of book learning. Asha knew in the pit of her stomach that she was right.

"To confront Argoss's wickedness, She taught him her sorcery. When he needed to fight, She taught him to wield a sword and bow. When he was injured, She healed him. When he was lonely, She comforted him. She taught him how to love his wife."

Asha's eyebrows shot up into her hairline.

"She knew that Argoss was attempting to rival her godhood, amassing a horde of bastards. However the battle went between Argoss and Theron, however victorious he was and for all the blessings she had granted him, Theron was mortal. He would not be there to fight if the bastards and their descendants should rise."

"She bore him a *child?!*"

Eugenie shook her head. "It's not clear. Morgassen have been asking the runes that question for decades. Every time, the pattern suggests that the answer is…less than truthful."

Asha's mouth opened wide.

"Either way, Theron *did* have a child. A descendant of the Hero, blessed by the Goddess. One, to combat an army."

Asha's stance faltered, as if she'd been knocked on the side of her head with a hammer.

"All of his children's children were born of human mothers, at any rate."

That didn't really answer Asha's question. And yet…

"Do we know where he is?" she asked.

"We don't know *who* he is. There used to be a record, in the High Temple Faelia, of births, marriages, and deaths.

"How would *you* know that?" Asha interrupted. "How would you know what goes on inside the Temple Faelia?"

Eugenie smiled a strange smile. "We have always known the secrets of the other temples. You just never knew ours."

It didn't sit well with Asha. Not at all.

"It was not my secret to keep, nor mine to tell."

Asha swallowed her anger. But her confusion persisted.

"Even *within* a family, how would you know which one it was?"

"They were all single children. But the record was destroyed. The Faelians are trying to recover the knowledge. They have not yet succeeded. Maybe…maybe that's him." She pointed to a stone on the wheel. The runes scattered across the pattern bearing positive attributes were all in decline. All except one—courage. It cut across the tide, rising to face the calamity hurtling toward it. Given enough rotations, they were bound to collide.

"Do you really think it's possible, that we will find the child of Theron?"

"We must, if we are to prevent the return of Argoss."

"*Can* things happen the same way twice?"

It gave Eugenie pause. "I don't know."

"Why are you telling me this now?"

"Do you trust me?" she asked.

"Of course I do, Sister."

Eugenie smiled, and began painting runes in a deep inky dye up the length of Asha's forearm.

"What kind of ward is it?" Asha asked.

"Better you don't know."

* * *

When the walls of Lighura came into view in the far distance, Eugenie's mare was foaming. The trembling underneath Eugenie felt like an earthquake, and she feared the animal would collapse before they could reach their destination.

This did nothing to quell the storm raging in Eugenie's stomach.

It's just nerves, she tried to convince herself. But the closer they came to the Lighuran border, the more her stomach rebelled. Sweat poured down her sides beneath her Examiner's robes, and her breathing came almost to a standstill. Colors bled together before her eyes until the road that lay ahead of them was nothing but a blur. She closed her eyes and pushed the mare forward.

Moments from the stone gate marking the outer edge of the village, Eugenie yanked on the reigns for dear life and tumbled off the horse.

"Gin!"

Asha was right behind her, in time to pull her plaited hair back as Eugenie expelled the meager contents of her stomach and produced a black, rancid stain in the dirt.

"Are you alright?"

Eugenie didn't answer. She clung to Asha's robes and prayed the world would just stand still.

"You've got to stop this," Asha urged. "Look at what it's doing to you!"

"That's not it…"

When at last Eugenie opened her eyes, the sight of the village wall, or more precisely, what she saw beneath its Faelsday decorations, set her mind to shrieking. She couldn't bear to look at it, to face the ravenous void eating away at the village's core.

Asha didn't want to admit it, even to herself, but Eugenie's wild-eyed fear was contagious.

"What do you see?" she whispered.

"Something's wrong. Something's very, very *wrong*."

18

Sera was running out of patience. So when she saw a knife-throwing booth, it seemed like the perfect opportunity.

"Do you want to give it a try?" she asked. The stall was one of many that had cropped up overnight. Lysandro had called on her early as Faelsday dawned, and they'd snagged a freshly baked breakfast from one of the sweet tents erected in honor of the day. Their offerings washed the clean morning air in cinnamon and cloves, lending their spice to what promised to be a warm day. The village was agog with early morning shoppers and young children who wanted to take their first peek at the festival before their parents woke. Paper decorations in brilliant yellow, deep red and lush violet were strung up from every building, swinging low across alleyways and the broad avenue along which she now pulled Lysandro by the arm.

They approached the tent to find a middle-aged man wearing a faded patchwork tunic. He barked at the crowd, tempting them to sacrifice their coins for a chance at glory.

"Care to test your skill, Signor?" he asked, twirling a small knife on the edge of his index finger and flashing a wicked grin at Lysandro.

"I'm the one who's interested."

"You, Signorina?"

"That's right."

"Whatever you fancy," he said, handing her the knife. "Now, the way you do this is…"

Sera ignored him, and smiled at Lysandro. He lifted a curious eyebrow that threatened her concentration. Before the distraction of admiring his face grew pronounced, she flipped the blade in her hand, pinched it between her fingers, and sent it flying into the heart of the wooden target, barely bothering to look.

The knifeman's mouth hung agape.

"Was that about right?" Sera asked sweetly.

Lysandro pushed his lips to the side, trying to hide his smirk. "You're very good at that," he said low in her ear.

Sera cocked her head, coy as ever. "Didn't you already know that?"

The air about Lysandro shivered, but he didn't take the bait. His cool expression stayed in place, and he simply said, "you're always surprising me."

Sera was crestfallen. Had she imagined that he'd caught her meaning? She thought she'd seen understanding followed by naked fear flicker in his eyes, but it had happened so quick she couldn't be sure.

"Are you gonna let her show you up like that?" the knifeman asked.

A booming voice from behind Lysandro answered for him.

"Oh-ho ho! Sorry Signor, but not this one. He'd be as likely to hit *you* as he would your target." The large hand that clapped Lysandro on the shoulder was attached to a man Sera didn't recognize. "Doesn't have a taste for weapons, you see. Morning, Don Lysandro. Happy Faelsday."

Sera was about to say something in Lysandro's defense—what, she didn't know—but she didn't get the chance.

"I don't know," Lysandro said. "Perhaps if you repeat your instructions again."

Sera watched, intrigued, as Lysandro went through the charade, fumbling the knife and almost cutting himself while struggling to absorb the lesson. The other don just laughed. But when Lysandro threw, it was with confidence. The blade made its home right next to hers, carving a neat "v" into the center of the bullseye.

"Oh." Lysandro straightened his back, seemingly surprised at himself. The don nearly fell on his backside.

Sera smiled in satisfaction.

"Be careful with these two," the stall keeper chuckled. "Luck is on their side today." He reached into one of his many pockets and produced two hemp bracelets with a small gem woven into the center of each. He wished them a Happy Faelsday then turned his attention to the next cluster of people.

"Which do you like better?" Lysandro asked, holding both bracelets out to her.

Not a hint of mischief showed on his face; he was very good at keeping secrets. It didn't sit well.

But how much more direct could she be, without flat-out telling him that she already knew his biggest secret?

I want him *to tell* me, Sera thought. *Why doesn't he?*

He waited for her to choose as she pondered what else he might be hiding. She selected the one with the milky white stone for herself and tied the pale green one around his wrist. Her fingers lingered on his skin. She missed him. Even though he was right there with her, he seemed far away. It felt like ages ago that they'd shared that night on the cliffs, though it had only been days. The Shadow had not called upon her since. Every minute of those days, she had longed for the press of his arms around her waist, the taste of his mouth.

Lysandro noticed the shift in her mood almost immediately.

"Are you alright?"

"Fine."

"Are you sure?"

No. Not really. But what could she say? Here, of all places, where anyone could hear them?

"Yes," she said and forced a smile. It hurt. She didn't realize it would until she'd done it, and by then it was too late.

They continued on their stroll through the middle of the thoroughfare, not stopping to look at anything too closely as they passed.

"Are you tired?" Lysandro asked.

"No."

"Hungry?"

"No."

He stepped in front of her, blocking her path, and turned to face her. "Won't you tell me what's wrong?"

Sera felt her heart race; her mouth was going to betray her, and she felt powerless to stop it.

But they were interrupted again, this time by a rather odd-looking pair of women—one slight, with fair hair and a haunted face, and the other a copper-skinned giant, who stooped as she helped steady the former on her feet.

It's a bit early to be that *drunk*, Sera mused.

The smaller woman walked right up to Lysandro and stared wildly into his eyes.

He tipped his head toward her, curious. The small gesture seemed to shake the woman from whatever had compelled her to approach him. She licked her lips to speak.

"Happy Faelsday to you. May the Goddess bestow on you Her many blessings." As she said this, the woman grabbed Lysandro's left hand and began to trace an indiscernible pattern on his palm with her index finger.

Upon closer inspection, the woman was not as old as Sera had first thought. It was the pale shade of her hair, so blond it was almost white, and the deep hollows under her eyes that made her look so. The intensity of her expression as she gripped Lysandro's hand made Sera uncomfortable.

She could feel Lysandro growing tense as well. But he didn't retract his hand or turn her away.

"You'll have to excuse my sister, Signor," the bigger one said, dipping her chin toward her companion. "She hasn't been well." She lifted the smaller woman up, almost off her feet it seemed to Sera, and pulled her away. They were gone as quickly as they'd come.

EUGENIE COULDN'T BELIEVE HER EYES. THE RUNES HAD NOT LIED; THE AGE of Darkness was truly upon them again, but so too was the Age of Theron, if the hero of legend could be seen walking in another man's shadow. She'd sensed a glow about him from a distance, a sort of glamour that suggested he was more than what he seemed, but she hadn't truly *felt* him glow until she'd gotten closer. He radiated strength, and kindness…and courage. Being in his presence had felt like basking in the naked sunlight.

"What is it now?" Asha asked. "Who is he?"

Eugenie smiled a dreamy, far-off smile, her world once again filled with hope. "We've found him."

"Who?" Ashe paused. "The Child of Theron? Why didn't you say anything?" she hissed. She turned to approach the couple again, but Eugenie took hold of her wrist like her life depended on it.

"No."

"Why not?!"

"I have a very strong feeling…that we mustn't say anything to him."

She wasn't saying it right. It was more than a feeling. It was a command, one that thronged inside her head—deeper, it seemed—and set her whole body trembling.

Asha's eyes went wide. "Then what in six hells are we *doing* here? If Argoss does rise, we'll need him! And what about the task *we* were charged with?"

Eugenie's eyes slid to the ground, to where Theron's Child had stood just a moment before. The impression she had seen was still there, but it was faint, and stretched out after him in a thin, glimmering veil.

"He doesn't know who he is," she murmured. "And we mustn't tell him."

"Yes we damn well must!"

"No! It is not yet time!"

Eugenie's strength was giving out; what the runes foretold crashed over her in tumultuous waves. The force of their telling was so overwhelming it threatened to bring her to her knees. Before she slumped to the ground in the middle of the road, Asha caught hold of her, and tried to steady her on her feet.

"Eugenie. Are you *sure?*"

"I've never been surer about anything in my entire life. We must not interfere. Elsewise we rush to our doom."

Asha's bracing arm tightened around Eugenie's middle, and hauled her upright.

"Alright," she whispered. "Alright. But we'll watch him. The minute he needs us, or we need him…"

At Asha's pronouncement, the storm in Eugenie's mind began to subside. She slowly found her own balance again, the world no longer teetering toward calamity. She nodded.

"What did you do to him?" Asha asked.

Eugenie swallowed hard. "I'm not sure it will work."

"What?"

"I opened his eyes."

"LYSANDRO?"

He was still staring at his palm, pondering the pattern the woman had scrawled on it. Whatever thoughts crossed his mind, he brushed them off, curling his fingers inward and letting his hand drop to his side.

"Homesick?"

"What?" Sera asked.

"Are you homesick? It would be natural, on a day like today."

"I suppose I am." That wasn't what was bothering her, but it would do.

"What can I do to cheer you up?"

Her mouth quirked up. "A drink would be nice."

Lysandro smiled. "I still can't imagine you drunk."

"Oh, I'm pleasant." Sera smiled back. This time, it was genuine. "I think I've lost the majority of my brain matter to this holiday."

"That can't be. You're the most intelligent woman I know."

The compliment rolled off him so easily, Sera knew he meant it. Her smile deepened.

"I used to be a genius," she replied. "Now I'm just clever."

He flashed another of his affectionate smiles, but then something over her shoulder caught his attention.

Lysandro pulled a broadsheet off the outer wall of a nearby building, and examined the edict. In crisp, tiny letters, Marek demanded any villager with information regarding the identity of the criminal known as the Shadow of Theron to step forward. Anyone who cooperated with his office would be compensated. The reward: one lyra.

"You'd think that if Marek was serious about apprehending the Shadow, he'd offer a serious incentive," he said.

Sera could see the battle waging on his face. He didn't know whether to be incensed or amused. She trod carefully.

"Why would he do that? Print up a notice, just to make an ass of himself?"

Lysandro's eyebrows rose at her choice of words, and a boyish laugh escaped him.

"If I had to guess, I'd say it's a misprint." A furtive grin played across his lips.

"It also implies that Lighurans' loyalties can be bought," Sera added.

Lysandro paused, the smile gone. "You're right. He *would* think that." The words came out so deep he was almost growling.

The notices were plastered over every wall and building. But they were hard to see under the swell of decorations celebrating Theron's miraculous recovery on the eve of his triumph. If they hadn't been mostly lost in the merrymaking, the sheer number of them would have cast a cloud of discontent over all of Lighura, misprint or no.

Lysandro crumpled the notice and shoved it deep into his pocket.

"Where is our illustrious magistrate today?" Sera asked, scanning the crowd subconsciously.

"Holed up in his office, I imagine. He doesn't go to the temple. Why should he celebrate a temple holiday?"

That doesn't mean he won't start trouble, Sera thought.

Lysandro must have seen the worry in her eyes. "It's alright," he said, taking her hand and pulling her closer to his side. "I'm right here."

Whichever side of him was talking to her, Lysandro or the Shadow, she felt comforted.

"Too many people for him to make a scene," he reasoned. "He still cares about how he's perceived. I don't expect he'll show his face outdoors at all, public sentiment being what it is. Plus he'll have his hands full once the chief magistrate arrives, which I imagine will be very soon. Come on. Let's enjoy the day."

She did feel better, as they walked along. Lysandro had not released her fingers from his own, and she reveled in the tender little back-and-forth motion his thumb made across her skin, so smooth and reassuring that she was lulled into forgetting about Marek. She soaked in the joyful atmosphere of the village. The rest of Lighura was no doubt trying to do the same.

Sera's hand separated from Lysandro's only when they came upon a large tent displaying costumes for sale, and she stopped to inspect their craftsmanship.

"Come, come! Try on something beautiful. Or something daring!" The proprietress of the stall danced at the edge of the tent, beckoning them inside for a closer look. She was dressed in layer upon layer. Billowing white sleeves peeked through a tangerine vest of luxurious velvet. A slatted purple skirt that fell to her knees covered a longer robe beneath of sunshine yellow. Ankles clad in green stockings poked out from the hem and hid themselves in gilded slippers of deep fuchsia embroidered with golden thread.

The chestnut tendrils that cascaded from her head were obviously a wig, topped by a broad-brimmed hat of sapphire blue and trimmed with an oversized speckled feather.

It was a riot to Sera's eyes. She didn't know where to look, and turned her gaze away.

"No thank you," she said.

"Walk in the shoes of a necromancer! Or a queen! Become a star in the night sky! The finest silks, the lushest colors!" The woman followed Sera from behind the table. She crossed the path of a crone dressed all in black, hunched over a garment in the back of the tent. The proprietress tripped over her as she pressed her wares into Sera's hands.

"No, thank you," Sera repeated.

The woman stepped beyond the front flap of the stall and called after them. "Fine, fine. I understand, you're so wrapped up in your beau you don't have eyes for anyone else, can't even see who's speaking to you."

Sera stopped. She spun on her heels and eyed the woman again. She was still staring after them, standing halfway into the street.

"Sera?"

She didn't hear Lysandro's query. Her heart was pounding too loudly in her ears as she retraced her steps, and stared the woman straight in the eye.

She knew those eyes.

A grin curled at the corner of her mouth, and she entered the tent, coming to stand behind the woman shrouded in black. Only her hands were visible as she worked on the embroidered cloak in her lap, her face completely covered by a voluminous hood.

Watching from the edge of the tent, Lysandro cried out as Sera did the unthinkable.

"Get up, old woman!" she shouted in Mirênese, and kicked the crone in the rump, knocking her forward.

The woman uncovered her face, exposing a scowl.

"Old woman?!"

"Oh Maman! I thought you were—"

Sera's face drained of all its color as she realized her mistake, and reached out to help the woman who'd done more than anyone else to raise her. As she did, a man in a billowing dress with a wreath of flowers atop his head snuck up from behind.

"You kicked my nursemaid?"

Sera screamed at the sudden voice at her back, then jumped into the man's arms. He lifted her off the ground and spun her, consumed by laughter.

"Sera, Sera, Sera!"

"What are you doing here?" she cried at last.

"What do you think?" Fabien put her down and took her cheeks in his hands. *"You should have come to me. I never would have let you go! Never! You know that, don't you?"*

Sera nodded, tears spilling down her cheeks. They embraced again. The vibrantly dressed woman, who was not a woman at all, stripped off his excess clothing to reveal a slender, well-muscled man with blond waves that came just to his chin.

"I almost had to run after you," he said, wrapping his arms around Sera and Fabien both.

She looked up and stroked his cheek in greeting. *"Pirró."*

"Good to see you, girl."

"Not so good for me," the doge's maid said, struggling to her feet and brushing herself off.

"I'm so sorry Maman," Sera called out.

"I thought I wanted to see you again, but now..." she approached Sera, and

cupped her face in her hands. Tears welled up in the woman's eyes. *"Now my heart is full of joy."*

They laughed, and the trio formed a tight ring around Seraphine.

At last, she was home.

LYSANDRO'S MOOD TURNED BLACK. THE WAY THE STRANGER PUT HIS MOUTH to Sera's like it was nothing turned his guts to ash. He didn't know which of the men squeezing her was the doge of Mirêne, and which was the king, and it didn't much matter. He was going to kill them both.

Sera finally remembered that he existed, left standing mute in the middle of the road and wallowing in his own agony.

"Lysandro! Lysandro come here!" She broke from the pack and reached her hand out to him.

He had half a mind to sling her up over his shoulder and run far far away. Before he could, the man with dark curls that framed his face, the one who'd kissed Seraphine, clasped him tightly with both hands, trapping him by his forearm and shoulder with an exuberant smile on his face.

"Hello! Happy Faelsday! You must be Don Lysandro de Castel. I'm so pleased to finally meet you. Sera's told me such great things."

She has?

Lysandro shuttered the thought, not allowing himself to hope.

"This is Fabien, Doge of Mirêne," Sera said, grinning. She didn't seem phased in the slightest by what had passed between her and the doge seconds before. It had only been for a fraction of a moment, but even that had felt painfully long to Lysandro's heart. Long enough to remind him that she was never meant to be here. Never *wanted* to be here.

"Fabien, please," the doge insisted, oblivious to Lysandro's turmoil. He gestured to the blond man. "This is Pirró."

The man wrapped his arm around the doge's waist in a way Lysandro had never seen a man do to another man. His eyes narrowed.

Pirró said something Lysandro didn't understand.

"In Andran, please," Sera said.

"Cheh?"

Fabien smacked the back of his hand against Pirró's chest. "Because it's rude."

"Oh. I see." Pirró turned a devilish grin toward Lysandro. "Sera has told us so much about you. Shall I read?" He snatched a well-leafed letter from the folds of Fabien's dress and held it up to the sunlight.

Sera's face turned ghostly white.

"It's quite poetic, really. In Andran, let's see…his hair—"

Fabien ripped the pages from his hands and held them at arm's length as Pirró reached for them. They argued in their own tongue, but Fabien was taller, and his words sharper. Pirró relented.

Beside him, Sera exhaled in relief.

"Sorry about that," Fabien said. "He's just cranky. It was a long journey, and he was sick most of the way." He turned to Pirró, who grimaced. "He's promised he'll behave. I hope you will still join us for lunch."

Lysandro was forced to concede the day to the doge. "Go on then," he said to Sera. "Have fun."

She looked at him as if he'd said the oddest thing in the world.

"It's alright. You haven't seen them in—"

"I'm not going without you."

His heart gave a little flutter. Her smile was warm and reassuring. And real. He drank it in.

"Excellent! Hold the fort, Maman!" Fabien cried.

She grumbled in reply.

"Lead the way," Fabien said to Lysandro. He wrapped his arms around Pirró's shoulders as they fell in line behind Sera and Lysandro.

Again, the gesture seemed out of place. Lysandro had expected the doge to shed his costume, the dress and wreath, as the other man had done before departing. He didn't.

Sera stretched up to him to whisper in his ear. "I told you…Fabien can't marry the one he loves."

His eyes darted to her and she returned a knowing look.

"Oh."

The doge's kiss had been no more than a greeting between friends. Lysandro still hated the man for offering Sera a convenient, loveless marriage, and for making her believe that was the best she could hope for. Never mind that, in her eyes, he was guilty of the same.

Still, one thing kept repeating.

"My hair is poetic?" he asked.

Sera's cheeks turned a bright red, and her gaze dropped from him.

"I can't recall…" she murmured.

"I see. You don't mind, then, if I cut it all off?"

She took in a sharp breath, then shrugged. "It's *your* hair. I'll never talk to you again, but—" she lifted her face to his, and a smile flashed across her eyes. "Do what you like."

Lysandro's heart set off at a mad gallop. Never before had she given any sign that she found him attractive. But the heat in her face told all. Before the doge had snatched it away, Lysandro had seen many pages in the letter Sera had written him. He had the strongest desire to tackle the doge to get his hands on them, to devour her words. Anything to know he held her favor. There was genuine affection in her touch. When she reached for his fingers and threaded them with her own in full view of Fabien, he had all he ever wanted.

Sera's mouth dropped open as they entered the tavern. The place was bursting with members of the doge's court. They all cheered and tipped their glasses at her arrival.

Fabien smiled wryly. "As you see, I've brought a few familiar faces with me. We discovered this absolutely charming tavern on our way into town." He called a barmaid over and ordered a first round and a veritable feast—a boiled chicken, stewed lamb, creamed potatoes, a bowl of cherries, and a whole tray of mincemeat pies.

"And bread," Fabien called after the maid. "Bring lots and lots of bread."

"Is that the trick, then?" Lysandro said to Sera.

"Got to soak up all that liquor with something."

Foaming mugs of ale were served, but before Sera could bring hers to her lips, Fabien reached across the table and put his hand over the mouth of her glass.

"Did you forget what day it is?" He produced a bottle of liquid as dark as glowing embers from the hidden folds of his dress.

"Oh Goddess, please no—"

"Shame on you! What's Faelsday without a little fire water?"

Sera groaned as Fabien passed her the vial. Even the small swig she took produced tears in her eyes. She gagged and passed it to Pirró, who did the same and then passed it back to Fabien. After his own swallow, he shook the remainder of the contents at Lysandro.

"What do you say, Don Lysandro? Care to celebrate like a true Mirênese?"

"Don't listen to him," Sera said. "You'll regret it."

"I'll have what she's having."

Fabien voiced his pleasure in his own language and handed the vial to Lysandro.

It was as potent as its name and reputation suggested, and burned all the way down his throat, like he had consumed the spit of dragons.

Sera coughed. "Oh, I hate that stuff."

"You *have* been gone too long. Have another!"

"Oh no. *No,*" she insisted when he tried to foist another swallow upon her.

"You're lost to me already, aren't you?" Fabien asked.

"If that means I'm sober more often than not, then yes."

Fabien mocked a frown. "Alright. I'm off to the little girls' room."

Pirró moved the bowl of cherries closer to himself and began to graze.

Sera leaned in. "How is he?" she asked as Fabien crossed to the other side of the tavern.

Pirró spoke between bites. "He and His Royal Highness are not talking to each other. He broke the king's nose."

Sera tilted her head from side to side. "It did need a bit of adjustment." She said it coolly and without malice.

Pirró's eye's crinkled. "How did you get so witty?"

She batted her eyes at him. "I had a good teacher. I'm surprised he let you come."

"Uh-huh." Pirró tore off a piece of bread from the loaf with his teeth.

Sera took in his words and looked around. Fabien had brought his *entire* court with him.

"Oh, boy."

"That's the point, isn't it? Fabien wasn't asking." His eyes darted between Sera and Lysandro. "He wants you to come back with us. You know that, right?"

Sera fell silent.

For Lysandro, that silence was filled with great hope.

Pirró took the hint. "Anyway, he's been obsessed with the drawing you sent him of the fourth panel. He's had a sketch done up of all the images together except the first. He's more determined than ever to find it, but—"

"Hey."

Pirró stopped and took a breath.

"I'm sorry you got caught in the middle," Sera said.

His shoulders slumped, but he kept his smile. "You're the only one I'd be willing to share him with. I know, I know," he said, not giving her time to protest. "All the same."

She clasped his knuckles as they lay clenched on the table just as Fabien returned.

"I was just telling her about your sketch."

He pulled it from his satchel and unfolded it across the table. "I have everything now, except the first panel."

Sera leaned forward to examine the work. "Then you have enough to figure out what the first panel holds."

"If only that were true. I can't trust that whatever is in the first panel lies north of what is depicted in the fourth panel. We already know from eight and nine that geographic logic doesn't apply across the panels."

The wind left her sails. "Aren't there other clues?"

"Not that I can see. The first panel stands alone. There's nothing here to suggest where Morgasse is pointing."

The Sister Peaks.

Lysandro didn't know what made him think that. He didn't say it aloud. All the same, the feeling persisted. The skin of his left palm grew tight, and he brought his other hand up to scratch it.

"Do you have any new leads on where the first panel might be?" she asked.

"I've sent out my inquiries, I'm just waiting now. We're almost there. I can feel it."

"You always think that."

"This time I mean it. We won't have our prize today, at any rate." His gaze turned to Pirró. "Did you ask her yet?" he asked.

"I didn't get the chance. How long do you think it takes to piss?"

Pirró bent over and rummaged through the bag at his feet. He pulled out a thick stack of bound paper and a blue tricorner hat trimmed in white fur. It was the sort Mirênese officers had worn in the last war between them and Andras, the one Lysandro's father had fought in as a young man.

Sera eyed the hat with suspicion. "What's that doing here?"

"I was hoping you would reprise your role," Fabien said.

"He's been working like mad on this," Pirró said, pushing the script across the table at her. "Just read it."

Sera sighed in resignation and flipped open the first page. What she saw there took her by surprise. Lysandro could tell how absorbed she was when she dropped out of the conversation altogether, and her breathing grew shallow.

"Many of the scenes you know already. I just never put them together in quite this way before," Fabien said. "For the music, I thought we could use songs the audience would already be familiar with. And—"

Sera held up a hand to silence the doge as she turned another page. Lysandro had seen that look before. It had come over her when she'd leaned over the railing and let *The Lady in the Lake* overtake her. He knew that she wouldn't come up for air until she'd read the whole script through.

The table fell into an awkward silence while Sera read. Lysandro filled the void by filling his belly. The doge and his lover followed suit.

"Our entourage is too large for the tavern to fit, so we've commandeered the playhouse," Fabien explained. "You and your friend are welcome to join us for a bit of revelry."

"My friend?"

The bench shook with the sudden arrival of Sancio.

"Hello everyone. Happy Faelsday."

Lysandro introduced Sera's friends.

"Aren't you going to introduce me to…" his eyes fell on Seraphine, who hadn't noticed a thing.

"Later. What brings you here today?"

Sancio blinked. His stare shot pure venom at Sera. Lysandro twisted in his seat to block Sancio's view of her to shield her from it.

"I have to talk to you," Sancio said.

"Don't mind us," the doge interjected. He and Pirró turned inward on each other and commenced a conversation in their own tongue.

"What is it?" Lysandro asked.

"Beatríz is going to confront Marek," he said in a hushed tone.

Now he had Lysandro's attention. "When?"

"Tonight. She's finally convinced that he's responsible for the window."

"What changed?"

Sancio shrugged. "I didn't tell her anything I hadn't already. Maybe—"

Sancio stopped short. His gaze turned toward Fabien and Pirró, who were sharing a kiss at the other end of the table.

Lysandro jostled him with his elbow. "Come on. Don't stare. Maybe what?"

"I...um..."

The lovers broke from their embrace when they saw they'd garnered unwanted attention. Sancio tore his gaze away.

"Sorry. What was I saying?"

Lysandro furrowed his brow. "What's wrong with you?"

"I know!" Pirró chirped.

Lysandro felt Fabien kick his lover under the table. "*Shut up.*"

Pirró said nothing further, but his devious grin remained.

Whatever private exchange they were having, Lysandro didn't understand it. He prodded Sancio.

"Marek?"

"Yes. Yes, of course."

Lysandro thought for a moment. "Is she sure that's wise? He still has that dagger."

"That's why I'm telling you," Sancio said. "In case you're needed."

Lysandro turned to Sera. Her eyes were glistening. As she rapidly neared the conclusion, she gasped in surprise.

"C'mon," Sancio jibed. "You're just a fifth wheel here anyway."

That put Lysandro's blood up.

"She's my betrothed. I can't—"

"She's what?"

"Well, close enough. I can't just leave her alone with them."

"With people she's known all her life?" Sancio retorted.

"They invited you too, you know."

"And like you, I have more important places to be."

"Seraphine may not be important to you, but she's everything to me."

"*Everything?*" Sancio reeled in his chair.

"I can't defeat Marek on my own, remember? Your words. What can I do that a high priestess of the warrior temple or the ever-elusive Examiners can't?" He overemphasized the point on account of his anger.

Sancio stood, exasperated. "Fine. Do nothing then." He turned abruptly and left.

Lysandro couldn't be in two places at once, and he had to make sure Sera was safe. She came first. As she should, if she was to be his bride. Why didn't Sancio understand?

Sera turned the final page and looked up as Sancio left.

"So?" Fabien turned to Sera. "What do you say?"

She shook her head slowly. "What have you done?" she whispered.

He winced. "Is it that bad? I mean, I know I'm a little attached." He stopped when he saw her mouth quirk; she picked the tricorner hat up off the table and donned it with pride.

"You have your captain."

"Fantastic! We perform at the end of the festival."

"What?!" Sera cried. "That's *tomorrow*. We'll never be ready!"

"We *will*," Fabien insisted, pounding his fist on the table. "I've come prepared. *You* already know most of it. What better time to premiere a play about love than on the close of Her grandest holiday?"

Lysandro saw the trio exchange glances. What they were all thinking, but nobody said, was that performing the play in Mirêne wasn't possible. Not without the king's permission.

Sera took several deep breaths, then stretched out her fingers. "Give me some more of that firewater."

"Ha! *There* she is."

Saying the doge had commandeered the playhouse was an understatement. Everywhere Lysandro turned, there were flowers. Satin pillows took the place of high-backed chairs on the marble floor meant to seat the audience. A full orchestra practiced in the corner, weaving their way through the bars of multiple songs Lysandro recognized—some of war, others of love—and scores of people bustled about preparing for a grand spectacle.

Fabien leapt up on stage and turned outward to face him and Sera. His voice echoed off the walls.

"In the first act, when the desert prince, played by yours truly, is seducing the girl, they'll be sand on the floor. Pirró, if you please?"

Pirró hopped to his feet and joined the doge as he dug his hand into a large sack in the corner and scattered the pink sand of the Maghreve across the wooden floorboards. The orchestra, fully attuned to the doge and his whims, transitioned from the percussive dynamism of battle to a soft, low song full of longing.

"As we dance..." Fabien grabbed Pirró by the waist and twirled him around, kicking up dust and creating a pink mist at their feet. At the snap of his fingers, a strong lantern beam shone down on them from above. The overall effect was an ethereal scene; the couple appeared to be dancing atop the dunes, glittering in the moonlight.

Lysandro was impressed. Sera was moved, drinking in the nascent wonders of the theater.

"I want the performance to be as immersive and as natural as possible. You've been Captain Duhamel for years now, so we need not rehearse *those* scenes. But the script should not be strictly followed, understand? We must attempt to capture its spirit."

Sera nodded. "I know my part."

"Good! How are your sword skills?"

"*Sword* skills?" Lysandro asked.

"Same as you left them, why?" Sera asked.

"You're going into battle, as a leader of men. You must look the part."

Fabien advanced, drawing his sword as he did so. Sera stepped back.

"I'm still in my dress."

"As am I."

"I've just eaten!" she cried. "And you're drunk!"

Every hair on Lysandro's body stood at attention. He moved to protect her, ready to relieve the doge of his weapon. And his head, if required.

Fabien let out a battle cry, but the sound of swords clashing erupted over Lysandro's shoulder. He spun round and found Sera engaged in combat with Pirró. He rushed to step in, but Fabien hauled him back by the arm.

"The blades are dull," the doge assured him with a smile. "It's only a play, remember?"

Lysandro swallowed hard. Sera was doing remarkably well against

Pirró. She was small and agile, and managed several faux strikes against her opponent. But Lysandro couldn't help imagining Marek in place of Pirró, and what would happen with just one little nick…

Sera cracked Pirró across the nose with her elbow. At least, she made it look like she did, and ended the match. Pirró flopped onto his back.

"No," Fabien shouted, "this is war, not some duel for your sweetheart."

"Yessir!" Sera saluted him.

The dead man giggled, which made Fabien even more cross. "That last move should have come much sooner. Don't do anything fancy. Just survive. Fight dirty if you must, or you'll catch another man's blade in your side. Again."

"Gods. I'd forgotten what a tyrant you are."

It went on like this for hours. They fought, they sang, they drank, they went over lines a thousand times until even Lysandro, reclining on a mountain of pillows set in the center of the floor, knew the scenes by heart. Though it was as the doge said—their lines and positions on stage were a little different each time. No matter how long he watched, each performance felt fresh.

Fabien and his people welcomed him into their circle without question. And Sera—he loved Sera more than ever before. She'd let him see. Her love of the theater ran so deep it wasn't enough to observe. She needed to be a part of it. The more he knew of her, the more he loved her.

I have to tell her. I need her to know me too. I can't live with this secret between us anymore.

Where, when, and how he would confess everything began to unfold in his mind as Seraphine sat with her legs folded on the stage. Murderous rage overtook him again as Pirró laid his head in her lap, his character mortally wounded.

"You smell nice!" he said.

She smacked him upside the head, and he sat up again.

"*Fabien…*" he whined.

"Stop annoying her. We're working here, you know."

Pirró muttered something under his breath, then settled down.

"Remember Sera, you've got to sing in your lower register. Celine's a soprano, and you've also got to compete with the canon."

"*Canon?!*"

"Didn't I tell you?"

They all rose from their places and followed Fabien out the rear door of the theater, where a heavy steel canon with a long narrow nose waited at the ready. Three attendants nearby prepared to fire.

"I know you're aiming for realism, but you're going to blow up the theater?" Sera asked.

"They're blanks," Fabien said. *"Really* Sera."

"When you said the doge was excessive, you meant it," Lysandro said.

Fabien turned, shocked. Lysandro's grin turned wry. "She told me a little something about you, too."

He chuckled. "It's just for the second act. We'll roll it up the hill a bit for your song, you know, so the sounds of war are far in the distance. Then we'll roll it back down again for the big battle. I'll time it to—"

Sera waved him off. "Don't tell me. But how, exactly, am I supposed to be as loud as that?"

Fabien shrugged. "Find your inner strength."

Sera could only laugh.

Lysandro had to admit, if Sera wasn't safe here, in the presence of heavy artillery, she wasn't safe anywhere. He called her over to his side.

"Is everything okay?" she asked. Throughout their grueling rehearsal, she had minded him every chance she got. It warmed his insides.

"Everything's fine, but I have to go."

Her eyes questioned him. "Are you bored?"

"No, no it isn't that at all."

"I know today probably didn't go the way you'd planned, but—"

"No, sweetheart." His breath caught in his throat. He hadn't meant to say that out loud. But she only smiled at him. He smiled back. "Nothing's the matter. I just have somewhere else I have to be."

"Okay," she said after a pregnant pause.

"Goodnight, Seraphine. I'll see you tomorrow."

He felt her tugging at the edges of his coat, pulling him closer to her.

"Be careful," she whispered.

There it was again—she spoke as if she knew he was walking into danger. This morning, it had taken everything he had not to give himself away; the only way he would know that she could hit a target with a knife was if he'd been on the cliffs the night Marek massacred those men. Maybe she did know.

"I will." He felt as if they were seeing each other for the first time. And it felt right.

He cupped her face in his palm and pressed a gentle kiss to her cheek. She released him, and he turned to face Fabien before he changed his mind.

"Bring her home when you've finished for the night."

"Of course."

"To her door, you understand? The streets are not safe here."

The doge nodded. "You have my word." Lysandro knew that Fabien would protect Sera with his life if it came to that. Lysandro shook his outstretched hand and headed quickly toward the temple. He did not want to be late.

19

LOTHAN DIDN'T CARE FOR FESTIVALS. HE HATED THEM, ACTUALLY, especially when they were in honor of the whore goddess and her precious goatherder. But this time around, the festival kept rioters away from his door.

Let them revel in their blind loyalty to a false god, he thought. It would be the last time.

He considered the summons from the Aruni high priestess in his hand. It was not a request, but a command. Lothan hadn't yet decided whether to humor the bitch when two of his brothers burst through his door.

"We've searched their homes. Nothing was out of place," the younger one said.

"Our brothers would not run from this," the other insisted. "They are loyal to you, Lord Lothan. We all are."

The man's sniveling was almost too much to bear.

"We questioned their neighbors. No one's seen Hairo or Dima for days."

And they never would again. However they had reached their end, Lothan had been immediately aware of it as he felt his magic increase. But it would not do for him to reveal how little their lives meant to him. At least not yet.

He did not relish the idea as he once might have. The satisfaction it would bring was an illusion, a false prize that would evaporate almost as quickly as it would come. The feeling of calm that using the accursed blade gave him shrunk with each life he stole, while its need rained down upon him like a torrent. He had already cut into his own ranks to sate its lust, but it had not gained an appropriate measure in return. The Sword of Argoss, (no, it was *his* sword now) was a hungry master. It left *him* hungry in turn, and set his teeth on edge.

Perhaps it was because the lives he had fed it were of such little consequence. His bloodlust spiked as he pondered what the life of a warrior priestess might yield. Yet he resisted. There were other ways to increase his power without prostrating himself before the blade's will.

Lothan pulled it from its place at his hip and wrapped it up again. The kerchief was soaked in red before he could turn the key in the drawer and lock its hunger away. He set his mind to other matters.

On his desk lay a map. Its borders stretched from the eastern tip of Andras where their little village hugged the coast, down to the Forbidden Desert, north to the Sister Mountains and west until it once again met the Boundless Sea. The temples of the three goddesses were clearly marked. Beside that lay a smaller scrap of paper constituting all the details he was able to glean from the Aruni *Histories* regarding the temples of Anruven. It wasn't much. That a cult dedicated to a mysterious, bloodthirsty god had existed in the age preceding Theron and that, together with Morgassen sorcery, it had been the source of Argoss's magic, was all he knew. That was more than anyone knew, it seemed. All his queries had come up empty. There were no books, no images, no spells or records of any kind at any of the repositories of history within a week's ride of Lighura, save for the few stone tables like the one moldering in their own museum. The men he'd sent further afield, to Lareina and the mountain regions, had yet to return. The chances of them finding what he sought were bleak, given what the men who had already returned had told him—that there was nothing to find.

The cult of Anruven had been obliterated in the aftermath of Argoss's defeat, their secrets never again meant to be conjured by human hands. Any arcane knowledge Anruven's priests had once possessed had died with them.

The blade hummed to him from inside the drawer. He ignored it and tossed the maps to the ground. A head of shaggy brown hair poked tentatively into the room.

"Lord Lothan?"

"What?!"

"The printer."

About time. "Get him in here."

His nose was a perfect target for Lothan's rage. It cracked under the force of his fist, and spurted forth blood that dribbled down the printer's chin and onto his clean white shirt. The scent of his own brutality caused Lothan to salivate. He seated himself and stretched out his legs as the printer choked on his own gore.

Lothan pinched a copy of the broadsheet against the Shadow between his fingers.

"See this?"

STEFANO DIDN'T. HE COULDN'T POSSIBLY, AS HIS EYES WERE FILLED WITH THE sting of hot tears.

"Do you think me a fool?"

Stefano gurgled in the negative.

"*Do* you?"

Lothan's voice rose, along with his fist. The printer shook his head to stave off a second blow. The rapid motion rattled the contents of his skull and set the world spinning at a dazzling pace.

"You will print these again, at your own expense." Lothan towered over him. "And it'll be done by morning."

At the risk of his brains spilling out of his ears, the printer shook his head again, this time slower.

"I can't," he protested. His words were wet and tangy.

Lothan's eyes flared like burning coals.

"Not enough paper."

Lothan narrowed his eyes and punched the printer again, sending him sprawling onto the floor. Stefano was relieved to be on the floor, and away from Marek's fist. He'd told his wife what he'd done, and she knew what to expect when he came home tonight. She'd clean him up and have a hot meal waiting for him.

It wasn't as bad as he'd feared. That, and his nose had always been a bit crooked to begin with. He would wear his wounds like badges of honor. He staggered home, but behind the blood streaking his face, he was smiling.

LOTHAN HAD NO DOUBT THAT THE PRINTER HAD BOTCHED THE BROADSHEET on purpose. But bringing the printer to justice went a little way toward lifting Lothan's spirit. But he'd been assured by his lieutenants, multiple times, that de Castel's titles and his family's position provided an impenetrable shield, and that to flout the law in this instance would serve to bring the chief magistrate down on his head. That was a headache he did not need. Besides, de Castel was nowhere to be seen. Most likely courting that girl of his, the one with the impudent mouth and an idiot for a father. It occurred to him that his revived "charms" could work just as well on her as they had on the mob that had gathered on his doorstep. That would fix Lysandro better than a prison cell, although pummeling him to death the old-fashioned way would be intensely satisfying.

The blade beckoned him again. It was so loud he thought he saw the desk vibrate with its echo. Like an organ that he had extracted and left in a drawer, he was bound to it by an invisible coil that tugged all the tighter as he tried to resist it. Its call could not be ignored. In time, he would destroy Lysandro. But first, to the temple.

BEATRÍZ KNEW WHAT SANCIO WAS GOING TO SAY BEFORE HE EVEN OPENED his mouth.

"No answer?"

"No, High Priestess."

"You're sure Marek received it?"

"I put it into his hands myself."

A shadow crossed Sancio's face when he said it. She suspected that the magistrate and his officers had treated him with less respect than an Aruni deserved, but Sancio was the only one who knew Marek was responsible for the breaking of the window.

"Alright," she said grimly. "Back to your duties."

He nodded and headed off down the corridor toward the training grounds.

Beatríz made her way into the nave of the temple, taking up the guard post she had set for herself every night since Marek's invasion. Sancio had hounded her about what he'd heard—or rather, *who* he'd heard, every day since it had happened. She couldn't get out of her mind that if she'd only listened to him from the start, when he'd first brought the Shadow of Theron to her door with stories of a hidden cave and dark relics, the temple window might have been spared.

There was only one man in the whole of Lighura who would trust Sancio as an ally and messenger, only one who regularly snuck into the temple house to see him when he thought she didn't notice. She wouldn't have believed it of him if she hadn't seen it with her own eyes. But the more Sancio refused to reveal the Shadow, the stronger her conviction became.

If her conjectures were correct, it didn't take a Morgassen to see the signs, that what once was might be again, and that the Shadow of Theron wasn't a shadow of anything. That she had already returned the temple's relic to his father was no small consolation.

A shuffling sound at the front of the temple tore her attention away from her thoughts.

Marek stood at the threshold, alone. He hesitated there, then, with a grunt, transgressed the boundary marked by heavy columns.

His eyes cast a wicked gleam in the moonlight, and the stench of blood filled the air. The hair on the back of Beatríz's neck stood at attention. Any doubts she had been clinging to fled. Everything the Shadow of Theron had told her was true.

Marek turned his head toward the newly laid floor of the prayer booth, where the cavity underneath now lay empty, then turned slowly back to her, wearing a knowing grin. There was no pretense now.

Beatríz's skin shivered as she reached for the hilt of her sword. He was no warrior; if she was lucky, it would be over before it began.

She rushed forward with her sword aimed at his head. He didn't flinch. But at the last minute, he pulled a small blade from his hip—a blade that dripped with blood. She leapt to the side to avoid the dagger and released a powerful swing aimed at the point where the back of Lothan's neck met his skull. He ducked and chanced a quick swipe at her legs. But she was wise to the move, and jumped out of the way of his arm. She landed a kick to his face and sent him sprawling across the floor.

Her longsword provided her enough room to keep Marek at bay while she worked out how to disarm him. A well-placed jab to the wrist would knock his grip loose, but she couldn't afford any mistakes. The tiniest cut would mean her life.

She didn't like it, but she knew she needed help. Even if some of the Aruni fell, they would not all—and it would be over. Working her enemy in wide, deliberate circles, she fought her way toward the bell that would alert her sisters.

He needed to get close to use his weapon. The magistrate tried to duck and weave his way toward her and away from the tip of her sword, but he was untrained, undisciplined, and she swatted him away with ease. She anticipated his moves before he even knew them himself. But she didn't relax. His lack of skill made it easy for her to spin him in circles, but it also meant he was unpredictable. Beatríz didn't dare blink. When he charged again, almost crawling with his head tucked low, she caught him in the shoulder and sent him reeling backward.

Marek reached for where she'd sliced him, but he didn't relinquish his grip on the dagger. If she was more daring, she could have advanced for a fatal strike. But Beatríz kept her eyes on the river of blood in his hand. It was unclear if its poison would extend beyond the jagged edge of the metal, should he flick his wrist and send a spray in her direction. But it was just enough of an opening to call the others. She raced to the bell as Marek clutched his butchered shoulder. She saw fear and recognition register on his face as she slammed the broad side of her blade against the smooth bronze. Its deep, resonant gong had never been more satisfying.

SHIT.

Lothan had minutes, maybe less, before the Aruni descended upon him. He was no match for the expert swordswoman. He cursed his own arrogance for ever allowing himself to believe that he was.

Even enchanted, his blade was diminutive. To inflict a wound, Lothan had to be nearer than the high priestess would allow.

He could see a sliver of glistening white out of the corner of his eye. He tried not to look at his rent-open shoulder. Another blow like that would kill him. She knew the stakes of the battle they waged and wouldn't be tricked into faltering. If he threw the dagger at her and missed, he would be dead before he could retrieve it.

But the metal in his hand screamed for blood, heedless to the seemingly insurmountable challenge it demanded. It hissed in his ears, suggesting that he do the unthinkable. But its talons were sunk deep. He slid to the floor and surrendered to its will.

He sensed the priestess's approach. Had he bled out? Lothan wasn't sure. It felt that way. His limbs became dull and leaden, but at the same time, thinner than air.

Then something happened that the high priestess could never have anticipated. The shard attacked her of its own accord, rising from the floor and flying out of Lothan's hand with inhuman speed.

It bit into her calf. Even with his hands empty, Lothan felt it go in, felt her energy collecting on the sword's edge. It called to him from across the floor as the daughter of Arun collapsed on top of him.

"Son of a bitch," he groaned, and shoved her off of him. He rolled onto his stomach and got slowly to his feet. The dense cloud that had settled over him lifted.

The horror and shock on the woman's face made the blinding pain in his shoulder disappear. Veins of black already traced her eyes, but he wasn't done with her yet. Not after the time she'd given him. Lothan grabbed her by the hair and dragged her across the temple with his good arm, stooping to retrieve the dagger along the way. Its pleasure seared into him, like a tremor racing down his spine.

With a howl, he pulled her up the unforgiving corners of the steps and onto the altar. The life drained from her until there was only a wisp of it left; she was a dead weight in his hand. She couldn't fight back, didn't even flail when the back of her head crashed against the honed marble edge of the last stair. He didn't care now how fast the Aruni came upon him. It wouldn't be fast enough.

Lothan slashed the priestess's face to ribbons, and watched the rivulets of blood stream down the folds of her garments and onto the floor with smug delight.

When the band of Aruni finally arrived at the front of the temple, it was empty.

20

SANCIO'S WINDOW WAS OPEN. WHETHER THAT WAS A SIGN OF HIS FRIEND'S trust in him, or simply habit, Lysandro didn't know. Whatever the reason, the room was empty. He had expected Sancio to lead him to the impending encounter between Marek and the high priestess, show him where best to hide. But he was nowhere in sight.

His bed was unmade, the room dark save for moonlight. Lysandro struggled to examine the bedsheets, the writing desk, anywhere where Sancio might have left him instructions. He saw a shadow out of the corner of his eye as he lifted the pillow. He spun round, drawing his sword. The door was open. Darkness spilled into the room from the empty hallway. Lysandro took in the whole of the room—Sancio had quit his bed, and had done so in a hurry.

Sword still in hand, Lysandro poked his head out of the room and listened. There was only silence. No, not silence. Underneath the quiet there was a faint, low sound, far away. Wailing.

He rushed to his left, following the sound out of the Aruni's sleeping quarters and toward the nave of the temple. He sheathed his sword as he found the holy warriors clustered around the altar. There was no conflict here, no enemies to fight. Only sorrow.

The weeping priestesses took notice of him and shifted listlessly to either side to let him through. The smell of blood in the air was thick. Lysandro knew what had transpired with a grim certainty before seeing it. But the knowledge of what he was about to see was not enough to prepare him for it. Tatters of the high priestess's robe lay atop the altar in a blood-soaked heap, its proud blue besmirched with ash. His stomach fell, his chest became hollow.

Kneeling in a puddle on the floor was Sancio. His hands and face were soiled with what remained of the high priestess.

His expression as he lit upon Lysandro turned his insides cold. He saw a flurry of loss, anger, confusion—and blame.

Murmurs among the Aruni encroached on the silence.

"We've already lost our window, now Beatríz. What's left?"

"What are we going to tell people?"

"The Examiners must hear of this."

"But where are they?"

One of them looked at Lysandro. "What about *you*?"

Every head in the room turned to regard him.

"You claim to be Theron's heir, his *shadow*," the woman sneered. "Theron was an avenger of the Goddess. What will *you* do?"

He said nothing, unsure of what he should say. What he could do. But the pain in her voice was unbearable. Her anguish seemed to reach out and grip him by the throat with both hands.

The air became charged, and he no longer felt welcome. Lysandro retreated out of sight.

"Let him go," Eugenie whispered, hooking Asha by the arm before she could take off after him. She kept her eyes on the floor as they hid themselves at the edge of the Aruni. "We're needed here."

The brisk night wind lashed at Lysandro's cheeks. The world passed him by in a blur, spinning wildly on its axis as he raced atop his stallion through the streets. His anger swirled like a tornado. Anger at Marek's flagrant, escalating violence, anger at the world falling apart around him, anger at himself, for stealing away time with Sera when he'd had none to spare. He felt the Aruni's accusing stares on him still, demanding that he assume the full mantle of his nighttime namesake. They wanted a miracle. They expected it of him. Even Sancio. How could they expect him to be more than he was, more than any man was capable of? Marek was no match for Lysandro's skill with a sword, but Marek wielded a dark relic. Even that fraction of Argoss's sorcery had been enough to bring the Aruni to their knees and had stilled Lysandro's hand.

Lysandro was angry that he agreed with them. He had not been there. The death of the high priestess lay at his feet, and they both knew it. It didn't matter that he didn't know what he could have done to stop it. He was angry that he wasn't what the Aruni wanted. What Lighura needed.

Marek's actions demanded an answer. Lysandro would be Goddess-damned if he didn't give him one.

He leapt from his horse, leaving the panting, foaming beast atop the hill that lay behind the magistrate's office and out of sight. He took with him the satchel stuffed full of Marek's notices against the Shadow, ripped from the town's walls as he'd torn through it like a raging demon.

Lysandro slid down the edge of the hill noiselessly, and caught a glimpse of Marek in his office before crouching down beneath the window. He'd been injured—a deep cut to his left shoulder. The high priestess had taken a bit of him with her, it seemed. Good.

Using the raucous noise of the men inside as cover, Lysandro shoved wads of the printed paper into the gap between the edges of the building and the uneven ground on which it had been built. He did this on every corner of the squat building, encasing its foundation in paper. He littered the kindling with gunpowder and struck a dagger hard and fast across the pages until one of them sparked. He fed the flame, and passed it along the line. His hands seemed to move of their own accord, his mind made blank, filled with white-hot fury.

The ink of the broadsheets proved spectacularly flammable. It flared a brilliant red that reflected in his eyes. Soon enough the flames began to smoke, digging into the structure and breathing into the corners of the wood in its mad race to consume and grow. The fire turned ravenous as it slipped underground and reached into the floorboards. It had its head now. Lysandro made his way to the front of the building. Ears pricked in the darkness, he drew his sword, and waited.

"Touch me again and I'll fucking kill you!"

Lothan shoved his lieutenant hard. He stumbled across the floor, scrambling away from Marek as his legs got tangled beneath him. His brother had been inspecting the damage to Lothan's shoulder, and his ragged, dirt-crusted fingernail had suddenly scraped against bone as he plumbed the depths of the wound. The unbidden touch had made Lothan shiver. He pressed another rag to his torn flesh to soak up the blood. It didn't flow as freely as it had before, but still. Lothan was running out of rags.

He was too drained to enjoy his hard-earned victory just yet, and he cursed himself a second time for maiming Lighura's only healer. At this point, Lothan would have taken the man blind. His hands would still have known what to do better than the imbeciles who now surrounded him.

"The gap's too big to stitch closed, Lord Lothan," Jenner protested. He stepped carefully toward his master with a small bowl of green goop in his hand. "At least let me dress it."

Lothan let out a low growl as the slimy substance mingled with his blood to form a runny paste the color of shit. The stink was not much better. He turned his face away from the stench, but the severed muscle connecting his neck to his shoulder screamed in protest and forced him to endure it.

It wasn't just his neck. The fingers of his left hand were numb, and refused to obey when he bade them harden into a fist. They trembled and shook but would not fold in on themselves. Without proper care, Lothan knew the loss of sensation would be permanent—if the limb didn't rot and fall off altogether.

"Here," Gorin said. He strode up to Lothan and yanked his arm upright. He pulled at Lothan's arm like that of a broken doll. Marek's vision winked out at the sudden surge of pain. He howled.

"Hold it!" Jenner shouted, seizing his chance to sew the wound shut as it smashed against itself in a crooked, ugly line.

Lothan breathed heavily through his nose and tried to imagine how the village would react in the morning as the needle plunged repeatedly into his shoulder and back out again at a vicious speed. He let out a sigh as his brother tied off the last stitch with his teeth, but when Gorin released his arm and Lothan tried to lower it, he couldn't. Even so, the weight of his arm strained at the edges of the stitching. He heard a wet snap, and screamed.

Jenner's face turned pale. "Oh! Forgive me My Lord!" He moved furiously to undo his work, pulling the coarse thread through Lothan's skin like a worn leather boot.

"I'll do it again, not so tight this time."

"The six hells you will! Let go of me!"

"You have to close it up somehow," Gorin snapped back.

The air took on an acrid quality. Lothan crinkled his nose and blinked to block out the sting. Then he saw the flames.

"What fresh hell…"

A blazing tongue flicked at the corner of the room, creeping up from the ground to taste the brittle wood underneath his feet.

"The building's on fire!" Jenner shouted.

"I'm not blind! Put it out!"

His men scrambled to douse the flames. They stamped at the corners of the floor and tried to smother the fire with hastily discarded clothing, but just as they seemed to get a handle on things, the other side of the room flared up.

Lothan screamed orders like a wild man. Then he heard his name called from the street like a battle cry. He ground his teeth. Theron's bastard *would* make an appearance now. If he answered the call in his current state, with his arm halfway off his body, Theron's Shadow would finish what the high priestess had started. Just when he thought his circumstances couldn't get any more wretched.

At the sounding of his name, all movement inside the little office had ceased.

"It's the Shadow of Theron," they whispered among themselves.

Lothan saw red. "Don't just stand there like jackasses!" he roared. "Quash this fire! And you!" he turned to Gorin and one other, the two biggest of the lot. "Get out there and bring me his head!"

The two men barreled out the front door. Lothan turned his attention to the rear wall of his office, where the flames were making a rapid ascent up the wooden paneling.

"Fuck!"

He backed away to the center of the room as the searing heat blistered and bubbled behind him. His men had retreated from the walls as well, and clustered around him.

"We can't stop this," one man cried.

"He's going to burn us alive!" screamed another.

"*Enough!*" Lothan shouted above the chaos, taking more of the smoldering air into his lungs than he meant to and suffering for it. With every shuddering cough, his body tore itself further apart.

"Lord Lothan, we have to escape." Jenner shoved the abandoned desk against the wall and threw open the trap door underneath. "*Now* Lothan, before it collapses!"

An ominous splintering echoed above his head. Revenge would have to wait.

THE ROOF CAUGHT.

Lysandro watched the wild shadows of the men inside through the glistening windowpanes as pandemonium erupted. He called out over the din.

"Marek!"

He tightened his grip around his sword. The opportunity to use it seemed upon him when the door swung open moments later. But it was not Marek himself that charged into the street.

Coward.

Lysandro gave them no quarter. He slashed hard at one and then the other as they came at him, opening their flesh from neck to navel. Both men crashed to the ground. They did not get up again.

Lysandro kept his eyes trained on the door, growing impatient. But Marek did not appear. Then he heard the cracking and splitting of wood, and the roof collapsed. A plume of smoke billowed up from the ground and swallowed the magistrate's office in a single gulp. Lysandro watched the hills to the rear of the burning rubble, but he spied no movement, no attempt at escape. When the inferno's rage began to subside, he approached the wreckage with caution. Tears welled in his eyes from the columns of black smoke and ash seething through the open gaps and charred boards. He hid his face behind his arm as he drew near.

There were no screams piercing the night. Nor any groans or signs of even the slightest movement. But something was missing—the smell of burning flesh.

He moved to inspect the ruined interior through a singular window that had not been shattered. But before he could put his face to it, he heard a slick pop, and a searing arrowpoint of pain sliced through his left bicep. He leapt back and raised his sword. Relief shuddered through him when he realized it was just an ordinary cut; the cloud of death that had ensnared him when Marek had last struck him was absent.

The night remained still save for the slackening blaze. It had not been an attack—the windowpane had burst from the intolerable heat, and a fragment of the offending glass had embedded itself in his arm.

If there was anyone left in the building, they were not alive. But Lysandro also knew that the collapsed building was empty. Abandoned. Somehow, without him seeing, Marek had fled. Lysandro's attention strayed to the insidious sting that crawled up the length of his arm like the kiss of a scorpion. Setting his sword between his teeth, he extracted the glass with his free hand. A well of blood bubbled up in its wake. He clamped down on it, clenching his jaw against his steel to stifle the pain. He reached awkwardly for a handkerchief out of his right pocket to tie off the bleeding before he turned to go.

Hurricane stood pawing the ground, waiting to take him home. Lysandro tried not to look at the faces of the two men on the ground as he walked past them. But he couldn't help himself.

Their unseeing stares followed him.

* * *

Lysandro would have given his fortune for just an ounce of the doge's firewater. He'd already drunk two full cups of the bitter tea Rafael had brewed to dull his senses while the surgeon rooted around in Lysandro's muscle. But every second was more excruciating than the last.

"Sorry Lysandro, but it's got to be clean before I stitch you up. Goddess, you'd think the window hadn't been wiped in a decade."

Lysandro braced himself for the onslaught of agony as Rafael again doused his arm in alcohol. It didn't burn any less than it had the first time. Or the fourth. Lysandro ground his teeth, convinced that it would have hurt less to cut off the limb and be done with it.

Rafael moved quickly to dab at it with a cloth and peer into the deep puncture.

"It's clean! It's clean."

Lysandro allowed himself to breathe. The tea thankfully began to do its work as Rafael worked a small needle at the fraying edges of the wound, pulling it closed.

"I know it hurts, but it should heal relatively quickly. You may not even scar."

That was something, at least. Arun knew he had enough of those already.

Rafael tried to steer his friend away from the tugging sensation at his skin.

"You're sure he didn't run out the back when you weren't looking?"

"Positive. But he was there. I saw him with my own eyes."

"Hmm. It's a mystery, I'll admit."

Rafael's words triggered thoughts of Sera. She would know. She would have sussed Marek out in an instant. He closed his eyes and conjured her image.

What would you say?

"A secret passage…"

"What?" Rafael asked.

"He *was* there, but then he wasn't. So he must have left."

"Through a secret passage," Rafael repeated.

"He had a secret hideout in the caves. I didn't even see it until I was standing right on top of it."

On top…

"There must be a tunnel underneath the building. Damn!"

"You couldn't have known," Rafael said. "And anyway, how would you have gotten to it? You did effectively drop a house on it. Not to mention your arm."

"I can fight."

Rafael tucked the needle back into his makeshift pack and began to wrap his handiwork.

"I'm sure you can. That doesn't mean you should."

"It can only be avoided for so much longer."

Rafael's mouth fell into a thin line. "I know. I would just feel better knowing you were at your best when the time comes."

Lysandro couldn't argue with that.

His thoughts again returned to Sera. It hardly took effort. But Rafael's words had reminded him of her, and of the worried look in her eyes as they'd parted for the evening. It was late. But was it *too* late?

He got to his feet the moment Rafael released him.

His friend shot up after him. "Where are you going?"

"To check on Sera. Make sure she got home okay."

"She's fine. You shouldn't be going out again tonight."

"She might be awake. I haven't seen her since..."

His voice trailed off, not finishing a thought he realized was best kept private. He hadn't called on her as the Shadow since that glorious kiss. The last thing he wanted was for her to think he'd lost interest, or that his sweet words had only been a ploy to elicit her embrace.

"It's not safe," Rafael insisted. "If the high priestess couldn't defeat him..."

Lysandro was thinking the exact same thing. He understood now, better than ever, why even though Theron was said to vanquish monsters with a swing of his sword, it was the Hand of Arun, the golden bow and arrow, that had triumphed over Argoss and his cursed blade.

Lysandro knew nothing of archery.

But he had his mind set on Sera, and could think of nothing else.

"What if Marek spots you?" Rafael pressed. "He could be anywhere, and he's already killed once tonight."

So have I.

The thought came unbidden, and Lysandro pushed it away as soon as it came. He conjured Seraphine again, and fixed his wary mind on her.

"I have to see her. I *have* to."

Rafael took a step back. "Good Goddess, Lysandro. You really love her."

"I really do."

Scaling the trellis outside Sera's window with one hand while endeavoring not to make a sound was more difficult than Lysandro had anticipated. But he managed it, and alighted on the balcony to find the doors to Sera's bedchamber left open. The pale gauzy curtains swayed to a delicate rhythm in the breeze.

Lysandro's breath caught when he saw Seraphine asleep in her bed. She looked like a dream.

The lightness of the curtains and their gentle dance lifted his heavy spirit. Had she waited up for him? Kept the doors open in the hope that he might appear?

He was overcome by the desire to fall into bed beside her, envelop her in his arms, and not let go until morning. Or perhaps ever.

He lingered only for a moment, as long as it took for this precious image of her to sear itself onto his soul. He retrieved the token of his affection that he'd carried between his teeth and laid it across the marble banister. As he did so, he spied a darkened spot on the cuff of his sleeve— an errant bit of blood that had been missed in his diligent attempt to make himself clean in her presence. He banished it with the pad of his thumb, rubbing vigorously. In a moment, his coat was clean. But still he imagined he saw the blackened stain there. It leeched from him the sense of peace that the tranquil scene before him brought. He could not bear the thought of Sera, so gentle and innocent, being touched by the night's violence.

He left her to her dreams and prayed that soon his own nightmare would face the dawn.

Sera woke to find an amaryllis, glistening with the morning's dew, laid with care at the edge of her balcony. Its silken beauty called to mind the graceful features and tender heart of its sender and brought a brilliant smile to her lips that would not fade for all the world.

21

SANCIO WIPED THE TEARS FROM HIS FACE. IT WAS AN EMPTY GESTURE THAT only smeared the blood and soot on his cheeks further. Not that he cared.

"He can't deny us now," one of the sisters said behind him. Sancio didn't bother looking up to see who it was. His gaze stayed fixed on the blood-soaked folds of the garment in his hands. The bereaved priestesses conversed over his head.

"Who can't deny us?" another asked.

"Magistrate Marek. Inside the temple or not, he can't argue that investigating murderers is not his business."

Sancio wanted to laugh. But he couldn't bring himself to it. Whenever he thought he was close, he feared he might vomit.

"He *is* the murderer," he said.

"What? What are you talking about?"

"I said, Marek *is* the murderer!" He was shouting now, but that no longer seemed to matter. "Can't you see what's right in front of your eyes? Beatríz was killed with the Blood Sword of Argoss. And Marek was the wielder."

Shouts of disbelief and outrage echoed all around him. Sancio ignored them. "*He* is the one who's been stealing relics from the temple, *he* is the one that destroyed our window, and now, he's murdered the high priestess."

"That's insane! How could you even think such a thing?"

"Because I was *there!*"

The room stilled, long enough for Sancio to catch his breath and reclaim his composure.

"You were where?" Varia asked. Her voice was low and urgent.

"I was in the temple the night the window was broken. I heard Marek's voice. He gave the order."

"Why didn't you tell anyone? Because of *you*, our priestess is—"

"Beatríz knew. That's why she summoned him here tonight."

Varia stepped back, unbelieving. "Why would she confide in you, a good-for-nothing novice who only knows how to eat?"

"Because she knew I wouldn't go charging to my own death like you."

Varia's eyes narrowed to slits.

"That's what you're thinking, isn't it? To go after Marek? Make him pay?"

Her stance said it all. Sancio scoffed. "You really do have bricks for brains. He already killed the high priestess. You think you will fare better against the Blood Sword?"

"He doesn't have the Blood Sword."

"Oh yes. Yes he does. The Shadow of Theron saw him use it."

"The Shadow—"

"The Shadow came to this temple days ago and told Beatríz everything. She confronted Marek, and he used the sword against her." Sancio lifted the tattered robes in his hands. "This is the proof."

Varia faltered, but only for a moment. "He can't kill us *all*."

"He can kill enough of you. Then what?"

Varia didn't have an answer for that.

"So...what do we do?" another asked, weathering Varia's hard stare.

Sancio made to rub his hand across his forehead again but stopped himself. "We can't confront him alone. The Council of Three sent Examiners to deal with the theft of the relics. They'll be prepared to combat the one who has taken them."

"But—"

"We'll send out riders, like we said. As many as we can spare. We can't wait any longer."

"That won't be necessary," an unfamiliar voice said.

"What? Why?" Varia asked aloud to no one in particular.

"Because we're already here."

At that, Sancio finally lifted his head.

"I'm Eugenie, Examiner of the Temple Morgasse. This is my sister Asha."

"I am one of you," Asha said. "And I feel your loss as if it was my own."

So many voices bombarded them at once that Eugenie thought her head was going to explode.

"Please, Honored Sisters, what should we do? Sister Asha, we are at your command."

At Varia's prompting, the Aruni dropped to one knee and laid their weapons on the ground in front of them.

Asha tensed.

Eugenie had anticipated this, but it seemed Asha had not. Eugenie could see a cloud of anxiety forming over Asha's head. She was confident in herself, but wary of leading others. Eugenie laid a gentle hand on her sister's forearm.

"We *will* stand with you against this threat," Eugenie assured the warriors, "but first we must understand our foe. What's your name, Brother?" Her gaze landed on the male acolyte bent over the foot of the altar. He was the only one who seemed to have any sense.

"Sancio." He bowed.

"I would speak with you about this Marek."

"I can tell you much."

Eugenie nodded. "I suspect so."

"But what should we *do*?" Varia asked, stepping forward.

"Prepare the way for the high priestess," Asha said. "That her body was taken will not stop us from bestowing on her every honor."

Varia nodded and turned to her sisters.

"That'll keep them busy, for now at least," Asha said in a low voice to Eugenie.

"Good. Sancio, lead us somewhere quiet."

He led them to his own room. Before he even had time to sit, Eugenie was on him.

"Who is the Child of Theron?"

"Excuse me?"

"The Child of Theron. The masked man who was here before. You know him."

"I believe you mean the *Shadow* of Theron, Madam Examiner."

"I mean what I say, Brother."

Shadow indeed. Eugenie knew who echoed in his footsteps.

The novice had an odd habit of rubbing the tops of his legs to soothe his nerves. Above his head, she saw a flurry of indecision. Eugenie picked at the threads of it in her mind, trying to glimpse what lay at the center. One by one, she unfurled his thoughts as he sat mute before her—fear, anger, jealousy, and betrayal all coiled around the central object that he clung to for dear life.

"He is your friend," Eugenie said at last. "The only one in the world."

Sancio's mouth gaped open, then closed again wordlessly.

"It's alright," Eugenie prodded. "His secret and yours are safe here."

"Don Lysandro de Castel," he said in a small voice. He blinked, not believing his own ears.

Eugenie drank in the name. "Yes. That's right. De Castel. And the story you have to tell me…he is at the center of it, yes?"

Sancio was visibly shaken. "Yes, Madam Examiner."

"Anything you refuse to tell me, the *slightest*, thing, could be of vital import. Do you understand?"

Sancio nodded.

"Good. Now tell me all."

He did. When he was finished, Asha was the first to speak.

"Fetch him, boy. This instant."

Sancio leapt from his chair, but crashed back down to it again at a wave of Eugenie's hand.

"No, Sister. That is not the way of things."

Asha's eyes darted from Eugenie to Sancio and then back again. For all the restraint she mustered in Sancio's presence, Eugenie heard her roar like a lioness.

"We've wasted enough time tracking our quarry. Now *he's* here, and *we're* here, and if de Castel is what you say and he has the sacred relic, then we can finish this."

Sancio dared to interrupt. "Our temple's relic is not *in* his possession. Not exactly."

"So give it to him! If you told true, then Marek is no longer willing to hide what he is. Your friend *must* challenge him."

Eugenie interceded. "Did someone say to Theron, 'you are called to be the Goddess's champion, and you *must* answer'? He will come to it of his own accord or not at all."

Asha raged like a bull. But when she did not charge, Eugenie knew that she had won over her mind, if not her heart.

"We cannot force the hand of fate. The wheel that brings de Castel closer to his destiny is already turning. But it may yet go awry."

Eugenie imagined she could hear the grinding of teeth.

"We must stand idle then?" Asha asked.

"No. There is much to be done that he cannot do."

"Like what?"

"We will be there when de Castel raises the call. For now, we prepare his army."

"His *army?*"

Eugenie nodded. "Darkness is returning. And it returns first to Lighura."

Sancio stared at her. "Do you mean to say, *Argoss* is returning?"

Eugenie wished she knew. But the signs were not clear.

"And you think Lysandro is…"

She watched the pieces fit together in his mind. He ran a bloodied hand through his hair as shock rippled through him.

"We must prepare ourselves to aid the Child of Theron, but we must also restore the villagers' faith. We can start with the window."

"The window?" Asha asked.

"I beg your pardon, Honored Sister, but the blacksmith has called upon every craftsman and artisan there is. No one remembers how to forge a sacred window."

"Of course they don't. The knowledge was never theirs in the first place."

Eugenie got to her feet and dusted off her robes. "Stoke the brazier. Asha, gather what warriors you can, the strongest among them. The night is no longer young."

ASHA WAS STRIPPED DOWN TO THE WORN BANDS OF FABRIC BENEATH HER robes. Sweat poured from her back in shining rivulets as she and the Aruni melted a handful of the shattered grains of colored glass and refashioned them into their former shape. She'd been doubtful when Eugenie first suggested she craft the window from memory, but as Eugenie sat cross-legged on the floor of the temple chanting, Asha found that she knew it well enough. Every angle, every curve, every shade of green and gold came to her as if from a dream. Thrumming between her ears was Eugenie's incantation. It transformed into an incessant tone that seemed to come from within her own mind.

The heat stung Asha's eyes. It could not have been hotter if she'd been standing inside Morgasse's forge itself. But on she worked, the night banished by the blinding white fire of the brazier with its mouth open wide. The Aruni working the makeshift bellows were no less tested by the strain, but their minds stayed clear of all but Eugenie's chant. Asha's body answered screaming to the task, feeling it was she who was being forged, molded by the leaping tongues of flame into a sacred windowmaker of old. When the dawn came, a shaft of light sought out its lost perch and found it again. It pierced through the diamond tip of the golden arrow that heralded the triumph of Theron.

"LYSANDRO."

Sancio cleared his throat as his friend came to the door.

He is *my friend*, he insisted to himself. *Whatever else the Examiner believes him to be.*

"Sancio. Won't you come in?'

The formality in Lysandro's voice cut right to the core of him. But he supposed he deserved it.

"Some breakfast?" Lysandro asked.

"No, thank you."

"You're sure?"

"I ate already, thank you."

That was a lie. Sancio couldn't remember the last time he'd eaten anything. His head was full enough. The mere thought of food made his stomach roil.

He sat in the chair Lysandro indicated and rubbed his knees as he tried to find the right words.

"The Aruni have decided not to make the high priestess's death public."

"What?"

"Not yet at least. I thought you should know, before you said anything."

Lysandro nodded. "Anything else I should know?"

Sancio shook his head stiffly. It was all he could do to keep from saying all he was forbidden to say.

"Will they do as you said? Try to seek out the Examiners?"

That shook him. Hadn't the Morgassen said she had met him? Perhaps she hadn't revealed herself. If that was the case, it was hardly within his purview to do so now. He'd delivered the one message he was permitted. Stretching their conversation beyond that put him on dangerous ground.

"I...expect so," he said.

Lysandro's eyes slid from him in contemplation.

"So, are you engaged yet?"

Lysandro hesitated before answering. "I'll know tonight."

"I'm sure you will be."

Lysandro remained taciturn.

Sancio wanted to apologize. He'd been in such a foul mood when Lysandro had chosen the girl over standing guard against Marek. Chosen her over what Sancio, his lifelong friend, had asked of him. Would it have gone another way if he'd come earlier? Or would there have been two heaps of ash on the altar instead of one?

The Examiner had said Lysandro's time had not yet come. Perhaps that was true. But it didn't make Beatríz any less dead, or do anything to heal the rift that Sancio felt widening between them.

He was not alone in this, Sancio saw. Lysandro's mouth worked as if to say something. But whatever he was thinking, it was not given the shape of words.

"Alright," Sancio said at last, and rose from his seat. "That's all I had to say."

"I *am* sorry," Lysandro said to his back as he reached for the door. "For the high priestess."

It's not your fault. He thought it, but Sancio couldn't bring himself to say it. He would never know what might have been.

"I know." Sancio turned back one more time and allowed himself a quick smile. "And um, you might want to stop by the temple."

Lysandro raised an eyebrow. "Why?"

"You'll see."

LYSANDRO COULDN'T BELIEVE HIS EYES. THE WINDOW WAS EXACTLY AS HE remembered it. It was as if, just this once, time had reversed itself.

Others seemed to feel it too, from the snippets of conversation he overheard in the street opposite the restored window. An Aruni in full battle regalia spoke with a cluster of people, spear in hand.

"If the long hand of Argoss has seen fit to undo time, then this is Arun's answer."

Those who surrounded her nodded in agreement. She was all pride; nothing in her tone or expression gave away her grief. It was the same for all the Aruni. No one would think they felt anything but triumphant on this day. Lysandro wished he could feel the same.

Marek was nowhere to be found. Lysandro moved through the crowd toward the blacksmith, who stood near a larger group of onlookers. He rubbed his jaw.

"It looks just as it was. You've kept your word, and more," Lysandro said, admiring the window.

"That's just it," the blacksmith replied. "I didn't do it."

Lysandro turned to face him. "What?"

"I did what you said, Signor. I called artisans from everywhere there is." He gestured with his hands to the dumbstruck crowd gathered around him. "But none of us could make hide nor hair of it."

Lysandro blinked. "What are you saying?"

"I'm saying, I have no idea how that window got there."

They both turned to contemplate the window. But it was beyond comprehension, and it made Lysandro uneasy.

"I know you said you'd pay for this, but...it doesn't feel right, Signor, not when it's not my doing."

"I'll pay you for your trouble, at least, and that of the artists you've gathered."

The blacksmith bowed. "That's more'n fair."

Lysandro left the man to ponder the sacred image, tearing his own gaze away to head for the playhouse.

There was no doubt, when he arrived, that the raising of the curtain was only a few hours away. Musicians tuned their instruments. Sets glistened, their painted locales still wet. High-backed chairs filled the house, and the middle-aged woman Lysandro remembered from the market was in a corner, surrounded by brightly colored dresses, convincing military attire, and finely woven Maghrevan robes of ivory and gold. It seemed none were finished to her satisfaction. She grumbled a curse, threw a costume in the face of one of her assistants, then went back to grumbling again, seeing to them herself.

Fabien was on stage, whirling the slip of a girl playing his lover in his arms, while the real one sat beside Seraphine in the middle row. She wore a soft, simple dress of pale lavender that looked sweet against her peaches and cream skin.

"Stop, stop, stop!" she cried to the feigning lovers. "The high notes are not right. You must find the balance between otherworldly and...shrill."

"I am not shrill!"

Behind the girl, the doge cleaned out his ear with his pinky finger.

Sera ignored the girl's protests and directed her gaze at Fabien. "*You* have to turn her out, so we can see her face."

Lysandro took the other seat beside Sera and was greeted with a smile from Pirró across the way.

"How am I to fall in love if I can only see her neck?" Fabien shouted back.

"*You* must fall in love, yes. So must the audience. You expect *them* to love her neck?"

The girl, whose name Lysandro didn't know, clamped a pale hand down on her quickly reddening throat. Her eyes went wide as saucers.

"What's wrong with my neck?"

"Oh, for the love of—"

"Nothing dear, your neck is perfect," Pirró cut in. Lower, so only Lysandro and Sera could hear, he added: "It's a hangman's dream."

Laughing was about the last thing Lysandro felt like doing. But he couldn't help it.

The girl was fit to be tied now, and covered her sobs with her hands. Fabien just shifted on his feet and stared at the rafters.

"You're horrible," Sera said to Pirró.

"You started it. And now we'll get nothing done today."

"Good morning, Sera."

She turned such a bright smile to Lysandro that it made his heart race, but it was quickly replaced by the furrowing of her brow. Lysandro squirmed in his skin as she studied his face.

"What's wrong?" she asked.

Her ability to detect the somber shift in his mood was uncanny. Her exquisite features, turned to worry at his expense, made him want to purge the previous night from his mind all the more. He shook his head in response; she was his safe haven, a balm on his soul. It was a burden he would bear alone.

"Do you want to get some fresh air?" she asked.

"Thank you, but I'm fi—"

She was out of her seat before he could refuse. Her hands were warm in his, and soft as silk as she pulled him to his feet and toward the door.

Fabien stepped forward on the stage. "We've only just begun here!"

Sera's sharp retort echoed through the theater. It was in Mirênese, so Lysandro couldn't understand it, but from the shocked look on Fabien's face, and the way even Pirró gaped, it wasn't anything good.

Fabien threw up his hands as Sera led Lysandro out the front doors to sit on the steep outer steps.

She clasped his arm with her hands and folded their fingers together on his lap. A deep sigh escaped him when she laid her head on his shoulder. It was the first time he had sat still in hours. But the world was still spinning, and he was cast adrift in the torrent of recent events. The frenzied beating of his heart slowed, finding a calm in the storm as he laid his cheek upon her rose-scented hair.

Though they were alone, she whispered to him, soft and gentle as a morning breeze.

"What's the matter?"

"Just...stay with me, for a moment?"

She squeezed him tighter, and he felt the weight of his guilt settle on him in the silence. He'd killed two men. And his impulsive anger would only provoke Marek further.

But Seraphine was safe, and by his side. He allowed himself to breathe.

They remained that way for longer than Lysandro dared. Soon he felt compelled to speak.

"I finished the novel you lent me last night."

"That's what you ran off to do?" she asked.

"I couldn't sleep."

She wanted to ask why. He could see the question forming on her mouth as he peered down at her. But she bit her lip instead.

"How did you like it?"

What to say? As the book had drawn to a close, he'd found he'd been walking in the steps of a murderer. And he had stepped into the same shadow that very night.

It had affected him like no other book before. Its dark mood had reflected his own, and he had seen more of himself there than he liked. Perhaps that had been the point, the author's subtle reminder that darkness dwelt where you least expected to find it.

"It was deeply moving," he managed to say. "Truly."

"I'm glad you enjoyed it."

Lysandro wouldn't have put it quite like that.

It was then that he noticed the flower he'd left for her in the night tucked into her hair. It had opened in the sunshine, and brought out the fiery strands in her tresses of spun gold.

"That looks lovely on you."

"Thank you."

"I can't stay. I just wanted to see you."

"You will come tonight, won't you?"

"Of course. I need to see how it all fits together. How it ends. You've been quite secretive about that."

Sera smiled in admission. "There *are* scenes we only do when you're not around…but with good reason. Can't take all the magic out of it."

"Will I see magic on stage?"

"Only time will tell. If Celine can stop shrieking."

"*You'll* be singing. That's magic enough for me."

He relished the rosy blush on her cheeks, then turned to go.

"You're sure you're alright?" she asked.

"I'm better now. Thank you. I'll see you tonight, Sera. Good luck." He pressed a kiss to her hand and departed.

Lysandro wanted her so badly, he couldn't stand it any longer. She was his shining light, his anchor in a world gone mad. He couldn't envision a future where she rejected him—if she were going to, she would have already done so. Still, he had not truly expressed his feelings. He needed to fix that.

This Faelsday was deeply personal. Faelia had blessed Theron with life so he could fight another day. Mere days before, Lysandro had survived the Blood Sword's blow, just as Theron had in ages past. He hoped that, like Theron, the Goddess smiled upon him, and wished him success in ridding Lighura of its great evil.

But the day was also a triumph of love. He would honor Faelia and give thanks by celebrating Her holiday to the fullest.

The shopkeeper rushed to greet Lysandro before his foot even crossed the threshold.

"Welcome, Don de Castel! I feel as if I've waited a lifetime for you to pay me a visit."

The jeweler's smile was framed by a sharp face and a neatly groomed mustache and beard showing the first signs of silver.

"I've had no reason to come before," Lysandro replied mildly.

"Is there something in particular you're looking for?"

"Particular? No," Lysandro answered. "Might I look around first?"

"Of course, Signor, at your leisure."

The little shop was well-stocked with rings, bracelets, brooches, every manner of adornment, all glittering in the sunlight that poured through the open windows. Lysandro passed a thoughtful eye over them all, but nothing sang to him. After some minutes, the shopkeeper inched up behind him, but he was careful not to intrude. He was rather like a fox stalking a rabbit in its den.

"Anything catch your fancy?" he asked, his tone so casual Lysandro could almost believe that his reply didn't matter to him in the slightest, that he'd only asked as a harmless amusement to while away the time.

"Do you have anything—" Lysandro paused, unsure of what he meant. The jewelry was all very fine, but in their cases, they felt as if anyone might claim them. He intended a gift meant for Sera alone, something that reflected the sense of wonder and enchantment she sparked in him.

"Do you have anything special?" Lysandro asked. "Something unique, or..."

"I believe I know exactly what you mean, Signor. Allow me." The man disappeared into the back and returned in a moment with three boxes covered in soft black fabric. He laid each one on the counter facing Lysandro.

"I don't display these because no one in Lighura can afford them. Well, almost no one," he added with a wink.

Lysandro raised an eyebrow in challenge. "But are they worth the excess cost?"

The man bowed his head in an attempt to appear humble.

"That will be for you to decide, Don de Castel. You will take this one, I think," he said, tapping the box in the middle, "but the choice is yours." Again he shrugged, but he could not hide his ravenous grin.

Naturally, Lysandro opened the boxes at the ends first. One held an elaborate choker studded with a cascade of emeralds—stunning, but not for Sera. Another housed several strands of pearls in pristine ivories and grays. This was at least an option. But the third...

The third box revealed a teardrop pendant with a luminous pink gemstone the size of an egg, hung from a shimmering golden chain. Almost immediately Lysandro thought of their night at the theater, and how Sera had stolen his breath away in a glistening gown the color of a gilded rose.

"It's a sapphire," the owner supplied when Lysandro didn't speak. "From the Selonia region. The color is exceptional. In quality, it's one of a kind."

Just like her.

Lysandro conceded to the man's prognostication.

The jeweler smiled. "As I said, Signor, I've been waiting a long time for you to grace my doorstep. I'm glad this piece will finally receive the attention it deserves."

Lysandro parted with a not insignificant portion of his fortune and made his way home, where another surprise awaited him. His father's coach stood paused at the entryway. Sitting on his front steps was the man himself.

"You're back earlier than I expected," Lysandro said.

"The chief magistrate didn't wish to waste any time."

Lysandro's head shot up as if a great weight were suddenly lifted from his shoulders. "You brought him then?"

Elias nodded. "As good as."

"Excellent. Things have gotten quite a bit worse since you left."

"I don't want to even imagine."

"Come inside," Lysandro said as he held open the door and bade Marta bring them lunch. He didn't rest as easy in the knowledge of the chief magistrate's impending arrival as he thought he would. The more he thought about it, the more it worried him. What could the chief magistrate do that the high priestess couldn't? He was not the superior warrior by any measure.

By that logic, were there any who could challenge Marek now, and succeed?

He felt a tugging in his chest, an urgent nagging that made uncomfortable suggestions. There was too much to risk now, confronting Marek alone. It had already proved fatal once, if not for the Goddess's intercession.

But Lysandro had escalated things with Marek to such a reckless degree. Locking him away would not stop the spread of his wickedness through Lighura like a cancer, and Marek would not be long for his cage. If anything, Lysandro feared that the worst was still ahead of him. He couldn't shake the sense that, for Marek to be truly stripped of his power (and his life), Lysandro would have to be the one to do it.

His father concluded his tale and partook of the cold side of lamb and hard, pungent cheese laid out.

"The only foreseeable problem will be finding Marek's replacement," he said. "It will be a tall order to restore confidence in his office, and I suspect the corruption goes all the way down."

A bit of meat got stuck in Lysandro's throat, and he had to force it down. The tang of blood on his tongue turned rancid.

"The sacred window has been restored," he said.

"Yes, I saw. Marvelous work that."

Marvelous indeed.

Elias cleared his throat. "I couldn't help but notice you've been to the jeweler's."

Lysandro felt the corners of his mouth quirk upward. "I have."

"I'd ask to see it, but bad luck and all that. I take it then, that things are progressing well?"

Lysandro could hear the restraint in his father's voice. He wanted to ask a lot more than that. He was worse than a schoolboy with that eager look on his face, ready to wade knee-deep into his son's romantic affairs.

Somehow, Lysandro no longer minded.

"They're progressing wonderfully," he answered.

His parent's smile widened as he wolfed down his meal. "Happy to hear it."

"Do you have plans tonight?" Lysandro asked.

"No. Should I?"

"There's a play to mark the end of the festival. Sera is singing in it. She has the voice of an angel."

"Does she? Who is she to play?"

Lysandro grinned. "An army captain."

Elias stopped chewing. "A what?"

"It's a new play, by the doge of Mirêne. Join me later?"

Elias swallowed. "Well. It certainly sounds interesting."

"It will be that, at least."

22

LOTHAN SLEPT POORLY ON THE SPARSE PALLET OF HAY JENNER KEPT HIDDEN in a sub-level of his house. The damp coming off the walls aggravated his shoulder. It was on the mend, finally, but only on account of the two men the Shadow had cut down. They'd been the best brawn Lothan had after losing Jair. Now he was left with a bunch of wiry nitwits.

The thing that really set his blood boiling was the silence his enemies kept. Their high priestess was dead, bled out in glorious fashion over the sacred altar. He had expected mourning bells and weeping and people throwing their arms up fruitlessly to the sky for succor. Any one of those would have made the destruction to his office and his body worth it.

But there had been nothing. The day had dawned just as it did on any other, the mass of them ignorant of his triumph.

He didn't know what those witches were playing at.

The minute he realized the temple was concealing their loss, he'd sent Jenner to sniff around. That was more than two hours ago. He'd already decided he would snap Jenner's neck and give his shoulder the extra push to knit itself together when the deputy stumbled through the door. His face was so pale and his eyes so wild, he looked like he'd seen a ghost.

"Well?"

"Umm...ummm..."

"For fuck's sake what is it?!"

"The w-window, Lord Lothan. It's…back."

Impossible.

Lothan bolted through the door and set off on the main road, not bothering about the clods scrambling after him.

"You better let me out here."

Aleksander pulled back the curtain of Elias's carriage and peered at the tavern about half a mile down the road.

"We're half a day yet from Lighura," Elias said.

"I'll hire a horse. I can at least try to maintain the appearance that I've come of my own accord."

Elias leaned back in his seat. "Of course."

The chief magistrate turned back to him as he descended the steps of the carriage. "I won't run, if that's what you're thinking."

"It was the furthest thing from my mind."

"Sure it was."

"My home and my table are open to you, as always," Elias said. He closed the door and ordered the coachman to drive on.

The tavern was crowded at midday, but with a little effort, Aleksander found a seat and dug in to a portion of boiled chicken and carrots served alongside a robust wine.

He attracted some attention; more precisely, the gold pin on his vest that marked him as Chief Magistrate did. A group of toughs in the back corner eyed him, though they pretended not to, checking on him every so often as they consumed their meal. They were big and nasty-looking, and just what he needed at the moment.

He left his seat and made his way over, keeping the accusatory glare he'd honed over the years trained on the one who had been spying on him from over his shoulder.

"Something bothering you?" Aleksander asked.

In tell-tale fashion, the man's gaze, marred by a jagged scar stretching down from his left temple, dropped to the pin for a flicker of an instant before rising again to meet his stare.

"Not a thing."

"No, Honor," the one tucked into the very corner of the room answered. "Just playing a friendly game of cards, we are."

Aleksander doubted that, but he didn't care. "I've got a job for you. If you're any good at it, it might even be long-term." He tossed money on the table—twice as much as was in the pot.

The men seated round stared at the coins hungrily. It was the one closest to the magistrate who asked: "What we gotta do?"

"Not much more than you're doing now. Follow me to Lighura. When we get there, stand behind me and look mean."

The man's face turned into a snarl.

Aleksander nodded. "Like that."

They deliberated in silent glances. It was only a moment before the five of them quit their seats, taking the money on the table with them.

Aleksander passed through the gates of Lighura with his makeshift army behind him, ducking his head to avoid the bright decorations strung across the entry to the village.

Underneath the banners and paper lanterns, he saw a notice from Marek's office, offering a reward for information about someone impersonating Theron. All the things Elias had accused Marek of were listed on the notice. A measure of relief crossed his mind at the possibility that someone other than his appointee was responsible for Lighura's troubles. Deep in his gut though, he knew better.

As these thoughts swirled the lunch in his stomach, he spied Lothan ahead on his left, surrounded by a half dozen of his deputies. A chill wind raced across his skin at the sight of him. He shook it off, convinced himself that it was all in his head, that time had magnified his last encounter with Marek in his mind. Aleks was not the man he used to be. The weight of its authority felt right on his shoulders.

Marek had his back to him. Aleksander called out with a voice full of gravel.

"Lothan Marek—"

He turned at the sound of his name, and found the chief magistrate glaring at him. So. The old de Castel had been able to pressure him into coming after all. Lothan smoothed away the scowl on his face before it had time to fully form.

"Yes?" he answered in a calm, unaffected tone.

"You've been accused of a series of high crimes, and you must answer."

"Of course. Shall we go to my office?"

Onlookers gasped and murmured as Lothan led him down the road to the wreckage he had yet to clear.

"What in six hells…"

"After you, Chief Magistrate," Lothan said, gesturing grandly toward the blistered wood that used to be the door.

Aleksander shivered with rage. "You'll give me a straight answer, Marek. What in Arun's name happened here?"

Lothan maintained his eerie calm, which incensed the chief magistrate all the more.

"Surely you don't think I destroyed my own office," Lothan said.

"Don't tell me what to think. If things have gotten to this point, you're still to blame. You're the keeper of the peace, are you not?"

Lothan had no ready response for that.

The chief magistrate's cheeks turned a mottled purple. "The courthouse, then. Move it!"

His deputies made to follow them, but the chief magistrate shot them a hard stare. "Back off."

The men Aleksander had brought with him took that as their cue, and stood closer to him. They had the desired effect, rooting Lothan's deputies in place.

Lothan turned his head in the direction of his men. He barely registered that they were there. Confusion swept over them, but they kept their distance as Lothan walked ahead of the chief magistrate toward the courthouse.

Lothan didn't mind the stares. He relished them, the fear imprinted on their faces long past due. But one face in particular caught his eye.

Across the way, still as stone, stood Lysandro de Castel. His hard glare was more than Lothan thought possible for him to muster. But the young don's eyes kept level with him as he and his captor crossed the square. He was rooted to the ground, and it put Lothan's hackles up. If he didn't know any better, he would have said that Lysandro was poised to strike. There was something in his expression that seemed familiar, but he couldn't place it. There was an iron will to the grim set of his mouth he had not seen before. It rattled him, and he turned away from it.

They passed beneath the restored window. Nausea overwhelmed him. Its very existence made a mockery of him. He thought he saw a grin in the hero's countenance. The pain in his side flared.

What right did de Castel have to be so smug? It took no strength or cunning to call upon his aging father to drag the chief magistrate down here against his will.

It *was* against his will. Lothan felt the man's reluctance reverberating off his skin. He could use that.

As for Lysandro: he'd get his. Imagining how sweet it was going to be put a wicked smile on Lothan's face. He aimed it at his rival and bared his teeth.

THE SUN DIPPED BENEATH THE HORIZON AS THE CHIEF MAGISTRATE PUT Marek in a courthouse cell reserved for those standing trial. He didn't make a fuss. Aleksander was grateful for that.

He stepped outside to face an even larger crowd than the one that had followed him through the square. They stopped chattering amongst themselves and looked up when they saw him.

"Starting tomorrow, anyone who wishes to speak against Lothan Marek is asked to come forward. All will be heard."

He closed the front door again and barred it. At his elbow was Gareth, the largest of the men he'd picked up from the tavern, the one whose nervous behavior had first caught his attention.

"Anything else you need?" he asked.

"Why, you want to stay on?"

The hulking man shrugged. "It's as good a way as any to make a living."

The respect from standing with the magistrate isn't too bad, either, Aleksander mused.

"I need two teams of two watching him throughout the night."

Gareth raised an eyebrow. "He the magistrate here?"

"He was."

"And he needs eyes all night?"

"In pairs," Aleksander repeated. "Don't underestimate him. I'll pay you at a junior deputy's salary."

"Mmm. His job, though…"

"Will go to the right man."

Gareth thought it over. "We'll figure out the shifts."

"Good. No one comes in or out except me."

The man grunted his assent.

Being a magistrate only required someone willing to follow the law and ensure others did the same. He'd learned a long time ago: no one knows the law better than a criminal. And no one is better at catching criminals than one who knows their trade.

Who knows, he thought, *I might have found the right man already.*

With nothing to do until morning, Aleksander found himself wanting a drink. He remembered Elias's offer; he always kept an excellent bottle of port handy. But Aleks couldn't ignore the optics. He'd have to rent a room at the inn. But for tonight, at least, the chair in the back office would do.

23

THE MOMENT HE CROSSED THE THRESHOLD OF THE PLAYHOUSE, LYSANDRO was transported. The lights were down low; they gave off just enough illumination for the patrons to find their seats. The orchestra was already playing a soft melody. It was probing and mysterious, as if they were discovering the music, rather than creating it.

"Don de Castel. What a surprise to see you here."

Lysandro and his father turned to find Sera's parents entering the row behind them.

"Good evening." Elias answered for them both when it became clear that Lysandro had no interest in conversing with Don Carlo.

"You must be so proud of your daughter's theatrical accomplishments," Elias said.

"Oh yes," Doña Alvaró replied. "We had no idea that such esteemed connections were to be a part of her education. Imagine—a doge!"

Elias and Lysandro exchanged an awkward look. Just as the woman seemed to realize her misstep, Elias said, "Enjoy the show, Signora. Signor," and turned back around to take his seat. Lysandro couldn't suppress a wry smile.

Elias absorbed his surroundings. "I must say, the show hasn't begun yet, but already the tone is quite different from what I'm used to."

"That's the point. It's striving for unprecedented realism."

"I've heard of it, but not experienced it."

"It's become quite popular in Mirêne."

"Under the doge's direction."

"Mmhmm."

"This doge—is he going to cause a problem for you?"

"Not at all."

Lysandro glanced down at his program. It described the play as performed in three acts: The Seduction, the War, and the Reception. It did little to spur the imagination for such an obviously lavish production. Perhaps that was part of its mystique. Lysandro didn't pretend to understand Fabien's reasons for the things he did. But he was a kind and generous soul, and saw only possibility when he looked upon the world. Lysandro couldn't help but like him.

Elias leaned back in his seat, mollified by Lysandro's quick answer. "It's good, to be doing this. Arun knows the village needs to forget its worries for the night. Marek was taken into custody, did you hear?"

"I saw."

"It will be interesting to hear what he has to say for himself. Do you think Theron's Shadow might be convinced to testify?"

Before Lysandro could absorb his father's question, the theater went dark, and he heard the reedy noise of the pipes popular in the markets of Maghreve thread its way into the melody. Its twang became overwhelming until it was the only instrument playing. Its master, kneeling on the floor, appeared at the left edge of the stage as the curtain rose. A soft golden glow lit the stage, thickly laid with rich carpets and an abundance of silver trays and goblets. From Fabien's personal treasure horde, Lysandro imagined. A pale luminous fabric graced the edges of the scene, inviting the audience into the desert caravan at the close of a meal.

"Thank you again, Prince Ishar." A robust man dressed in the garb of an Andran don spoke to Fabien over a platter of fruits and candies. "It has not always been easy between us, but granting us safe passage through your lands and showing us such hospitality earns you much esteem in my eyes."

"The honor is mine, Signor," Fabien replied. He was wrapped in dark robes trimmed with golden brocade. Lysandro had no doubt that it was genuine Maghrevan silk. His head was covered, and his eyes were outlined with kohl in the desert style. As he spoke to his guest, Fabien kept his eyes on Celine, seated at the don's side.

Ishar's interest in her was apparent as the company of gentlemen from both sides resumed their easy conversation. He kept his eyes on her no matter whom he spoke to, and did not answer questions put to him immediately, though of course none of the other players paid his distraction any mind. Celine, for her part, returned his stolen glances. She pretended to hide her mutual curiosity by ducking her head or turning to her father whenever Fabien's eyes met hers. Ishar served the girl himself, crossing the stage and pouring a glass of dark wine from his own jug when she neared the end of her cup.

"Thank you," she said in a soft voice, looking up at him and daring to hold his gaze.

"You are most welcome, Signorina." His smile was wide and sincere. After a beat, he said: "I cannot allow you to leave."

The girl's father looked up at that, but the prince caught himself, and restrained the passion in his voice. His smile stayed in place when he added, "not without first having experienced our night sky."

Celine bowed her head again in her coy way, casting her eyes to the floor then back at Fabien. Years spent in the Mirênese court, Lysandro observed, made her the perfect coquette, all innocence.

"I admit, in all the time we've been here, I've been—"

She stopped, then looked to her father, who gave a warning glance. "I have not ventured out of the tents you have so generously provided after dark."

"There are more stars than you can even imagine."

"So I have often heard."

"I would be honored beyond words to be your guide this night. That is, if your father will permit it." Ishar looked to the man who drank his wine and ate his food, and smiled. To refuse such a small request would be unseemly under the circumstances. Yet the don looked uneasy, casting about for a glimpse of his men. They were all deep in their cups, and not at all ready to safeguard his daughter's virtue.

"Please, Father," she interceded, tugging on his arm in the way a child might when begging for a new plaything. "If I do not go now, I fear I will regret it for the rest of my life."

Her father caved, as fathers do when put upon by their beloved children, and the prince took her by the hands and helped her to her feet.

"I would lay down my life before I let harm come to her," he said to her father. "Of that you have my solemn pledge." As he led her out of the tent to the right, it receded offstage, giving the appearance that the pair were walking beyond the confines of the encampment and onto the open desert. Their footsteps kicked up the sand piled up on the floorboards and bathed the air in a hazy pink starlight.

A play put together as swiftly as this one ran the very serious risk of appearing slapdash. But it was sumptuous and deliberate, and likely everything Fabien had envisioned. Lysandro found himself entranced.

Celine stared out with wonder at the air above the audience's heads. Glass chandeliers glittered above the audience, giving them a glimpse of the same night sky the desert prince showed to the object of his love. While Ishar was seducing the girl, the doge was seducing Lighura. It was working.

Fabien stood behind Celine, his gaze fixed on her. The music shifted, and became quieter, more furtive, more delicate.

Taking a deep, awed breath, the girl said, "it's the most beautiful thing I've even seen."

Ishar approached her at a steady pace. "I can no longer say the same."

Before she could turn her head, Fabien spun her around and kissed her. Even when Celine pulled away, she did not leave his embrace. Ishar brought his hand up to caress her face.

Lysandro was convinced, as were the females in attendance at tonight's performance, if their sighs were any indication. Fabien exuded charm, and at that moment Lysandro was grateful that his attentions were directed toward members of his own sex.

The girl protested that a romance between her and Ishar was impossible, that their families would never allow it, that these feelings would fade once she and her retinue were gone from the desert and its mind-bending heat. But nights in the desert could be bitterly cold, and she wrapped her arms around herself as she turned away from the forlorn prince. He draped his outer robe around her shoulders. Her fingers explored the luxurious fabric, and Ishar resumed his entreaties.

"I can shower you with jewels. I will make you a queen, set so far above all others that no one would dare touch us."

She tried to pull away but Ishar caught her wrist and drew her near again. "I am prince of my people. Yet I am nothing if you leave."

He sang, low in her ear at first, then with enough strength to reverberate off the theater walls. His voice was clear and powerful, the like of which Lysandro was hard-pressed to call to mind. Lysandro heard Fabien's soul carried on the music. Celine joined in his sweet serenade, an old Andran love song, and Fabien pulled her into a dance as they sang. The effect of their circles across the stage were enchanting. Fabien *did* turn her out, and she looked (and sounded) lovely, earning a robust round of applause. Fabien kissed her again as the music took a dramatic turn. The crowd gasped, and there were even some screams, as the prince whistled and an obsidian stallion, much like Lysandro's own Hurricane, trotted onto the stage from the right. The orchestral strings sounded a note of warning as Ishar lifted the girl onto the beast, still wearing his outer robe, and bade her hide herself from view. She did so willingly as he mounted the stallion behind her.

Shouts from the don's men echoed on the left. The stallion shifted his legs at the sound, adding to the audience's suspense—the string was pulled taut.

"I won't let them take you from me," he vowed. The stallion bolted back into the wings as the don and his men charged in pursuit.

"Good Gods!" Elias whispered in Lysandro's ear. "There's a horse in this play! If this is the new style, it's rather exciting!"

Wait, Lysandro thought. *It's only just begun.*

The desert was gone when the curtain rose on the second act. Out strode Pirró, taking in the painted backdrop of an army encampment with wonder. Lysandro didn't think Pirró could ever look so innocent, but he managed it beautifully. All signs of mischief were gone from his grin. The change made Lysandro all the more eager to see how Sera would assume the role of the captain.

Pirró came upon a group of uniformed soldiers at the far left of the stage and greeted them cheerily.

"Good morning, Signores, and brothers at arms! Might you tell me where the new recruits are to report?"

No one answered him immediately, but the man standing closest snatched the paper from his hands, read it once over, then groaned in commiseration.

"Ah, unlucky you!"

Pirró's grin widened. "Actually, I volunteered."

That earned him a round of laughter. "Men have been dying by the thousands for nigh on ten years, and you *volunteered?*"

Pirró faltered. "I wanted to see more of the world."

"Maybe you think you can do better, huh?"

"Now you're here, and we can *all* go home!"

The men laughed again. Pirró's smile weakened, but he played along with his erstwhile comrades.

"What's your name, farm boy?"

"Gascon."

"Let me give you your first lesson, Gascon. You won't survive Duhamel."

Gascon turned his head to each man in turn. "Is he our nearest adversary?"

"More or less. He's our captain."

Lysandro's ears pricked up.

Gascon chuckled. "Surely you jest." His voice was high-pitched and saccharine, as if he truly believed those boyish tales of battle and glory.

"The man is mad! He'll just as soon shoot us as look at us!"

"Every day he's plotting ways to kill us."

"I don't doubt it," another man concurred. "He's a rabid dog off his leash."

"He's been here from the start. At Verdennes, he slaughtered a hundred men single-handedly!"

"He's meaner'n a raging bull, but conniving as a fox."

"Nay, not a fox. He's more like a phantasm. He can sneak up on you without making the slightest sound…"

As they traded tall tales, the man (woman, really) in question approached from the right without notice. Lysandro drank in the sight of her. He'd expected her to be dressed in a captain's uniform, of course, but the concept had never truly taken shape in his mind. Her shape now filled his vision. The pants were tailored close. He could trace the curve of her thighs, her hips and backside in perfect profile in the prim white pants. Her blue coat was lined with red trim and shiny brass buttons. Black leather boots hugged her legs up to her knees, and across her chest lay a collection of a half dozen throwing knives that looked every bit a real menace. That's when he noticed something was missing. *Two* somethings. Lysandro made a silent vow that, when he discovered who had bound Sera's sweet, heavenly breasts, he would run them through. But not before gouging out their eyes.

Sera's footsteps across the floorboards were silent as she crossed the stage where the specter of her character took on more and more the shade of a demon in her men's eyes. She came to stand directly in Pirró's shadow, listening as her men spun enough yarns to turn her new man's cheeks pale.

"I heard he was in a madhouse before the war. Killed his maid because she overcooked his eggs!"

Gascon's eyes went wide.

"They weren't overcooked," Sera said with an eerie calm. "They were over-salted."

At the sound of her voice, a full octave lower than normal, the men jumped to attention. Pirró spun round.

"Who are you?" she growled.

"Gascon." He handed his captain his enlistment paper. Duhamel took it, and then Gascon stretched out his hand in greeting. Sera ignored it, earning a few chuckles from the audience. She sighed.

"Another bumpkin. Well, the canons are hungry beasts."

The farm boy started. "Surely you—"

As he spoke, a pair of soldiers were gabbing off in the corner. It had been going on all the while, but now their voices grew in volume. Without a glance at the farm boy, Sera reached for one of the blades at her chest and launched it at them, pinning one of the men's hats to the wooden frame of the stage behind him. A handful of the audience members cried out in alarm. Some of them ducked. Sera's daggers had teeth. It was an impressive stunt, and Lysandro found himself smiling. He didn't know what it was, but something about the way that woman threw knives ruffled his feathers.

"Fall in!" Duhamel shouted, and Gascon scurried to the end of the line.

The lights pulsed on and off to mark the passage of days. Each time the day dawned, Lysandro's eyes instinctively searched for her as she beat her soldiers into shape.

It wasn't just Lysandro. The way she spoke and how she moved demanded attention. She soaked up all the light on stage, and was mesmerizing to watch. Lighurans, worshippers of the warrior Goddess, gravitated to her character naturally. They found Duhamel's brash temper endearing, and his insults and curses gained their trust and deep-seated allegiance.

She barked insults as often as she did orders. At one point, she stood in the corner, shaking her head in disappointment.

"Faster," she warned the men as she loaded a pistol. She ripped the paper cartridge open with her teeth, poured the powder, and spat the remnants out over the edge of the stage before taking aim center stage and firing at her own soldier's heels. They jumped as sparks and smoke flew. So did the audience; they had been watching her actions in suspense, and some shrieked at the echoing report of the empty firearm.

When the final day of training dawned, the captain's soldiers stood in a proud line, ready for inspection. Duhamel passed by them all with his hands behind his back. He looked Gascon up and down at the end of the line. Gascon stood tall and proud, in the regimental colors at last. He turned to face his captain with a bright smile.

In response, he said, "When you die—"

"Don't you mean 'if,' Captain?"

"Try not to get blood on the coat."

Again, the crowd responded with mirth.

"Don't worry about the captain," the man standing next to Gascon whispered in his ear. "You're coming with us tonight."

Gascon considered. "Duhamel will kill us."

"He's going to do *that* anyway," the soldier jibed. "At least we'll have a little fun before he does it."

Darkness fell on the stage, punctuated by a dramatic shift in the music. Drums ushered in a bawdy, playful tune.

"Oh!"

Beside him, Lysandro's father erupted in nervous laughter as the stage was bathed in red light, showing the lavish furnishings and scandalously clad women of a bordello.

"I haven't heard this song in years."

"Father!"

"Lysandro." Elias gave him a sideways smile. "I was never unfaithful to your mother. But I did not go to my bridal bed a virgin."

The explanation mollified Lysandro little. Upon inspection, a large majority of the males in attendance were shifting in their seats and airing out their collars, to the chagrin of their wives and mothers. Lysandro was glad to be excluded from such a club, and tried to ignore his father's fingers, tapping out the tune on his leg as the soldiers on stage paired with the women. They disappeared giggling behind the voluminous curtains, whose fluid, undulating shapes suggested bodies mingling.

When the drinking and carousing was in full swing, Duhamel stormed onto the set, swinging wide the door on its hinges and knocking it into the wooden frame of the stage.

"What manner of devilry is this?!"

But the soldiers were already too soaked to care. They needled him.

"Come on, Captain! We go to war in the morning!"

"You won't make it to the morning." Duhamel stepped forward with murder in his eyes, startling his subordinate and causing him to cower behind the woman who'd been showering him with attention. But the captain was caught at the wrists by the house's madam.

"Come now, my dear Captain. Won't you sit down and have a drink with us?"

Two more girls were upon him in an instant, pawing at the officer's uniform like a rare prize.

"Unhand me!" he cried. Sera's limbs flailed, but the girls only tittered and laughed, and succeeded in slipping her coat halfway off her arms and relieving her of her hat. Golden red tresses came tumbling down to her shoulders. The unbuttoned coat revealed a plain white shirt and coarse linen bindings across her breasts. The girls clawing at the captain stepped back in shock, in tandem with gasps from the audience. Just as quickly as those flashes of femininity had come, they were gone again. The women of the bordello instinctively surrounded her to shield her, her instant confederates. A skinny girl with light brown hair on Sera's left reached out a tentative hand to assist her.

"Don't touch me."

Sera tucked her hair back into her hat and rebuttoned the coat, smoothing any wrinkles before the men could see.

Lysandro cocked his head. He'd supposed Sera was simply playing the part of a man. Or a woman captain—which he supposed she was, just not in the way he expected. The turn was one of great intrigue, marked by the unsuppressed reaction of the audience, made party to the captain's secret.

"Won't you have a drink, at least?" the madam insisted. "On the house."

Sera begrudgingly took the bottle offered her and sat at the edge of the scene, dangling her legs over the side of the stage. The brunette sat beside her.

As the sounds of the bordello echoed across the stage, the brunette brushed her hand against Sera's cheek. Sera caught her by the wrist and squeezed hard, making the girl flinch.

"Oh, my dear," the brunette said sadly. "Sooner or later, love comes for us all."

At that moment, the captain turned her head pointedly across the stage, to where Gascon had finally chosen a partner from a ring of eager candidates. Duhamel's eyes fell again to the drink in her lap. She took a long swallow. The music played at an ever-increasing pace, ascending new heights of debauchery as ensnared couples lent their voices to the song. The soldiers carried on, and Duhamel's companion proceeded to roll a cigarette and take long, lazy drags. When Pirró's voice was added to the lovers' mix, Sera inclined her head toward the brunette and stole a drag from the cigarette, licking her lips as she released a plume of white smoke. She took the cigarette in her own hands and pulled again. When Pirró's voice bellowed above the rest in triumphant release, she flicked away the errant ash with the tip of her thumb. Untold fathoms of emotion and intention were concentrated into that single square inch of flesh. The subtlety of Sera's performance rocked him to his core.

She held the cigarette out for the brunette, who laid her head casually on Sera's shoulder and pulled more smoke into her lungs.

When the curtain rose again, they were back in the desert, with

Duhamel and his men crouched in the dunes before a tent guarded by two spear-wielding warriors. Inside the tent was Celine, pacing nervously.

Huddled in the sand on the leftmost edge of the stage, one of Duhamel's soldier's cried out at an entirely inappropriate volume: "Do you think we should sneak up on them?"

The audience laughed, but Duhamel was having none of it. She bashed the man on the head and sent him sprawling to the ground.

"I would rather take a herd of bloody elephants!" she hissed.

"It's only two, Captain," Gascon said. "We are six."

"You only *see* two, farm boy," Duhamel replied. Then after a moment, she asked: "Did you ever catch any rabbits on that farm?"

"Plenty."

Duhamel nodded. "With me."

They wriggled on their bellies and overtook the guards before they could raise the alarm. Gascon placed a helmet on his head and took up the watch at the front of the tent while Duhamel crept inside.

"No! No!" Celine cried as she became aware of the intrusion. "You can't take me from him! I'll die before I go back!"

Sera slapped her hard across the face, making the audience flinch. When Celine stood upright again, her cheek flashed a bright red.

"Do you know how many good men have died so that you could satisfy your...*curiosity?*"

"Did any of those soldiers *ask* me if I wanted their shields? Their lives?"

"That choice was not yours."

"I will not go back." The girl grabbed a cheese knife from a nearby pedestal and pointed it clumsily in the captain's direction.

Duhamel closed the gap between them in an instant. She snatched the diminutive blade from the girl's hand and sent it skittering across the stage. Celine crumpled at Sera's feet and covered her face as anguish flooded her voice.

"I cannot live without him." She began to sing in a high, plaintive voice, of how all the hopes and dreams of her life rose and fell upon her lover's smile, and all the ways in which she would die if she was forcibly separated from him. It was a song Lysandro knew well, from *Elard and Galaine,* in the scene where she is told he is dead, though it is a lie.

Celine's voice was beautiful; it was perhaps the best rendition of the song he'd ever heard. Duhamel's expression softened, and she seemed to listen to the girl's pleas not to separate her from her prince. But the final note and the audience's rousing applause were both cut short when Duhamel threw a large sack from a nearby pile of silks over the girl's head, slung the princess over her shoulder, and dashed off the stage.

In the following scene, the tent was gone but the desert remained. Duhamel entered again from the left, with the sack containing the girl wriggling over her shoulder. The hooves of a horse sounded, and Ishar appeared astride his stallion. A wave of relief, followed quickly by confusion and shock, rippled through the crowd. Duhamel released her captive.

"Ishar!" the girl cried. He pulled her up onto the beast and embraced her with great passion. Then he turned his attention to Duhamel.

"You have returned my wife to me at great risk to yourself. From the bottom of my heart I thank you."

The captain nodded and stepped back as Fabien wheeled the stallion around.

"Will you go home?" Ishar asked.

"I go to the battle," Duhamel said, as if it were obvious.

"But—why restore her to me then?"

"Men make war for their own sake, not yours."

"Why do you?"

"Because my soul is contrary to my nature. Go. Ride far and fast. We will be upon you come the dawn."

Fabien spurred the horse and they disappeared offstage. Sera retreated the way she had come, toward the sounds of war.

At the first report of the canon, the men and women in the audience screamed. Lysandro felt his father jerk upright in his chair. Swords clashed offstage, with the sound of men in roaring combat occasionally drowned out by the canon.

When the stage was lit again, it was drenched in blood. There was a ruckus on the other side of the theater. A woman had fainted at the sight of the glistening gore and had to be carried out. At the center of a mass of fallen bodies and drifting sands painted red sat Duhamel. In her lap, she cradled Gascon's head.

Sera had not been spared the blood. A large swipe of it marred her left cheek. She ran her fingers coaxingly through Pirró's hair as the battle continued to rage in their ears, but still he did not wake. The canon was softer now, further away. Seraphine's voice rang out over it.

"We're going to lose the light soon. Any chance of you getting up?"

Alone, Sera took off her hat, setting it to the side and letting her hair fall down to her waist. She set her gaze on the fallen soldier and started singing.

It was an old song, one sung by soldiers in the throes of drunkenness. The words belonged to those who had died in battle, forgotten by their comrades. It reminded the survivors that those who had perished were waiting for them as they grew old, that they would be there to meet them and be their guides across the river into the next world, where they would be brothers again. The pain and loss of the lyrics were normally smoothed over by the boisterous, full-throated camaraderie of brothers at arms. But Sera sang with such sincerity that its impending promise became unbearable. Lysandro was transfixed; only when her song came to a baleful close did he spy his father clenching and unclenching his jaw out of the corner of his eye, fighting back the water pooling in his eyes.

Sera waited for the applause to quieten before replacing her hat atop her head and tucking her hair back into it with determination. Then she did something that made the air in the playhouse go still. She reached for the pistol in her coat and cocked the weapon.

It wasn't part of the script—was it? Lysandro fended off a chill.

She considered only for a moment.

"Ah, the hell with it." Sera craned her neck and put the barrel of the gun under her chin. The audience reacted, crying out in protest. But in that same moment, the sound of horses drew their attention. Sera's head snapped to her right. She tucked the gun back into her boot as her countrymen approached. It was a silent, subtle gesture. But everyone in the audience saw it.

A soldier leapt down from the horse pulled to a stop at her side and examined Gascon.

"He's breathing! Stubborn bastard."

Duhamel nodded. "Always has been."

They lifted Gascon off of her and laid him on a litter, to be carried into the wings. Duhamel got to her feet.

"We've got the desert swarm cornered by a ridge two miles from here. General Black is mustering for a final push. It'll all be over come morning, and he needs every man."

"He'll have to settle for me."

The scene that followed couldn't have been any more real. Bodies crashed into each other on the stage, spraying new bouts of blood across the sand and bringing the audience to the brink of rioting. But they were riveted. Sera's costume was the only thing that distinguished her from the masses of combatants. Lysandro counted nearly two dozen soldiers downed by her hand as the orchestra reached a frenzied pitch and the canon's bellows increased again in intensity. Horns and drums sounded a funeral march. Someone sliced Duhamel's leg open, and she hit the ground. The crowd gasped. Such a wound was death. But the captain kept up the fight, pressing her back to a dune and fending off her attackers like an enraged tiger. The sounds of chaos mounted ever higher as sunlight fled the battlefield. The war raged unseen, louder and faster without end until suddenly, all was quiet. Elias gripped the arms of his seat hard.

Then, a piano was heard playing. Its saccharine melody seemed to come up from the darkened edge of the stage unbidden. It grated. The moon rose over the stage, its weak blue glow showing the havoc wrought. From either side, men in plain black garb swept away the blood and sand. The bodies of the fallen disappeared into stage pits, shoved and tumbled over each other into oblivion.

Lysandro had seen many plays depicting war and love, but they had always been kept at arm's length. This was not that. The scales of reality had shifted, and the audience had become bound up in it, somehow.

As he watched another dead soldier turned over to meet his grave, he saw the faces of one of the men dead at his own hands. For one dizzying, terrifying moment, Lysandro thought he was going to be sick. The sensation slid away from him as quickly as it had come as a new day dawned on the stage, illuminating a well-appointed parlor.

"Welcome, welcome everyone. Thank you for coming to honor these brave warriors and their fallen brethren."

A large man bearing the insignia of a general was speaking to a polite audience. They raised their glasses to him and the handful of guests dressed in uniform.

They looked like broken men. One kept his arm in a sling, another had a bandage over his left eye. None of them stood upright. Not even Gascon, who lurked in a corner, his chest bandaged up to his neck underneath his newly washed coat.

"We are grateful to you, General Black," one of the guests declared to their host. "If not for your strategy and cunning, this war would be going on still, and these brave men would have faced yet another harsh winter. Now, they can rejoice in their victory in the bosom of their families."

Another round of drinking followed the toast.

"Speaking of family," the general answered, setting down his glass, "may I introduce my daughter, Signorina Ilona Black."

Sera never ceased to shock the onlookers when she took the stage. She was bound by an enormous, elaborate dress of dusky pink satin. The dress wore her; it was visibly restrictive, and her movements were stiff as she made her way to her pretend father's side. She walked with a limp, obscured by the handmaiden who clutched at her arm and steadied her steps.

Naturally, she drew the attention of the young soldiers on stage. Any one of them could have been under the captain's command; now, any one of them might be given the general's blessing to take the captain to wife and force her to submit.

When one such suitor bowed and kissed her hand, making a great production of the gesture, she narrowed her eyes, and audibly crushed his fingers in hers. He withdrew hastily and said nothing more.

One of the maids serving the guests turned to close the shutters. It caused a loud clamor at the back of the set. The soldiers on stage flinched. So did Elias.

Behind Sera, two men exchanged greetings as she moved to a table set in the foreground and fixed herself a drink.

"Did you hear? General Black caught up with the desert rat and his stolen bride at Galatz. Their heads are on display there now."

Duhamel fell forward. She braced herself on the table, but not before knocking her glass off the table. It tumbled off the stage and shattered.

"All that, and they didn't even bring her back alive," the second man said.

"Well she went mad, as I heard it. They snuck up on them, killed him first. She turned on them, and killed one before she killed herself."

Duhamel's maid tried to steady her, but she pushed the girl away. Her hands were trembling.

"Oh," one of the men said, finally noticing her. "My apologies, Signorina, I didn't see you there."

She turned from him without a reply, moving as fast as her injury would allow. She exited the scene then entered again downstage as a gauzy curtain, painted as an exterior wall laden with windows, separated her from the gathering. It took her a bit, but she made it to the center of the stage where a bench marked the entry into a garden. She seated herself with a sigh, and stretched her leg out in front of her, wincing as she did so.

The guests were still visible through the gossamer windows, but their conversation was no longer intelligible. Lysandro watched as Gascon's silhouette moved through the party, then came outside to where Duhamel sat alone with her thoughts. She sat upright and assumed a ladylike posture on noticing his approach.

"Excuse me, Signorina. Do you mind if I join you? The air in there is a bit too..."

Gascon cocked his head at her and furrowed his brow.

"Strange. I feel as if we've met before, inside a dream. But that dream is of war and death, where there is no place for beauty." He paused. "I'm not bothering you, am I?"

Duhamel remained silent. Miraculously, snow began to fall. Duhamel and Gascon took little note of it. Gascon turned his head to the revelers inside, then back at the general's daughter.

"It's maddening, isn't it?" Gascon began to pace. "The world has ended, and yet that damned music keeps playing. The dancers go round and round...it is a lie. This is insanity, to pretend everything is alright, that it can ever be alright again. Everything feels wrong. *This* is wrong," he said, pulling at his fine clothes. "My scars are the only thing that stops me running wild in the street." He sat beside her and dropped his head into his hands. "I should have died in the desert. Perhaps I did."

Sera swallowed hard, her face shifting to a haunted expression. Her transformation back into the captain was complete when she opened her mouth and said, in his familiar, gritty voice: "So did I."

Gascon lifted his head and looked at her. After a moment, she returned his gaze. Their faces became obscured by a gale wind laden with snow. The final curtain fell on the storm, and in the same beat the orchestra kicked up its pace, sliding effortlessly into the time-honored song every village and city danced to from here to the ends of the Allied Lands on the feast of Faelsday.

The crowd vibrated with jubilation as the actors took their bows, first Celine, then the doge, followed by Pirró and last, Sera. Lysandro and his father applauded wildly as she curtsied in her impossibly stiff gown. Pirró unsheathed his sword, tucked it behind her back, and cut her free. She stepped out over the dress, revealing her captain's uniform to even more raucous applause. She turned her head to the left, where an invisible hand tossed her her hat. She caught it with ease, and took a grand bow.

Lysandro caught her eyes. She pursed her lips in a rueful smile.

Fabien stepped forward and took an additional bow as the play's author and director. Pirró and Sera closed ranks behind him, so when he turned to rejoin them, he was surprised by a formal bow from his own cast, the one reserved for royalty. He turned back to the audience then, his expression one of sheer delight.

"Thank you, from the bottom of my heart, for welcoming us into this absolute *gem* of a village, and for allowing me to share this bit of my soul with you, this story of a man born in the wrong skin. Please stay! There's wine and refreshments enough for everyone."

His pronouncement was met with sound approval. He smiled from ear to ear, grabbed Pirró, and bent him into a dip, kissing him fiercely. Where Lighurans paused in confusion, the sound of the cheers onstage couldn't get any louder, until finally the village rejoined in the celebration. Then two decisive thumps on the floor made the players freeze. A deep voice bellowed out:

"The king!"

Every hand in the audience stilled, except for a single pair of royal hands.

"Congratulations, Brother."

"Thank you, Sire."

Fabien touched his knee to the ground. *All* the actors on the stage did. All except Sera. Lysandro watched her fingers stiffen to stop themselves from coiling into fists at her side.

The king cocked his head at her, impatient. The man beside him barked at her.

"You will kneel before your king!"

"You're not my king."

It seemed the time for Sera to draw gasps from the crowd was not yet over. All eyes settled on her. Lysandro silently pleaded for her to look his way. But her gaze was fixed on the king of Mirêne. Lysandro watched her straighten up inside her coat, gaining power from it as if Duhamel's courage was borne from somewhere outside herself.

"Aren't I?" the king pressed.

"You're mistaken," she announced in a clear voice. "I am Lighuran born, a child of Arun—and we kneel to no one."

"Oh I *like* her." Elias smirked.

His father's response was one of resounding consensus; there were nods and murmurs of approval wherever Lysandro looked.

The king appeared to realize he'd stepped into a viper's nest, and withdrew.

"So it seems. You played your part well."

The corner of Sera's mouth upturned ever so slightly.

At a glance from their monarch, the orchestra hastily resumed their jubilant playing. In a sweeping, put-on gesture, Sera extended the king her hand as he approached the stage.

He ignored her and ascended the stage on his own to assume his place at the center of the dance commencing on stage. As Lysandro watched, he caught a glimpse of the world in which Sera had lived before returning to Lighura, this world of artifice and deception where whole conversations were carried out in subtle gestures and furtive glances. The dancers' eyes shifted to Sera and the king whenever the steps dictated they be partnered. She executed her part well, but all the same, Lysandro could sense the animosity radiating off them. And the attraction. But the last bit was one-sided; the king seemed to relish the game. There was a wolfish gleam in his eyes that Lysandro did not like.

Sera departed his company the minute the song ended. Lysandro was on his feet to search her out. But his father was quicker, pulling him toward Fabien and capturing both his hands in his own.

"My dear doge, I simply must congratulate you. It is a triumph! I've been to the theater many times, but never in all my years have I seen anything that moved me so much as this."

"My sincerest thanks," Fabien answered. "I hope I did right by you as a soldier, Don de Castel. You have my greatest respect."

"You did indeed," Elias assured him. "I can't think of a better honor. And you—" he turned to Seraphine. She appeared from behind the stage in a pale golden gown that painted her like a sunbeam. "You beautiful, ingenious creature, well done!" He cupped her head in his hands and laid a kiss upon her cheek. Lysandro wasn't sure if his father congratulated her on her performance, or on bringing his son to his knees.

At any rate, Lysandro cleared his throat. First Fabien and Pirró, now his father, even the king of Mirêne had kissed Sera, Faelia's sake.

But before he could step in, the king of Mirêne appeared from behind his back and pulled Sera away. Lysandro was a second behind her, but he felt Fabien's hand pressing against his chest. Fabien shook his head in an almost invisible movement then retracted his hand. He took Elias by the shoulder and led him in the opposite direction toward the feast.

"Trust her," Fabien said in Lysandro's ear as he passed.

It wasn't *Sera* that Lysandro didn't trust. He came just within earshot of where she and the king stood. They spoke in Mirênese, which left Lysandro flustered, but Sera's cold response was obvious. She dismissed the king and moved to rejoin the celebration, but he grabbed her by the wrist and spun her around to face him again.

A shiver of rage ran down Lysandro's spine. He strode up to them with rapid steps and put himself between Sera and the king.

"I'll thank you to leave my fiancée alone."

The king raised an eyebrow; he slid effortlessly into Andran. "Ah, yes, Don de Castel. I've heard of you."

Sera bristled, which seemed to bring him pleasure. "I have my spies too."

Lysandro fixed the king with a hard stare.

Fane looked amused rather than threatened. Lysandro felt it high time the king's face received another adjustment, to put it in Pirró's terms.

"An Andran don in a pretty, out-of-the-way little village on the coast. What do you intend to give her that I can't?"

"My unwavering loyalty and affection, all the days of my life."

The intensity of Lysandro's words shook the air. He cast an earnest glance at Sera over his shoulder. Her expression was unreadable.

The king seemed suddenly ill at ease. Rolling his shoulders, he turned his gaze to Sera.

"Well? Will you spend the rest of your days in this village? With him?"

Lysandro curled his fingers into a fist. He was going to pummel him, and to six hells with the consequences. But before he could strike, Sera stepped closer into Lysandro's shadow, and slipped her hand into his.

"You're a good king, Fane. But Lysandro's a thousand times the man you are."

Fane blinked and stepped back. The blow hit him harder than any swing of Lysandro's arm could. Lysandro felt his chest puff up like a ship's sails, buoyed by Sera's high praise.

"I believe the lady made herself clear."

The king straightened his back and strode off without another word.

Lysandro felt Sera squeeze his hand. When he turned to face her, the room suddenly became too warm, the air too thick. He raised a single eyebrow in an attempt to relieve the tension.

"A thousand? Seems a bit much."

"Did it? I was afraid it wasn't enough."

By Faelia—she was serious.

He drew courage from her as he reached into his coat and pressed the jewel he'd purchased into her hands like a secret.

"This is for you."

She opened her palms like a flower in bloom. Her eyes grew round at the sight of their contents, reflecting the gem's rosy brilliance. His name was a sigh on her lips. The sound raced across his skin as he lifted the pendant and moved to adorn her with it.

"May I?"

"Please. Thank you, Lysandro. It's incredible."

"No more so than you," he answered. He ran his fingers through her hair and swept it over her shoulder in a caress before fastening the necklace. His fingertips lingered at the nape of her neck.

"Lysandro?"

"Hmm?"

He didn't recognize the sound of his own voice. It was an odd sound, subdued, and yet...primal.

"This is not the sort of gift one gives to a bride of convenience."

His hand drifted down to the place where her neck met her shoulder. His other arm encircled her waist as she stood with her back to him. She fell easily into the embrace, and set his heart pumping like a madman's. It took all he had to stop his voice from cracking, and to whisper in her ear as smooth as velvet.

"Is that what you are to me, Sera?"

She shivered in his arms, but he only held her tighter. Her voice came softly on the night's breeze.

"No."

She inclined her head toward him, giving Lysandro a splendid view of her profile etched in starlight. She was a vision—sheer perfection. The slight parting of her lips seemed an invitation.

They came together on swift impulse. The little sound that escaped her set his blood on fire. He could feel her heart fluttering against him as he drew her closer.

Everything felt right in the world. Kissing her was like coming home. They knew each other here, here there was no pretense. Only desire. The thrill of their embrace sizzled through him from his fingertips to his toes. When she ran her fingers though his hair, it sent his heart spinning in its cage. His breathing hitched as their tongues met and their kiss deepened. It had been so long since he had tasted her. Gods, how he had missed her.

He could have worshipped at her sumptuous mouth forever. But his paradise was shattered when she clutched his forearm and her fingers pressed unwittingly into his stitches. He tore himself away from her in agony. The speedy retreat of pleasure for pain was dizzying, and he swallowed against a wave of nausea that threatened to overtake him.

"Lysandro, your arm!" Her fingers reached for the spot where moisture was seeping through the stitches and turning his shirtsleeve sticky.

He shook it off quickly. Too quickly.

"It's nothing, I—I knocked into a corner."

Silence fell like an anvil between them. Sera stepped back. He wanted to rush to her, to wash away what he'd said in a moment of pure idiocy. But he froze, and didn't dare look her in the face.

"How did you hurt your arm?"

The cold fury in her voice spooked him. He couldn't tell her the truth. Not now. Not like this. But he would not utter the lie again. So he stood rooted in place, as silent as stone.

The raging storm in her eyes broke, giving way to hurt as she turned and fled.

No.

"Sera. Sera wait!"

But she was already gone. Panic flooded him as she melted into the crowd. He couldn't chase after her here. It would only serve to embarrass her. She shielded herself with all the patrons who wished to congratulate her and cut herself off from him entirely.

Tonight.

He forced himself to steel his nerves against her well-deserved wrath and the way she pointedly avoided looking in his direction. Tonight, he would go to her, and everything would be right again.

* * *

He'd smooth things over first, soothe her ire, and then, tell her. That was the plan. If he could bring a smile to her face with the mask on, then perhaps he could keep it there once he removed it.

The curtains to her room were swaying in the breeze. That was good. Or so he thought. It left him completely unprepared for her quarrel with him to pick up exactly where it left off.

"Signorina," he called out in a low tone. He was met with a sharp stare.

"*Now* you come." she scoffed and turned away from him.

"Signorina," he pleaded, taken aback, "have I done something to offend you?"

That cruel snort again that turned his blood to ice. "*Did* you?"

"Darling, I—"

"Don't."

Lysandro bit his tongue. His words only seemed to stoke the fury in her eyes. She turned the full heat of her stare on him, and he felt his skin prickle.

She was so far away. He stretched out his hand to her. He wanted to swallow her up in his arms and soften her sharp tongue with a sweet caress, but she took a step back. Lysandro's heart sunk from his chest and settled somewhere in the vicinity of his knees. His hand dropped to his side.

"Take off your mask," she said.

Lysandro swallowed. How could he, now? It would only make things worse, though he wasn't sure how much worse things could be. He wasn't keen to find out.

"Take off the mask!"

He shuddered.

Sera pressed her eyes shut to control her anger. When she opened them again, Lysandro saw them glisten in the moonlight.

"You...you promised..."

Lysandro's heart broke into a thousand pieces.

She turned away from him.

"...Signorina..."

Look at me. Please.

Her breath hitched. "Please. Please just go." She disappeared behind the curtains and out of sight without casting a backward glance. The sound of her sobbing assailed Lysandro's ears.

He held his crumpled mask tightly in his hands.

He ripped it off again upon reaching his chambers. He didn't make it to the bed; he slid to the floor with his back against the door. He'd almost had it. He'd almost had her heart in his hands. Her kiss had felt like heaven. That was ruined. All ruined. He tried to rend the mask in two as he sat on the cold floor, the room dark as pitch. But the fabric wouldn't yield. He succumbed to the hollow sensation of his heart eating itself from the inside, and wept bitterly.

24

ALEKSANDER HAD EXPECTED THE COURTHOUSE TO BE FULL. WHAT HE hadn't expected was the witness box itself to be crammed with people.

When that many villagers had cause enough to accuse someone of a crime, that someone was guilty. Of what, Aleksander had to figure out.

He had slept poorly—naturally, as he'd slept in the judge's chambers with his feet propped up at the desk, stretching and contorting his back at a hideous angle. There was nothing to speak of for breakfast, and his coat crinkled in all the wrong places as he walked the few feet from the office door to take his place at the raised dais.

Caterina spoiled him. She'd have had a warm, invigorating meal waiting for him, his clothes pressed and ready to make the impression a chief magistrate should. But he wanted her and the girls as far away from here as possible and had packed in haste on his own. She'd be mortified to see the figure he cut now.

Gareth brought Marek into the room and sat him down in the box designated for the accused. He was clapped in irons. Marek did as he was bidden, and looked out calmly over the courthouse. Aleks expected Marek to be outraged, or defeated, or something—*anything*. Instead, Lothan sat as docile as a lamb and looked on with a detached air, as if this were all perfectly normal.

Aleksander perused the gaggle of Lighurans jostling each other for a seat in the witness box. There were so many of them that they couldn't figure out how they were all going to fit. One gentleman looked about to lose his temper, but the woman behind him pulled on the cuff of his sleeve, and the provoked bluster deflated into grumbling.

Aleksander thanked the Goddess that Elias was not among them. He sat by himself in the back row on the magistrate's right. It would have been awkward to accept testimony from him, given that their friendship was not a secret. If they even were still friends.

Aleksander tired of waiting for the witnesses to sort themselves. He pounded the desk with the flat of his hand. The sound echoed off the wood, and the attendants stiffened at attention. The witnesses stopped squirming and squeezed shoulder to shoulder. Aleksander never got tired of the effect such a simple gesture could have.

He turned his eyes to Marek, who looked back with a patient stare that grated on his nerves.

"Lothan Marek, you stand accused of dereliction of your duty as magistrate of the village of Lighura—among other things."

Aleksander snapped his head in the direction of a shout. It was the wizened witness, of course, the one who'd been kicking up a fuss.

"I'll get to you, in my own good time," Aleks said.

The grumbler was sufficiently chastened.

"What about you?" Aleksander asked, turning back to Marek. "What do you have to say for yourself?"

Marek seemed to consider the question, but ultimately, he decided to remain quiet.

"Fine."

It was enough to push Aleks over the edge of grouchy into downright irritated.

He looked again to the witness bench. He didn't know these people. Trying to organize them by the severity of their accusations or their credibility would be an impossible task without a lengthy delay. Aleksander didn't bother.

"Who's to be first?" he called.

Let them figure it out.

The grumbler shot up from his seat, of course. But he wasn't quick enough for the stern-looking woman to his left. She hissed something Aleksander was grateful not to have heard and shoved a thin young lad, her son by the look of him, ahead. He stumbled toward the magistrate with a bewildered, embarrassed look on his face.

"What's your name?" Aleksander asked.

"Don Fernando Carras, son of Don Aldo Carras. He was murdered when a thief entered our home."

"I hung the man who killed your father," Marek said. "Not sure what more I could have done to punish him."

He speaks.

Lothan's dismissive reply shook something loose inside the young don, for the retort that came back was sharp.

"That may be true, but what he isn't telling you is that we'd been complaining for weeks about break-ins and thievery, and he'd done nothing. He said he was going to do something about it, but he never did. He didn't come around asking questions, didn't arrest anyone. More and more houses were robbed, and when my father found one of the thieves in his study and confronted him, he was killed. A few days later, the magistrate hung one of his own men."

His own man?

"Was it the man your father encountered?" Aleksander cut in.

"I can't say. I never saw him."

Fair enough. It spoke well of the lad that he hadn't embellished.

"He told us the man had confessed, but he put up some fight. Screamed that it was *Marek* who killed him. Right up until they hanged him."

Did he now...

Aleksander shifted his gaze to regard Lothan. His eyes narrowed to slits.

"What were the man's exact words, Don Fernando? Do you remember?"

"Exactly? No. One of the others might remember better. But I do recall that he was really worked up."

I can imagine. Hard not to be when you're being hanged for something you didn't do.

"He called Marek a liar and said that *he* was the one who murdered my father. If Marek had done his job in the first place," Fernando continued, "my father would still be alive."

"These others you mention, the ones whose houses were also stolen into—can you name them?"

"They're all sitting right there," he said, pointing his chin back toward the witness box.

It aligned with what Elias had told him, as far as Aleks could remember. He'd only been half paying attention, distracted by the fact that Elias hadn't looked him in the eye as he'd spoken. His gaze had occasionally landed on his shoulder, above his head, or on his magistrate's pin. But never in the eye.

Anyway, it was more important to wipe his mind clean of what he'd been told and hear it straight from the source. Elias was one of the few noblemen whose house hadn't been attacked. The only one, it seemed, except his and Don Lysandro's.

Carras's testimony had the gears turning in Aleksander's head, certainly, but his story alone would not be enough to see Marek on the business end of a rope. There was much that Marek could explain away if he so chose. He could argue that the murdering thief had eluded him, despite his best efforts, but that he'd caught him in the end; the man in question would not be there to dispute it. That the condemned had been ensconced in Marek's own offices was more problematic, but corruption was not a hanging offense. Marek was already stripped of his title regardless of anything else, but that wouldn't be enough to keep Lighurans safe from the wrath he expected was simmering just beneath the surface.

Aleksander hoped that the young don's claim wasn't the best evidence the village had to offer.

He thanked the boy, who nodded and rejoined his mother.

"I'll go next, if you don't mind."

The man who approached Aleksander was of an age with him, thin, and well-groomed. He sported a ring of purple under his right eye, and his nose had the distinct look of being broken but not properly reset before it began to heal.

"My name is Stefano Morici, and I own the print shop."

"What have you to say against this man?" Aleksander asked.

The printer gestured toward himself. "My face, and most likely some of my ribs as well, were broken by him."

Aleksander looked up from his notes. "Eh?"

"He ordered me to print a wanted notice for the Shadow of Theron. But—"

"The what?"

"The Shadow of Theron, Honor."

"What in six hells is the Shadow of Theron?"

"He's…our local hero. He is called such for his defense of the honest people of this village, and for standing against the plague sitting over there." He cast a cold glance at Marek.

The multitude of heads occupying the gallery bobbed in unison. Aleksander furrowed his brow.

"But who is he?" Aleksander asked.

"No one knows, Honor. He wears a mask about his face, and is sly as a fox, as elusive as a phantom."

"He destroyed my office!" Marek shouted.

"As I was saying…"

Aleksander knew that Marek hadn't done *that* himself. Whatever else Lighurans thought of him, that did make the so-called Shadow of Theron a vandal. But he gestured for the printer to continue.

"I was ordered to print the notice, but there was a mistake on the type, regarding the reward. When the notices were distributed with the error, Marek sent his goons to summon me."

"You deliberately humiliated me," Lothan growled.

Stefano shook his head. "I take great pride in my work, Honor, but all men make mistakes."

The smirk creeping at the edge of his mouth, and the barely suppressed snickers of the gallery, told Aleksander the true shape of it. But the printer wasn't finished.

"Do you mean to argue that a simple misprint merits such a severe beating as I have endured?"

"Certainly not," Aleksander answered in Marek's stead. "You're *sure* it was him?"

"It was the man himself, Honor. I was called into his office for that express purpose."

Hard to mistake that.

Aleksander scribbled on the paper in front of him.

"And as to what Don Carras said, I do remember the day Marek hung one of his officers. He said, 'murderer—you're just as guilty as me.'"

"Thank you, Signor."

"My pleasure," he said, and shot a final barb at Marek before taking his seat again.

Marek did not return fire. It was so odd that he wasn't fighting back. But things were definitely getting worse, and the witness box was packed with people chomping at the bit to have their turn at him. Aleksander wondered what it was going to take to rile him up.

Lothan could barely keep his eyes open. The swirling nausea caused by seeing the temple window's mysterious restoration was compounded by his possession of the Cerulean Key. He'd shoved it grudgingly in his pocket before leaving his house at the last minute, trying at intervals to build up his immunity to its agonies enough to use it. But then he'd been confined to a cell before being able to rid himself of it.

It was like a shackle around his throat. It robbed him of any rest and produced horrific nightmares of Theron's Shadow taking the form of his predecessor, his black charger trampling him into the ground. By dawn, he had been bathed in a cold sweat, and utterly drained.

He managed to slip the key under the threadbare mattress of his cell before being collected for his trial. His fingertips still throbbed from the direct contact as if he'd gripped a red-hot poker.

With the peace of being away from it came the overwhelming urge to sleep. But even that was interrupted by the howling in his veins to be nearer the Blood Sword. He couldn't soothe that ache until he could hold the key in his hand long enough to open his cell. He was being pulled in so many directions his skin felt on the brink of splitting apart. Not to mention that he was being closely guarded, and all of Lighura was itching to stone him.

All except de Castel, the man who had put him there. It galled him, that Lighura's princeling cared so little about the trouble he'd caused that he couldn't even be bothered. He was probably off sticking the Alvaró girl. An image arose in his mind, of the two of them laughing as they fornicated on de Castel's fancy bed in his fancy house.

The picture was chased away when an overstuffed Aruni jostled his way out of the witness box and moved to the front of the courthouse. Lothan craned his neck to snap stiffened joints, and his vision flashed white. He saw stars as the still tender muscles keeping his arm attached to the rest of him screamed.

"I am Brother Sancio of Temple Arun and I've been sent as their representative. When the damage to our sacred window was discovered, this so-called magistrate refused the high priestess's call for swift justice. Many of the people gathered here can attest to that."

The fat warrior paused and took a stuttering breath. "But what they don't know is that Marek himself was the one who destroyed it and took the life of our high priestess."

The gallery erupted in outrage. Their clamoring voices ran together like an ungodly shriek deep in Lothan's skull, and he fought hard to keep from shielding his brain from the sound with his hands.

"Brother...?"

"Sancio," he supplied for the chief magistrate.

"Have you proof of this?"

The warrior (it made Lothan snort to think of him as such) nodded.

"I was there when it happened."

Lothan would have laughed, if he thought his body wouldn't fall apart from the attempt.

How could I have failed to notice you?

"I was in the nave when I heard them enter. I hid myself in the private prayer booth. I heard him give the order."

Fuck.

The chief magistrate looked surprised. It was rather unbelievable, even though it was true. Maybe he would get away with it.

"Why would he do that?" the chief magistrate asked the priest.

"For spite, I suspect. The Shadow of Theron had just recently discovered that Marek was the one stealing sacred relics from across Andras. The Shadow was working in tandem with the high priestess, and I was his contact.

Fuck. Fuck.

The priest nodded to another Aruni in the gallery, who stood and lifted a wooden chest onto the magistrate's desk. It was where Lothan had kept a log of his dark trade and some of the smaller, useless relics. That is, until Theron's Impostor had sent the mouth of the cave crashing down on itself. He'd assumed the chest had been buried in the rubble.

"I wouldn't touch any of its contents, Honor," the priest warned as the chief magistrate reached into the box, then retracted his hand just as swiftly. "Something in there almost cost the Shadow his life."

"You mentioned the high priestess."

The priest ducked his head. "High Priestess Beatríz. The Shadow told her of what he'd seen when he retrieved the chest before you. And I told her what I had witnessed in the temple. After Marek refused to see justice done, she summoned him to the temple to confront him."

The second Aruni pulled something out of her robes—a bloodied, filthy blue rag. Sancio held it up for the chief magistrate to see.

"This is all that's left of her."

The courthouse fell silent. It was a single moment of peace, the only one Lothan was allowed.

"Honorable Magistrate…"

"Yes, Brother?"

"I have been directed to tell you, that you cannot hang Lothan Marek."

The chief magistrate raised an eyebrow. "Can't I?"

The priest shook his head. "He murdered one of us. His blood is ours to spill."

"I won't argue with you on that point."

"Did you witness the murder of the high priestess?" Lothan asked.

The priest hesitated, but the chief magistrate directed him to answer.

"No. But after what the Shadow told her—"

"Who knows what the Shadow told her? For all you know, *he* is the murderer you seek, not me."

"It was *you!*" the witness insisted. "And it was you who stole the relics from the Goddess!"

Lothan shrugged. "What need have I of relics? I've never been a devotee of the temple. Isn't it more probable that a man who impersonates a god would seek to possess items of a supposedly sacred nature?"

"Watch your tongue, Marek," the chief magistrate warned.

Lothan took a deep breath and focused the trickle of energy he had left into his soothing tone. "Have I said anything wrong, Honor? How are you to accept the second-hand testimony of one who, by his own admission, was not present for the crimes I stand accused of?"

"But I heard you—"

Lothan ignored the braying man and squared his gaze on the magistrate. He had only a few seconds to turn this in his favor.

"If this Shadow has seen so much, let him come forward, without his mask, and give testimony against me. You can hardly refuse to question this man before handing me over to the temple. You must hear from him directly. You cannot deny me that."

If it had been anyone other than the chief magistrate, Lothan would not have been strong enough. But he had preyed on his weakness before; he already knew the way in. And as for the Shadow—he wouldn't dare. The minute he took off his mask, Lothan had him.

It had been necessary, but Lothan pushed himself too far. He clenched his fists so hard that his nails sliced into his palms. But without something concrete to divert his attention, he was going to faint.

What he heard next put a smile on his lips.

"Brother Sancio, are you able to contact the Shadow?"

He hesitated. "He has always been the one to contact us, Honor."

"But *can* you get a message to him, and convince him to present himself?"

The priest hesitated even longer. His eyes drifted to the priestess who'd carried the chest to the magistrate. She struck Lothan as too thin to be a warrior, with a bony face and pale hair that was almost white.

A fine pair of warriors—a pig and a waif.

The waif made an almost imperceptible dip of her head. Lothan raised a curious eyebrow.

"I can," the priest said at last.

Lothan glared at him.

You're going to die, piggy. I will enjoy making you squeal.

LYSANDRO FOUND THE DOORS OF THE PLAYHOUSE LOCKED. HE POUNDED ON the wood and called out for Sera. But it was Fabien who answered. Lysandro slumped in his boots.

"Gods," Fabien said. "You look awful."

"I need to see her," Lysandro said. He could scarcely hold himself upright in the entryway and braced himself against the marble columns.

Fabien looked behind him, muttered something under his breath that Lysandro didn't understand, then stepped out into the open, closing the door behind him.

"It's not a good idea," Fabien said.

"Fabien," Lysandro begged. "I have to see her."

The doge sighed. "It will do more harm than good. Give her time. Give *me* time."

"You can't keep her from me."

Fabien tilted his head, his eyes full of sympathy. "Lysandro. I love her. I love her as much as a man like me possibly could. I offered to make her a dogessa. She's told you that, hasn't she?"

Lysandro wanted to retch. But he simply nodded.

"That offer still stands. I could take her from here and you'd never see her again. I'd do my duty by her, get with child, and then—" Fabien shrugged. "She'd be free to have as many lovers as she desired."

Lysandro was definitely going to retch.

"She'd be miserable for the rest of her life. She wants..."

"What does she want?"

Fabien blinked. "I seem to recall something about unwavering loyalty and affection, all the days of your life."

Lysandro held his breath. Had Fabien overheard, or had she told him what he'd said? What did it mean if she had? Lysandro shook his head; this conversation was making him lose his mind.

"How can I give her any of those things if she won't speak to me?"

"She will. But...not now. I'm sorry. I *am* on your side in this."

Lysandro doubted that. He didn't try to hide it.

"I wish for her happiness above all else. Look, why don't you go eat something? You look as if you've missed a meal or two."

A full stomach wouldn't bring Sera back to him. He didn't see the point.

"Go now. I'll do what I can."

Lysandro put his weight on the door, holding it open. "Broken glass."

"What?"

"Tell her, it was glass from a broken window. She will understand."

Lysandro almost collapsed when the door closed in his face.

FABIEN RETURNED TO THE STAGE, WHERE THE LUSH PILLOWS THAT BELONGED to a make-believe desert camp were strewn about the floor. Pirró sat up as he entered.

"How is he?"

"Why do you care how *he* is?" Sera snapped.

Fabien ignored her. "Like he's been struck by a runaway coach."

Sera's face went white. "What do you mean? Is he hurt?"

"I thought we didn't care," Pirró said.

Sera clucked her tongue.

"He's fine," Fabien answered, reclining beside Pirró. "In body, perhaps. In heart and mind, though…" Fabien shook his head.

Sera dropped back onto the silken pillows. Her headache was creeping in again. She had thought she didn't want to see him. But now that he'd come and gone, she regretted sending Fabien to the door. Lysandro's devastatingly handsome face, marred by sorrow, was etched on the back of her eyelids. The impression made fresh tears threaten to fall, just when she thought she'd finished crying.

He'd reached for her, in those last moments, but she'd backed away, stung by his broken promise to end his masquerade. Remembering the pain in his eyes as she had done so sliced right down to the bone.

This is his fault, she told herself once more.

"He's sorry, Sera," Fabien said. "He's falling apart without you. What more could you want?"

She wanted Lysandro to tell her the truth. To look her in the eyes and confess to being the Shadow of Theron and explain why he had courted her night and day with the promise that he would reveal himself, but yet still refused, even when she could stand it no more. Why? Why the mask, and the secrets? She could think of only one reason.

"He doesn't love me."

"Oh, yes. Yes he does," Fabien said.

"He wants me to believe that."

"Come now, girl. You're being ridiculous."

"He lied to me," she insisted.

"Did he? Did he ever tell you something that wasn't true?"

"He didn't tell me all."

Fabien laughed. "That is not the same. Believe me, there is an ocean between those things. Secrets are often necessary. Sometimes they hurt. It's a sign of how deeply involved you are with another person." Fabien gestured to Pirró. "No man alive has hurt me more than he has."

Pirró grimaced, but Fabien smoothed it away with a gentle hand. "But what hurts most is his absence."

Fabien was right about that. It was killing her to push Lysandro away. All she wanted for him was to catch her in his arms and never let go. But she had to know his heart.

"He's desperate to talk to you. He wasn't even making sense."

"What do you mean?" Sera asked.

Fabien folded his hands behind his head. "He said to tell you it was glass from a broken window. Said you would understand. Do you?"

His arm. The bleeding.

Sera stifled a sob. The only broken windows in Lighura were buried in the rubble of the magistrate's office. Only one person could be responsible. There was no way to admit to that without also admitting he was the Shadow. Is that what he would have done, if only she'd come to the door?

Merciful Faelia, what have I done?

"I'd say she does," Pirró said to Fabien as Sera sprang from the floor. But she came back down just as fast again, and hard, as her ankle snagged on the ropes of their imaginary tent.

SANCIO TOOK A LONG, CIRCUITOUS ROUTE TO LYSANDRO'S HOUSE TO AVOID any prying eyes. Time was, this winding path would have left him purple in the face by the time he'd reached his friend's doorstep. Now, with only a few steps more to go, his body ached to run.

He was shocked to see the surgeon open the door.

"Why are *you* here? Is he sick?"

Rafael tilted his head. "You'd better come see."

The surgeon led Sancio to Lysandro's rooms. They were bathed in darkness, though it was midday. Sancio saw his friend crouched on the floor with his back against the wall, his eyes closed.

"He won't eat, or drink… you'll be lucky if he speaks to you."

"I'm not hungry."

"You haven't eaten in almost two days. You must want something."

Rafael bit his tongue as Lysandro flinched, and tears pricked his eyes.

"Sorry. I didn't mean—"

"Lies."

Rafael furrowed his brow. "What?"

"All those poets, Morçan, Al'ataine, de la Vega…they sing songs of the great triumph of love, its tenderness, the way it fills your soul…"

"Lysandro,—"

"They lie. They never said how much it hurts."

Sancio pressed his lips into a thin line. Lysandro's pain was palpable as he spoke, choking on his own words. Seeing him like this made all kinds of complicated feelings churn in his gut. But he didn't have time for any of that.

"I'm sorry Lysandro. Truly. But at least now you can focus on more important things."

Rafael shoved him with his elbow. "Don't be so callous."

"It's not callousness. It's the truth."

"More important things…" Lysandro said faintly.

"Yes."

"Like what?"

"Like *what*? Like putting the nail in Marek's coffin, before he raises Argoss?"

Lysandro shot him a hard look. "He is not Argoss reborn," he said firmly. "He's just a man. An insidious man who happened upon an insidious weapon."

"And can *wield* it?"

Sancio bit the inside of his cheek to stop him spilling his guts in retort. Instead he answered in the only way he could.

"He might get away with everything. He's demanded that the Shadow testify in full view of the village and the chief magistrate agreed."

"Why in Arun's name did he do that?" Rafael cried.

"Because he's the chief magistrate. He must be seen to be fair. My words weren't enough. It wasn't *me* who's seen the worst of what he's done."

He couldn't tell the whole village who he was. Not when Sera still didn't know.

"What will he fear if you don't?" Sancio pressed. "What *more* will he do to exact revenge on those who tried to hang him? Or your father, who brought him to the chief magistrate's attention?"

Lysandro's legs shifted on the floor. Sancio's words had the intended effect. But Lysandro wouldn't admit it now, not until his hurt and his angry pride subsided. Sancio knew that.

"You know what you have to do, you don't need me to tell you," he said as he turned to leave. "Just be quick about it, before it's too late."

"Sorry," Rafael said when he was alone again with Lysandro. "If I'd known he was going to be like that I wouldn't have let him in. He does have a point though."

"Rafael—"

"You have to stop this," he pleaded. "You're going to end up killing yourself."

"Rafael," Lysandro repeated.

"Yes?"

"Go away."

He shook his head, then did what he was asked without saying more.

LOTHAN WATCHED AS TWO OF THE MEN WHO HAD BEEN HIRED TO KEEP AN eye on him almost came to blows.

"Ah, shut up, will you? Just 'cause you got the keys don't make you better'n me."

"If it doesn't, why don't you have 'em then?"

"I'll tell you what I have, a right hook that'll knock that stupid grin off your face."

"You're just upset because you've gotta answer to me now."

"I'm not answering to *nobody*—"

"Shove it. The both of you."

The biggest of the men came stomping through and put an end to the squabble with a quick swipe at the keys that returned them to his own pocket.

"Aren't you the teacher's pet?" the first man asked.

"We've been hired to do a job. It's honest work and the pay is good. You don't like it, go back to the tavern."

The man newly bereft of the keys snorted.

"You ain't the boss of me either."

"*Out*, I said."

They'd be back. Lothan counted on them being put on shift together again at least once. He could use that; it was much easier to draw on people's innate characteristics than it was to convince them of something they found contradictory. It was as good an opportunity as any. But first, he had to subdue the effects of the damned key. He groaned at the thought of touching it again. It already heated the mattress so much that it was like lying atop a furnace.

Wasn't it enough to be so near?

No, of course not. He needed to master its power, and he couldn't do that by cutting corners. He screamed as he lifted it from its hiding place and returned it to his pocket. It was like sticking his hand inside the mouth of a raging volcano. His reaction was so severe it made him heave. That got his captors' attention, as they were forced to clean up.

The key was heavier than a block of granite in his pocket. He felt it drawing him down, trying to push him into the floor, and likely through it into the darkness beyond. Sweat beaded on his brow, but he ignored it, gripping the lumpy edges of the mattress to brace himself for the night's terrors.

25

MARTA GASPED AT HOW DARK THE ROOM WAS AT THIS HOUR, EVEN THOUGH it had been the same the day before, and the day before that. She mumbled her disapproval and rushed to pull the drapes aside and let daylight in.

"Leave it."

Lysandro heard her breathe heavily through her nose in protest, but he didn't apologize. She let her hands fall to her sides, walked across the room to where he crouched, and pulled a gleaming ivory envelope from her pocket.

"A letter came for you."

"Please, Marta. Let me be."

"But…" She turned the letter in her hands. "Don Lysandro, it's from her."

His eyes locked with hers. A letter? What could it contain, other than a seal on his fate? But then, why write to say what he already knew?

With equal parts hope and terror, he snatched the paper from Marta's hand and tore open the envelope.

Lysandro,
I need your help. I'm ashamed to ask for it, especially after how we parted. I would have come in person if I were able.

My parents are leaving this evening to visit my mother's sister. Normally I would be expected to accompany them, but I suffered a fall a few days ago. A minor injury, wrought by my own carelessness. All the same, I cannot get around easily on my own at the moment. A journey is out of the question. So is being left by myself in this house.

Can I stay with you while my parents are away? They've agreed on condition of your answer.

I'll understand if you refuse. I'll never bother you further, if that is your wish. I apologize deeply for the imposition, but you've always been generous to me, and I hope I can depend on you.

Yours, Sera

Lysandro read and reread the letter until the words blurred before him.

"Lysandro?"

He folded the paper and rose to his feet.

"Make the house fit to receive the Goddess Herself. Bring in fresh flowers from the garden."

"Which ones, Don Lysandro?"

What says, 'I'm at your mercy and will do absolutely anything you ask of me'?

"I'll leave the details to you."

She nodded and hurried away.

Lysandro's heart raced as he bathed and dressed himself. He recounted every syllable of Sera's note in his head. She claimed to depend on him still, even after everything had fallen apart.

Yours. Was she his? Merciful Faelia, how he prayed it was so. But Sera offered to release him, if he wished it. As if he could *ever* wish to be free of her. As he thought on it, he realized that her words gave no clue as to what she herself wanted. But there would be time, at least. Time to talk, to beg her forgiveness. If what she was truly asking for was a chance to reconcile, he knew it would be his last.

But he was barely presentable. The visage staring back at him through the looking glass belonged more to a ghoul. His face was thin, with deep fathoms under his eyes that told of sleepless nights and hours spent staring into an empty future.

It was impossible to respond to her in writing without pouring his heart into a missive of epic proportions and inundating the paper with enough tears to return it to pulp. In the end, he sent his carriage to fetch her without further word. Whatever he was going to say, he would say it to her directly. If he could manage.

He didn't feel ready when he heard the carriage coming back up the path, carrying the only woman he would ever love inside it. He rushed to meet her nevertheless. When she opened the carriage door, the nervous air that had been buzzing around him stilled. Perhaps it was the time spent forcibly apart, but her beauty destroyed him. Her face was almost unbearable to behold. But something was amiss; she looked as forlorn as he. She had not wished for this, he reminded himself. If not for her fall, would she be here now? But—she could have relied on Fabien. She simply hadn't.

She's choosing to be here.

There was a heady silence as they considered each other. Lysandro was desperate to understand the quiet uncertainty in her eyes. His gaze dipped downward, where he noticed that she stood balanced on one foot, the other held aloft mere inches from the ground. Her hands tensed around the edges of the carriage door as she contemplated her descent.

Instinct took over. He reached her in one stride and swept her into his arms. His heart thudded hard against his ribs when she laid her head on his chest and relaxed in his embrace. Then his steps faltered; she was wearing the pendant he had given her. He imagined for a moment that the path he trod did not lead to his home, but to the edge of eternity. He would never feel the loss of her if they could go on like this forever, wrapped in the scent of roses and citrus from her sun-kissed hair. But a few moments were all fate afforded him as he laid her down atop the plush bed coverings of his largest and most well-appointed guest room, bathed now in the lavender glow of twilight. The room was awash in flowers, all white. The color of surrender. He heard the shuffle of Marta's feet discreetly behind him.

"Can I get you anything?" Lysandro asked.

"Some tea, maybe?" Sera answered in a small voice. He merely turned his head over his shoulder, and Marta skittered away.

"Thank you."

His arms felt empty without her. He chased away the agony of it by rearranging the pillows on the bed. He kept in constant motion, his eyes riveted on his self-given task. He could not bring himself to meet her gaze. He felt like a fool. He didn't know what to say, or how to destroy the barrier that had risen between them. But the silence was excruciating.

When she spoke, it sent shock waves through him.

"I'm so sorry Lysandro, I—"

"*No,*" he said, not thinking as he placed his fingers on her lips to stop her. "No. I am the one in the wrong."

Her lips parted ever so slightly under his fingertips; he was still touching her mouth. He retracted his hand from that sensuous place and tore himself away from her intense gaze that he could not decipher. He walked to the foot of the bed, and gingerly rested his fingers on the slipper adorning her good foot.

"May I?"

She nodded, and he removed her right shoe. She tensed as he reached for her left. The ankle was three times the size of the other, and flared an angry red.

"Oh… Sera…"

"It's a bit tender, but it's fine. Really."

"No…I don't think it is. Don't move. I'll—"

She lifted an eyebrow.

Where's she going to go, idiot?

He winced. "I'll be right back." He raced to fetch Rafael from his room and returned in an instant. "Sera, this is Rafael. He's a surgeon."

Beside him, Rafael blinked. "This is Signorina Alvaró?"

"Yes," Lysandro answered.

Rafael sighed. "Of course it is."

Lysandro's eyes narrowed at his friend, but he only received a wordless expression in response.

Sera's eyes grew round as saucers. She sat straight up on the bed and clutched at the bedclothes.

"No. I said I'm fine." Her voice was tight.

"I'll be the judge of that," Rafael said, approaching the bed.

Sera looked ready to scream.

Lysandro started at a sudden realization. *She's afraid.*

"Sera," he said, dropping his voice and daring to sit at the edge of the bed. Her gaze scattered, not knowing where to look now that he had blocked her view of Rafael as he moved to inspect her ankle. "Sera look at me. He's not going to hurt you. I'm not going to let anyone hurt you."

She pressed her lips together to stop them from trembling.

"Look at me Sera," he pleaded. She dragged her gaze to his.

"Lysandro..." she murmured, releasing her grip on the bed and reaching tentatively for him. His heart gave a little leap as she dug her nails into his sleeves.

"I'll take care of you," he whispered. "I'll always take care of you. I told you I would, remember?"

Her eyes took on a glossy shine. He couldn't make sense of why she cried—out of fear, or perhaps with the realization that he had, in effect, just told her everything.

"Signorina?"

Lysandro turned to regard Rafael, but his friend looked right past him and into Sera's eyes with a rare look of pathos and outrage.

"What did they do to you, to make you so afraid?"

Sera blinked. "It..." She turned her head to the side, in that tell-tale way of someone not willing to examine their own demons. "It was a long time ago."

Rafael's mouth settled into a grim line. "I'm just going to look, and I'll only touch you if you permit me. Alright?"

Sera swallowed, and sought Lysandro's eyes. His gaze settled on her and didn't let go. She drew in a ragged breath and nodded.

She held his stare and tried to breathe. He'd never seen her like this. The way she had called out to him in her terror broke his heart. He would murder whoever had instilled this fear in her. But she had called for *him*. She wouldn't have done that if she no longer trusted him, no longer regarded him with the same high esteem as when she'd rebuffed the king and put her hand in his. She had never corrected him when he'd called her his intended—his bride to be.

Lysandro shook free of his runaway thoughts as Rafael turned Sera's attention to him. "I'm going to lift your skirt—"

"You'll do no such thing!" Lysandro barked.

"To your *shins*, Signorina, so that perhaps I can see the ankle. Okay?"

Lysandro glared at Rafael with murder in his eyes. Rafael ignored him, which made him even more enraged.

Sera gave a slight nod. Lysandro twisted his body so he could focus on Sera *and* watch Rafael out of the corner of his eye. The movement inadvertently increased her anxiety. Her palms opened, searching restlessly for an anchor. Lysandro brushed his fingers against hers, not sure if she would accept his offer, but she clutched him eagerly.

"Can I test your ankle? Just a fraction?" Rafael asked.

She licked her lips. "Okay." She squeezed Lysandro's hand. He squeezed back.

"What hurts more, this…or this?"

"That—*that*," she moaned.

"Stop, you're hurting her!" Lysandro demanded.

Rafael shot him a look. *Which one of you is the patient?*

Lysandro was aware the timbre of his voice bordered on the hysterical, but the sound of her suffering was intolerable.

"It's your muscle that's hurting, not the bone. But the swelling is a concern, likely because you've been walking on it."

"I haven't had much choice."

Lysandro growled under his breath. Had her parents been so absorbed in their own plans that they hadn't recognized Sera's pain? Or had they simply not cared? They were, after all, the same parents who had sent her away from her home, away from anything she'd ever known, to mold her into something they considered more suitable. As if she hadn't been worth enough to them just as the Goddess made her.

Rafael, ignorant to Lysandro's inner rage, continued.

"We need to reduce it. Now." He pulled a glass syringe out of his case.

Sera whimpered at the sight of it.

"Wait! Is that really necessary?" Lysandro interjected.

Finally, Rafael looked at him. "Would I have suggested it if it wasn't?"

"Do it."

Lysandro turned to look at Sera. A sheen of sweat covered her forehead. "Sera—"

"Quickly, *please*."

Rafael complied.

She winced, and turned bury her forehead against Lysandro's chest as the needle pierced her skin. Lysandro cradled the back of her head and tried to steady her shaking. In a moment, it was done. Her anxiety waned when she heard the needle being snapped back into its metal case.

"I'm going to soak some rags in arnica to bind it with. It'll be uncomfortable at first, but it's meant to restrict your movement to allow the ankle to heal itself. I want you on your back—"

Lysandro started.

"Off your *feet*—today and tomorrow. I'd also like to give you something for the pain. Ah, thank you Marta, perfect timing. Just a moment then."

Rafael cleared his throat, and actively avoided his friend's face as he added a dark black powder to Sera's tea.

"Thank you," Sera said, regaining a true sense of calm now that Rafael was leaving.

"The pleasure is entirely mine."

Lysandro practically shoved him out the door. "I ought to pummel you," he hissed.

"Mm. Maybe later. I'll only be a minute with those bandages." Rafael sighed. "Goddess damn you. Damn you and your exquisite taste."

The tea did its work quickly. Sera slipped into a deep sleep only minutes after imbibing it, leaving Lysandro to dine with Rafael in an awkward silence. Sera was there, in his house, but that wasn't enough. He needed to breach the gap that stretched between them. He passed by her room on his way to bed to see if she might be awake and perhaps willing to talk. But as he came nearer to the door, he heard a muffled groan from within.

"Sera?" He opened the door a crack. "Are you well?"

Her answer was another noncommittal groan. He opened the door a bit wider. "Can I—"

"Yes," she answered.

He entered the room and assessed her with a quick glance. "Is everything alright?"

Her cheeks flushed, and she averted her eyes. But her discomfort was plain. She bit her lip, and at once Lysandro became intensely jealous of her own mouth.

"It's just..."

"Is it too tight?" He gestured to the bindings that had stiffened around her ankle, now held aloft by a mountain of pillows.

"It's my corset," she confessed. "It's hurting my back, and I can't—" She twisted at the waist, but not enough. "I can't undo it."

Sweat trickled down Lysandro's spine.

"I'll fetch Marta."

"No," she cried as he turned to leave. "She'll be sleeping now, don't wake her." She drew in an awkward breath.

He couldn't leave her like that.

Lysandro moved to the bed without a word. She couldn't bend her knees to sit cross-legged with her ankle propped up; it left Lysandro with no choice but to position himself between her legs.

Gods.

Lysandro scooped Sera up by the shoulders and pressed her tight to his chest. He kept his eyes locked on hers as he lifted up the back of her dress.

"Lysandro—"

His gaze that bore into her eyes, and never once strayed to her body, was his only reply. Sera pressed her lips together and leaned into him, resting her chin on his shoulder.

She smelled so good. He closed his eyes to better take in the fragrance, and stretched out his fingertips to assess the bindings that kept Sera's body from his. He wasn't sure where to begin. The pads of his fingers lighted on loops upon loops woven in an intricate, invisible pattern, but they could not spy a starting place. His cheeks burned.

"I'm not...um..." He cleared his throat. "I've never done this before."

"I'm glad," she whispered in his ear.

Lysandro's blood thundered between his temples.

With her assurances, he took the time to explore the intricacies of the bindings with his hands, and finally discovered a fastening that offered some give. He slipped a slender finger into the loop, teasing it loose. It complied, unsurely at first, but then with greater ease, and he was able to undo the first fastening with two alternately tugging fingers. An image began to form in his mind about the nature of what his hands confronted, and his progress grew smoother as he worked. Sera let out a sigh as the garment loosened around her ribs. But the looser it became, the more her body tensed beneath his fingertips. She swallowed hard, and the breath that warmed his shoulder grew ragged.

Into the fraught silence she murmured, "This is not how I pictured this."

Merciful Faelia.

He stared at the ceiling, and mustered the courage to ask, in a low voice, "How did you?"

She lifted her chin. "What?"

"Picture it?"

He could *feel* the heat that rushed to her cheeks. She uttered a wordless response and tucked her face back into the crook of his neck to save herself from answering. His heart pounded as the possibilities flickered across his mind.

With another tug, he had her free of the bindings. He pulled her gaze back to him as he gripped the form and slid it away from between them, revealing her bare back to his touch. He inhaled sharply at her soft skin. He had no reason to, but Lysandro lingered, tracing a furtive path with his fingertips up the length of her spine and settling at the base of her neck.

It was too easy to imagine how it would be to hold her just like this, their bodies pressed skin to skin. It saddened him. Lysandro didn't know whether he would ever again be permitted this intimacy.

But Sera didn't shrink away. Her curves fell softly against him with uninhibited breaths. She did not ask him to leave, but he knew he must. Lysandro withdrew his hands and replaced her cotton dress over her skin.

"Good night, Seraphine."

He left the room without giving himself a chance to change his mind. He leaned against the opposite side of the doors as he pulled them closed, and savored the words she had let slip. She'd thought about them— together. The corners of his mouth drew up into a smile.

* * *

Lysandro made up for Sera's missed dinner the next day with a sumptuous breakfast served at her bedside, with fresh eggs, sizzling bits of bacon with ripened tomatoes, oranges, and warm bread. This morning, the stretches of silence were softer, more comfortable.

After she'd had her fill, she reached for the book she had placed on the table beside her pillow. Then she grimaced and put it back down again.

Lysandro cocked his head. "Is the story not to your liking?"

"I like it fine," she answered, "but the medicine makes the words swim on the page."

After a moment's thought, Lysandro picked up the book and found her place. Sera laid her head back onto the pillow as he began to read. A few pages in, Lysandro felt her fingers brush against his at the edge of the bed. He intertwined them with his own as he tried to keep his voice even.

The better part of an hour had passed when Lysandro noticed that Sera had fallen asleep. Seeing her delicate features in repose, with her hair radiating outward onto the silken pillow, Lysandro was struck by the portrait of her, like a sleeping princess locked in the topmost room of the tower, dreaming in vain of someone worthy to come and awaken her heart.

She had given him so many chances to win her love, and he'd squandered them all. He had not proved strong enough, honest enough. Brave enough.

He dared to stroke her brow with the pad of his thumb. Still she did not wake. A lump formed in his throat, and fresh sorrow seared his eyes. He had failed her. If she returned to Mirêne with the doge, her heart would stay locked away, lost to him forever. Without her, he would wither and die. She deserved so much from him, that the truth was the very least of it. He had to tell her.

* * *

After what felt like an eternity, Seraphine's eyes fluttered open. Lysandro felt his heart might stop before she noticed. At last her brow crinkled, and she looked down at her hands and unfolded the Shadow of Theron's mask laid across her lap. She turned her eyes to his.

"I never meant to lie to you. Never to you. But when I heard you crying that day, after that terrible conversation with your father...I hated being the cause of your tears. I couldn't leave you like that. I just couldn't."

Sera was listening, intently so, but she made no move to respond.

"Say something. Are you angry still, or...disappointed?"

He'd said it—his worst fear was laid out before her. He held his breath as he waited for her to reply.

She looked unsure of what to say. What she did *not* look was surprised.

"You *knew?* But h-how did you...how *long* did you—"

Sera scrunched her face. "I did warn you, that I am particularly observant."

Lysandro covered his face with his hands. His mind raced through all the moments they had shared. She had known full well who he was when he had refused to reveal himself. Even when she begged.

Oh Gods...

"I can do better," he promised. "I can be better." He couldn't keep the pleading out of his voice. He didn't try.

"I knew who you were, but I didn't understand why you wouldn't tell me. I didn't know if you...if you meant..."

He searched her eyes. They began to glisten, and her words got tangled in her throat.

Understanding sunk him like a stone. How could he have been so stupid?

"I meant *every* word. Seraphine...I am madly in love with you."

Sera released her breath. He hadn't realized until then that she'd been holding it. His gaze swept over her face with a pained expression. She looked so lovely it hurt.

"You're so beautiful, Sera. So beautiful. I can't think straight whenever you're near. I was too afraid to tell you my heart. I didn't think you'd want me."

He blew out a heavy breath, the burden of holding it all in lifted from him and replaced by an overwhelming dread. A tremor rippled through him as Sera released her hold on his mask and pressed her palm to his cheek. His eyes closed heavily at her touch, trying to imprint the sensation on his skin before it faded forever. He bit his lip.

"It was your eyes," she said.

He opened them to her again, his irises clouded with confusion.

"Your eyes gave you away. Their soft, gentle gray. Those streaks of blue like lightning."

His heart tumbled over itself as he took in her words. His brain stopped working altogether when she pulled on him, bringing him dangerously close.

"The way that the Shadow...the way *you* make me feel...I couldn't bear that it might not be real. I love you Lysandro. But I want *all* of you, not just pieces at a time."

He took in a sharp breath. Had he heard right? Impossible. Lovesickness had addled his mind.

His skin tingled at the feel of her fingers roving in his hair, beckoning him to her as she covered his mouth with her own.

Lysandro lost all semblance of himself and fell headlong into her kiss, taking her lips between his own and telling her everything he could not with words. Wanting burned bright and undeniable between them. He surrendered his soul to her, wrapping strands of her hair around his finger and clasping her tight, refusing to let even a sliver of light pass between them.

He could have lived in her embrace forever, if not for his lungs and their stubborn demand for air. He denied them as long as he could. But they were traitors both.

He and Sera parted, but still he held her, pressing his forehead to hers.

"Marry me?"

He reached for her hands and pressed little kisses to her fingertips. She trembled ever so slightly against him and inhaled with a shudder.

"Will you be my bride, Sera?"

She gave a subtle nod. It wasn't enough.

"Will you?"

"Yes," she whispered.

"Yes?" he pressed, tasting her sweetness again, drawing it out of her. "Yes?"

Her cheeks were flush from their passion, her lips turned a rich berry pink that made them all the more enticing.

She reached for him, but he pulled away and let his mouth fall to the crook of her neck. His lips brushed against her porcelain throat, traveling tortuously slow to the hollow behind her ear. His voice was deep and desperate in her ear.

"Say you will, Seraphine. Say you'll be mine. Please."

"Only if you kiss me again."

He obliged. Grasping at her hair, he plundered her mouth, seeking with every inch to be near her, to become a part of her.

"I am yours, Lysandro," she said at last. "You were right, that day in the museum. You *are* my everything."

His smile was too big for his face. "And you're mine. On my soul, I will never hide anything from you again." Lysandro pulled her upright on the bed wrapped his arms around her, burying his grin in her hair.

Sera beckoned at his lips. "Did I say you should stop?"

Lysandro's blood reached a fever pitch.

"My sincerest apologies. It won't happen again."

They were thoroughly enmeshed when Rafael swung open the door.

"I see you're feeling better."

They pulled apart instantly.

"I really don't like you," Sera said.

"No. I suspect you don't."

"We're going to be married!" Lysandro cried.

Rafael grinned. "Let me be the first to offer my congratulations! You deserve every happiness." He shook Lysandro's hand, then pulled him into an embrace. "Now let's have a look at the bride, shall we?" He unbound Sera's ankle, and found it returned to its normal size.

"That looks much better. How does it feel?"

"Like I can get out of this bed."

"Wait a while, yet." He rotated her ankle, watching her face to see if any pain registered. She only looked mildly uncomfortable. "You're on the mend, but I wouldn't rush it. If the night is clear, maybe you can take her for a short walk in the garden after dinner."

Lysandro nodded with enthusiasm.

"Alright." Rafael raised an eyebrow. "I'll leave you to it then."

Sera narrowed her eyes, but Lysandro only let out a sigh of relief. "I thought he'd never leave." He leaned over again to kiss her, but she stopped him with an index finger pressed to his lips. He groaned.

"I want to know what the Shadow of Theron knows."

Lysandro's expression shifted.

"Everything."

When Lysandro finished, she knit her brows together, and didn't say anything for a long time.

"I didn't mean to kill them," he said.

Sera cocked her head. "Yes you did."

And just like that, she'd gotten right to the heart of what was eating at him.

"I did," he admitted. "In that moment, anyway. But Marek is the one who deserves it. They were just following him."

She gave him a hard look. "Marek was not the only murderer on the beach that night."

He grunted.

"They would have killed you?"

"Yes."

"Would you prefer to be dead?"

Lysandro stilled. It was that simple. Even if it didn't feel like it. "No."

She shrugged. "Nothing to feel sorry for then."

"I suppose not," he said with a sigh.

Her gaze softened, and she reached up to stroke his hair. He leaned into the caress. "It makes me love you all the more, though."

"Say it again," he pleaded.

"I love you."

He expected her to say more on the matter of Marek. She was whip smart, and he was keen to know what she thought. He was disappointed, but not surprised, that her first instinct was to ask a question.

"What happens now?"

"The chief magistrate has called for the Shadow to come forward and to offer proof of Marek's calumny."

"You should."

His eyebrows shot up into his hairline.

"He must not have the blade with him, or he would have already used it. This may be your best chance to stop him while it's out of his reach."

"But if I reveal myself, you'll be even more of a target. *And* Sancio. *And* my father. I won't take that risk."

"You don't have to."

"But didn't you just say I should unmask myself and—"

She cut him off with a wave of her hand. "I didn't say that."

Lysandro blinked.

"But will the chief magistrate accept that?"

"I'm sure you'll find a way to convince him. But you have to convince everyone *else* that you are the Shadow."

An image flashed across Lysandro's mind. He smiled, relieved to find a path through the current morass that would satisfy Aleksander and preserve his privacy. "You're quite clever."

"Mmm. Now where were we?"

"Here, I think." He pressed a tender kiss to her lips.

"Not quite," she whispered.

"Here, then." Lysandro parted her lips with his tongue, taking in more of her sweetness until it coated the back of his throat.

She gave a soft sigh, her breath slipping between his lips as they parted from hers. "You're getting closer."

"How much closer shall I get?"

The sultry challenge in her eyes made his hair stand on end.

"GODS, YOU LOOK GOOD."

Lysandro adjusted his attire as he readied himself to appear before the chief magistrate. He pulled her into a kiss with a gloved hand, encircling her waist and cupping the back of her neck. She was magnificently flush when he finally surfaced.

"Are you sure?" she asked. "About your father?"

Lysandro nodded. "He'll tell everyone who's willing to listen."

"If you say so."

"I'll be back soon," he said to her and Rafael as he mounted Hurricane and rode off into the twilight.

Out of the corner of his eye, Rafael saw Sera wrap her arms around herself, her eyes creased with worry.

"He'll be fine," he assured her. "The Goddess walks with him."

There was a long silence before she answered. "I know."

26

ELIAS COULDN'T STOP SMILING.

"I'm thrilled for you, Lysandro. Positively thrilled." He gripped his son firmly by the shoulders and pressed a kiss to either cheek.

"Thank you. Although your reaction is not in the least bit surprising."

Elias smirked. "I didn't make it easy for you, I know. But I was just so eager for you to be happy."

Lysandro beamed, his joy genuine. "I am."

"And now," Elias laughed, "with the question of your marriage settled, think of all the time we'll have to talk of other things!"

"Like Marek's trial, for instance," Lysandro replied.

"I couldn't believe that you'd miss it."

"I never intended to. But I needed to sort things out with Sera first."

"And are they sorted now?"

That brilliant smile again. "Better than I could have possibly imagined."

"I'm so glad. So *very* glad. You'll stay for dinner of course. But wait— where is the dear girl? Why didn't you bring her?"

"She wanted to come but was unable. There'll be time enough for that later."

"Yes of course." Elias was anxious to know his daughter-in-law, and to acquaint himself with the *taste* of her cooking this time, rather than just the smell of it.

"About Marek," Lysandro said as he took his customary seat at the table.

"So much has come out already. Really damning stuff. I had no idea Sancio was so involved. Did you?"

Lysandro's head snapped up. "How do you mean?"

"He gave the most remarkable account of Marek's movements. He claimed to have *been there* the night the window was shattered. He said Marek had done that, and that he was the one stealing from the temples. I know you hate Marek, but did you have any idea?"

Lysandro answered in a low voice. "No."

Elias shook his head. "Our town is too small for such dark, wild things." He put a bit of pork into his mouth and chewed.

"Where do things stand now?"

"There are many more who wish to speak against him. But what everyone's really waiting for is to see if the Shadow will appear and give truth to Sancio's claims. You'll come to the courthouse tonight, won't you?"

"I'm afraid not," Lysandro sighed. "I have a marriage contract to settle."

Elias's eyebrows shot into his silvering hairline. "Shouldn't I be present?"

"No. This is something I need to do on my own."

"But...surely that can wait?"

Lysandro flashed his father a wry smile. "After all your complaining, you wish to wait longer for me to be wed?"

Elias had no answer.

A smile crept up Lysandro's lips, reaching his eyes. "Nor do I."

Elias made his way to the courthouse to hear the last testimony of the day before court adjourned. He kept his distance from Aleksander, as had become his habit. Though his friendship with the chief magistrate was no secret, he suspected that Aleksander's refusal to visit with him was a matter of propriety, and he respected that absolutely.

This evening it was less of a chore. He was brimming with Lysandro's good news, and shared the announcement of his upcoming nuptials with everyone within earshot. Only when he was surrounded by the curious and their questions did he realize that the girl's own family was absent, and that perhaps he had overstepped his bounds. He attempted to withdraw himself tactfully.

"Well, I'm sure Lysandro will tell you all about it himself when he returns."

"He won't be here, you mean? I thought that he of all people would be present for this," Montes replied.

"Not today I'm afraid. Love waits for no man."

Montes took his seat as the chief magistrate approached his place and summoned yet another local man to tell of Marek's utter disregard for his troubles with thieves. Though the man was vociferous in his speech, Elias became distracted by the sound of thunder approaching. It was a peculiar storm, acute in its intensity, and seemingly headed for the courthouse.

Elias glanced over his shoulder, and noticed that others seated in the back rows were doing the same. He wasn't imagining it; something was racing toward them. As it came nearer, Elias discerned the clack of hooves on cobblestones.

A terrible black beast burst through the doors of the courthouse. Men and women screamed; the chief magistrate jumped to his feet. But Elias sat perfectly still, with the ebony monster breathing down his neck.

Astride the great demon sat the Shadow of Theron. He was covered in black from head to toe, and his wide-brimmed hat cast an ominous shadow over his masked face. He urged the demon forward toward the magistrate.

"You called for me, Honor?"

"So I did. Can you keep that, that—" he waved his finger at the stallion — "*thing* right where it is?"

The Shadow dismounted with ease. He shocked Elias further when he held out the reigns to him.

"Hold him for me, will you Signor?"

That voice.

Elias took the reins offered him without a word, and looked up.

He'd never seen the Shadow of Theron before. Up close, Elias saw his mouth curve into an amused smile. Just like his mother's.

Almighty Arun...

The Shadow moved with that familiar, lithe grace that was

unmistakable. Elias's heart pounded wildly in his chest, but the stallion tugged on his reins, seeking more freedom for his neck, and Elias couldn't give order to his jumbled thoughts.

That boy always did love his horses.

Elias rubbed his chin. His son had known he wouldn't be able to keep his mouth shut. He was too clever by half. All the same, Elias had been right all along; Lysandro wouldn't have missed his chance at Marek for all the brides in the world.

The chief magistrate settled himself in his seat again, and the wooden benches of the gallery creaked as people stretched their necks to gape at the Shadow. But Marek was having none of it.

"What good is the word of a man who hides his face?" he raged.

"Were my identity known, my loved ones would be in the gravest danger." The Shadow pulled a small slip of paper from his clothes and extended it to the chief magistrate. "This should satisfy you."

Aleksander unfurled the paper, read it, and almost fell out of his chair. "Th-this can't...I mean—"

The Shadow dipped his head lazily to the side. "Honor? Are you convinced?"

Aleks cleared his throat and nodded.

"If you please, then."

He seemed to return to his senses. "Of course." He rolled the parchment up and fed it to the candle burning at the corner of his desk.

"This is outrageous!" Marek screamed. "How can you expect—"

"Oh, *shut up* Marek! If you have a problem with the way I do things, take it up with the Chief Magistrate."

The gallery shook in raucous laughter. Marek looked ready to erupt.

"The Shadow of Theron has entrusted me with his identity, and his proofs are beyond doubt. I will hear him."

Elias listened as the Shadow recounted in horrifying detail all he had seen, and how close he had come to death. When he came to his near-fatal encounter with a shard of Argoss's Blood Sword, Aleksander interrupted him.

"Careful now—to be struck by the Blood Sword of Argoss and survive is something only Theron has done. Do you realize what it is you say?"

There was a pregnant pause as the Shadow considered his answer. When his voice came, it was clear as a bell.

"I do, and I did."

The villagers trembled at his response, muttering prayers and stretching their palms upward to the heavens. Elias sat still as a stone, his mind racing too fast for him to make any sense of anything.

"Lies!" Marek cried. "What of my office? Ask him of that!"

Aleksander turned to the Shadow. "Did you destroy the magistrate's office?"

"I did."

"Ha! You see?!"

The Shadow of Theron spread his arms to either side of him. "I will gladly rebuild it with my own hands when you appoint someone worthy of it."

Subtle though it was, Aleksander narrowed his eyes at the implication. He *had* been the one to appoint Marek, after all.

"I'll be right next to you!" Stefano shouted, standing on his feet.

The whole village joined in the chorus.

When the Shadow made to depart, he turned to see bowed heads as he walked back to his horse.

"I am not Theron," he chided them in a crisp tone.

Elias's blood pumped furiously in his veins.

I have to tell him.

Their heads rose in admiration as he took back the reins of his steed.

"Thank you, Signor," he said, touching the brim of his hat in a sign of respect.

Elias swallowed hard, too choked with the pride and terror warring inside him to speak.

The Shadow of Theron mounted the great beast, wheeled him around with ease, and disappeared.

FOR THE FIRST TIME, LOTHAN DUG IN HIS HEELS WHEN IT WAS TIME TO return to his cell.

"No! *No!*" he roared.

With a final shove, Aleksander and Gareth broke Lothan's iron grip on the bars and locked the door as he stumbled to the floor of his prison.

Aleksander pulled an old handkerchief out of his pocket, no more than a rag now, and mopped the sweat from his forehead.

"That was something, wasn't it?" Gareth asked. "I've never been much for religion, but…"

Aleksander nodded. When he woke up that morning with a stiff neck and a curse on his lips, he never would have guessed that the trial would take such an unbelievable turn. Never in a million years would he have believed that his best friend's mild-mannered son, a boy he'd known for ages, would be at the center of it. He couldn't make sense of that at all.

"Guess Marek's not the magistrate anymore," Gareth said, shaking Aleksander from his own thoughts.

"You still want his job, eh?"

"You can hardly do worse."

The man had a point.

"Look, I get it. I'm not your first choice. But I've been a help to you, haven't I? You could at least put in a good word for me with whoever you do pick. I'm not likely to be welcome to stay otherwise."

Aleksander saw something reflected in the man's face then that he hadn't expected to find there—a reminder of a much younger man.

"Nothing is set yet," he said.

Gareth nodded and was about to say something else when there was a knock at the door.

"Expecting company?"

"No," Aleksander answered, drawing his sword from his belt.

Gareth followed behind him with nothing but his bare hands.

What now? Aleksander thought as he made his way to the front office. Bad enough that he had a thieving, murdering bastard of Argoss in a cell, and had the unpleasant task of figuring out which of Lothan's officers knew of it. He didn't need them banging down the doors before the Aruni claimed him.

The knocking came again, more insistent this time.

Murderers don't knock.

"Aleks? Are you in there?"

He swung the door open wide at the sound of his wife's voice.

"Caterina! You're here!"

"Of course I'm here. Have you eaten yet?"

Just like her. Feed him first, *then* berate him for leaving her behind. He smiled.

"I've missed you."

"Naturally. That's why we came."

"*We?*"

"I wasn't going to leave the girls *by themselves*." She looked over her shoulder as the girls followed with baskets of bread and wine and roasted chickens on their arms.

"Caterina, allow me to introduce Gareth. He's helping me out here. Gareth, these are my wife and daughters, Carmen and Ilisa."

Gareth's eyes fell on Carmen.

"She's your daughter?"

"I just said that, yes."

Gareth nodded. "She would be."

Aleksander raised an eyebrow, but said nothing.

"Come inside girls, this is no place for you to be." He herded his family away from the line of cells. "Go and get yourselves settled. I'll be right in."

The women cast furtive looks at Lothan, but shielded their eyes just as quickly from his quiet madness and moved into the judge's quarters to lay the table.

Aleksander approached Gareth. "Will you be alright on your own for a bit?"

"Fine," Gareth answered. "Don't know about that guy though."

They both turned to consider Marek, shivering and incoherent.

"Should we do something?" Gareth asked.

"Like what?"

"I don't know. Call the surgeon?"

"What for? He only does that when he's in here. And besides, he's a dead man no matter what we do."

"Mm. It's odd though, isn't it?"

Aleksander shrugged and went to join his wife.

Gareth stood guard at a distance, staring at his ward with open curiosity.

After a time, Carmen emerged, carrying a plate of food.

"We thought you might be hungry."

He turned his head to the side and grunted.

Her shoulders slumped. "You could at least say 'thank you.'"

He grunted again and kept his eyes on the floor.

"Is there a reason you won't look at me?"

He said nothing. Carmen left the plate on the table with a sigh and turned to go.

"I never know what to say…" Gareth called after her.

She turned. "Excuse me?"

"I never know what to say around pretty girls."

"Oh."

He looked at her then. Gareth approached the meal she had brought for him and picked up the bread, stuffing it into his mouth. He swallowed hard, then took another mouthful. The conversation was over.

"You're welcome," she said.

Gareth grunted.

Sera was on him before Lysandro even dismounted.

"Oh, thank Faelia. What took you?"

"I wasn't gone that long," Lysandro answered. "It's a lot to tell. Glad you're feeling better."

Sera ignored him. "Marek could have killed you."

"The Aruni will kill *him* as soon as the chief magistrate hands him over. It is as you said. He doesn't have the Blood Sword."

"Still."

Lysandro tilted his head. "Weren't you the one who told me I should do this?"

"I know!" She pressed her head to his chest. "I just…"

Lysandro wrapped his arms around her and stroked the back of her head. "I know, love. I know. I'm here now."

"Don't do that again. Even if I tell you to."

Lysandro chuckled and kissed her hair. "Alright." He inclined his head toward Hurricane. "I've got to stable him. Come with me?"

He took Sera by the hand and led her to a darkened corner of his sprawling house, where there was a smaller stable that looked to be original to the building. Hurricane entered his stall without a fuss and took the carrots that Lysandro offered him. When Lysandro suggested that Sera try feeding him, she declined.

"He won't bite you."

"Tell *him* that."

Lysandro laughed. "He's saved my life more than once."

Sera seemed to reconsider the animal. "He's just as terrifying as I remember him. But I'm glad you have him."

They left the stable and entered the room where Lysandro transformed into the Shadow of Theron, and where he often slept after venturing out into the night.

"I've wanted to show you this for the longest time," he said. The dark stone floor and wrought-iron fixtures were so very different from the appointments of the rest of the house. "I wanted you to know me. I'm so sorry it took so long for us to get here."

Sera tugged on the front of his shirt, pulling him down to her in a warm embrace. "You're forgiven," she murmured. She slipped her thumb under the mask and tossed it to the floor. Lysandro's dark hair fell across his shoulders.

"You can't know how long *I've* wanted to do that."

Lysandro pulled her close, pressing her body to his and feeling her soft curves. He noticed immediately that they felt closer than usual. He broke from their kiss and stared into the fathoms of her eyes.

"Seraphine…what are you—"

She interrupted him with another fervent kiss. His pulse quickened as her fingers fiddled with his belt. Lysandro pulled her hands up to his lips and kissed her knuckles.

"Sera. Sweetheart. We're not—"

"You have my promise, and I have yours."

"But—"

"Where has the rogue who climbed my window gone? I was hoping he would make love to me tonight."

With a shrug of her shoulders, her dark robe drifted down around her, leaving only a thin nightdress. Lysandro could make out the shape of her full breasts through the gauzy ivory.

He swallowed, his throat suddenly dry as a desert. Sera stretched up on her toes to kiss him. When her tongue slipped possessively into his mouth, his resistance evaporated.

His tongue rose to meet hers as he cupped the back of her neck. Sera did away with his hat, and pulled the gloves from his hands one finger at a time. A growl escaped him when she undid the clasp of his belt and whipped it around his hips in one swift motion and sent it clattering to the floor. His mouth gravitated downward at her body's insistence; she sighed at the soft strokes of his lips and tongue along her collarbone and the tops of her breasts. He dampened her nightdress as he took her nipples into his mouth through the veil of fabric. When he sucked, the sound of his name became an urgent prayer on her lips.

He got down on his knees, pressing kisses to her navel and between her thighs. Lysandro's lust spiked as she clutched his hair.

In a surprise move, he gripped her by the bottom and tossed her off her feet. She landed with a yelp on a bed laid with lush, dark furs. A grin spread across his lips.

"Screaming already, Signorina?"

The smile vanished as he felt the warm press of her fingertips beneath his shirt, relieving him of it. He licked his lips and lifted Sera's shift up over her head. He drank in the sight of her.

"So beautiful," he murmured.

Her cheeks turned a glorious shade of pink.

"I love making you blush."

Her flush deepened as his voice thrummed in her ears.

"Just like that." He nuzzled her warmed cheeks and kissed the tip of her nose as their skins collided, and Lysandro nestled himself between her hips.

Sera drew in a sharp breath as he thrust forward. He froze, and his eyes questioned her.

She clapped her hand on the back of his neck. "Don't stop."

He turned his head to press a kiss to her palm, and began to move in slow, gentle strokes, earning every precious inch. Sera's breathing eased as their hips met, and their mouths collided, eager and wanting as they found a tantalizing rhythm. She dug her knees into his flanks, spurring him onward.

When her desire became too much to bear, Sera turned him onto his back without breaking their stride. She pulled at his very soul with every grazing of their bodies. He rose to answer her call until there was nothing left of him that wasn't hers. When she sat upright, he beheld a sublime view of her nakedness, shimmering by candlelight. Her golden red hair floated in and out of his vision in undulating waves. His hands explored her curves in the darkness. He gripped her hips, then let his hands travel up her slender waist to her breasts. She moaned as he cupped her soft flesh; his thumbs drew lazy circles around their tender centers, and he felt a shiver run through her. Her hips ground into him more surely. She ran her fingers through the dusting of hair on his lower abdomen leading to his sex, calling out to him as her crisis unraveled her. She collapsed on top of him, bringing her nose down to the crook of his neck.

Lysandro flipped her over. Freshly tumbled and panting for breath beneath him, she'd never looked so perfect. He had to be nearer, closer, deeper. He cradled her bottom in his hands and dug and dug and dug and dug until he cried out. Sweet release buzzed through him. The tension in his muscles dissolved, and he drifted down to her, nestling against her collarbone to soothe his frazzled heart.

"I love you Seraphine," he murmured against her glistening skin.

He withdrew with a shudder and settled on his belly, lifting his arm to let Sera in as she wriggled into his embrace, their noses touching. The sweet smell of earth mingled with the fresh night air and the rosewater perfume of her hair. Lysandro closed his eyes to take it in, and let sleep come.

27

Dawn roused them. Lysandro rolled onto his back as Sera stretched herself across the broad planes of his chest. He traced the length of her spine with the gentle brush of his fingertips.

"You smell so good," Sera said, drawing in a deep breath.

Lysandro couldn't help but smile. "Do I?"

"Mmm. I smell fresh-cut grass, and warm spices. Is that... juniper, in your soap?"

Lysandro raised an eyebrow. "Mmhmm."

"Hm. It's comforting."

He wrapped his arms tighter around her, and she pressed her cheek into the notch in his throat.

Sera's fingers traced a furtive path over the darkened line of flesh on his bicep, the site where his life had leeched out of him, and almost didn't come back.

"Does it hurt?"

He caressed the worry from her face with the pad of his thumb. "It's only a dull pain, but it goes right through me."

She withdrew quickly and kissed a spot lower down on his arm.

"I have my strength back now. And I have you."

Sera smiled. "Yes you do," she said, and brought her mouth to his. Lysandro ran his fingers through her hair, bringing her closer.

"Will you come someplace with me this morning?" he asked when they parted. "We could bring a lunch."

"Of course. Should I make us something?"

"You don't *have* to…"

Sera's eyebrows shot up, and he laughed.

"Would you *like* me to make something?"

"Oh please."

"Then I will. Do you have any requests?"

Lysandro shook his head. "Surprise me."

Sera's eyes took on a seductive glint. "I thought I already did."

"Oh, you did." He kissed her again, with more fire in his belly.

She nuzzled his nose and stirred to rise, but he clutched her tight, and pressed their bodies together.

"Not yet. Let me hold you just a little while longer."

It was late in the morning when Lysandro helped Sera up to his mare's saddle and settled in behind her.

"She's a much milder horse," Lysandro assured her. "She'll let you lead her."

"I don't really know what I'm doing," Sera confessed.

"I never would have guessed. You were so poised on Hurricane," he teased.

"He was going faster than I could think."

Lysandro laughed. "You get used to it."

"*You* get used to it."

"I could teach you, if you like."

They traveled at a leisurely pace, the gentle sun shining down on them like a warm caress.

"Here," he said, offering her the reins. "I'm right behind you if you need me."

It left Lysandro's hands free to roam. He temped her with light touches to her hips and thighs until they reached a gated garden leading to a sprawling structure of white stone—a Faelian temple.

Sera realized why he'd brought her as Lysandro leapt down from the horse and gripped her by the waist to help her down.

"You didn't need to do this first thing in the morning, Lysandro."

He looked at her with earnest affection. "Yes I did. My promise is genuine. I need you to know that."

She traced the fine lines of his cheek with her fingertip. "It's beautiful," she said.

"I come here sometimes when my prayers are not suited to Arun."

Lysandro retrieved a roll of papers from his saddle bag, then walked with Sera, fingers entwined, to the portico at the front of the L-shaped complex.

A tall woman with silver threaded through her chocolate brown hair came out to greet them.

"Good morning to you both. How might the Goddess assist you today?"

"Good morning. I'm Don Lysandro de Castel, and this is Signorina Seraphine Alvaró. We wish to be married."

"Splendid. Come with me, please." She led them around the porticoed outer walkway to the back of the temple, covered in exquisitely manicured gardens.

"It's too pleasant to go inside. For such a joyous occasion, we should revel in the beauty of Faelia's creation. Don't you agree?" The priestess gestured to a circular stone stable surrounded by benches and took a seat opposite the couple. She pulled a small pair of wired spectacles from her robes and adjusted them on her face.

"Now then, let's see."

She held out her hand, into which Lysandro placed his papers. Seraphine went quiet.

"She will gain half of my estate, which includes my residence in Lighura and the adjoined lands, the ancestral de Castel holdings upon inheritance from my father Don Elias de Castel, and its lands, and the attendant annual income. In the event of my death, full possession will revert to her. She will have the power to grant inheritance on any children we may have however she sees fit.

"Fine." The priestess looked to Sera.

"Um...can we have a minute in private?"

"Yes of course. Take as long as you need."

Lysandro followed Sera as she moved to a corner of the garden overtaken with creeping vines covered with pale blue blossoms. He looked down to find her wringing her hands.

"What's the matter?"

"Lysandro, I don't have…my father can't—"

He stopped her right there.

"Am I here with your father? Or mine, for that matter?"

Sera stopped fidgeting and looked up into his eyes. They looked so perfect in the sunshine.

"This is between you and me. I'm giving you everything because I want you to have it. I don't want you to have to ask if you need anything. And, if something happens to me, you'll be protected." He cupped her face in his hands. "I don't want anything. Only you."

The gleam in her eyes softened around the edges.

"That was a lot better than the first time you asked."

"Oh Sera. I'll spend forever trying to make that up to you."

Sera wiped her face and returned to her seat at the table. "Can I put down my undying love and fidelity?" she asked.

Lysandro smiled, as did the priestess.

"That's lovely."

The priestess affixed her signature with a practiced flourish, then turned the contract over to Lysandro and Sera. She looked over the details of the wealth Lysandro was conferring to her. With a saucy expression, she said, "You forgot the theater box."

Lysandro shot her a sideways glance.

They inked their names at the bottom, then the Faelian rose to her feet.

"My sincerest congratulations to you both. We have a section of the garden set aside for wedding feasts. Come."

She showed them a wide open plain with enough room to host the whole town, bordered by flowering trees that decorated the ground with delicate pink petals.

Lysandro folded their fingers together and squeezed; it was the sort of wedding he'd always wanted.

With their marriage contract signed and the date of the ceremony set, they left the temple and found a secluded cove to lay out their picnic.

Sera had only been an hour or so in the kitchen, but still she amazed with pies stuffed with meat, potatoes, and bits of pungent, melty cheese that fit in the palm of Lysandro's hand. She'd even made bite-sized cakes, filled with elderberry jam and finished with an elegant, shimmering glaze.

Lysandro let his mind wander to the future as he filled his stomach.

"We can hire more staff for the house, if you like."

"What for?"

"I don't know. I prefer not to use a valet, but if you want a lady's maid, you can have one."

Sera took a swallow of the fruity wine they'd brought with them. "If you can dress yourself just fine, I'm sure you can handle dressing *me* too."

"I foresee a problem with that…"

She laughed at his boyish grin and kissed him.

"Are there any changes you want to make?"

"Like what?"

"You could pick new furnishings, or perhaps different artwork…"

"I like your house."

"Yes but it's *my* house. It's meant to be *our* house. It should reflect both of us."

Sera saw his point. "If I think of something, I'll let you know."

"Thank you." Sera held the last of the little cakes in her hand, soaked with strawberry liqueur and topped with crackled sugar. She had taken the tiniest of nibbles, and left the tantalizing bit in her hand, completely forgotten. It was more than he could stand.

"There's something on your hand."

"Hm?"

She looked down and yelped as Lysandro caught the remainder of the confection in his mouth, and a couple of fingers in the bargain. Her blood pounded as he licked the jam from between her fingers.

"So good."

Sera tried to control the rising heat in her cheeks that accompanied the jolt of desire between her legs, but it was no use. Sera dragged her thumb across his mouth, and Lysandro cast her a wicked smile as he cleaned his lips with his tongue.

"I'll let the tailor know too," he said, frazzling her nerves with the sudden change in

subject. "Whatever you need for the wedding he can put on my bill."

"Oh no. Fabien will murder me if I let anyone else dress me on that day."

Brushing her hands clean, Sera found a grain of sand under her fingernail. She dug it out, flicking it into the sea with disgust.

"I fucking hate sand."

Lysandro laughed out loud.

"I stayed in the Maghreve with Fabien for a month once. Never again. It got *everywhere*."

"Why didn't you say something?"

Sera shrugged.

"Well...do you want to leave?"

"No. It's nice here. It's a nice view." She stood and untied the ribbons on the front of her dress. Lysandro's eyes bulged out of his head.

"What are you doing?!"

Sera made a big show of looking around, and stretched her arms out to either side of her. "There's *no one* here." She cupped her hand to her mouth. "Hello! Anybody out there? I'm taking off my dress now!"

Lysandro tried to shush her, but was stymied by his own nervous laughter.

She pulled the dress over her head and tossed it onto the blanket, leaving only a thin shift of plain white. She looked down at Lysandro's stunned face and smirked.

"Are you coming or not?"

The sea was a cool crystal blue. After swimming in the calm waters, they sunned themselves on a nearby outcropping of rock. Gentle waves broke into foam at their feet.

Lysandro rolled onto his side to admire Sera as she napped, her hair drenched and her white shift floating almost translucent around her. She looked like a siren that had been caught unawares in her private pleasure.

He leaned over her and woke her with a kiss. Her eager response stirred him, and he peeled her soaked dress away from her skin to cup her breast.

She moaned into his mouth. Desire raced down his spine until he trembled with it. On impulse, Lysandro pushed her dress hurriedly up to her waist. He needed her—now. He slid effortlessly into her as a bracing wind raced across his back. Lysandro made love to her with brisk abandon, the growing warmth between them rising to a searing heat. When she raked her fingers through his hair, he felt like a god. She opened her eyes to him, and he was overcome.

"You're all I've ever wanted."

Their mingled cries echoed into the sea.

ASHA SURVEYED THE DAMAGE LYSANDRO HAD DONE TO THE CLIFFSIDE. IT was an impenetrable wall of fallen granite.

"Do you see a way in?" she asked.

Eugenie couldn't see any weak points. She chose instead to follow the sound of whispering that tormented her at night. It led back up the hill to the roof of the cave, where the insidious voice was the strongest. She scanned the ground.

"There," she said.

The place she pointed to looked like little more than a rabbit's burrow. But when Asha put her full weight on it, the hollow fell in on itself, and they were able to slip down into the space below.

The setting sun did not follow them. Eugenie sensed a powerful malice through the void. The voice was louder and more insistent than ever.

"Asha," she whispered, grasping blindly for her in the dark.

"Shhh!"

Eugenie felt a firm grip on the front of her robe. Asha pulled her close into her own shadow.

Asha's body had gone stiff, and Eugenie heard her sword scrape out of its scabbard.

The twilit wind whipped across the opening above their heads, and produced an unnaturally high whistle, like a wind blown straight from the mouth of an icy hell.

Just as the contours of the cave began to take shape, the shadows to their left seemed to darken. The blackness assumed a solid form, edged in a deep purple mist. The small hairs on the back of her neck stood on end.

"Asha!"

Asha swung her weapon fast and high. It collided with the wall in a shower of sparks, and something unseen fell to the floor with a crack.

The whispering stopped.

"Give me the lantern," Eugenie insisted, fumbling with the light tied to Asha's belt and opening the slats.

A skeleton in rags lay toppled at Asha's feet. Just beyond it was the head, snapped clean off.

Eugenie watched the skull teeter on the ground. As it stilled, she saw a blackened tongue loll out.

She shut her eyes to it, pressing her lids together tight.

"You alright?" Asha asked.

She opened her eyes. The tongue was gone, the skull devoid of life.

"Fine," Eugenie answered.

Asha pivoted her head in every direction, but found no further enemies. The lantern cast long shadows on Eugenie's face.

"You've got to eat something Gin."

"You know I can't."

"I know you *won't*. But you'll end up like him if you keep this up." Asha jutted her chin toward the crumpled skeleton.

Eugenie didn't like her reflection in the mirror any more than Asha did. But it was what Morgasse demanded of her to keep Her sight, and she couldn't stop now. Not with the next turn of the wheel so close. She could feel it creeping along her veins.

Eugenie swept the light before them, illuminating slivers of the cave at a time. There was not much to speak of; it was an ordinary cave with some larger calcium formations. A few feet ahead of them was a circular depression in the dirt, littered with desiccated snake skins. They glowed a bright blood-red, crisscrossed with a black and white diamond pattern shriveled in decay along the scales. Asha stretched out a tentative hand.

"Don't touch them. The poison is housed in the skin," Eugenie said.

"Why eldur vipers? Or is it snakes in general?"

"Eldur vipers are believed to draw the power of their venom from Anruven.

"So...Anruven is the volcano?"

Eugenie shook her head. "He dwells *inside* the volcano."

Asha crouched down to get a better look.

"He is a hungry god. According to his followers, he demanded a constant flow of sacrifices. When the volcano erupted, it was understood as a sign that Anruven was making the world over to reflect the desires of his devotees, and overwhelming their enemies with rivers of blood. But the cult of Anruven shrouded themselves in mystery. The only records we have of them are the one or two written by our priestesses. It might all be conjecture."

"But what use would Marek have of such things?"

"Perhaps Lothan and his followers believe that if they are bitten and survive, they can draw on that power. A sign of their bastardy, perhaps?"

"But that's to do with Anruven, not Argoss."

"I suspect they are greatly confused by the two. Argoss absorbed cult practices into his own sorcery. Without records to distinguish them…"

Asha poked at the darkened skins with her sword. "That's a dangerous game to play."

Eugenie agreed. "Destroying every temple to Anruven in the aftermath of Theron was a fatal blow. Starving him of followers was meant to ensure he could never challenge Morgasse again. Without understanding what he's doing, Marek has the potential to do something catastrophic."

"And this is all in your *Histories*, is it?"

Eugenie nodded.

Asha frowned. "It isn't right."

"Eradicating all memory of Anruven?"

"Keeping secrets from your sisters."

"That was neither my choice nor yours."

"You know what my high priestess told me, before I left? She told me not to trust a Morgassen. That they never say what they mean."

Eugenie shifted on her feet. "Do you feel that way?"

"You've shared your secrets with me. And we're stronger for it. How much stronger would we be if we had a Faelian with us?"

Eugenie shrugged. "Guess you're stuck with me."

"You know I didn't mean it that way."

The stretch between them grew awkward. Asha tried to smooth it over by focusing on something else.

"I can't hold the Aruni back much longer. They want Marek's blood. But *we* need to recover the relics as well. We know Don Lysandro ingested the Sorrow Stones, and Marek still has the shard of Blood Sword hidden somewhere—it's not *here*, right?"

"No," Eugenie confirmed. She hadn't been sure before, but it was clear now. The nauseating power that had drawn her to this place had been the skeleton. With the skull separated from its spine, she could no longer sense its lurking presence. Perhaps tonight, at last, she could rest without fear of nightmares.

"We traced the books," Asha continued. "What else is missing?"

Eugenie closed her eyes and recalled the map marked with all the temples that had been targeted, trying to remember what it was they were forgetting.

The stones, the pages, the shard, and...

"No."

"What?"

Eugenie's eyes bulged. "Nonono—"

"What is it?!"

"He has the Key!"

HIS JAILERS WERE AT IT AGAIN. LOTHAN DIDN'T KNOW WHAT THE ARGUMENT was about this time. He didn't care. They were so absorbed in their own foolishness that by the time Lothan's screams drew their attention, the door to his cell was already open.

They charged him as one. Lothan dropped the Cerulean Key the minute it rasped in the lock. Activated, it was like trying to hold a fireball in the palm of his hand. He channeled the blistering pain into fury and barreled through them. He knocked the smaller one to the ground with a blow from his good arm, then spun as the bigger man came at him. Lothan lunged for the dagger the warden kept at his belt and plunged it right into his throat. The man sank like a stone, clutching at his neck as the life gurgled out of him.

"Fargas," the little one groaned. "Fargas..."

Lothan rolled his eyes and stabbed him in the chest, getting the blade stuck in one of his ribs in the process. He tried to pull it free, but it was no use, so he left it there.

Panting, Lothan ground his teeth. All of this blood, and not one drop of it to slake his own blade's thirst. He had to get it back. That was the first thing. Then he was going to pay Don Lysandro a visit. Lothan pulled a handkerchief from the expired jailer's pocket and soaked it in the blood spilling out of his chest before using it to retrieve the Cerulean Key from the floor. He didn't know what made him think of it, but it eased the agony of handling it. With the bloodied key tucked safely in his pocket, he strode calmly out the front doors of the courthouse and into the empty street.

THE SALTY BREEZE FROM THE SEA CURDLED INTO THE SMELL OF BLOOD. SERA woke with a start at the sudden turning of her dream. But her awakening had not chased the rancid scent from the air.

"Lysandro?"

She quit the bed and ventured down the hallway to her left, guided by the horrid smell. The second door to her right opened onto a small but well-appointed study. She grimaced; she had thought she was walking into the sitting room. Sera realized then how unfamiliar she was with the home that would be hers. But now was not the time to explore. Not when something smelled wrong.

Down the hall, she heard the scraping of metal against metal. Something in its quality turned her insides cold. She quickly eyed her surroundings and lifted a long, sharp letter opener from the desk. She tucked it into her sleeve before entering the hallway again, this time trying the third door down from the left.

Sera found herself in the grand foyer.

She was not alone.

"Lysandro!"

Lothan clucked his tongue as he approached.

"If you wanted someone strong enough to protect you," he chided her in a low, husky voice, "you chose wrong."

He was on her in an instant, too fast for her to use the letter opener. The stench of the charnel house was overwhelming.

His hands were everywhere. Sera struggled to break free, but she couldn't see the source of the smell; she was terrified of twisting in the wrong direction.

"It'll serve that smug sonofabitch right if I take you here in his own house," Lothan growled in her ear. "I'm going to enjoy this."

Sera's elbow connected with his nose, and he lost his grip on her.

Blood seeped from between his fingers as Sera scrambled away from him.

"You're going to regret that," Marek snarled.

Sera screamed for Lysandro again, but before she could reach for the letter opener, a pair of strong hands clapped her on the shoulders and lifted her from behind, away from Marek.

She turned to find Rafael.

"Run!" he cried.

Marek's eyes went white with rage. "*You!* So you didn't know him, eh?"

Rafael's voice shrank. "*Run...*"

"You had no idea!" Marek lunged at him, wrapping his blood-stained fingers around the surgeon's throat.

"I never would have dreamed it was possible. And yet..." He squeezed Rafael hard, turning his face a mottled purple.

Lothan retrieved the dripping sword from his belt and raised it over his head.

Sera hurled the letter opener with deadly accuracy. It pinned back Marek's wrist; Rafael crashed to his knees.

Lysandro raced toward Marek from behind, materializing from another hallway with ungodly speed. With a fierce cry, he raised his sword high over his head and sent it back down again, severing Lothan's hand at the wrist.

Lothan screamed and crumpled to the floor. Gore spurted from the wound at an alarming pace, spraying the foyer with violence.

Lysandro aimed his blade at Marek's heart. But he rolled away at the last second, and the tip of Lysandro's sword cracked the bloodied black and white tiles at his feet.

Behind Lysandro's back, Sera could see the cursed dagger quivering, as if it intended to rise.

"*No!*"

She rushed forward and clawed at Lysandro's knees, dragging him off his feet as the dagger slid across the floor and sought out its master.

Lothan grasped it with the outstretched fingers of his remaining hand. He stumbled to his feet and toward the door.

Lysandro broke free of Sera's restraint. But as he did so, Sera heard a voice she did not recognize.

"Lysandro!" the voice called from beyond the door."Lysandro he's escaped! He's—"

The door swung wide on its hinges to reveal Sancio. He froze in the doorway as he came face-to-face with Marek.

Lothan disappeared into the street behind him. Sancio blinked, holding his intestines in his hands as a crude red line blossomed on his shirt like a devil's grin.

"Sancio!"

Lysandro rushed to him, and Sera made to follow. She was stopped by Rafael's firm grip on her shoulders.

"Help him!" she screamed.

His answer came low in her ears, so only she could hear it. "There's nothing I can do."

LYSANDRO TRIED DESPERATELY TO SHOVE HIS FRIEND'S GUTS BACK INSIDE HIS belly. But no matter how hard he tried, they refused to stay where he put them, and slipped out of the cavity into a mess of bloody coils beside him.

"It's going to be alright," Lysandro stammered. "Just hold on, Sancio."

Blackness crept along his intestines and started to take root inside him. Sancio twitched as the blood in his veins turned to soot.

"Listen to me," Sancio pleaded. "You'll need the thing…the thing that's yours, but that you've never seen."

Tears ran down Lysandro's face. He'd given up putting Sancio back together again, and clasped at his friend's hands.

"What?"

"Ask—"

Sancio blinked, trying to beat back the poison clawing at the whites of his eyes.

"Ask your f-father…"

"Sancio," Lysandro begged. "Brother. Don't go."

Sancio's voice was barely a whisper. "Go. Go be the Hero. The beautiful Hero." He stretched a disintegrating hand up to stroke Lysandro's tear-streaked face.

Lysandro started.

"It's alright," Sancio smiled. "I'm dying anyway."

Lysandro couldn't speak. He could only stare at the boy he'd known forever.

"Ask...E-Elias..."

Sancio's tongue turned to ash in his mouth. Then his eyes.

28

RAFAEL'S HOLD ON SERA FINALLY LOOSENED. SHE CROSSED THE ROOM TO reach Lysandro, kneeling in a puddle of blood and staring at his hands as his friend turned to ash and spilled between his fingers.

"Lysandro..."

She pressed her hand to his shoulder, but he didn't respond.

"He isn't hiding what he is anymore," Rafael said behind her in a tremulous voice. "And now he knows who you are."

Sera shot Rafael a sharp look. He pressed his mouth shut.

"Get Marta in here," she said. "Now."

Rafael rushed to do her bidding.

Sera squeezed Lysandro's shoulder more forcefully, and finally drew his attention.

His eyes snapped to her with wild panic. He scanned every inch of her, frantic to confirm that the blood staining her dress wasn't hers.

"Did he hurt you?!"

"No."

His voice dipped. "Did he *touch* you?"

Sera hesitated a moment, then decided on the truth. "He tried."

Shadows pooled in Lysandro's eyes, but she pressed her forehead to his.

"I'm here," she assured him. "I'm still here."

He wrapped his arms around her tight with his hands fisted behind her back, careful not to soil her clothes with his hands. His grief came in fits and sobs.

"Oh Lysandro. I'm so sorry."

When it seemed like his crying might never end, she whispered softly in his ear. "Come. Come away from here." She pulled him to his feet and guided him to a chair at the far end of the room. His hands were shaking.

Marta screamed when she entered and stretched her hands up to the sky before pulling them close to her heart.

"Marta," Sera murmured, coming to stand beside her. "Marta, I hate to ask you this—can you take care of Don Lysandro's friend?"

"But how can I?" she sobbed. "There's nothing left of him!" She covered her mouth with a handkerchief and wailed.

Sera looked around and spied a painted flower vase on the mantel. She emptied its contents into the hearth and handed Marta the empty vessel.

"There is *something*," she said gently.

Sera knelt between Lysandro's knees as Marta collected what remained of Sancio into the vase and placed it with great care back on the mantel.

Without warning Lysandro shot up from his chair.

"My dad! I have to get to him!"

Sera held his legs tightly, and wrangled him back to his seat.

"Marek won't hurt anyone else tonight," she said.

His mouth gaped in disbelief.

"Lysandro. You cut off his hand. Without someone to help stop the bleeding…" she looked up at him through veiled eyelids. "He'll be dead by morning."

Lysandro looked to Rafael.

"She has the right of it."

I think.

Lysandro took the surgeon at his word. His gaze fell on the severed hand on the floor, its graying fingers stretched upward like a dead cockroach.

"I don't want that…*thing* on my property."

"Right. Shall we…I don't know, throw it into the sea?" Rafael offered.

"Burn it!" Marta cried.

"Yes." Lysandro stood and walked to where it lay.

"Don't touch it," Sera cautioned.

"We can't light it on fire right here," he answered.

Sera's gaze drifted upward as she considered. "Marta, you know that tin in the cupboard where you keep the tea?"

She disappeared into the kitchen. In a moment, she returned with the receptacle and handed it to her master.

Lysandro crouched on the floor, careful not to step in the vermilion pool that had not yet been wiped away. He opened the tin wide on its hingers, laid it out over the hand, then snapped it shut quickly, as if he were caging a tarantula.

Tin in hand, he looked to Rafael and jerked his head in the direction of the garden.

"I'm coming with you," Sera declared.

"You don't—"

"I'm not leaving the two of you alone. Who knows what you'll try."

"She might be right about that," Rafael said.

The men made quick work of hollowing out an out of the way corner of the garden. Lysandro tossed the sullied tin into the pit, and added kindling to feed the fire.

The metal casing glowed a hot red, and slowly began to melt. Then the flames got their first taste of the decaying flesh within. As they did, the smoke curling up into the night sky turned violet, and an alien stench assailed their nostrils. Lysandro spun Sera away from the site, tucking her face into the folds of his coat to shield her from the miasma. He listened to the hissing and popping of the skin. It reminded him of the skeleton he'd encountered at Marek's hideaway and its dark whisperings, and instilled in him the fear that the severed hand before them was more than just dead flesh.

They stood guard over the fire until there was nothing left but charred bits of bone, then resettled the soil. Reentering the house, Lysandro called for a washbasin. As he dipped his hands into the tepid water, turning its contents pink, Sera moved to assist him. He retracted his hands as if he might contaminate her.

"I've got it."

She cupped his face in her hands. "Let me help you."

Lysandro's emotions crashed over him in a great wave, and his eyes grew glassy again.

"Don't mar those beautiful hands with this ...with that man's..."

"I've gutted pigs. This is no worse than that."

He was implacable.

"I am not some celestial being in danger of being tainted, Lysandro."

"You are to me."

"I'm flesh and bone, as are you."

She opened her outstretched hands and waited for Lysandro to place his bloodied fingers inside them. Reluctantly, he did.

His gaze rested on her calm, focused expression. The gentle touch of her hands as she washed the blood away was the only thing stopping him from falling apart.

"Thank you," he murmured. When at last his hands were clean, Lysandro pulled Sera close. "I don't know how he escaped, or how he got in here. But I *will not* let him hurt you."

That's when Sera remembered.

"He had a key."

Lysandro straightened. "That's impossible."

"I *distinctly* heard him turning it in the lock. But something about it sounded...sounded wrong."

She hooked her arms under his shoulders and nestled her head under his chin.

When they finally laid their heads down to rest, Lysandro kept his left arm wrapped snugly around her, and his sword grazing the fingertips at his right. It took some time, but eventually he felt Sera's breathing grow slow and steady against his chest.

He did not sleep.

LOTHAN HOWLED IN AGONY. HE'D BOUND UP THE STUMP OF HIS RIGHT ARM with his shirtsleeve so tightly that he'd lost sensation in it for a while, but now it ravaged him, and he screamed until his throat was raw. He slipped in and out of consciousness, always slapped back awake by the incessant gnawing at the edge of his mangled wrist. The fingers of his right hand were crushed by the binding and would sink back into the flesh if he didn't release them. Or so he felt, no matter how many times he had to remind himself that those fingers were no longer there. But the sensation persisted, and the blinding pain along with it.

The fire in his veins peaked. Lothan was certain that if he didn't unwrap his wound to release the torturous oppression sprawling up his arm it would throttle him. In the back of his mind, he knew that to unleash the flow of blood again would be his demise, but he was heedless to his own counsel. He scrabbled at the blood-soaked fabric with his teeth, mad to be free of the knot now that he'd set his mind to it.

What he saw stilled his crazed mind. In a span of days (or had it been hours?) the bones of Lothan's right hand had reconstituted themselves. The fleshless hand uncurled before him, strung together by sinew alone. He twisted it and made a fist, and shuddered at the foreign feeling of bone scraping against bone. He unclenched his hand again and felt sensation flow down to his pointed fingertips. He didn't recognize the manic laugh that rang out.

His hazy mind shifted its focus to the revelation that de Castel was his nightly tormentor.

That fucking coward.

Lighura's princeling had never challenged him with anything more than words in broad daylight; he only dared to taunt him behind a mask at sundown. But it had all been for naught. Finding Lothan in his own house, de Castel had tried his damnedest to kill him. He had failed.

Marek reached with his left hand into his pocket and found a worn-down pair of leather gloves. He pulled them on quickly before the world went black again.

SANCIO WAS GIVEN THE HONOR OF A WARRIOR'S FUNERAL. HIS PYRE, TOPPED with his ashes and the bloodied remnants of his clothes, was erected right beside the one for High Priestess Beatríz.

Lysandro squeezed Sera's arm as they stood watch. She squeezed right back. She looked up at him and watched the flames flicker on his cheek. He was trying so very hard not to cry.

Anguish and vengeance warred on his face. There had been no sign of Marek, dead or alive, for days. His deputies had scattered. But none of that was enough to settle the village and ease their fears. It wasn't enough to cool Lysandro's rage. She knew she couldn't stop him from hunting Marek down, to the edge of the world if he had to. But the terror of losing him burrowed its way into her heart.

With Sancio's parents dead, Lysandro and Elias were his closest family. Villagers approached them to offer their condolences. Lysandro endured it in a sullen silence until one of the mourners caught his attention—the odd woman who had spoken to him at the Faelsday market. She looked as distraught as he felt, and did a much poorer job of concealing it.

"I didn't know," she pleaded with him.

"Didn't know what?"

He strained to understand her over her sobbing. The other woman with her put her arm around her and tried to lead her away.

"I'm sorry," she said to Lysandro. "Truly. It is a terrible loss."

Lysandro looked again at the smaller, fair woman, at her drawn face.

"Is she alright?" he asked.

Her companion's face became unreadable. Without answering, the pair of them turned away.

Lysandro shifted to face his father.

"I've known him all his life," Elias moaned. "I will miss that little boy sneaking into my cupboards." The thought seemed too much for him, and he gripped Lysandro hard by the shoulders.

"I lost my wife. I don't want to lose my son."

They embraced, and Lysandro could no longer hold back his sorrow. But thinking of Sancio as his father held him sparked his memory.

"He said to ask you."

"What?"

"Before he died, Sancio told me to ask you, about…"

Elias stilled.

"About something that's mine, that I've never seen."

His father stood tall and wiped the tears from his face. "Yes."

The recognition on his father's face startled him. Sancio's dying words had not been a delirium borne of his pain, if his father understood them.

"Go home," Elias said. "Go to the cottage on the southeastern edge of your land."

Lysandro shook his head. "There's no—"

"*Go*," Elias urged him. "Bring me what you find."

* * *

Lysandro had never seen another house on his property, however small. This corner of his land was thick with overgrowth, almost completely returned to the wild. He found the twisted trunk of a fallen tree and sat down to rest, trying to calm his mind. He filled his lungs with clean, sweet air and stared into the sunlight, wondering how he could be so happy, and yet so full of sorrow. The prospect of marrying Sera without Sancio there sharpened the ache in his chest.

A glint of metal caught his eye. It was the brass hinge of a door, set into a very wide, very tall tree. The door was covered in moss. There was no sign or carving to indicate who had lived there. It just was. His heart pounded in his chest as he opened the door.

He took in the entire room in a glance. It was full of ordinary things being steadily overtaken by mold and greenery. A ladder led up to a small, plain bed covered in dust. Beside it on the floor was a thick handsewn book bound in leather. He opened it to find it covered in minute, neat script.

Verne got out again today. Built up sinking corner of the fence. Traded Hecter three baskets of cheese for side of deer.

Delivered four kids just before dawn. Three survived. All on the small side but doing well. Mother's spirits low. She put up a fuss before allowing them to feed. Buried the fourth on the other end of the field so she won't smell it.

The tinker passed through. Bought three yards of copper wire, received fifteen lyra for five stacks of firewood.

Lysandro read page after page of incidental details, wondering why his father would send him here with such urgency. Then an entry caught his breath.

Bad storm last night. Had to patch Kenna's roof. Her smile was so bright when it was done, it made my hands sweat. Said she felt safer knowing I was nearby. Spent the rest of the day smiling.

Kenna was the name of Theron's wife.

He read the entry again, with knowing eyes and a sense of wonder. How had this place been forgotten by the centuries?

The corner of Lysandro's mouth quirked upward. He felt a natural affinity for this man, this legend, recording the simple act of falling in love.

He kept reading, but didn't find anything else of interest. Except one thing; a passage that seemed out of place with the gentle, unassuming voice that had filled the pages.

I hate her. I'd kill her if I thought I could.

There was more. About how she always lied, and twisted things to suit her. How she threatened Kenna. Whoever "she" was, she was most definitely not his wife. But he never referred to her by name.

With nothing else to discover, he descended the loft bedroom and headed toward the door. On the way out, his foot caught on something heavy hidden beneath the rug. He threw it back to reveal a trap door affixed with an iron rung that led down into the tree's roots.

It was rusted shut with age. Lysandro tugged hard, and was blasted by the smell of damp earth when it came free. Lysandro descended the narrow ladder dug into the wall. What he saw when he reached the bottom more befitted his idea of Theron. The gentle giant had become a master of war. Enormous maces hung from the wall, tipped with dried blood. Axes, spears, and crossbows kept in sturdy wooden racks were well worn, their handles wrapped so many times in leather as the original wood underneath was eaten away. A length of chain mail big enough to lay over a charger hung on a rack in the corner. Perched on a spear stood a full suit of armor. It towered over Lysandro's head; the breadth of the shoulders was twice the size of his, or more.

It unsettled Lysandro to see how the quiet, happy life recorded above had been disrupted. Theron had never wanted this. He hadn't asked for fame, or wealth, or to be hailed as a god. He had been just a man, who lived to make his sweetheart smile. The one who had written in that journal and the one who had amassed this arsenal were two completely different men. A knot formed in the pit of his stomach.

Some preternatural sense turned his attention to a large wooden chest tucked into a corner. It grew stronger as he approached it.

He opened the chest to find a magnificent sword with an intricately carved handle of gleaming white bone, threaded with gold. In the darkened underground, the blade of the weapon seemed to glow.

"Do you know what that is?"

Lysandro turned to find his father. He hadn't heard him approach, didn't even see from whence he'd come.

Elias dipped his chin in the direction of the chest, waiting for an answer.

Lysandro hesitated. He lifted the sword out of its velvet casing, and was surprised by the lightness of it in his hand. It was like grasping air, but it cut the wind with the slightest flick of his wrist. The grip of the handle fell easily into the grooves of Lysandro's hand.

He couldn't believe his eyes. But it couldn't be anything else.

"This is Theron's sword."

Saying it aloud didn't make it feel any more real to Lysandro. But he couldn't deny the thrum of power pulsing through his hand, the mark of the divine. Lysandro was dimly aware of a small tugging at the very furthest corner of his mind, a faint yet distinct feeling that the weapon was familiar to him. Like a half-remembered dream, he imagined for a moment that he was, at long last, being reunited with it. Lysandro pushed those thoughts away.

"That sword belonged to my father," Elias said.

Lysandro's brows knit together.

"And to my father's father. And his father before him. Theron is your ancestor."

Lysandro inhaled deeply.

"When I was a boy," Elias continued, "my father would bring me down here for training. 'We must always be ready,' he warned, 'to take up Theron's mantle.' It's why I gave you this land."

Elias pointed to the sword. "I'd never seen that before a few weeks ago. It had been kept in the temple since long before my father's time. But after the temple was destroyed, it was returned to me, for safekeeping. For you."

He stepped closer to his son. "Is it true, what you said? That you were cut by the Blood Sword and lived?"

Lysandro averted his father's inquisitive stare. He hadn't expected his father to recognize him in the courthouse. But it didn't bother him the way he thought it might.

"Yes," he answered.

Elias looked visibly shaken by his response.

"Your mother begged me not to tell you. She didn't want you to fight. But you *must*."

Lysandro made to put the weapon down again and leave it in its chest forever. But something stopped him. An instinct rushed upon him that he didn't understand. But he immediately felt that to relinquish the sword would be a mistake. He gripped the handle more firmly, and was reassured by the feel of it against his palm.

"Take it with you. The Goddess wills it so."

* * *

Lysandro felt his blood quicken in his veins as the coach bearing Sera's parents approached.

"You belong with me." His grip around Sera's waist tightened. "I can't protect you here."

"We're not married yet."

"In my heart, we are." The thought of her leaving his side for even a moment terrified him. "It isn't safe," he pressed. "What if he comes for you? I won't let him do to you what he did to Sancio."

"Lysandro—"

He squeezed her in protest. "I couldn't save him."

"Marek hasn't made any noise in over a week. He's lying dead, somewhere. I'll be alright." She pressed a fervent kiss to his lips. "It's over now. And we're both still here."

Lysandro wasn't convinced, but there was nothing more he could do as her parents' carriage stopped in front of them. He reluctantly released Sera and waited beside her as she greeted her parents and told them of their engagement.

"I'm happy indeed to hear such news," her father said, coming forward to shake Lysandro's hand.

Lysandro didn't really want to, but he knew it was not the time to make a fuss.

"We can go tomorrow to the temple to settle your contract."

"Our marriage is already settled," Lysandro replied.

Alvaró's brows drew together. "What do you mean?"

"The contract's already been signed. By me and my bride." He reached for Sera's hand. She took it eagerly and folded their fingers together with ease.

Her father was very obviously put out. He had traded his daughter's childhood for a bride price. And sweet, darling Sera—she had been worried she shouldn't have enough to give *him* her dowry, after the Mirênese custom. Lysandro had done what no bride, and certainly no father, would have ever expected; he'd given her the whole of his fortune. But Carlo would get nothing.

Lysandro smirked.

Alvaró was about to say something, but his wife interrupted him.

"Oh, how romantic! My dear, clever Seraphine, you will be the most radiant bride Lighura has ever seen."

"We're to be married at the Temple Faelia at Beloquín in three weeks," Sera said.

"Three weeks! That's not *nearly* enough time to—"

"Three weeks," Sera said, more firmly this time.

Three weeks had never seemed so long. Lysandro cursed the fact that he couldn't make camp beside Sera's bed. He wanted to help Sera fend off her mother's designs on their wedding celebration, but he declined an invitation to stay for dinner in favor of spending the time with his father. They had so very much to talk about.

* * *

Long after the sun had set, Lysandro ascended Sera's window. His heart leapt into his throat when he found it open.

"I wasn't sure you'd come," she whispered. She flew into his arms, and he covered her in hot, fervent kisses.

"My house is empty without you," he whispered against her skin. "As is my heart."

Making love to her on her soft, airy bed was everything Lysandro dreamed it would be. Their goodbyes were long and bittersweet, but when dawn broke over the horizon, Lysandro was gone. Then he was back again, primly dressed and perfectly composed, the glint in his eyes as he called at her front door to invite her to breakfast the only hint of their midnight tryst.

THEY CARRIED ON LIKE THIS FOR DAYS UNTIL, ONE MORNING, LYSANDRO arrived to find the door to her house forced open.

"*Sera!*"

Furniture was overturned everywhere he looked. In the study, papers were scattered over the floor, smeared with blood and ash. A set of clothes large enough to fit Sera's father lay crumpled against the wall.

"Oh Goddess *Seraphine!*"

He flew up the stairs to her bedroom. As he went, his eyes darted into every corner of the house. Bloodied mounds of plain servants' clothing dotted the house. He dreaded that any second, he would spy a dress he recognized.

Sera's door hung off its hinges. There were scuff marks on the floor leading to her writing desk, where it had crashed into the wall after failing to barricade the door. The room was in a great tumult, but there was not a drop of blood.

Like a madman, Lysandro ran to the playhouse, hoping against hope. But he already knew the truth.

"Fabien!" he called out as he bounded across the entryway. "Pirró!"

A man he didn't know approached him. "*Shir, domaine?*"

"Where's Fabien?"

The man offered him an apologetic look and called another man over. His Andran was so thick, that between this and Lysandro's own frenzy, he could barely understand.

"Where's Fabien? Is Sera with him?"

"Seraphine? I didn't see. Some women came for His Highness this morning, took him to…"

The man hesitated and began to converse with the man beside him in Mirênese.

Lysandro grabbed him by the shoulders.

"Where?! Where?!"

"*Qui modar…*ah…how do you say…the art house. With the statues?"

Lysandro spun on his heels and sped toward the gallery, heedless of the uproar stirring behind him.

"YOU SEE? THE FIRST PANEL IS THE KEY; THE REST MERELY POINT THE WAY."

Eugenie stood staring down at the collection of images the Doge of Mirêne had spread out on the floor. After having convinced the curator to take the panels from Temple Theron down from their suspended perch, the doge laid them flat against the marble tile with great care. Then he filled in the blanks by placing detailed sketches, rendered to scale, of both the panels that he possessed and the ones he had tracked down in his quest to uncover the hero's secret tomb.

The result was remarkable; the alignment his artists had been able to achieve between the panels bordered on the uncanny, even down to the interwoven pattern that served as a nearly unbroken border along the image's edge.

The window's composition exhibited a level of detail that set it apart from those of the Goddess's temples. Eugenie wondered whether that was simply a result of changing practices regarding the forging itself, or if the distinction was deliberate. If that was the case, it was for a purpose that Eugenie couldn't easily fathom.

Together, the panels depicted Morgasse, framed by the thunder strikes characteristic of her since before the Age of Theron. So were the golden sigils that comprised the hem of her garment, stained a deep blue purple, the color of storm clouds. She was bestowing the Cerulean Key upon Theron, astride his horse. They were facing the Plains of Valere, toward the Forbidden Desert and the Lost Fortress of Argoss. With her left hand, Morgasse pointed upward, toward the first panel, and with open mouth she foretold his final resting place.

The nearly complete picture made Eugenie's skin prickle, and her stomach turned in sick anticipation. But before she could bring herself to complete the image, she shuddered. Behind her, a deep voice shouted, followed by the echo of rapid footsteps pounding across the marble floor. It had already begun.

"Fabien? Fabien!"

Don Lysandro rushed in on them, almost colliding into the doge's shoulder.

"Fabien is Sera here? Is she with you? Please!"

The doge was at a loss. "No. I—"

A cry of anguish pierced the air, and the Child of Theron sank to his knees.

Eugenie stepped forward. "What happened?"

Don Lysandro looked up at her. "Who *are* you?"

"My name is Eugenie. I am the Examiner sent from the Temple Morgasse."

He blinked. "The Examiner?"

"Yes. This is Asha, of Temple Arun."

"Lysandro, what's *wrong*?" Fabien cut in. "Where's Sera?"

"He has her," he wailed.

"Who does?"

"Lothan Marek," Eugenie answered, "the bastard of Argoss."

"But why would he take Sera?" Pirró asked, stepping forward to grip Fabien's arm. "What does he want with her?"

"He knows who I am," Lysandro answered. "He knows that I'm the Shadow of Theron and that I love her. He took her because of me."

Saying it out loud brought him fresh agony.

"We'll get her back," Asha said. She stepped in front of Eugenie and pulled Lysandro to his feet. "He'll want to force you to witness whatever he has planned. She'll be safe until we can get to them. Do you know where he might have taken her?"

"We know exactly where he's taking her," Eugenie interjected. "He needs the Eye to ascend to his place of power. He'll look for it where it was seen last."

She kneeled on the ground at Lysandro's feet and reached for the rune stones at her hip.

"You knew…"

Eugenie looked up at Lysandro. His breathing had slowed, but his eyes were wide and bright. The blue gray of them flashed like lightning. She started.

"What?"

"You knew who Marek was. You knew what he had done…"

Eugenie hesitated for a moment. She ducked her head to avoid his stare, and focused on preparing to cast the stones.

"Yes."

"And you did nothing," Lysandro snarled. "You *had* him. Why didn't you kill him when you had the chance? Now he has Seraphine!"

In the same moment that the stones left Eugenie's hand, Lysandro kicked them aside in rage. The rune for the Hero Theron skidded across the floor and landed beside the stone bearing a half-circle etched with a line through the middle, the sigil indicating Arun—a bow and arrow.

"Asha." Eugenie gripped her sister's arm. She saw, and her eyes grew round. The wheel was turning now. *Fast.*

Eugenie craned her neck to consider Lysandro. He tensed his right hand into a fist, then released it again. In the interval, the phantom of a bright weapon flickered in his hand.

"You will need more than Theron's sword if you are to do battle with Argoss and his bastard."

Lysandro stared queerly at her. "How did you—"

"Do you know where it is?" Asha asked, rounding her shoulders to face Eugenie.

Eugenie held out her hand, into which Asha placed the missing panel. When she unwrapped it, Fabien's eyes went as wide as saucers.

"By the Three-Faced Goddess, is that—"

Eugenie laid the panel on the floor, and made the image whole. The rumble of thunder echoed in Eugenie's ears, and a stark winter wind stirred her hair. The panels, both glass and paper, shimmered to life. Dark clouds rolled across the plains, and the winds off the distant mountains made the grass quiver. Eugenie heard the sound of hooves as Theron's stallion charged across the desert. Her gaze was drawn to the topmost corner, to the eyes that haunted her dreams with their piercing stare. She had only guessed before at the name of the snow-capped mountains. Now she was sure.

"The Sister Peaks."

"The Sister Peaks? That will take days. Lysandro needs us here, *now*."

"I'll never make it on my own. Asha—I need you."

Asha breathed deeply. Then she turned to Lysandro. "We will help you all we can. But right now, you must travel alone."

"What the hell good are you? You were supposed to help—supposed to *stop him*, before he hurt anybody. Before he kidnapped my wife and killed my best friend!"

"I'm sorry. My blood is screaming to ride with you. But the Goddess wills it, and I *must* yield. I can offer you my warriors—"

Lysandro wrenched his arm free of her. "I've wasted enough time already." He turned away from the Examiners to Fabien. "Are *you* coming?"

The doge didn't look up. The sacred image before him held his unwavering gaze.

"*Fabien!*"

He was oblivious. His lips were moving, but no sound came out—none that even Pirró, kneeling close beside him, could decipher. He swept a lock of hair out of Fabien's face, then turned to Eugenie.

"What's wrong with him?"

"His eyes cannot see what he was not *meant* to see."

When Eugenie had placed the final panel, she had completed the chain of wards that comprised its border. Like a thick fog, the nine panels cast a cloud of confusion over themselves; Fabien had been caught in their snare.

Pirró's gaze flickered between Fabien and Lysandro. He set his jaw in a grim line, and turned to Lysandro. "Go."

Lysandro left the village with all speed, with Hurricane his only companion. The stallion charged through meadows and valleys as if Lysandro's urgency was his own. But Lysandro knew that if he pushed Hurricane beyond his limits, he would never reach Sera. The Examiner's words, that Marek would not harm her unless Lysandro was there to see it, were of little comfort. There was much Lothan could do short of killing her. He could beat her. He could—

Lysandro kicked Hurricane again, driving him at a furious pace.

He tucked into a small town on the edge of a looming forest as the sun began its descent and dyed the sky a pale, sickly purple. If he didn't stop and rest Hurricane now, he didn't know when his next chance would come.

He brought him around to the stables attached to a tavern then took for himself a plate of bread and a cold shoulder of lamb, a meal that could be eaten quickly.

"You'll be needing a room then," the proprietor said as he laid the food before him, more a statement than a question.

Lysandro shook his head and swallowed. "I'll be riding through the night."

"You don't want to be doing that, Signor."

"Why not?" Lysandro asked, not interested enough to look up from his food.

"There's an old tale, told to children mostly, about Sar Arwan. A hobgoblin that used to hide in the woods and comes to steal 'em away at night. But he come back. Every night this week, we've found one of our animals slaughtered."

"Plenty of animals are accustomed to hunting at nighttime," Lysandro countered.

A small woman with rounded shoulders approached them from a nearby table and stood behind Lysandro's stool, clutching her hips.

"I never heard of an animal what wasted their feast, just scattered the innards about in a great mess!"

Just then the surface of Lysandro's drink rippled in his cup, and he heard the rattling of glassware behind him. His chair shook on its legs and he stretched out a hand to steady himself. A cry of alarm went up among the patrons. Some scrabbled under the tables and clasped at their heads.

It was over in seconds, then the world went still again.

"Arun bless us and save us, there it is again," the proprietor said.

"This has happened before?" Lysandro asked.

The man nodded. "It'll be fine one minute, then the next the whole of the ground'll be quaking under your feet. It's what brought Sar Arwan back to us."

"Argoss is pushing through the great seals! You mark me—his chains will no' hold him much longer. The world'll break apart and *all* his torments will be upon us again."

The woman turned a steely gaze at Lysandro that traveled to the double swords strapped to his back. His own, the one he'd used for years, and his ancestor's, that felt at home in his hand.

"Last night, it took a boy."

Lysandro said nothing.

"If you're brave enough or fool enough to go through there on your own at night, then perhaps you might rid us of our affliction."

Grunts of agreement came from every corner of the room.

Lysandro set his jaw, and stood up. The woman followed.

He exited the building and walked with brisk steps to the stables to retrieve Hurricane and climbed into the saddle.

Hurricane reared his head in protest when the woman stepped in front of him and took hold of his reigns.

"*Please*, Signor. We have none else."

Sera. He had to get to Sera.

Lysandro rounded Hurricane, shaking free the woman's grip on him.

"I'm sorry."

He jabbed Hurricane in the ribs and sent him galloping into the forest.

Lysandro did not travel by moonlight, for the sky above him was sewn up tight by the dense canopy. He lit an oil lantern and strapped it to his saddle, but the shafts of light bounced off thick trunks that conspired close together, and did little to guide the way.

He cut a circuitous route through the wood, moving slow and unable to cross into the next field as fast as his blood urged. The sounds of nature about its business acted as a shield until, without warning, the forest fell quiet.

Hurricane pressed onward out of implicit trust for his master, but the beast became increasingly agitated. His hard, unsteady breathing was the only noise that reached Lysandro's ears.

Hurricane whinnied as he traversed something wet. The ground squished under his hooves, and Lysandro heard something pop. The air stank of waste and decay; Lysandro covered his nose and mouth with his sleeve to keep the stench out. When he cast the lantern downward, he saw his horse's legs were steeped in blood. He fought the impulse to turn around and see what it was they had come through.

Lysandro stiffened in the saddle and kept his eyes alert for any slight movement hidden by the dark. Tree branches lay snapped and broken across the forest floor, and glistened in an eerie yellow glow. It appeared as if the forest itself had succumbed to infection.

The undergrowth was spotted with blood, so thick in some places that it formed obsidian puddles among the roots of ash and cedars stretching their limbs up into the night. Bits of bone and teeth gleamed back at him in the darkness, stripped clean of flesh. His blood jumped in his veins when the lantern light reflected a horned animal staring back at him. It was several seconds before he realized the eyes were hollow.

He wondered if Sera had come this way, if her and her abductors had been beset by whatever was terrorizing the little town at the wood's edge. Every second that Lysandro did not overtake them instilled him with a gnawing sense of dread.

A low rumble moved through the forest, making the leaves in the trees shiver. It quickly built into a peal of thunder. The ground did indeed feel as if it was opening up beneath them and might swallow them up.

"Easy, easy!" Lysandro called as Hurricane skittered backward and refused to continue. Once the tremor had passed, Lysandro ribbed him hard and shoved his nose forward through the trees, but Hurricane wasn't having it.

Lysandro dismounted and urged him onward by hand.

"Come on. Never seen *you* scared before."

The horse snorted, pushing a puff of warm breath through Lysandro's hair. He followed reluctantly as Lysandro kept a close grip on his reigns. He stepped carefully around the haphazard mounds of shredded bark and leaves piled up like burrows. The old woman had been correct in that, at least; Lysandro couldn't conceive of a creature that would construct its home with such great haste and with so little care. The undergrowth was in complete disarray.

He was grateful when a dense fog rolled over them. It came nearly to his knees and hid the forest floor from view. It seemed to rise up from the soil itself, seeping from invisible seams of the earth, now split apart. But the boon turned instantly to a curse when he heard, very close to his ear, a wet hiss and the sound of chattering teeth.

It leapt at him with a screech. Lysandro drew his blade as he dodged. The unseen creature sailed over his shoulder and landed on the ground near Hurricane's feet. The stallion stomped and kicked furiously, but the little thing came at Lysandro again, leaving the ground and jumping up as high as Lysandro's chest. He swung his weapon in a wide arc and knocked it back, but it was not sliced in half, as it should have been. The creature seemed to recognize this and gave that chittering laugh again as it got to its feet and readied for another charge. It opened its mouth wide as it came for him, revealing several rows of unnaturally long, flat teeth. Lysandro thrust forward to spear the thing, but it latched onto the top of his blade. It growled and scrabbled with small, fast claws, and tried to shut its jaw and snap the sword point off. Lysandro dropped the sword and the monster both, and drew the second sword at his back. At the sight of Theron's weapon, the creature made of shadows relinquished the sword in its mouth and clutched at its head, ripping out tufts of hair from behind its pointed ears. A shrill howl pierced the night. It curled itself into a ball and then unfurled again, facing away from Lysandro as it took flight up a nearby tree. Lysandro launched the blade into the air. It bit into the trunk and hit its mark. The foul thing let out a single, inhuman scream, then the darkness that congealed around it and gave it its form thinned and dissolved into the night.

A sickly luminescent ichor dripped from the spot where the sword had pinned its prey to the tree.

Lysandro pulled it loose and examined the blade in his hand. It shone against the moonless night, made seemingly of light itself. He retrieved his own sword and returned it to the sheath at its back, keeping the sword of Theron drawn as he mounted Hurricane and rode on.

* * *

Morning broke across Lysandro's eyelids. He lifted his head from Hurricane's flank and stretched. Judging from the sun's position in the sky, he had slept a mere four hours. Maybe less. At his feet rushed a small stream. He bent over it to splash water on his face. Beside him on the bank lay a large stone, surrounded by a series of smaller ones. He was struck by the queerness of their arrangement; the grass was depressed beneath them, not grown up around the sides, and the circle surrounding the center stone was nearly perfect.

Lysandro couldn't say what made him lift the stone in the center, but he cried out as he did. On its smooth underside, in Sera's familiar hand, was a single word scrawled in a thin, crimson script.

South.

Tears of relief burst forth unbidden. With that single word, she had told him a thousand.

"I'm coming, Sera," he whispered.

30

SOUTH. THEY WERE TRAVELING SOUTH. TRACKING THE SUN'S MOVEMENT IN the sky was harder than Sera thought. They weren't moving in a straight line, and her head had been turned about a few times, but now she was really sure.

They'd been walking for hours. But for how *many* hours, Sera couldn't tell.

She knew her father was dead. She'd heard him cry out when Marek had come crashing through the door of their home, but he hadn't been dragged along with them. She couldn't find it in herself to cry. He had been too cold and distant a father for his loss to sting. Sera didn't like this about herself, but she understood it. What she didn't understand, and what made her heart ache, was that her mother didn't cry either. She simply did as she was bidden with a blank expression.

Marek's men herded them like cattle over hills and grassy plateaus. Marek himself rode on horseback, jutting ahead of them for long stretches at a time before circling around again to complain about their pace and shout orders at them to keep moving. She was relieved whenever he took off. She hated the smell of the Blood Sword tucked into his belt. She hated even more when his eyes fell on her.

Every once in a while, she would see him take a fold of papers from inside his coat pocket and consult them before heading off. Sera hadn't been able to catch a glimpse of the pages yet. But what puzzled her most was the fact that Marek was hiding the loss of his hand from the others. He kept gloved whatever he had under there working as fingers—wood, she supposed—so that they wouldn't see. If he was in pain, his face did not betray it. But it was a distinct disadvantage. She saw it in the way he struggled to keep his horse in line, and the way he fumbled his papers and nearly dropped them more than once, cursing to himself when he thought no one was watching.

But no matter where they were headed or why, she had to find a way to slow them down. A solution was not forthcoming. The constraints of her situation consumed Sera's thoughts as they walked without food and without rest until one of Marek's men stumbled upon a patch of wild mushrooms with round, bright red caps. Sera held her breath at the sight of them.

"Lord Lothan, look at these!" The man bent over to smell them. "We could make a soup from this."

Marek ignored him and urged his horse forward.

"But—Lord Lothan," a second man pleaded. "We need to stop and eat."

"Fine. But I'm not eating those mushrooms."

"I'll find something," another said, and scurried off.

Marietta exhaled loudly and pulled a handful of mushrooms from the ground. "Thank the Goddess."

Sera pinched the soft flesh of her mother's hand, causing her to drop them.

"Ow! What—"

"Don't eat those," she muttered under her breath.

Her mother turned to her wide-eyed, but Sera kept her expression even. They both turned to watch as Marek's man gorged himself on the fungus. He didn't even bother to brush the dirt off.

* * *

Perhaps he hadn't eaten enough of them. Perhaps she had been mistaken. But Sera's doubts evaporated as sweat began to pour from the young man's face, and the others started to notice as they gathered around a meager fire, sharing the meat of the two small rabbits one of them had managed to catch.

Sera shifted in place, and something stabbed her suddenly under her arm. She'd forgotten it was there. She'd grabbed the long sewing needle and slid it into the seam of her nightdress when she'd first heard the screams from downstairs. But it did her no good where it was, tucked into her dress where she could not reach it quickly. Keeping it hidden along the inside of her arm, she reached up to pin her hair at the nape of her neck, and deftly shoved the needle into the knot with no one the wiser.

"What the fuck's wrong with you?" Marek snarled, glaring at the man whose insides were a bomb waiting to go off.

The man's face flickered purple in the firelight.

"I think I…I've got to…"

He stumbled to his feet, but didn't make it to the tree line before the vomiting started.

Marek rolled his eyes, but it got serious quickly as the man lost control of his bowels, and his body fought to purge the poison from both ends. Marek didn't move a muscle; he only looked annoyed at the inconvenience. But the others scrambled to their comrade's aid, wanting to help but not daring to get close enough to actually do any good.

"What's wrong with him? Lord Lothan—quick, before he shits his brains out!" one cried. Marek blinked. "What *exactly* do you expect me to do?"

Sera and her mother were left alone with him around the fire as the rest crowded helplessly around the sick man. Their shouting peaked when he began to seize.

"Oh my. Can't you do something?"

Her mother wasn't looking at Marek. She was looking at *her*. And now, so was he.

Shit.

Marek's eyes narrowed as he left his perch and moved toward her. "What did you do to him?"

"Nothing," she answered truthfully. But that didn't satisfy him. "If I had the power to do that, why would I kill *him* instead of you?"

"Who said anything about killing?"

"Your man is dead," she said. Sera looked over her shoulder to see that the screaming had stopped and the man on the ground, covered in his own waste, was no longer moving. But Marek seemed to know it without being told, closing his eyes and inhaling deep as the man expired. He opened his eyes again and trained them on her.

He grabbed her by the elbow and pulled her away from the fire. Her mother leapt to her defense.

"No wait! Please!"

Sera drowned out her mother's cries of protest and kept a cool face as Marek tore her away from the others and whipped her around to face him. The forced silkiness of his voice made the bile rise in her throat.

"You really did choose the wrong man. It's not too late to change your mind."

"You're a dead man walking," Sera spat back.

"Am I?" he sneered. "Do you really think de Castel has the balls to face me? He knows what I can do."

Sera raised an eyebrow. "You're the one running."

He squeezed her throat with a hand she knew was not really there. But whatever he was hiding under his glove, the pressure on her throat was all too real. With his free hand, he unfastened his belt.

"After I've had you, your don won't want you anymore."

Sera laughed in his face, and its effect on him was immediate. She had encountered men like him in Mirène—she knew what he wanted. She'd be Goddess-damned if she was going to give it to him. Sera leveled him with a stare.

"He's had me before you. He'll have me *after* you. It'll be like you never existed." She turned her head to the side, and waited.

He breathed down her neck like a raging bull, and squeezed her throat until she saw stars at the edge of her vision.

She'd only told him the truth. It would haunt her, but she would find solace in Lysandro's arms. And Lysandro would kill him; she was sure of that. All the same, her breathing eased when he released her.

When Sera opened her eyes again to meet his gaze, his wicked grin widened.

"I wonder if your mother feels the same way."

Sera's heart pounded.

"Bring me the widow," Lothan ordered. "She must be in need of some company."

"No—*stop!*"

Sera rushed forward as Marek turned from her and approached her mother, but he shoved her hard, and she landed on her backside. Marietta flailed and kicked furiously, trying to get a toehold in the dirt, but the men holding her by either arm dragged her forward relentlessly.

"What are you doing? Sera!"

"*Mama!*"

The men that handed Marietta to Marek were now on Sera, pinning her to the ground as Marek bent her mother over, hiked up her skirt, and shoved himself inside her.

Her mother's screams were an agony. Sera fought against the hands that held her down, but they were too strong.

"Mama! Mama!" she sobbed.

Over the chaos, Sera heard Marek's laughter. One of her captors gripped her by the chin and forced her to look. Marek's wild eyes were trained on her, his teeth gleaming in the moonlight as he pounded into her mother relentlessly.

You're a dead man, Marek. A dead man.

When he was finished, he tossed Marietta to the ground, where she fell face-first into the dirt. He turned his body toward Sera, flesh in hand, his seed dripping into the soil. Then he left them there with a grin on his face and sauntered back to the fire as he fastened the closures of his pants. His men released her.

Sera crawled on her hands and knees to her mother's side as she scrambled to cover herself.

"I'm sorry Mama. So sorry." They embraced, and wept.

Sera and her mother huddled together on the cold hard ground, with nothing to keep them warm as the night deepened. So did Marek and his men. They had been so intent on getting to wherever it was they were going, that they hadn't considered they might need things like blankets, or a reliable source of food. At least they'd had enough brains to stop for the night near a riverbank. Their snores meant there would be no more trouble tonight. But still Sera couldn't sleep. She turned over on her side and found that, like her, her mother was still awake.

"I'm sorry, Mama," she whispered again. She'd said it so many times in the last few hours, but there was nothing else she could think to say.

"Enough, Seraphine. I would gladly endure that, from him and the rest of his men too, to save you from it."

"Mama…"

"You are for Don Lysandro. Your father and I didn't spend all that money to make you a suitable match for him, just so you could be soiled by the likes of Lothan Marek."

Soiled?

Sera's face crumpled.

"Just pray that he sets the chief magistrate on our trail."

"He'll come himself," Sera said defensively.

Her mother snorted.

Now she was angry. "What, Mama? Why wouldn't he come for me?"

Marietta made a clicking a sound with her tongue, the kind one makes when they're forced to endure the naïveté of others.

"You've chosen well for a husband. Dozens of others couldn't bag him. But to come riding out chasing after you, and to face Marek himself? He simply isn't that sort of man."

Her mother's words rattled her so much that her mother had turned away from her before she was able to formulate a reply.

It enraged Sera not to be able to correct her.

There was no doubt in Seraphine's mind that Lysandro was racing toward her at that very moment. But he'd need her help if he was going to catch up to them. She was still mulling over in her mind how she could slow Marek down when she felt a rough, uneven pressure underneath her arm. She shifted to find a handful of rocks tucked under her side. Their smooth white edges shone in the dark.

Her eyes drank in the moonlight as her thoughts coalesced.

She pressed her hand to the ground to stand up, lifting the small stones on the way and tucking them into her palm as she got to her feet. She kept her fingers closed but relaxed as she walked toward the river, where a lone officer was standing guard. He didn't move as she approached. She kept her footfalls light, and peered at his face.

He slept leaning against a tree, but his eyes opened just a slit as she tried to back away. Once his gaze settled on her, his pupils widened to attention.

Damn.

"What are you doing?" he demanded, peeling himself off the tree and planting his feet more firmly on the ground.

"I came for a drink of water."

"You can drink in the morning. Get back over there. Now."

"I'm not running away, here. We walked about nine hours today, and your idiot leader didn't think to bring any food."

The man snarled at her, but she could see the hunger in his eyes.

"All I want is some water. How happy do you think he'll be tomorrow if we pass out on the road and you can't go anywhere? I doubt he's brought me along just to leave me for dead on the side of the road."

The man hesitated, weighing her request against Marek's temper.

She shrugged and made to turn. "I'll just ask *him* then."

"*No!*" the man shouted, loud at first, then quieter. "No. Just take the damn drink, all right? But be quick about it."

She reached the riverbank and knelt in the grass, sure he was watching her. The only thing he couldn't see was the patch of grass directly in front of her. Sera stared at the soil, searching for what she needed to make this work. She found it right on the edge of the bank. A large stone had lodged itself into the edge of the river, its surface made smooth by the eternal tide. She yanked it free and dried it on the grass before settling it into the earth. Then she dropped the stones with her left hand and carefully arranged them around the larger stone while she brought water to her lips with the right.

She couldn't write a whole missive, even if a thousand thoughts were running through her mind. Between the size of the stone she had to work with and the man getting impatient over her shoulder, she had to be brutally sparing. What one thing could she say that might actually do some good?

She settled on the final bit of her little scheme, and splashed some water on her face. She stretched her fingers up to her hair, searching for the sharp end of the needle tucked away somewhere in her tresses. She bit her lip when she found it, then brought her finger fast and hard back to that place. She scrawled her finger rapidly across the flat underside of the stone before the bead of blood that welled up on her skin ran dry.

Sera washed the wound and pressed her thumb against it as she laid the stone in its place and made her way back to her mother's side. All she could do now was pray.

Merciful Faelia, bring my love to me swiftly and keep him safe. All-Seeing Morgasse, guide his steps. Almighty Arun, lend him your power.

DAMNED ARUNI. DAMN THEM AND THEIR RIDICULOUS RIDDLES.

Lothan tilted the page in his hand, trying to get the sun to reflect off the golden ink etched across it. The paper, torn from the *Histories*, bore an illustration of a twilit desert with the hidden fortress of Argoss looming far in the distance. The lines on the illustration were so fine that they looked more like the shifting of the sands in the wind than deliberate markings. Lothan had to squint to see it. Even when he could make out the images nestled in the dunes, the fucking thing still made no sense.

The formation of rocks jutting out over the sea *looked* like a woman bending over with her arm outstretched, reaching down into the water. It also just looked like rocks on a cliff. How was he to know if this was the outcrop he sought, or if it had been the one he had spotted a mile back, but had dismissed? For all he knew, the one depicted on the page was three miles ahead, beyond his sight.

If he turned from the coast now and was wrong, it would take days to retrace his steps. And he'd be traveling right in de Castel's path. He didn't doubt that the little Alvaró bitch was right. De Castel would be on them in an instant if they were forced to circle back. Lothan was aching for that fight, and to plow Lysandro's beloved right before his eyes, but not until he was ready. Not until he found what was calling to him from the depths of Argoss's fortress. He lifted his gaze to the horizon again, studying the cliffside and trying to decide if its shape was woman enough for him to set his course by. But he just wasn't sure.

He wouldn't be sure of his way until the soil at his feet turned to sand. Even then, the Forbidden Desert was vast, and if legend was to be believed, the outer walls of the fortress were enchanted, made invisible to the world by a nest of forgotten spells.

Would the Lost Fortress recognize him as his master? Would its spires and turrets glisten on his arrival, its unseen hands throw down the gates? Even if he could find the fortress—which, at this rate, was far from certain —would it be for naught?

Disappointment festered. He'd half-expected that the river of blood rushing along his blade would guide him, whisper in his ear and reveal the path to Argoss's stronghold. But it was silent. The river ran more slowly now; it had been too long since it had drunk. The blood along the edge was darkening, growing stale from unfulfilled lust.

Perhaps if he offered it the fresh life it craved, it would share its secrets. They'd already lost one man along the way; what was one more?

* * *

Lothan was running out of men, and running out of excuses for how their number had dwindled from a dozen at the start to now only four. Even if he slaughtered the rest of them, it wouldn't be enough. His sword stubbornly kept its silence. It was starving. Without blood, its magic would dry up, and it would be no more than a broken bit of steel.

* * *

The Shadow of Theron stalked his dreams. He chased Lothan without rest, hunting him like a demon born from an endless night. When the demon overtook him, the shadows parted to reveal Lysandro's hardened face.

Lothan walked along the heavy outer wall of the fortress as he slept. It was cold and unfeeling as he lay dead at the threshold, barred from entering, its powers and mysteries forbidden to him. He looked down at his own body, laying broken and discarded at the feet of the Shadow.

His pursuer stood over him with a sword in his hand, glowing bright as a white-hot flame. The sight of it, and the humming vibration that radiated from its edge, made Lothan scream. It sliced through the night and tore his body asunder.

Lothan woke in a cold sweat. Even awake he felt Lysandro coming, bringing *it* ever closer—the gleaming white sword that would cleave him in half. He swore, and rolled onto his side. But when he closed his eyes again, the demon Shadow was waiting.

* * *

Lothan was seeing things.

That's what he thought, when the high stone wall leading to the Lost Fortress disappeared from sight, then flickered back again in the blink of an eye. He stretched out a tentative hand, and felt the hard, pitted surface materialize against his palm. Then it shimmered, trembling in the sun and turning slick before vanishing. Lothan retracted his hand quickly.

"What should we do, Lord Lothan?"

They'd crossed into the Forbidden Desert three days ago. The last time they'd found fresh water had been the morning before.

They were standing at the edge of Argoss's fortress. They had to be. But something was wrong. Whatever spells or incantations that hid the fortress from sight couldn't possibly have been designed to work like this. The magic had grown brittle, unpredictable. When it finally gave out, Lothan didn't know if the structure would remain solid, or wink out of existence altogether. He wondered what that might mean for anybody who happened to be inside.

But if he couldn't penetrate the fortress and find something to drink, they were all going to die.

"Move it," Lothan snapped.

They traveled along the wall for over an hour, and finally came upon a narrow opening that allowed for them to enter into the complex one at a time. He shoved the three men he had left ahead of him. The Alvaró girl and her mother had nowhere to run; they followed behind without complaint.

The walls were so high it was impossible to see over them. A strong wind whistled far above their heads, racing over the top of the labyrinth, but aside from its shrieking whistle, all was quiet. Even the smallest creature of the desert knew not to venture here.

There was no way to tell which direction they traveled in, or if they were getting any closer to the entrance of the keep. Every turn and corner looked like every other, and turns branched out into two and sometimes three avenues. Many led to dead ends, forcing Lothan to retreat and start again. More than once, the walls faded into the air, and they were left standing in the wide-open desert. The sun had reached and passed its ascendance in the sky before the labyrinth at the base of the fortress reappeared again, and they could move through it. Lothan could have been at the center of the maze, or a mere two steps from where he'd begun. There was no way for him to know. And with his stomach howling and the Blood Sword shriveling at his side, what little patience he had left withered.

Then the walls disappeared again, and Lothan cursed out loud.

"This is insanity!" he screamed.

"More insane than coming here in the first place?" Sera's voice drifted up from behind him.

Lothan swung at her with the back of his hand and sent her sprawling. When her eyes met his again, he could see the murder in them. But her gaze inevitably dropped to the sword at his belt. She knew better than to fight back.

His lips settled into a smug satisfaction.

As night drew on, the maze passed in and out of reality more quickly. But Jenner, now the thinnest among them, was becoming increasingly agitated, and began to pace as they waited for the maze to open back up to them.

"Isn't there some way for us to go on? When it disappears, I mean. Couldn't we *aaghnn*—"

The walls of the maze had pulsed back to life, materializing in the middle of his body. His left half dropped to the ground.

The women screamed. Lothan stepped quickly back. There were only two brothers left to him now. Both gaped at their bisected kin, then clustered around Lothan and begged for his protection. Their eyes were wild. Descendants of Argoss or no, the fortress showed no mercy.

"Enough!" he roared. With much shouting and cursing, he managed to climb atop his brothers' shoulders. From there, his fingertips could just reach the top of the wall.

"Lift me up!" he called. The men below shifted his weight, so that each of them held one foot high above their heads. They were so weakened by the journey that they nearly dropped him, and he cracked his jaw against the unforgiving edge of the wall. The impact blackened his vision for a spell, and it took untold restraint not to kick their teeth in. When his eyes cleared, he looked out over the labyrinth.

Ahead, little more than half a mile, a staircase hewn out of stone spiraled upward to two metal doors that flashed crimson. He marked the spot in his mind's eye.

"Down!" he shouted again.

"What did you see, Lord Lothan?" the two men left standing clamored after him. "Did you see the path ahead?"

He did. But what good did it do him, when the labyrinth never meant to let him leave?

An insane idea crossed his mind.

He grabbed Sera by the wrist.

"Let go!" she screamed.

"Shut up."

She clawed at him with her free hand and gouged the flesh from his left cheek. Pain flared beneath his eye, but he became numb to it as the walls shifted and faded again. He dug his nails into her arm and raced forward.

"What are you doing? *Stop!*"

Within seconds, he'd already decided that if her arm came out of its socket, he would just dump her. Lothan felt the heat of the walls, sensed them growing solid again and closing in around them as they sped across the open desert. But he didn't stop. He hurried onward to the place he had imprinted in his mind, trying to ignore Sera's terrible screams and the fact that he was racing straight to the Abyss. At any moment, he could crush his own skull in, if he were just a few inches off his mark. Or if the staircase didn't appear where he had seen it last.

He arrived at his destination and dug his heels into the sand, screeching to a halt. Sera slammed her face into his back from the sudden standstill. They both stood panting, their faces red from exertion. Then her arms flailed outward as the ground shifted and rose beneath them, and she stumbled as the sand hardened into stairs that climbed high into the air. When they finally stopped, Lothan drew in a deep breath, and smiled in triumph.

"You stupid jackass!" Sera cried. "We could have both been killed! We still might be."

Just like that, she had spoiled the moment.

"Such a sharp tongue. I have no idea how de Castel stands you."

"He's going to kill you."

"So you keep saying. But he'll have to get through *this* to do it, won't he?"

The color drained from her face, and Lothan found his victory.

They climbed the steep stone steps until they reached the first summit, marked by two towering columns that framed a pair of double doors. The metal glowed red in the blistering heat. Lothan recognized them as the ones from his dreams. He dropped his gaze to the ground, terrified that he would find himself lying there lifeless. His breath shuddered in his lungs when he did not.

Lothan turned and spied his men huddled with Alvaró's widow in a remote western corner of the maze.

"Left!" he called down to them.

Their heads spun at the sound of his voice.

"Lord Lothan? Lord Lothan!"

The maze shimmered, but this time, it remained faintly visible. Lothan swung his arms to get their attention.

"Up here, you idiots!"

They craned their necks straight up to the sky.

"Fucking numbskulls," he growled under his breath.

Seraphine murmured to herself.

"What?"

Sera didn't respond. Lothan clutched at her arm and squeezed her until she winced.

"They can't see us," she said at last.

"What do you mean?"

"From here, you can always see the maze. Even when they cannot."

Lothan shifted his attention back to his brothers and narrowed his eyes. They were standing still, waiting, as if they labyrinth had winked out again, even though Lothan saw it plainly. Then he observed a subtle shifting in the light and shadows, and his men went on as before—though in the wrong direction.

"Left!" he called out again. They didn't look up this time. They simply obeyed. With Seraphine's mother in tow, they reached the summit as the sun disappeared below the horizon.

It was only when Lothan finally turned to face the doors that he realized. There were no doorknobs, no rings, no handholds of any kind. Lothan pressed all his weight against them. It was as successful as pushing on a mountain.

"How do we get in?" one of them asked.

Lothan looked to Seraphine. "Well?"

She blinked. "How should I know?"

"Would you tell if you did?"

"Of course not."

The Blood Sword hissed. Lothan lifted it from his belt and held it reverently across his palms.

What must I do to gain entry?

A notion trickled into his ear. But that would kill him, wouldn't it? He could handle the sword without being threatened by its venom, but he couldn't—

Before Lothan could stop it, the stream of blood lashed out and struck him like the forked tongue of a serpent. The flesh around it rippled and flared from the shock of intense heat. His vision swam as the blood falling from the base of his thumb mingled with the gore pooling in his hands. He felt his life drain out of him, but then fill up again just as quickly. An army of souls filled him, and his skin felt stretched near to bursting. For an instant, he was euphoric. When it passed, he was able to focus on the blade again. He found it flashing a brilliant red, and grown to an impressive length. Lothan drank in its vermillion light.

The women backed away as his brothers knelt at his feet and pressed their foreheads to the stone. Lothan turned his bloodied hands outward, and pushed on the doors. They turned slowly inward.

Their small party entered a massive room with an impossibly high ceiling. Lining it were stone columns, with the spaces in between draped in a rich fabric dyed indigo. Darkened bones lay piled up along the edge of the floor together with rusted swords and broken bits of armor. The floor was inlaid with lapis and mother of pearl in a mosaic depicting celestial bodies. Suns, moons, stars, and planets were shown, but not in their natural alignment. There was something curious in their orientation, a sense of movement or direction that held some latent meaning just beneath the surface. Spread across the starry sky were sigils etched in gold, and connective threads weaving an infinite, inscrutable pattern.

Lothan saw nothing in the image at his feet that he recognized; in all of his midnight wanderings, he had never bothered to look up.

He leaned over to peer into the mural. His eyes lost their focus the longer he stared, and he imagined the floor to be moving, the golden lines racing onward to fulfill their secret destiny. He would have lost himself in the infinite space, pulled downward into its unfolding pathways, if not for the tugging he felt on his arm.

"Let go," Sera said. "It isn't as if I can leave."

He yanked on her harder, pulling her close and raking his tongue over her cheek. She struggled against him, but it was no good.

"I'll touch you how and where I want."

Only then did he release her and turn his attention toward the room again as if the whole thing hadn't happened. At the farthest end of the great hall was a throne carved in gold. Lothan approached it alone, taking in the masterful details that, when occupied, would give the impression of Lothan perched upon a mountain. Protruding from the armrest on the right side was a nest hewn from the same piece of gold as the throne itself. The depression was littered with fossilized bits of eldur viper skins and broken bits of shell the color of speckled amber. The basin on the left was filled with a glittering black sand—volcanic ash, he realized. He dipped his left hand into it and let it fall through his fingers. He was surprised to discover it had retained its heat through the ages. It was so intense it seared his fingertips. He had no clue as to its purpose, and so left it be.

Precious gems and stones sparkled at the base of the throne. On either side were iron cages large enough to fit a full-grown eldur viper. Or a man. He wondered who Argoss might have had cause to imprison, but he didn't much care.

He turned back and saw his underlings staring at the space with their jaws hanging open. He snapped his fingers to get their attention, then looked from one empty cage to the other.

"Make our guests comfortable."

There was a great kerfuffle at that, but ultimately Seraphine and her mother were shoved into the cages. As Lothan secured the hatch on Seraphine's cell, his eye caught sight of the heavy curtain behind the throne. It swayed in place.

"Stay here," he ordered the others, and tucked into the cavernous tunnel beyond.

The seeming obsession with earthen treasure continued into the passageway behind the throne. The rough-cut stones embedded in the walls let off a faint blue-purple glow. Arranged in a sharp rising and falling pattern, they gave the impression of a mountain range, with stones glowing a vibrant orange flowing through the heart of the ridge like a river of fire. The blackened stone in the heart of the lava flow, glass forged from the volcano's fury, was unmistakably meant to represent the Eye. In the centermost peak the orange stones surged, spewing forth in an upright stream from the mouth of the summit in a wide-reaching spray. It was the light from these rocks, lodged into the low ceiling above his head, that illuminated the way.

At the end of the tunnel were yet more gems and stones, some raw and uncut, still covered in dirt, other polished to a high luster. They all lay scattered over a humble wooden worktable. On either end of it rested two large stones, carved into skulls that gave off an internal glow like the warm yellow of embers. Draped around the back of the chair was a vest of dark maroon. The linen was threadbare with age, but even so, the master craftsmanship showed in the fine ivory stitching along the shoulders. Lothan discarded his own shirt, rancid with the sweat of days, and pulled the vest on. The open sleeves were wide enough to accommodate his brawny arms, and the hem fell just to the center of his knees. He ran his hands over the front of the garment, and felt a patch with that familiar, sticky sensation where the Blood Sword was accustomed to rest. It was as if it had been made for him. He tucked the weapon into its place and sat down at the table to inspect its contents.

On first glance, it looked like the workplace of a jeweler, or a metalsmith. There were small hand-held tools with various tips and edges, meant for crafting hard materials and bending them to the maker's will. Lothan removed his gloves and laid them on the table, exposing the bones of his right hand. The flesh had not grown back. Nor did Lothan suspect it would. The draft that settled onto his fingers after such a long confinement in the stifling leather of the gloves came as a relief.

He picked up a ring, forged in bronze, that was too small for even a child. At its center was a milky green stone Lothan hadn't seen the like of before. He put the ring down again and picked up a hand-bound book. The pages were smudged with blood, and filled with sigils and characters that Lothan didn't understand.

The sword's full length felt uncomfortable at his side—the handle nudged him in the gut. He removed it from his belt and laid it out in front of him on the far end of the table. When he turned his concentration back to the book again, the writing appeared different. The glow from the skulls shone now through the sword. Together they cast a fiery light over the open pages, revealing the full shape of the letters and words. Lothan experimented with the unfamiliar sounds until a rhythm emerged, and his mouth moved around the contours of the incantations more intuitively. In response, the miniature ring emitted a small but distinct hissing sound. Lothan picked it up again to examine it and turned it over in his hand. It made a sound like a great intake of breath, and the metal expanded. Lothan slipped the index finger of his right hand into the opening. The sliding of the softened metal against bone felt as if the digit was being swallowed. Then there was a deep exhale as the band settled at the base of his finger where it met the knuckle. Immediately, Lothan's swirling thoughts came into sharp focus. His innate abilities to sense and manipulate "accursed" objects, and to influence people, had always felt fuzzy and elusive. Now, they were at the tip of his finger.

The Alvaró girl's hatred of him, time and again, proved too great an obstacle for his own powers of persuasion. But with this? Perhaps he could inflict upon de Castel the greatest pain of all.

Taken together, the private space struck Lothan as odd. With all Argoss's power—his forging of the Blood Sword, and his ability to call up creatures from the Abyss—Lothan never imagined Argoss as a scholar. Yet evidence of just that was plain wherever he turned. There were books piled up in every corner of the room, some bound and folded together with books yet to be completed. Translations in progress. Most curious was the style of the writing itself. It reminded him of nothing so much as the *Histories* he had stolen from the temple. Flipping through the inscribed pages of the books being copied, it was clear where Argoss's interests lay.

Again with Anruven. Always Anruven.

Lothan didn't understand the fixation of this forgotten god, but he knew there had to be a reason for Argoss to seek him out. For that was the picture the collection of works painted—one of a sorcerer hungry for knowledge of Anruven wherever he could find him, regardless of how far and no matter how obscure.

To Lothan, this was a fatal flaw. While Argoss had been off seeking Anruven, he'd lost sight of the threat at his doorstep. Here, Lothan had an advantage; he could sense de Castel's approach. If Lothan were able to advance where Argoss had failed, he might yet find a way to avoid the fate that visited him nightly, and shatter the luminous blade that curdled the blood in his veins at the mere thought of it.

Lothan rummaged through the books for something he might actually be able to use, not caring if he lost the place at which Argoss's work had been interrupted. The book that had the most interest was one that appeared to be full of spells, guessing from the words that he *could* read. He laid the book open at a page entitled "Summoning." Other than the title, the script on the page was unintelligible, but he bullied his way through the sounds, coalescing his thoughts around calling the bastards positioned across Andras. He mastered its cadence as he came to the end of the incantation.

Nothing happened. He tried again, reciting it more smoothly this time, but still he could sense that his words had had no effect. Then he saw it— the pair of skulls inked into the page's border were not there simply for show.

"Son of a whore..."

He grumbled to himself as he laid his hands atop the glowing skulls and began again. He didn't question it when the teeth in their heads began chattering, echoing his words, and the palms of his hands felt a surging warmth. He closed his eyes and reached out to his remaining brothers with his mind. Scores of wretches with the blood of Argoss flowing through them would soon converge on the citadel that was their legacy.

As he reached the apex of the spell, the ground shook beneath his feet, and he could hear the screams of the others in the throne room ahead.

A rumbled of thunder followed, not too far in the distance. De Castel was getting closer. Lothan needed to be prepared. The brothers he had called upon would keep his sword well fed, but that wasn't enough.

He had torn the page bearing the map from the *Histories* and left the rest behind, but he remembered something from the bestiary, an illustration of a monster that thrived in the desert. He called it to mind as he placed his hands on the skulls again, and let his thoughts multiply. He flashed a rare smile. He neared the end of the incantation and felt the skulls cool as his words ceased.

Lothan stood and stretched his limbs, content with his progress. But his empty stomach rumbled to remind him of what was left undone. A putrid stench wafted up from a corridor on his right. Fresh food was out of the question, he knew, but there might be something he could salvage. He followed his nose until he came to a large storeroom, packed full with a feast long turned to dust. Game birds hung trussed up from their bones, their ribcages filled with cobwebs and spider carcasses. On one of the shelves rested a swollen wineskin.

Lothan had nothing to lose. He put the skin to his lips and took a daring swig. But the inner lining of the skin had degraded, and turned its contents into silt. Lothan gagged.

"Fuck!" he shouted, his voice raw and mangled. He wiped his mouth on his arm and thought of how fine a drink it must have been when it was new. As the thought crossed his mind, the ring on his right hand constricted. He focused his thought again—this time, with force. He watched with keen interest as the sack that he had spilt on the floor filled up again. Lothan retrieved it, and put his lips to it once more. The spiced wine was deep and fiery, the best he had ever had.

Lothan picked up two more skins, concentrated his will, and took a sip from each to test them. The results were not exactly the same, but were equally splendid. He retraced his steps to the great hall and tossed a skin to each of his men, who gulped them down hungrily.

Lothan stood before the cage holding Seraphine. She screamed when she saw the bare bones of his hand, but he ignored it and took a long, satisfying drink from his wineskin. When he had but a trickle left, he tipped it over, letting the droplets fall through the bars of the cage and down onto Sera's head. She scrambled to catch what little she could in her mouth.

Lothan laughed. "You needn't act so desperate. I'll let you out, if you're ready to play nice."

Sera mustered the liquid still on her lips and spat onto Lothan's shoe.

He kicked the front of her cage in reply and caught her fingers with the edge of his boot.

"Next time I won't be so generous," he growled. He would have tested the ring's strength against her will then and there, but his earlier efforts had drained him.

He left her nursing her hand and considered: he still had not found what he'd come for, the fathomless obsidian pendant that could work his will without end and make the world over again in his image. This might have enraged him, did he not suspect that what he sought lay right under his feet.

He cleared his mind of all else and begun to pace the floor, seeking to unlock its pattern.

SERA HAD THE PADLOCK TO HER CAGE SPRUNG OPEN WITHIN MINUTES. SHE slid the piece noiselessly into her hand, placed it in the corner of her cage, and checked one last time that she wasn't being watched.

After wandering the room aimlessly for what seemed like hours, Marek had thrown his hands up in frustration and stomped off again into the space behind the throne room. When she cocked her head in that direction, silence met her ears. Wherever he had gone, he was still there. The two men he had not yet killed lay hunched on the floor on the far wall with their heads together. Their deep, heavy breathing continued uninterrupted.

Sera gripped the bars of her cage ever so slowly, and swung it open on its hinges without making a sound. She caught her mother's eye as she stood up, but Marietta was wise enough to not voice her surprise as Sera slipped away through the main doors leading back out to the maze.

The doors were indescribably heavy; she was just about sure that the muscles in her neck were ready to snap from the strain as she finally caught a cracked bit of stone tile with her foot. She crouched down and wedged it firmly between the doors, leaving a small enough gap not to be noticed, but big enough that she could get back in. Once she was certain the doors wouldn't slam shut and cut her off from her mother, she stood upright and surveyed the desert beyond.

The landscape was empty. Below her, the maze continued its infuriating dance between seen and unseen. What Lothan had said about Lysandro having to cross the labyrinth had shaken her to her core. She had to warn him, somehow.

The tile that she had used to prop open the door was not the only one that was loose. Sera bent down and pried up another, its width roughly the span of both her hands, and flipped it over. It was smooth on the underside, and not terribly heavy.

She retrieved the elongated needle hidden inside her coiled hair and tested its point against the surface of the stone. When she saw rough white marks appear, she was elated. Scooting forward on her knees so as not to get bowled over by the next fierce wind, she peered over the edge of the tower and began scratching out the maze's pattern. With a final set of markings in the corner to indicate which end was up, she stood, turning the tile over and over in her hands to grasp the weight of it. She would need to be holding it just right to fling it clear across the maze, just as she had seen Fabien do with smooth polished stones across the Seeran River so many times before. That, and the wind had to be on her side.

Twisting her torso as far is it could go, she sprang back and released with all her might. The tile spun in the air, just the way she'd hoped it would, then crashed into one of the inner walls and shattered to pieces.

Damn!

She nearly cried out loud, but caught herself and stamped her foot in futile fury. She could repeat this with every tile, and still she would not reach the sands beyond the first turn. It was simply too far. Even if she were thick-headed enough to try, she would be found out long before that, and then where would she be? There was nothing lighter nearby to substitute for paper, and even then no way to ensure it wouldn't blow far beyond anyone's reach. She had to find another way.

Turning back around to search for inspiration to strike, she saw something she hadn't seen before—something *none* of them had seen. There was a slim space to either side of the heavy double doors.

Sera followed the path to her right until she was standing squarely at the back end of the tower. The ground was littered with long-abandoned nests. Some kind of snake, she guessed, by the layers of desiccated skins piled one on top of another. They must have gone on breeding and breeding among themselves until they'd run out of food, she mused.

A distant hissing sounded overhead, and the blood in her veins froze.

She backed up against the rough-hewn wall just as a flash of black and red streaked across her vision. It landed at her feet, facing the opposite direction. Without even thinking, she shoved the mass of coils over the side with her foot. It didn't plummet the way she expected, instead landing on another ledge below. By the wild swinging of its head, the creature was none too happy about it.

Could vipers scale a wall? Sera wasn't entirely sure. Either way, it seemed to disappear, slithering toward the tower and out of sight. There had to be a crevice that she could not see from where she stood. No doubt the thing would wait patiently for her to follow before striking, but she was too smart for that. She lay on her belly and waited, needle at the ready.

When at last it did poke its head out to see where she had gone, Sera didn't hesitate. She aimed for the spot on its head right between two bright red markings, and pinned it to the ground. Its body gave a little shudder and became still.

The drop down to the level below was not insignificant. In trying to grasp onto something on the way down, Sera skinned her left arm from her elbow all the way to the shoulder. It stung and flashed a bright angry red, but it wasn't bleeding. Yet, at any rate. She scanned the space behind her to discover she had been right; there was a crack in the tower into which the viper had secreted itself away. She did the same now, but not before retrieving her needle, now with a poisoned tip. That might be good for something.

It was so dark in the crevice, it was impossible to know if there were other serpents lying in wait. But the alternative was to stand at the threshold doing nothing, and every moment she tarried was one that brought Lysandro closer to that treacherous labyrinth. She tucked inside quickly, and promptly tripped over something in the darkness. She leapt to her feet prepared to fight, but whatever she had stumbled over wasn't alive. Never had been, by the feel of it. It was something wooden, like sticks strung together. She pulled its outer limbs out into the blistering sunshine, where wonder filled her eyes. It was a ladder. An old and rickety one, tucked away at the back end of the fortress, where no one would see. A picture began to take shape in her mind, one that left her dumbstruck.

This was the way Theron had come.

Sure now from the silence that the space she had disturbed lay empty of predators, she poked in again, searching on her hands and knees as her vision failed her. For a moment, the sun dipped into just the right spot to send a weak shaft of light over her shoulder, where it reflected on an object tucked deep into the corner. She scurried over to the place she had temporarily seen, and her hands met a satchel fashioned from leather, its contents spilling out onto the loose sand in front of it. She scooped up all she could find with her outstretched fingers and made her way back again into the light.

All remained quiet, save for the howling wind blowing sand in every direction. It seemed she had not yet been found out. Sera opened the satchel and found a series of glass vials, the things that had been strewn about. Most were empty. One had the dried, dusty remnants of some small creature or other. Whatever it had been, it had once had wings. Only one bottle held a liquid that had not dried up with age. It glowed a pale, luminescent green. Sera popped it open and braved a smell, but there seemed nothing toxic about it. The honey-like substance felt cool to her fingertips. She pressed the gel to her scraped arm, and found instant relief. She stoppered the bottle without using too much and secreted it away between her breasts before examining the rest of what had once belonged to the hero of old, what he had left behind to face Argoss in the Final Confrontation.

The bulk of the satchel was occupied by a book, bound by hand and fashioned with an astonishingly elaborate cover. It was the impressive half-orb in the center of the book, taking up almost the book's entire dimension, that had dimly reflected the light. Which was strange, now. Here, under the sun's full, unabating glare, it radiated darkness, drinking in all the light pouring into it from above with no reflection in return. Its inky center was as like a bottomless pit. Sera undid the brittle latch holding the pages shut with minimal effort and opened the binding to reveal page after page of strange markings, and diagrams so complicated they made little to no sense at all. She scrutinized the crude script all the same. It reminded her of the pattern carved in stone on the table kept in Lighura's gallery. They were in the same language; she was sure of it. Then she remembered the sharpened bit of stone that had been displayed nearby, and realized it was not a table at all, but an altar. To whom or to what, Sera did not know. But the book she held in her hands, and its encrusted skin with the gem that swallowed sunlight, had something to do with it, and nothing at all to do with the goddess.

He must not get this.

Sera worked quickly in the dark, scrabbling with her hands until her fingernails turned raw and bloody as they met harder stone beneath. She buried the book within the sands, piling it high and making it appear a natural effect of the winds for good measure. She tossed the empty satchel to the side, where one more item came dislodged and rolled its way out. A spyglass. At *last*, something she could actually use.

The ladder was ready to crumble at the slightest pressure, but Sera was light and quick, and made her way to the roof of the tower without too many of the rungs snapping beneath her feet. She grabbed the spyglass that she had clamped firmly between her teeth, put it up to her eye, and hoped against hope.

When she saw a dark figure astride a dark horse take their first steps onto the desert sands, both no bigger than the tip of her finger, she cried. He had never been far behind. That, she had always known, but to see him again, so close so soon, nearly robbed her of her wits.

Nearly.

She fiddled furiously with the lens of the spyglass until it popped free. Perfect. Now if she could turn it to just the right angle…

Sera's heart leapt in her throat as Lysandro raised one hand to shield his eyes.

Yes!

She had to keep the light in his face long enough for him to realize that it was more than a fluke. He had made it this far. Surely, he had seen at least some of the clues she had left behind? Now, once she got his full attention, how to actually warn him?

"Get back here you little bitch, or I will slit your mother's throat!"

No, no!

She was out of time. And with Lysandro standing stock still, staring at her. She could feel his gaze on her. Damn it all!

"Ten! Nine!"

Marek wasn't bluffing. Sera knew enough to know that. Even if she chanced it, he would do it for spite. And with only seconds left, she didn't know *how* exactly she could send Lysandro a message that could help him.

"Eight!"

She took one last look at where Lysandro stood—and then she saw it. As he moved, the swirling winds that danced and skittered in secret patterns across the wasteland peeled away from him in great tumultuous waves, as if in fear. Stuck in the thick of it, he probably didn't notice the shifting pattern. But she saw. The blade that pulsed light in his hand carved the path before him. He was headed straight for her.

"Seven!"

She had to go back the way she had come. If Marek retraced her steps and found whatever dark magic was in that book, it was all over. She hauled the ladder up onto the rooftop with the last of her strength and jumped down, then down again to the floor below and raced around the bend to the front doors, just as Lothan stepped outside. To all appearances, Sera had been standing there at the threshold the whole time. She worked hard to steady her breathing and schooled her expression.

"Where the fuck have you been?!" he barked.

Sera looked to one side of the vast expanse of sky, then the other, and spread her empty hands out in front of her.

"Is my mother dead?"

She was terrified of the answer, but the words came out as casually as if she'd asked about the weather.

He let her agonize over her silence for a bit before answering.

"Not yet. She will be if you try that again."

Sera nodded her understanding.

He stood closer to her. Not with the intention of menacing, she realized, but with the attempt to charm. At least, what passed for charm as far as he was concerned. When she averted her gaze from his, she noticed that he was toying with a ring, turning the milky green stone around and around on his finger.

That was new. Whatever it was, Sera surmised that Marek was using it to sway her to his side. Or so he thought. She did not have an abundance of options. There was nothing for it but to play along.

He licked her again as he had before. Slower this time, letting his tongue travel from her collarbone to the place just behind her ear.

It took everything she had not to flinch.

He was grinning with smug satisfaction when he resurfaced. How she wanted to kill him.

"Your would-be hero is on his way, I imagine," he said in an easy tone. "We should make ready for him."

31

THE NICHE IN THE MOUNTAIN FACE WHERE THERON FOUND HIS ETERNAL rest was impossible to see from any distance. It was even more impossible to reach, but Eugenie wasn't relying on her eyes to find it. She cut a jagged path west across the plains and north toward the Sister Peaks, following an invisible golden thread, fine as spider silk, that shimmered in the minutes before dawn and the fall of twilight.

She and Asha journeyed along its course unwaveringly for days, as fast as their horses would allow. When Eugenie's mare succumbed to exhaustion and lack of food, Asha shared her mount. Then they flew.

Eugenie's supply of the herbs needed to cast the Eyes of Morgasse was dwindling; soon she would be forced to eat. But then, they'd be left in the dark. There was little left of Eugenie when they reached the base of the peaks, save skin and sinew. Asha carried her on her back, clawing her way up the mountain by digging a pair of daggers she kept tucked in her boots deep into the rockface by degrees until they reached an opening just big enough to crawl through.

There was nothing grand about what they found inside. Missing were any sacred markings or adornments. The sliver of space etched into the mountain peak gave no sign at all that the hero of legend, favored one of the Goddess, lay entombed there.

Even his clothes were unassuming. Asha and Eugenie spied them through the sarcophagus carved entirely of ice. He wore the simple weave of a man from a small village. The pale blue tunic was worn, but stitched with care. His pants were darkened at the knees from long toiling hours. He had left the world as he had entered it—humble.

Eugenie sank to her knees at the sight; moisture gathered in the corners of her eyes. She mourned the loss of him as if it were fresh in her heart. Theron's fair hair lay across his brows as if windswept. The heather gray eyes that haunted her dreams were closed, their urgent pleading lost to her. Here, his expression was serene. With him was what they sought— the Hand of Arun. Theron's arms were crossed over his chest, holding the unstrung bow in one hand, and a single arrow with a shaft made of matching burnished gold in the other.

Eugenie and Asha bowed their heads in silent prayer.

"Which one of us should take it from him?" Asha asked after a time.

Eugenie knew exactly how she felt. It was inconceivable to separate Theron from the Hand—they were like two halves of the same soul. But Lysandro shared in that soul too. And his hour of need had come.

"You're the warrior," Eugenie said.

Asha seemed to summon her courage at that. She pressed her hands to the lid of the sarcophagus and shoved it askance, just enough for her to reach in and retrieve the weapon.

Eugenie flinched as she did so. She squeezed her eyes shut to convince herself that it was just her imagination, that those supple fingers had not just twitched at the loss of the bow.

"Thank you," Asha murmured, and left his empty hands folded peacefully across his broad chest. Awe filled her countenance as she beheld the relic in her hands. The bow was nearly as tall as she was, and so thick around that she couldn't close her fingers when she grasped it. It was forged for larger hands than hers; in Theron's grip, Eugenie imagined, the fit would be perfectly attuned to the contours of his palm. The shaft of the arrow was straight and true, marked with runes from the crystalline arrowhead to the golden fletching that flared in a double ridge sharp as eagle talons.

Asha propped the bow up between her knees to string it, but she couldn't exert enough pressure to bend it.

"Give me a hand with this, will you?" she ground out. Sweat dripped from her temples despite the cold.

Eugenie saw invisible characters flicker across the surface of the bow, flaring to life as Asha put her weight into it.

"I could give you a thousand hands," Eugenie said. "You still would not string that bow."

Asha released the relic and raked a hand through her hair. "Is there anything else I *can't* do to help Don Lysandro?"

Eugenie didn't know what to say in answer.

The wind was strongest at the mouth of the cave. As Asha strapped the Hand of Arun to her back and familiarized herself with its weight, Eugenie paced back and forth across the entryway, considering their next move. She was caught off-guard by a blast of wintry air. She slipped, and the tomes that she carried strapped across her chest slid off the edge, threatening to pull her down like an anchor.

"Eugenie!"

Asha leapt after her, catching Eugenie's sleeve in her right hand, and using her left to sink her dagger into the side of the mountain. They slammed into the rockface with terrific force; Asha felt something crack inside. She screamed. The weight of her own body and Eugenie's books, now shackled to her waist, threatened to tear her limb from the rest of her body and send them plummeting to their deaths.

The mountain shook. Veining cracks in the rock threatened the hold of Asha's dagger. The sound of it spread deep and wide, as if the whole of the mountain was splitting apart.

Through the sheer force of her will, Asha hauled Eugenie up over her head, back inside the safety of the cave. She struggled to find a foothold to pull herself up, but once she did, she was able to turn her body to face the mountain and climb back up the way she had come. But her focus shifted from her legs to her shoulders as she felt Eugenie tugging on her clothes. She couldn't find her balance with Eugenie pulling on her, and if she lashed out to catch herself, Asha would pull them both back down again.

"Back up!" Asha barked, not having enough breath to be polite. Eugenie obeyed, and scrambled back to give Asha enough space to fight her way back into the cave. Asha dug her nails into the frozen rock until they turned bloody. She slumped onto her back as she met solid ground, her breath ragged.

"Are you okay?" Eugenie asked, coming to her side.

Asha licked her wind-cracked lips. "Yeah. You?"

"Yes. Thank you."

"Uh-huh."

The minute Eugenie came to her feet, she screamed. Asha followed her terror-stricken gaze to the coffin. It had cracked down the middle and collapsed upon itself. But that wasn't why Eugenie had screamed. The coffin was empty.

Behind Eugenie's hysterical ramblings, Asha heard a deep rumbling.

"Do you hear that?"

Eugenie stopped. "Hear what?"

Asha listened again. And again she heard it. The sound chilled her to her core.

"Thunder."

They both turned to see black clouds stretching across the horizon, blotting out the sun.

Eugenie's voice reached a fever pitch. "We're out of time. He needs the Hand. *Now*."

Asha gaped at her. "And how do you suppose we get there? Just fling ourselves off the side of this peak and ride the wind?"

Asha saw Eugenie's eyes darken two shades.

"*Yes*."

Asha stared at the top of Eugenie's head as the Morgassen dropped back to her knees and began flipping furiously through the books that had nearly been their doom. She found what she was looking for, and started to make her preparations.

"Have you done this before?" Asha asked.

Eugenie didn't look up from drawing runes in the snow with her index finger. "No."

"Will it work?"

There was a pause before Eugenie answered that Asha didn't like.

"Three would be better. Three sisters, I mean."

It was not the first time that a complete circle would have aided their cause, Asha recalled. And in such dire times as these, that fact could not have been lost on the Council of Three. Yet they had chosen to send them to battle handicapped. She filed the thought away.

"Eugenie."

"What?" she asked, still focused on her task.

"Two is enough." Asha knelt opposite her and stretched her palms outward.

Eugenie's fingers stopped moving.

Asha smiled. "There's not enough room for anyone else up here anyway."

Eugenie smiled back at her, and nodded. She took hold of Asha's forearms and began to chant.

Asha tripped over the unfamiliar words, but she kept her eyes on Eugenie, and mimicked the way her mouth moved to produce the sounds. By the fourth round, she had it well enough to close her eyes and concentrate.

Their voices stretched and multiplied as if they had entered an echo chamber—or a tunnel. The wind whipped wildly around them, trapping them in a column of swirling snow that lashed at Asha's cheeks and the tips of her ears. The chant was ingrained enough in her mind now for another part of Asha's brain to question if the swirling of the snow might prove disastrous. Would the altered spell blow them back to the base of the mountain, but no more? Or back in *time*? There was no way to know where the wind would take them, if Eugenie's intentions as written out in the runes were obliterated by the churning winds. Eugenie seemed to recognize this too, and on instinct they tightened their grip on each other, inching closer in the snow until their knees touched, with the Hand of Arun pressed between them. Whatever was going to happen, it had to happen now, or not at all. Their words resounded, sharper and more insistent—a command, rather than a prayer.

Asha's thoughts scattered, and she felt the swirling chaos of the wind around and through her as the world darkened. Unforgiving cold turned to blistering heat on her skin. Lightning flashed across her eyelids. She opened them, and found herself in the desert, clutching Eugenie. The Hand of Arun still lay across their laps. It seemed unreal. Then the image before her faded to nothingness.

Eugenie's voice echoed insistently in her ear. Asha rejoined the chant until her sight and sensation returned, and Eugenie's face took on a tangible, permanent quality. She only stopped when she saw Eugenie's lips come to a standstill. Asha blinked, and released Eugenie's hand.

Another crack of thunder drew her gaze upward, where portentous clouds roiled against the topmost tower of the Lost Fortress.

Lysandro's voice rang out across the sky. *"Sera!"*

"We've got to get up there!" Eugenie cried.

As she said this, a ridge of sand shifted beneath her feet.

"Get back!" Asha shouted. She brought her sword downward with a heavy stroke. There was a high-pitched trill, and a dark gray stain blossomed under the sand.

Answering the call, a cadre of sand wyrms emerged from their hiding places and reared up on thick tails. They stood almost twice as tall as Asha. Moving in tandem, they closed in on the Examiners with terrific speed. Their open mouths revealed rows upon rows of gnashing teeth.

Asha pulled on Eugenie's arm.

"Get behind me Gin."

"Not a chance."

Eugenie drew out a golden medallion from a chain around her neck and begun to speak again in a forgotten tongue. She turned her hand upward to the sky, grasping at the power gathering in the clouds. The lightning obeyed, streaking down out of the heavens and into the palm of her hand. Eugenie closed her fist tight around it and brought it hurtling to the ground. The desert shuddered, widening the crevasses from which the sand wyrms came. They plummeted back down into the Abyss, taking with them the shifting sand that obscured the way with treacherous drops and unbreachable chasms.

Asha grinned. The narrow path ahead was still wrought with peril, but they were no longer running blind.

Another wave of sand wyrms crested before them as they followed the twists and turns of the labyrinth. Asha took the lead, swinging at anything that moved as they raced to the top of the citadel.

THE SWORD OF THERON LIT THE NIGHT. FOR TWO DAYS, LYSANDRO traversed the desert in search of Sera. But as the grassy plains gave way to sand, her clues had likewise dried up. She'd had precious little to work with, he knew; there were no river stones for her to rearrange, no trees whose inner bark she could use as parchment and then slide surreptitiously back into place. But the light that flickered in and out of his eyes as he first crossed into the desert was her doing. Of that he harbored no doubt. For the briefest of moments, it had been a beacon shining out between dark clouds gathering in the sky. He tried to hold fast to that point, but without her secret reassurances to guide his way, his mind gave way to panic that he would come too late. But as darkness fell once more, the blade of the ancient hero pulsed to life in his hands. It seemed to drink in the starlight, and grew warm against his skin. Above the howling of the desert, he imagined he could hear it whispering to him. Not in words—it was more of a feeling, an impulse that urged him leftward. He lifted his chin in that direction, and the blade hummed in eager anticipation. Lysandro pushed Hurricane forward.

Storm clouds gathered above him as the Lost Fortress of Argoss came into view. The thought of Sera trapped inside its accursed towers, entirely at Lothan's mercy, made him shiver.

Hurricane was not dumb to the danger either. He reared up on his legs as lightning split the sky and came hurtling down mere inches in front of him.

"I'm sorry to leave you," Lysandro said as he dismounted, and pressed the stallion's forehead to his own. "You kill anything that comes near you, you hear me?"

The horse snorted and turned his nose away. He didn't need to be told.

Lysandro drew his own sword with his left hand and moved forward into the labyrinth that opened before him. He was heedless to the way the labyrinth bent and twisted around him. Its pathways widened as it shrunk away from the light-filled blade in his right hand. The sands at his feet swirled into wide mounds as sand wyrms wriggled out of the Abyss. Those daring enough to lunge at him with hungry mouths split apart in the air as he leapt past them, giving them no more consideration than a flick of the wrist as he moved with swift, determined steps.

As he reached the base of the staircase that climbed in a tight spiral to the top, he heard Sera scream.

Lysandro bounded up the narrow stone stairs, turning back only once to separate the head of the sand wyrm that had slithered up behind him and stop it from biting at his heels. A crack of lightning came crashing down beside him. It tore off a piece of the fortress and cast everything in a stark white light, leaving the horde of wyrms that chased him blinded. A second bolt engulfed another wyrm as it leapt for Lysandro. The stench of its immolated flesh made him gag as he ran past. The storm raged as it prepared for another strike, echoing in Lysandro's chest as he raced through the open doors at the top of the stairs and found Seraphine, standing deathly still at the opposite end of the enormous room. Lothan had a carefree arm slung over her shoulder.

"*Sera!*"

Her dress was in tatters, her skin was battered purple on her arms and across her neck, and her face looked gaunt.

But she was alive.

He dragged his gaze away from hers to stare at Lothan. Marek's eyes shone with gleeful malice. Lothan's blade was a broken shard no more, its cursed metal longer than Lysandro had ever dared to imagine it, even in his darkest nightmares. Marek's lips twisted into a wicked grin as he greeted him.

"Theron's Impostor. We've been waiting for you."

The sword of Theron pulsed hot in Lysandro's hand.

"I didn't think you'd come. Or even if I did, I didn't think you'd survive the labyrinth. You really are a thorn in my side. But now that you're here, I must ask you…where did you get *that?*"

At this last, Lothan's grin turned into a vicious snarl. Lysandro spied a shiver race across his skin as Lothan's gaze dropped to the weapon at his side. His eyes grew wide at the sight, and the fingers trembled, weakening their grip on the blood sword.

Lysandro charged forward.

"*Stay back!*"

Sera's blood-curdling scream halted his momentum just as Lothan swung his blade in a wide arc and sent a spray of venomous blood in his direction. Lysandro dodged the attack, and retreated to a corner of the room.

Lothan turned to Sera as if she had just done the most inconceivable thing. He knocked her to the ground and swung again, and again Lysandro avoided the stream of blood that splattered across the room and ate into the tiles of the floor like acid. Lysandro twisted his body away from the spray with an effortless grace that pushed Marek to his breaking point.

Each successive stream was weaker than the last. As Lothan reeled and prepared to attack a fourth time, Lysandro rushed forward, sliding under Marek's raised arm and coming up behind him to slice across his back. Lysandro retreated again out of the venom's reach as Lothan spun to face him.

Lothan howled in frustration, but just as quickly regained his composure. His smile returned as he raised the jeweled bones of his right hand and snapped his fingers.

Lysandro had no time to gape in astonishment at the gruesome return of Marek's hand. The floor began to vibrate under him. From every darkened corner came the sound of bones rattling. The skeletons of warriors long dead rose to their feet, took up their abandoned weapons, and advanced on Lysandro.

He swung Theron's gleaming sword in a wide arc, removing the heads of the first five to lunge at him in one stroke. The next wave rounded on him; he cut through the shoulder of the one to his right down to the hip of another, while stabbing at a third with the sword in his left hand. But his own metal got caught in the ribs. The skeleton slid along the blade and came close enough to claw at Lysandro's face. He twisted his grip on the sword and sent it flying upward, scattering bones in all directions as he dismantled the ribcage. Lysandro barreled forward into the oncoming crush. Using his own momentum, he kicked off from the opposite column and sailed through the air. He came crashing down on their skulls and stomped them into the ground.

He wove through the mass of enemies in a deadly dance that sent them tumbling back. He spun and cracked the jaw of another, split open the clavicle of another. And another. And another…

LOTHAN SHIVERED WITH RAGE AS LYSANDRO TORE THROUGH HIS SKELETON army, splitting them to pieces and crunching them to dust under his boots. The distraction managed to keep the blade of his nightmares far from himself up until now, but once his soldiers met Theron's sword, they did not rise again. As the swarm of ensorcelled skeletons thinned, Lysandro turned his attention back to Lothan.

Marek plucked Sera up from the floor; a long, thin needle stuck out halfway from the lock of her mother's cell. Sera tried to lunge for it, but Lothan pulled her up by her hair, ignoring her screams as he kicked her knees out from behind her and positioned the Blood Sword a hair's breadth from her throat.

Lysandro froze, and Lothan cackled in victory. With the girl dead, Lysandro would be too broken to fight. But as he fisted his bony hand in Sera's hair and began to press downward, the lightning outside split the sky again, this time, striking fear straight into the heart of him.

Something else was coming.

"DON LYSANDRO!"

Lysandro couldn't tear his eyes from Seraphine; the lump that formed in her throat as she swallowed brought her skin that much closer to the river of blood. However fast he was, however powerful the sword in his hand, he could not undo what Lothan's vicious eyes promised. Lothan was seconds away from stealing her from him forever.

But someone else was calling to him, someone who was approaching rapidly from behind.

"Don Lysandro, quick—it's the only way!"

It was the Aruni Examiner. She fled to his side and tried to push something into his hands. It fell to the floor in front of him. Lothan's laughter split the air as he spied the object that lay abandoned at Lysandro's feet.

Only then did Lysandro look down to see the Hand of Arun.

Lothan taunted him as he dropped his swords and lunged for the bow.

The string became tangled in his trembling fingers as Lysandro's mind scrambled to piece together how it was meant to work.

"Are you a god now, Lysandro? Theron returned? Have you *ever* felt true power throbbing through your veins?"

Sera had less than seconds to live. Lysandro shook his fingers loose, grasped the end of the string with one hand, and curved the bow with the other until the two met.

The sound of the string pulled taut tolled like a distant bell between his ears. It resonated deep within his soul, and everything became clear. His mind emptied. Time stood still. With the innate sense of a child as it takes its first breath, Lysandro retrieved the golden arrow from the ground, nocked it, and released.

THE PORCELAIN STARS THAT DANCED AND SKITTERED IN THE COSMOS AT Lothan's feet stood still, frozen in fear as Lysandro took hold of the Hand of Arun and aimed it at Lothan's heart. Its crystalline arrowhead shimmered with a blinding light. But it was the bolt of lightning that flashed in Lysandro's eyes that turned the blood in his veins to ice. Mortal terror took hold of his throat. He was dead before he could scream.

"LYSANDRO?"

Lysandro blinked, and came back to himself.

"Sera?"

Their eyes met from across the room.

"Sera!"

He dropped the Hand and rushed to her, sweeping her into a tight embrace. He parted from her just enough to brush her hair out of her eyes and take in her sweet face.

"Are you okay?"

She nodded, leaning her cheek into his caress. "I left messages for you. Did you—"

"I did."

He smiled, and cradled her chin in his hands as their lips met. Her gentle fingertips brushed against the back of his neck, and he lost himself in their sweet reunion. With each brush of her lips, the world righted itself. It was the sort of kiss most only dream about but seldom find, the kind that binds hearts together until long after they've ceased to beat.

Then Sera remembered her mother.

She moved quickly to free her with Lysandro's help. Marietta stood and stared at him.

"Don Lysandro. Why are you dressed like the Shadow of Theron?"

Lysandro blinked. "Because I *am* the Shadow of Theron."

Her mouth dropped open.

"I told you, Mama," Sera said. "I told you he would come for me."

Marietta pressed her lips together in an approving smile as Lysandro's arm tightened around Sera's waist.

"Yes. I see."

They stepped with caution away from the fallen body of Lothan Marek, his face frozen in horror. In his right hand, he still gripped the Blood Sword. Lysandro lifted his blade high in the air, ready to smash it to pieces.

"Don't."

Lysandro whipped around and saw the Examiners, their heads bowed low.

"It may rebuild itself again in time. I must find a way to lift the curse," Eugenie said.

In the bigger woman's outstretched hands was the golden bow blessed by Arun.

Sera's eyes traveled from the weapon to Lysandro's clear eyes, the color of the morning sky. She tucked herself further into his embrace.

"Lysandro," she whispered, and tightened her grip on his arm. "What did you do?"

He didn't know how to answer her. The clarity and purpose that had washed over him in that moment felt like a dream. Now he was awake.

"The Goddess chose you," Asha said. As she passed Lysandro the Hand, he felt a surge of power. The weapon was heavier in his hands than it had been a moment before. It seemed a terrible burden. He gave it back to the

Examiner, who took it as a look of confusion and disappointment spread across her face.

"This doesn't belong to me," Lysandro said.

"But—"

Eugenie stepped forward and whispered in Lysandro's ear.

"You will know the day, and the hour. When you can avoid it no longer, come find me in the castle beyond the sea."

THE CHILD OF THERON TURNED TO TAKE ONE LAST LOOK AT EUGENIE AS HE and the others left the fortress. He met her gaze in a silent exchange. They would meet again. The time had already been set.

Asha spoke low in Eugenie's ear so only she could hear. "Does he know what's coming?"

"He will. In time."

"Then shouldn't we—"

"It is not our duty to interfere. We will prepare, and guard the Hand. For now, let him have this moment." She looked on with tenderness as Lysandro embraced the woman who held his heart. "Let him love his wife."

3 2

"Do you freely give this woman your deepest love and fullest devotion, from this day and into the hereafter?"

"I do," Lysandro answered.

The measure of silk binding his hand to Sera's tightened while all of Lighura looked on. But the only one who mattered stood right in front of him. Beneath the bindings, Lysandro stroked Sera's slender fingers in a tiny back-and-forth motion with his thumb that turned her cheeks crimson. His eyes flashed at the sight.

The Faelian priestess turned to Sera.

"Do you promise to love your husband, wholly and without restraint, to be his joy and his comfort for as long as the sun may rise?"

Sera beamed at him with a smile that shined brighter than any sun.

"I promise."

The Faelian tightened the silk for the third and final time, the knot that bound them together completed.

"Before Faelia, Arun, and Morgasse, Don Lysandro and Doña Seraphine are wed. Nothing in the world can tear them asunder."

The village erupted in cheers as Lysandro tugged unexpectedly on their bound hands, pulling his bride off her feet and catching her mouth in a kiss.

"You're a rogue," Sera chided.

His mouth quirked upward. "I know. I love you," he whispered against her cheek, steadying her in his arms as gravity threatened to pull them down. He kissed her again, with great passion, and didn't care one whit who saw.

The celebration lasted all day and all night, with enough food and wine to feed the hordes that had descended upon the temple at Beloquín to help Lysandro and Sera rejoice in their love for one another. As the feast raged on and stuffed mouths grew quiet, Lysandro gazed lovingly at his bride. She was resplendent in a gown of sparkling white, like a wishing star come to life. He stood and cleared his throat.

"I want to thank you all for coming here, after the many trials that Lighura has had to bear." He looked out over the villagers, and saw their loss reflected in their eyes, along with the hope that, finally, the storm had passed.

"I have something to share with you today…"

"Other than this marvelous feast?" someone called out, to the cheers of others.

Lysandro smiled. "I want to tell you that I'm—"

Sera stood and whispered quickly in his hear.

"Don't."

"Why?"

"Don't give your secret to them. Let them believe that the Shadow will return when they need him—let them dream of him. But from now on, your nights belong to me."

He smiled at his bride and caressed her face with his knuckles. "I want all of Lighura to know…that I'm the luckiest man in the world."

"We all *knew* that!" Rafael bellowed to a great echo of laughter. "I'll let you have this one, Don Lysandro." He winked at his friend. "The best man won."

"Damn right he did!" Elias shouted, tapping the bottom of his cup down on the table. In the seat beside him, Aleksander did the same.

Lysandro's cheeks warmed to be honored by his father in the old way, one soldier, one warrior to another. They exchanged a knowing glance. Elias's eyes shined with pride.

"May I have a dance, at least, Doña?"

Rafael approached the couple as they moved to join the revelers.

"I suppose."

"You are *not* dancing with the bride before me," Fabien interjected, stepping in front of Rafael and extending his hand to Sera.

"I guess that leaves us," Pirró said, putting his arm around Rafael. Rafael looked to Lysandro for help. None was forthcoming.

ALEKSANDER'S OLDEST DAUGHTER LOOKED ON WISTFULLY. IN A BLINK, HER vision was filled with Gareth. He cut a dashing figure in his best attire, his good looks only enhanced by his scar. His smile made her heart knock against her chest.

To her left, her father's heart stopped altogether.

"Signorina Carmen."

"Signor."

"Would you care to dance?"

She took the hand he offered her faster than Aleksander could stop her. Gareth spared him a quick smile over his shoulder.

"That smug bastard."

Elias just laughed. "Relax, will you? It's a wedding. She *should* be dancing. Here. Have some wine."

"She's not old enough."

"She was old enough when you thought Lysandro might marry her."

"They look handsome together," Caterina said. "Look how she's smiling."

Aleksander growled.

LYSANDRO TOOK SERA BY THE HAND AND LED HER TO THE CENTER OF THE festivities. "Dance with me?"

She clasped the back of his neck and pulled him into a kiss. His heart was still galloping when she released him.

"Always."

THE HEAD HIGH PRIESTESS OF THE TEMPLE MORGASSE WAS THE LAST TO arrive.

"Forgive me, sisters. I am feeling my age today."

Imelda walked with slow, uncertain steps toward her customary seat at the table. On either side of her were the other two Head High Priestesses. Together, they comprised the Council of Three, the highest temple authority in all the Allied Lands.

"Have you received word from Eugenie?"

The query came from Karin, the younger woman to her left, who served at the head of the Temple Arun.

"No."

Karin balked. "Are you not the least bit concerned that she has not communicated with you once regarding the recovery of our most sacred relics?"

"I received a letter from my head priestess in Lareina," Phaedra, the Faelian among them said. "Your two examiners came and went, and she had no indication that they were even close to tracking down the healing stones, let alone returning them to her."

"*Our* two Examiners?" Karin repeated, her tongue sharp.

"Is there a Faelian among them?"

Karin rolled her eyes and slammed her fists down on the table. "We've been over this a thousand times."

"All the same—they're *your* Examiners."

Karin growled.

Imelda sat back in her chair, cleaning the dirt from under her nailbeds as they bickered. These little meetings were always so productive.

"Well?"

Karin was looking pointedly at Imelda.

"Are you both finished?"

The other women shifted in their chairs; they did so hate when the Morgassen chided them like children. Which was exactly why she did it.

Imelda sat forward, feeling her spine stiffen in protest as she did. She ground her teeth to repress the pain.

"There's no need for Eugenie to report back until she has the relics in her possession. But they won't be going back to the temples."

Her sisters' faces contorted in outrage, but she stilled their tongues with a raised hand.

"I've been warning for years that their spread across Andras was insecure. Now you have the proof of it. They will remain here, with us, protected by our most powerful of spells."

"The most powerful of *your* spells," Karin replied.

Imelda flashed a self-deprecating smile. "No, sister. My power alone would not be enough to keep them safe. It will require all of us."

Karin shook her head. "I won't do it. They were spread across the hero's homeland so that they would not all fall into the wrong hands. You're inviting disaster."

"And what are *you* inviting, when you keep the sacred weapons out of reach for the one who may need them?"

Karin's eyes widened. "What do you mean?"

"Exactly what I said. The stones speak of the past once again becoming the present. Eugenie has seen it as well, I suspect."

Phaedra leaned in closer, whispering even though there was no one else around to hear.

"Do you mean to say the Hero Theron is returning?"

"He's already here."

"And...his adversary?"

Imelda pressed her lips together in a fine white line.

Her revelation sent her sisters reeling.

"Why have you not told us before?"

"I just came from the casting," Imelda replied thinly.

There was a pause.

"I'll do as you say," Phaedra said at last. "I'll allow the Sorrow Stones to be housed here."

Imelda hid her satisfaction behind a disaffected expression.

"And what will we do?" Karin cut in, "just hand our most powerful gifts from the Goddess into the hands of any young man professing to be Theron? How can we be sure of upon whom we bestow these gifts without knowing if he is in fact descended from gods?" She turned her head to Phaedra.

"Our efforts to recover the Hero's bloodline are not yet complete. But we must be sure. Anyone seeking the Goddess's favor must present themselves to us. Imelda, will you be able to read those who approach us for signs of divinity?"

This was going even better than Imelda expected.

She dipped her head in the affirmative.

"This is madness," Karin argued. "This is not what the Goddess intended."

"How do you know?" Phaedra said in retort. "Or do you now question the wisdom of Imelda's casting, too?"

Imelda looked up at her innocently to match her stare.

Can you see me?

The Aruni relented.

Imelda folded her hands placidly in her lap in triumph.

"Of course not. But..."

Imelda bit the inside of her lip to keep from scowling.

"Something's not right," Karin finished. "And if what Imelda says is true, we must discover what it is." She turned on her heel and left.

Imelda stood as well, and headed out into the brisk winds coming down from the north to make the long walk back from the Great Hall to her private chambers.

"You'll catch your death in this weather," Phaedra said to her back as she stepped outside. "Did you not bring a heavier cloak?"

"I'm quite comfortable, thank you."

"I don't think I've ever seen you wear your heavy robes, even up here." She wrapped her own woolen robe more closely around her middle as the wind howled between them. It was strongest here at the council's table, the highest point of the Temple of the Three and the place closest to the top of the mountain.

"Are you never cold?"

Imelda's lips twisted into a wry grin. "No."

She descended the long stairway etched into the side of the mountain to the confines of her room in the western tower as fast as her aging body would carry her. She slumped against the door as she latched it closed, and sank to the ground, panting heavily.

Maintaining her composure in the face of the others had wiped her out.

She mopped the sweat from her brow, and tore at her skin with her fingernails. With Lothan dead, his power had returned. There was simply not enough room inside the Head High Priestess's skin for both of them, and it threatened to tear her apart.

She managed to crawl over to the mirror edged in hand-hewn silver she kept tucked under the bed. She gripped its raw jagged edges, drawing blood from her palms as she stared down hard into its reflective surface.

Imelda's dull eyes burrowed into the ones staring back through the glass, flickering to life under the strain until the image shimmered, hardening the contours of the chin and nose, widening the mouth, and darkening the irises to reflect Argoss's sharp features. It was an illusion, no more, but it allowed him a few minutes of respite from the aging skin that was growing too frail to hold him.

He released his breath as the change took effect. He stretched back, exhausted, and slid the mirror back under the floorboards. A shudder rippled down his spine as his power expanded along his muscles and settled back into place. He reached for the decanter on a small nearby table, poured himself a glass of wine, and spread his limbs across a wide-backed chair.

Argoss absently moved the runes he'd cast earlier in a clockwise direction, being careful to keep them in alignment lest the young Examiner suspect they reflected anything other than the divine voice. They lay splayed out on a table inlaid with lapis and intercut with stars in mother-of-pearl that he kept well-hidden. He hadn't anticipated that the Child of Theron would move the stones out of his carefully laid path. He had taken great pains to separate them again. That it had happened at all made him wary.

He downed half his drink in a single gulp, and took stock of the situation.

Lothan Marek had proven remarkably effective. He had removed the relics from their safeguards, set them in motion, and had consolidated his power considerably. That might have proven much more difficult than Argoss had originally anticipated, if not for the ease with which Marek had killed his brothers. He even managed to retrieve the ring.

Argoss looked down at his hands, and saw its outline in its accustomed place. But the impression was faint. Argoss closed his eyes and poured all the energy he had regained from Lothan's demise into the conjuring. He felt the familiar squeezing around his flesh as the iron band answered his call. The cut and polished surface of the jade glinted in the candlelight. It was solid enough for him to remove from his finger and roll around in the palm of his hand.

The corner of his mouth curled upward. The jade would be invaluable, and could house his power in the absence of his scattered seed. Marek had done well to reacquire it.

But he had failed to reveal the Eye. That was an unforgivable disappointment.

Lothan's shortcomings stemmed from his own petty desires. But that force of will was also the reason behind his success. Argoss had the sense that his promise was unfulfilled, that Marek had been prevented from ascending the height of his power. He clenched his fingers into a fist, summoning the ring's strength in that old familiar way until he felt his consciousness shed its skin and radiate outward. The gem warmed the Morgassen priestess's long-dead fingers, keeping him bound to her shape as he settled into Lothan's body and tested the edges of it. If he could just...

In the farthest corner of his mind, he felt the fingers that had once belonged to him twitch.

Yes. There was a use for this skin yet.

He should have never relinquished the Hand.

Lysandro and Sera lay in bed, lost in each other's arms. Their bodies glistened. Sera's chest rose and fell gently against him, her hand splayed across his chest and her eyelashes brushing delicate kisses across his skin.

Lysandro had everything his heart desired. Yet his spirit was restless.

There was a tightening in his gut, as if there was a tether there binding him to the golden bow that stretched every time he thought of how very far away it was, left in the hands of the Examiners. It felt as though a part of his soul was leaving him, drifting further from his grasp as the night drew on and the Examiners set off across the sea.

He reached beneath the bed in search of reassurance. The sword of Theron met his fingertips. Its latent power thrummed against his skin. He exhaled, relieved to find it where he had left it.

Sera shifted in his arms, nuzzling closer and wrapping her fingers around his middle.

Lysandro smiled, and grew calm again. He withdrew his fingers from the weapon and wove them into his wife's hair, cradling her head while she slept. Soon he too slid into slumber.

But when he dreamed, he dreamed of battles long past, and those not yet fought, of charging through hordes of goblins across open fields, and of the day, drawing ever nearer, when he would be reunited with the weapon of his ancestor, and once again wield its awesome power to protect what he loved most.

* * *

Thank you for reading! Did you enjoy? Please add your review because nothing helps an author more and encourages readers to take a chance on a book than a review.

And don't miss more from Kathryn Troy with CURSE OF THE AMBER. Turn the page for a sneak peek!

Also be sure to sign up for the City Owl Press newsletter to receive notice of all book releases!

SNEAK PEEK OF CURSE OF THE AMBER

The sun seems to have forgotten Wales. I didn't think there was any place on Earth that could make me long to be in Egypt again, but I couldn't escape the memories that flooded me. I shivered in the absence of the Valley's merciless heat, where for summers on end its oppressive dryness sucked the life out of my lips and baked my skin into hardened, sand-beaten clay. That dryness had followed Ramesses, Amenhotep, Aken-aten, and his son beyond the world's suffering down to their resting place, and kept the divine kings ready in the dark, empty stillness.

But the day's oppression had always faded with the sun. The perfection of those nights on the Eastern Bank, at our host Hani's home—that was what I missed. Invigorated by the fresh, life-giving breeze off the Nile's surface and snuggled between my parents under thin woven blankets was a warmth I knew I would never feel again. The cold and damp of Britain, once the stronghold of the Druids, was relentless. The gnawing feeling at the pit of my stomach grew, and the thought I'd pushed away more than once made itself more insistent.

This was a mistake. I shouldn't be here.

My fingertips numbed to the statuette in my hand, a solid representation of the wet chill in the air. Its faceless form was as alien to me as the bog in which I crouched. The shape of the stone fetish was at least interesting, a long, slender column with a severe "V" etched into it. It held more promise than the dozens of thin rings fashioned out of iron, bronze, and even gold, heaped together in a tangle, the clay pottery, now in shards, and scraps of linen that appeared to be tossed desperately into the bog as a last-ditch effort to avoid Roman destruction. But I couldn't enjoy it for what it was. It was inscrutable, too disconnected from anything familiar. Its primitive, obscure expression reminded me of my own cold thoughts, and as I squeezed the chilled stone in my hand, I doubted if I would discover anything that had once been warm—made of flesh and blood. We were as deep down as the famous bog bodies had been, more so in certain places, and still we had nothing, or rather no one, to show for it.

I lifted my head, trying to shake off my melancholy and averting my eyes from the stone carving that would not reveal its secrets to me. I was too low down to inhale even a whiff of air that wasn't saturated with the grassy pungency of the bog wall. From my vantage point, huddled low in a deep, man-hewn pit, the sodden depression of the bog appeared even more overgrown on all sides. Birch trees poked out of humble clusters of willows, red-speckled buckthorn, and mountain ash. Except for these trees skirting its outermost edges, the sunken area was wide and open. The cauldron bog retained its secluded atmosphere, despite being carved into a series of waterlogged cavities.

My somber mood deepened when I saw my advisor approach. Up until then I'd been successful at avoiding him. I deliberately didn't linger, and always found a reason to visit another pit when the one we were in suddenly emptied of other researchers. I'd resisted the wrenching feeling in my gut too long, but as our excavation wound down, it was impossible to ignore, with nowhere for my thoughts to hide—there was nothing left of what used to be my life.

"How's it going?" Alex asked, and knelt beside me.

"Fine," I answered, not bothering to look up from the peat I was brushing off of a link of iron rings sunken into the over-saturated soil.

After a long, awkward silence, he said, "It's okay, you know."

"What is?"

"If you don't...if *we* don't find one."

I swallowed hard. The only place for my rising fury to go was back down.

"I just don't want you to think that this whole thing was a waste—"

"A *waste*?" I shot back. "I've got enough to keep me occupied for the next decade, thank you." It was true, but that didn't make the prospect of studying human sacrifice *sans* a human sound any better. Nothing would tell us as much about the Druids as human remains that had, willingly or otherwise, undergone their practices. It may have been more than anyone else expected, but the bar had been set impossibly high. A human discovery might have been the only way to exceed my father's own discoveries in the Valley of the Kings and earn the same level of respect in my own right.

"All right, all right," Alex said, contrite. "I didn't come over here to upset you."

"Then why are you here?" There was more bite in my voice than I meant, but he had that amused eyebrow raised again, the one that made my anger meaningless and painted me as a silly, wide-eyed novice with dreams of finding the next Tut.

"I thought you might need a refill." He offered me a cup of coffee.

A gruff "thank you" was all I could manage. My brain had reached maximum capacity for caffeine, but it went down easy. Milk and two sugars, just the way I liked it. Damn.

He reached out for me but caught himself before his fingers could find their way into my hair, frowning before he lowered his voice.

"Will you come tonight, Asenath? It'd be a shame for you not to see the room. You picked it, after all."

Memories of Alex's firm, feverish grip on my hips, his moans in my ear, passed unbidden across my mind. Some days it was so easy to look at him and just see the charming, somewhat quiet young man always at my father's side, more often than not covered in two-thousand-year-old dust.

"Will you tell *her*?" I asked.

His silence hit me like a stab in the gut. It was self-inflicted—those rosy pictures and all his stale promises were just a veil, a childhood infatuation. I saw him then as he was—his chocolate-brown hair had dulled, the sharp line of his chin softened; so, had the brilliance of his eyes, their dark fathoms fading. Small lines crept at the corners of his eyes and mouth. I bit my tongue as a distraction. The imprints of his touch on my skin would fade, if I let them.

I sipped my coffee again. It had a bitter taste the second time around. When I let the silence settle between us, he rose to his feet, stifling a groan on the way up. He disappeared again to the other side of the dig, and I went back to work.

I ended the day uploading my latest round of pictures as usual. Dr.

Pryce, the head of the Aarhaus team, walked into the makeshift tent and took up the seat beside me.

"Good evening, Miss Hayes."

"Hi, Dr. Pryce. I'm almost done here."

He nodded. "Time for your daily report. Carew was preoccupied, so he asked me to come in his stead."

"Preoccupied with what?" I asked, then mentally kicked myself the moment the words escaped my mouth. It was too familiar, but my patience with Alex was thin. Dr. Pryce didn't seem to notice, and only smiled, a sly thing with a hint of amusement. "Right," I answered, shaking my head. "Well, according to today's soil readings, we're anywhere from fifteen to twenty-five hundred years down, and some of the wells were definitely dug by human hands."

"Wells," Pryce repeated, bobbing his head thoughtfully, "but no mounds."

"That's right." I felt my face flush hot under the electric lamps swinging overhead. The Druids hadn't built permanent structures, making them an elusive lot. But I'd hypothesized that impermanent markers, made of dirt and mud, had been either destroyed or overlooked completely. The clunky peat-cutting that locals relied on for fuel had raised almost every bog body ever found by sheer accident. Any significant difference to the topography would have been ripped apart before anyone had realized its importance. I had at least hoped to map out some pattern to the ritualized deaths bog bodies had endured and give more substance to Julius Caesar's accounts of human sacrifice among the Druids. But without markers in the ground as a reference, or actual victims to study, deciphering the meaning of these haphazard bits and bobs wouldn't amount to a whole lot that we hadn't known before.

I think Pryce read the disappointment on my face, and tactfully changed the subject. "It's taking us longer than we thought to hit our marks," he said. "It's unlikely that we'll be able to complete the site, this time around at least."

I blew air out of my lips in a loud puff, deflated. He'd caught me. I had tried not to be concerned by it, but we *were* behind schedule. Cerriglyn Bog couldn't support the weight of bulldozers. The ground was too unstable. We'd been left to do the grunt work with smaller machines, sometimes only by hand. It made just reaching our intended depth a daunting task. I pursed my lips and wondered if I would ever feel the African sun on my face again, or see Hani's familiar, wizened face. He was probably still there, giving respite to obnoxious tourists, those he decried for destroying his homeland with their discarded water bottles and used-up film canisters. A hollow feeling deepened in my chest at the thought, threatening to swallow me up. I did my best to shake it off.

"Let's narrow the field, then," I finally answered.

Dr. Pryce smirked and pulled a copy of our working map from his back pocket. "I thought you might say that."

"Am I that predicable?" I asked.

"Predictable? No. But *capable*? Yes, you are that, Miss Hayes. So, what do you think?"

I examined the map centered around Cerriglyn Bog. Bordering its northeastern edge was the forest, with fainter lines indicating its prehistoric boundaries intersecting the topmost sectors of the bog. Along that corner crawled a small creek. Minus the geographic features, the map was blank. Staring at it was like gaping into an abyss, and that overwhelming feeling crept back up again, settling in my armpits and down the center of my back. I hoped Pryce couldn't smell my fear.

I closed my eyes, wishing for the meticulously plotted charts of the Valley of the Kings, its pristine, orderly rows and markers instead of this yawning nothingness. But it too, once, had been only a mass of nondescript, transient dunes. I looked at the map again, the one in my mind's eye laid over it like a transparency. The bog beneath came to life, reacting like watercolor paper dipped in ink. Invisible markers blossomed in neat, ordered lines, woven together by unseen pathways into a modest village, one as close to the wetlands as safety would allow.

"Let's pull it in here," I said, pointing to the northeastern sector where the environmental markers overlapped—where the bog met the forest and where it touched the bank of the creek. "Take half your team out of the south and move them to the center." Those in-between spaces would have been the most sought after, the ones deemed sacred. If we didn't find anything bigger than chicken bones there, I doubted we would find them anywhere.

"Will do," he said, restoring the map to his pocket. "You know, Miss

Hayes, I never really thanked you for thinking of us. This is the most exciting thing that's happened to our department in decades."

"Of course," I answered quickly. "You're right here. I thought it would be wrong not to. Although I'll admit that my intentions were not entirely altruistic—your Celts might be able to tell me something that the pyramids can't." That was the main reason I'd gone along with Alex's suggestion in the first place—I was seduced by the idea of bringing Druidism out of the shadows and drawing a line straight back to the practices that made pharaohs divine kings and praised wetlands as sacred.

Pryce smiled. "You *are* your father's daughter, Miss Hayes."

I turned my face from him and bit my lip. The sting of tears that should have run dry long ago tried to push its way forward again. I tried to console myself with the thought that, had I not already been thinking about them, it wouldn't have hit me as hard. But even I wasn't convinced.

Pryce cleared his throat. "I apologize, Miss Hayes. I—"

"It's fine," I assured him, blinking to clear my eyes. "Thank you for the compliment."

"I'd ask you to stay longer, if I didn't think Alex would have a fit. Lord knows he wouldn't get any work done without you." He rose from his chair and left me with a knowing grin.

* * *

Pryce's parting words left me wondering just how much Alex *was* supposed to be doing as my supervisor. I shifted restlessly in a moldy dorm bed, abandoned in the nadir of the academic year. Today was not the first time that Alex was seen to shirk his duty. Sneaking breaks and doing his utmost to *not* tire himself out as much as the next man was second nature to him. It stung to have my work, my conclusions, be subject to his opinion. But it was too late to switch advisors and explaining the more pressing reason for wanting the distance was out of the question.

In the starkness of the brisk night, my boots called to me. Their plush lining was irresistible at the ridiculously late hour. I'd never get any sleep if I didn't clear my head and at least try to keep warm. I pulled the barely upholstered desk chair next to the window. After pushing down on the window to confirm that, yes, in fact, the wind was coming *through* the closed frame, I set the chair in front of the window, so that the frame sat at the leftmost corner of my vision, leaving the rest of my view looking out onto the bog which lay in the distance. Thick grasses and clusters of myrtle clutched each other in the darkness, shivering violently in the wind. Moonlight bounced off their tangled, indefinable edges, and the more I peered into the Welsh countryside, the more it divested itself of its false bluntness. The bog and its surrounding brush revealed whispers of greens, blues, purples, and yellows in its multi-layered blackness. Calm crept softly over my frazzled brain as I roughed out the scene before me in charcoals, paying attention to the angles and proportions before treating its colors and textures. I willingly lost myself in the quick strikes of my hand against the paper. Thoughts of anything but how to render the window frame fell from my mind. I considered whether to keep the aged, peeling texture of the white frame intact, or to restore it to a gleaming pristineness set at odds with the watery chaos beyond. As I worked, the untarnished frame looked too unnatural, so I weathered it once more. I worked until my eyes became blissfully heavy and drifted down into sleep.

I was still working on the image of the bog in my dreams. My charcoal strokes had become bloated with water, bleeding my greens, my blues, my whites, and my blacks together until the bog was nothing but a dark mass, a bottomless chasm. Obsidian waves shifted and swayed—something was rising to the surface. I couldn't run, couldn't scream or blink the image away as the rising wave took shape and glided across the surface of the bog. A shrunken, wrinkled face emerged from the watery depths. Its twisted mouth wrenched open to reveal a blank expanse. Vacant eyes glowed an unearthly blue, staring straight into my soul.

I woke gasping for air and wiped a sheen of cold sweat from my forehead. Raindrops pattered onto the floor beneath the window, its brittle borders unable to keep either wind or water out. The edge of my picture, laid on the nightstand, was visible out of the corner of my eye. The rain glistening on the windowpane reflected on the paper in the moonlight, making the colors look blurry and wet—alive, almost. I was afraid to turn my head, afraid in the way that you can be only after waking suddenly, still too tied to your dreams to know they aren't real. Those glowing, luminescent eyes still stared at me, *through* me, at the edge of my mind. I held my breath and looked. The only things on the paper were what I had put there—high grasses peering into the window frame, that crumbling barrier against the creeping dark without. It was splintered and cracked, losing its power to keep the fen at bay.

* * *

Don't stop now. Keep reading with your copy of <u>CURSE OF THE AMBER</u>

Want even more from Kathryn Troy? Read CURSE OF THE AMBER and be sure to find her at kathryntroy.blogspot.com

* * *

A curse, a resurrection, and a centuries old witch hell bent on revenge.

Quintus is a dutiful son and soldier, sent to Britannia to improve his marriage prospects and ensure the Druids never rise again. Roman soldiers destroyed the last Druid stronghold in a battle of blood and fire. So, he never expects to be sacrificed to their sacred bog, trapped forever by the gods below.

Two thousand years later, Asenath Hayes discovers the most well-preserved body in history. And the last thing she needs is for him to wake up.

As the young archaeologist delves into Druidic rituals to grasp why Quintus was offered to a Welsh bog and then resurrected, she is forced to complete her research with the "missing" body, dodge her ex-lover and mentor with his own agenda, and keep her gorgeous new houseguest under wraps.

But, smitten with her as he seems, Quintus says he wants to go home.

Asenath is drawn to Quintus by the secrets they share, even if it scares her. As Asenath is pulled deeper into the mysteries of the bog, she must risk everything to keep him from hell's cold grasp as she uncovers forbidden rites, awakened deities, and an attraction that transcends the ages.

* * *

Please sign up for the City Owl Press newsletter for chances to win special subscriber-only contests and giveaways as well as receiving information on upcoming releases and special excerpts.

All reviews are **welcome** and **appreciated**. Please consider leaving one on your favorite social media and book buying sites.

For books in the world of romance and speculative fiction that embody Innovation, Creativity, and Affordability, check out City Owl Press at www.cityowlpress.com.

ACKNOWLEDGMENTS

Thank you to the City Owl team and all of the people that helped this book come together. Special thanks to my mom, Lysandro's first and best fan, and my Dad, an ancient Greek through and through, who shared his favorite stories with me and made those long-dead heroes come alive again. They are a huge inspiration for this book.

Thank you so much to my children, Annabelle and Adrian, whose awesome ideas led to the beautiful cover. The glowing eyes, Adrian- they are awesome! The flowers look just right Annabelle. Also: baguette.

Last but never least, thank you to my adoring hubby Andy, my happy thought, my calm refuge and the voice of reason among my chaos. I'd go crazy without you.

ABOUT THE AUTHOR

KATHRYN TROY is a history professor by day, a novelist by night. She likes to write what she reads —fantasy, romantic fantasy, gothic fiction, historical fiction, paranormal, horror, and weird fiction. Horror cinema and horticulture are her other passions. When she's not writing or reading or teaching, she's either gaming, traveling, baking, or adding some new weird creepy cool thing to her art collection.  She is a Long Island native with one husband, two children, and three rats.

kathryntroy.blogspot.com

ABOUT THE PUBLISHER

City Owl Press is a cutting edge indie publishing company, bringing the world of romance and speculative fiction to discerning readers.

Escape Your World. Get Lost in Ours!

www.cityowlpress.com

 facebook.com/YourCityOwlPress
 twitter.com/cityowlpress
 instagram.com/cityowlbooks
 pinterest.com/cityowlpress